"MATHEWS [ ] TALE OF INTRIGUE AND ESPIONAGE. . . . THE THRILLS IN THIS BOOK ARE IN ALL THE REALISTIC DETAILS. MATHEWS IS A FORMER CIA ANALYST WHO'S ABLE TO TRANSLATE HER EXPERTISE INTO A HIGH-ACTION THRILLER THAT KICKS OFF IN A LIVELY FASHION. CARMICHAEL IS ONE OF THE TOUGHEST FEMALE SECRET AGENTS WE'VE SEEN IN A LONG TIME. NO WONDER HER NICKNAME IS MAD DOG."

—*USA TODAY*

"RIVETING . . . [Mathews's] presentation of espionage and CIA tactics is impeccable."

—*Publishers Weekly*

"Francine Mathews's *The Cutout* is not just a fresh new voice in international intrigue, it's a brand-new vision— INTELLIGENT, PASSIONATE, AND UNCEASINGLY ENTERTAINING."

—Stephen White, *New York Times* bestselling author of *The Program*

"Francine Mathews writes with precision and authority. *The Cutout* is A TOP-RATE SPY THRILLER. I loved it."

—Ridley Pearson, *New York Times* bestselling author of *Middle of Nowhere*

THE

CUTOUT

Francine Mathews

BANTAM BOOKS
NEW YORK   TORONTO   LONDON   SYDNEY   AUCKLAND

*This book is dedicated with love to Rafe Sagalyn,
literary agent and friend,
who made me write it;*

*and to Barbara, the original Mad Dog.
I'd never have survived the Farm without you.*

Cutout: A third person used to conceal the contact between two people—usually an agent and a handler who do not want to meet because one or both may be under surveillance.
—NORMAN POLMAR AND THOMAS B. ALLEN,
The Encyclopedia of Espionage

ACKNOWLEDGMENTS

A tour through the Intelligence world is marked by a series of rituals. There is the initiation of the polygraph; the rite of passage that is tradecraft training; the ceremonial presentation of the first Certificate of Merit or presidential stickpin. And upon exiting, there is the moment when one is required to sign an oath of secrecy. That oath obligated me to submit *The Cutout* to the CIA's Publications Review Board, which is charged with removing classified material from text written by former employees. The board reviewed this work in both draft and final manuscript form, and I would like to thank them for their thoroughness, expediency, and professionalism—and for requesting me to change only one word.

The Cutout would never have seen the light of publication without the intelligent editing and heartfelt encouragement of Kate Miciak, vice president and executive editor of Bantam Dell Books. I have worked with Ms. Miciak for years now, on a variety of novels, but never have I valued her skill and dedication so much as in the present instance.

I would also like to express my deep gratitude to Dale and Linda Lovin, formerly of the FBI, and to Paul Gray, Chief of FAA Security at Denver International Airport. Their professional advice and willingness to assist a writer who was sometimes out of her depth were invaluable. Any errors unwittingly committed in the translation of their facts to fiction must be considered entirely my own.

My final word of thanks must go to all those women and men of the CIA who trained, befriended, and inspired me, and to my family, who endured my moods and temper during the long months required for this book's completion.

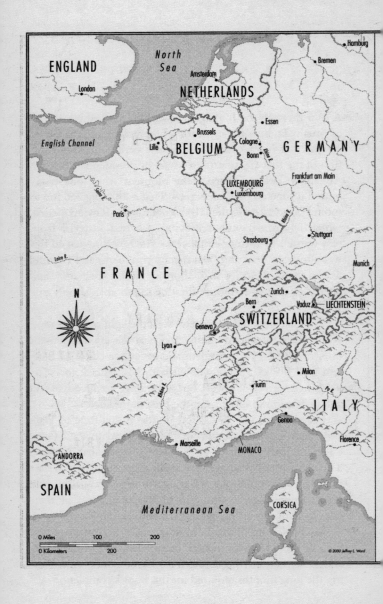

Part I
TUESDAY, NOVEMBER 9

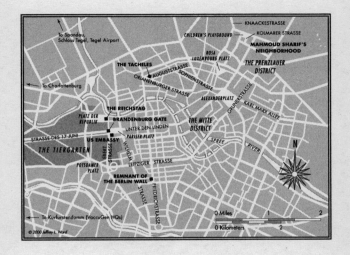

ONE

Berlin, 12:03 P.M.

S HE WAS A SMALL WOMAN; the press had always made much of that. On this crisp November morning in the last days of a bloody century, she stood tiptoe on a platform designed to lift her within sight of the crowd. They were a polyglot mass—threadbare German students, Central Europeans, a smattering of American tourists. A few Turks holding bloodred placards were shadowed, of course, by the ubiquitous security detail of the new regime. After twenty-four hours in Berlin, Sophie Payne had grown accustomed to the presence of riot police.

The international press corps jostled her audience freely, cameras held high like religious icons. The new German chancellor had not yet banned the media. Just across Pariser Platz, at the foot of the Brandenburg Gate, sat a tangle of television vans and satellite dishes. Sophie surveyed them from her podium and understood that she was making history. The first American Vice President to descend upon the new German capital of Berlin, she had appeared at a troubled time. The people gathered in the square expected her to deliver an *American* message—the promise of solidarity in struggle. Or perhaps redemption?

She had come to Berlin at the request of her President, Jack Bigelow, to inaugurate a foothold in the capital. Behind her, to the rear of the seats held down by the German foreign minister and the U.S. ambassador, the new embassy rose like an operatic set. Before it, Sophie Payne might have been a marionette, Judy playing without Punch, an official government doll.

The U.S. embassy's design had been fiercely debated for years. The trick, it seemed, was to avoid all visual reference to Berlin's twentieth century—that unfortunate period of persistent guilt and klaxons in the night. Comparison with the present regime might prove unfortunate. But neither was the nineteenth century entirely acceptable; that had produced Bismarck, after all, and the march toward German militarism. The State Department planners had settled at last on a postmodernist compromise: a smooth, three-storied expanse of limestone corniced like a Chippendale highboy.

It might, Sophie thought, have been a corporate headquarters. It made no statement of any kind. That was probably her job today, too.

But in the last thirty-six hours she had read the obscene graffiti scrawled on the new Holocaust memorial. She had met with third-generation Turkish "guest workers"—*gastarbeiters*—about to be repatriated to a country they had never seen. She had even dined with the new chancellor, Fritz Voekl, and applauded politely when he spoke of the rebirth of German greatness. Then she had lain sleepless far into the night, remembering her parents. And decided that a statement must be made.

Now she set aside her carefully crafted speech and adjusted the mike. *"Meine Damen und Herren."*

In the pause that followed her amplified words, Sophie distinctly heard a child wailing. She drew breath and gripped the podium.

"We come here today to celebrate a new capital for a new century," she said. That was innocuous enough; it might have been drawn from the sanitized pages she had just discarded.

"We celebrate, too, the dedication and sacrifice of generations of men and women, on both sides of the Atlantic, who committed their lives to the defeat of Communism." Nothing to argue with there—nothing that might excite the black-clad police or their waiting truncheons.

"But the fact that we do so today in the city of Berlin is worthy of particular attention," she continued. "The capital of Germany's past as well as her future, Berlin can never be wholly reborn. It carries its history in every stone of its streets. For Berlin witnessed Hitler's tyranny and horror, and Berlin paid for its sins in blood. As we dedicate this embassy, let us commit ourselves to one proposition: that never again will this nation submit to dictatorship. Never again will it shut its doors to any race. Berlin must be the capital for *all* Germany's people."

There was a tremendous roar—spontaneous, uplifting, and utterly foolhardy—from the crowd in the middle of Pariser Platz. A bearded figure waved his placard, chanting in a torrent of Turkish; he was followed by others, scattered throughout the square, and in an instant the police truncheons descended in a savage arc. Someone screamed. Sophie took a step back from the podium; she saw a woman crumple under the feet of the crowd.

Nell Forsyte, her Secret Service agent, was instantly at her side. "Say thank you and get out," Nell muttered.

Sophie reached for the microphone. And before the sound of the blast ripped through the cries swelling from Pariser Platz, she felt something—a vibration in the wooden platform beneath her feet, as though the old square sighed once before giving up its ghost. Then the Brandenburg Gate bloomed like a monstrous stone flower and the screaming began—a thin, high shriek piercing the chaos. A wave of red light boiled toward the podium where she stood, paralyzed, and she thought, *Good God. It's a bomb. Did I do that?*

Nell Forsyte flung Sophie to the platform like a rag doll and lay heavily on her back, a human shield shouting unintelligible orders. Somewhere quite close, a man cried out in French. Glass shattered as the shock wave slammed outward; the plate-glass windows of the luxury hotels buckled, the casements of a dozen tour buses popped like caramelized sugar. And then, with all the violence of a Wagnerian chorus, the massive glass dome of the nearby Reichstag splintered and crashed inward.

The chaos suspended thought and feeling. For an instant, Sophie breathed outside of time.

"You okay?" Nell demanded hoarsely in her ear.

She nodded, and her forehead struck the wooden platform. "Get off my back, Nell. You're killing me."

"Stay down."

"I'd prefer to get up."

The Secret Service agent ignored her, but Sophie felt a slight shifting in the woman's weight; Nell was craning her neck to scan the square. Sophie had a momentary vision of a pile of dignitaries—American, German—all crushed beneath their respective security details. She giggled. It was an ugly sound, halfway between a sob and a gasp. *If I could just get up, I'd feel better. More in control.* She dug an elbow into Nell's ribs.

The agent grunted. "When I count to three, stand up and face the embassy. I'll cover your back."

"Shouldn't we crawl?"

"Too much glass."

Nell gave the count and heaved Sophie to her feet. Only then did the Vice President notice that she'd lost a shoe. All around her, men and women lay on the platform amid splatters of blood, a hail of glass. The podium, Sophie realized, had miraculously shielded her from shrapnel. A tense ring of German security men surrounded the foreign minister; he sprawled motionless amid a heap of splintered chairs. Somebody—the embassy doctor, Sophie thought—was tearing open his shirt.

At the right side of the platform, maybe a yard from where she stood, a dark-skinned scowling man drew a machine gun from his coat and aimed it at Sophie.

She stared at him, fascinated.

Then Nell's pistol popped and the man's left eye welled crimson. He reeled like a drunk, his gun discharging in the air.

This time, Nell tackled her at the knees.

———

The medevac helicopter circled over Pariser Platz twice, ignoring the frantic signal of an ambulance crew from the rubble below. There was nowhere to land; survivors trampled the wounded underfoot, and the main exits to the Tiergarten and Unter den Linden were choked with tumbled stone and rescue vehicles. The chopper pilot veered sharply left and hovered over the roof of the embassy. Normally, a marine guard would have been posted there for the duration of the Vice President's speech, but the soldiers had probably rushed below in the first seconds after the explosion. The roof was empty. The pilot found the bull's-eye of the landing pad and set down the craft.

A two-man team scuttled out of the chopper, backs bent under the wind of the blades. They rolled a white-sheeted gurney between them. A third man—blond-haired, black-jacketed—crouched in the craft's open doorway. He covered the team with an automatic rifle until they reached the rooftop door. There, one of the men drew a snub-nosed submachine gun from his white lab coat and fired at the communications antennae bolted to the embassy roof. Then he blew the lock off the door.

A security alarm blared immediately. It was drowned in the clamor of Pariser Platz.

The blond-haired man raised his gun and glanced over his shoulder at the helicopter pilot. "They're in. Give them three minutes." He scanned the rooftop, the heating ducts and the forest of defunct antennae. Brand-new, state-of-the-art listening posts, all shot to hell in seconds. The CIA techies had probably been there for weeks installing them.

The helicopter rotors whined, and the man in the black jacket steadied himself against the door frame as the craft lifted into the air. The screams below seemed hardly to affect him. He scanned the square like a hawk, waiting for the moment to dive.

———

Machine-gun fire. It was the sound of her recurring nightmare—a dream about execution and a firing squad. Sophie struggled in Nell's grip, choking on the wave of oily smoke that had flooded Pariser Platz. It was impossible to see much—only the blank wall of the embassy looming. The agent lifted her under the armpits like a child.

"We've got to get inside." Nell thrust Sophie toward the dignitaries' chairs, vacant now as a theater on a bad opening night, shards of glass sparkling everywhere. Sophie could feel Nell's urgency nipping at her heels.

A marine guard thrust open the shattered main door. Then he fell, slack-mouthed and startled, dead at Sophie's feet. Nell's arm came up beside her. The agent fired at something in the shadows of the entryway. And then, with a sound like a punctured tire, Nell dropped to her knees. There had been no report from another gun. Someone inside the embassy had a silencer.

A clatter of footsteps, a gurney being lifted over the marine guard's corpse. Blood was spreading rapidly across the dark blue wool of Nell's suit. A rescue team in white coats surged toward Sophie, and she sank down beside the agent with a feeling of relief. Nell grabbed Sophie's waist with one arm and with the other raised her gun. As Sophie watched, a bullet struck the agent square in the forehead and she slumped over, rage still blazing in her eyes.

Sophie was cradling her, a dragging, bleeding weight, and screaming *Nell, Nell,* when they seized her from behind. Then night fell like the guttering of a candle flame.

"Get out of the way!"

The man at the head of the gurney shouted in German to the bewildered survivors at the edge of the platform. "We need room! Move it!"

The medevac helicopter hovered two hundred yards above Pariser Platz, a gurney line descending from the motorized reel. It took only seconds for the two men below to attach the stretcher. It rose slowly, smoothly, with its white-sheeted burden. A figure appeared through the swirling maelstrom of smoke—black leather jacket, blond head. He reached for the stretcher, steadied it, and swung it carefully inside.

A German newsman, his face smeared with soot, had his lens trained firmly on the chopper. Where it gripped the video cam, his right hand was slick with blood. "Who's on the stretcher?" he demanded.

The gurney team ignored him.

The newsman swung his camera into the face of one of the medical techs. Livid with anger, the man shoved it aside. The reporter dropped the camera with a cry of pain and clutched his wounded hand.

Shedding their white coats, now stained with blood and dust, the two men pushed through the crowd. An ambulance idled at the edge of the Tiergarten, strangely unresponsive to the hundreds of wounded in the square. They made for it at a run.

TWO

Arlington, 7 A.M.

CAROLINE CARMICHAEL BALANCED her coffee cup—an oversized piece of Italian pottery with *Deruta* stamped on the bottom—between the thumb and forefinger of each hand. Her gaze was fixed on the dull blue wing of a jay carping beyond her window. She may have seen the bird—may have recorded something of its petulance, the way its beak stabbed angrily at the sodden leaves. She may have acknowledged the rain streaming down into the defeated grass, and in some hollow of her mind determined which suit to wear to work; but for the moment she was content to sit nude beneath her oversized terry-cloth robe. It enfolded her like an ermine, a second skin. It had once belonged to Eric, and that alone made it precious.

The cotton loops smelled faintly of lemons. She closed her eyes and imagined him breathing.

Lemons. The groves of Cyprus, dry hillsides crackling with rosemary. Cyprus had come well before Budapest and was thus a place that Caroline could consider without flinching. Raw red wine and merciless sunlight, the sea a cool promise through the tumbled stones. She had bought the robe in a shop in Nicosia. He had worn it maybe four times. *I'm not a robe kind of guy,* he'd told her when she packed for home. *Take it with you. Really.*

And just what, Caroline wondered, was a robe kind of guy?

When Eric emerged from the shower, his hair a tousle of spikes and the night's growth of beard a haze along the jaw, he rarely reached for a towel. The drops beading his skin evaporated in the Cyprus heat, while he stood lost in thought, eyes fixed on nothing. Caroline never asked where his mind went in such moments. She was too well acquainted with Eric's demons—the fear that gripped him before certain meetings, the uncontrolled retching over the porcelain bowl.

Nicosia was bad. Budapest was worse.

She could have loved the craggy old city on the banks of the Danube were it not for the change in Eric. Some nights, working surveillance in the passenger seat beside him, she would lose herself in the spectacle of Buda Castle, floodlit and austere on its manicured slope. By day she plunged into the warren of Pest's back streets, where the buildings' grimy plaster facades, untouched as yet by the mania for renovation, hovered like the backdrop to a Bogart movie. Beneath the coal dust that penetrated every crevice of every shop, she found carved chests daubed with brilliant birds, embroidered linens, spurs once owned by a Magyar horseman. She fingered the cloth, stroked the splintered wood, and imagined a vast plain swept by wild herds. Later, when the incessant rains of March fell, she retired with a book to Gerbeaud's, the city's most venerable coffeehouse. She toyed with chocolate torte and eavesdropped on young Italian tourists.

Eric refused all refuge. He grew hollow-eyed from strain and restless nights; he spoke sharply when he spoke at all. When she referred to a time beyond Buda, he lost the thread of conversation. Always a creature of discipline, he became, if anything, an ascetic—forgoing sleep, the after-embassy drinks hour, even her body in the small hours of morning. The night meetings ended increasingly at dawn, long after she had closed her book and put out her light. She would awake early and dress for the embassy in silence, her husband an insensate stranger shrouded amid the sheets.

Three months before the end of their tour, Eric accepted temporary duty in Istanbul for the summer. Caroline decided to head for the States the same day he left Budapest. She had no reason to go on to Turkey with him, no duty in Istanbul. She would work in Langley and hunt for a house. Headquarters would be glad to have her back—they never asked inconvenient questions. And perhaps absence would improve Eric's frame of mind. Dispatch him from his present limbo, a restored creature.

I'll call you, he says as they stand in the echoing concourse of the Frankfurt airport. There are no lounge areas at the individual gates, no place to sit and talk. Bearded men too large for their tropical-weight suits are wedged between newspapers and duty-free bags, smoking endless cigarettes. Their wives pace the concrete floors in wrinkled saris, children curled in their arms like sacks of flour.

The international terminal is one vast waiting room between past and future, punctuated by drooping plants and security portals and guards with electronic sensors. Terrorism haunts the Frankfurt airport, because a decade ago a boom box wired by two Libyans was loaded from the tarmac into the baggage compartment of Pan Am 103. That flight ended in fiery chaos over a small town in Scotland. And now Frankfurt is determined to shut the barn door on the horse's ass.

It takes hours to process through security. Tourists disinclined to learn from history ignore the gate queues and raise their voices in complaint. Bags are opened, or x-rayed, or swathed in yellow twine. Forms are stamped. Cameras monitor. People stand and sweat and stare blankly with ill-defined tension. And at last, the baggage dismissed, they win the freedom of this concourse. Its sterility is almost harrowing.

Caroline clutches her boarding pass in her right hand, her carry-on in her left, when what she really wants is to hold Eric until the breath leaves his body.

"I'll be at the Tysons Marriott," she says. "I'll let you figure out the time change between Istanbul and Virginia."

She notices with half her mind that the Americans complain the loudest. They eddy in a tide of sweatsuits around the island that is Eric, convinced they deserve some sort of dispensation. They've paid in blood for world dominion, and this German obsession with order is an outrage. It smacks of cattle cars shunted to a Polish siding, of diversion to the death camp showers. Patience is a virtue Americans distrust.

Eric touches her cheek. Kisses her forehead chastely, as though in benediction. And turns away, his mind shifting elsewhere. Caroline stretches out her hand to his retreating back. But it is already too late. It is this she will remember, years later, when people ask. She will remember that they parted in silence.

Did he suspect what would happen that frantic April morning? Or did he go ignorant as a calf to his destruction?

Caroline drank the last of her coffee, the taste of sewage in her mouth. The jay beyond her window lifted its wings and flitted away; she was very close to being late for work.

When the news breaks, she thought, it's the one thing on everybody's mind, the question we never ask aloud. We shrug off disaster, hurl obscenities at the slow car in the fast lane, skip our workouts for a long lunch. But the question remains; it hovers like a priest's profile, half glimpsed through a confessional screen.

When a plane explodes five miles above the earth, how exactly do you die?

Over the past two years, she had pinned down some specific answers. Twelve of the passengers on MedAir 901 were found seventeen miles from the plane's point of impact, dead but still strapped into their seats. Five others—first-class passengers who sat directly over the forward baggage compartment, where investigators believed the bomb exploded—were incinerated at ignition. Seven of the taller members of the coach section were decapitated when a wing sheared off. Ninety-eight others never got out of the fuselage. But the worst of it, in Caroline's opinion, were the ones who were sucked from their seats, to swirl with the air currents like leaves or empty candy wrappers high above the coast of Turkey. At thirty thousand feet they would lose consciousness in seconds, suffocate in the thin air, freeze in the subzero winds. And disintegrate on impact.

Even now, when she closed her eyes at night, she saw the children. There'd been twenty-one of them on MedAir 901, some of them teenagers, some of them still in diapers. Candy wrappers, all of them, in their pastel Easter clothes.

Eric's was one of the bodies they never found at all. Two and a half years of probing the metaphoric wreckage, a thousand days of questions thrown out into the clandestine universe, and Caroline still did not know how her husband had died.

It was Eric she longed for now, in the rain of Arlington, as she tossed the dregs of her coffee in the sink and padded down the length of carpeted hall to her solitary bedroom. She longed for the tautness of a thigh, the delicate flesh above the hip. The rime of sweat that lived in the crease behind his knee. *All these,* she thought, *all these are denied me.* And the pain of it stopped her short in the doorway, to take a ragged breath, to calm herself, and to move then with resolution toward the closet door.

She was halfway up the George Washington Parkway when the news from Germany broke.

———

The CIA's Counterterrorism Center was in the grip of its daily frenzy. Tucked away on the ground floor of the New Headquarters Building, the CTC was a windowless three thousand square feet of stale air and blue industrial carpeting, where fifty-odd terrorism experts jockeyed for space and priority among a welter of cubicle partitions. It brought together CIA case officers, Intelligence analysts, FBI agents, and Secret Service detailees in a way that no government organization had ever attempted before. Turf battles and chains of command were set aside in the Center; here, the common threat took precedence. There were people who knew Farsi and people who knew explosives and people who knew where Moammar Qaddafi slept each night; people who dreamed in Arabic, or understood counterfeiting, or chemical precursors, or how storage centers were hidden in the hearts of mountains. Here the stuff of fiction was commonplace—the satellite images of guerilla training camps, the electronic intercepts of private conversation. In Caroline's mind, it was the most fulfilling and exciting three thousand square feet in the entire world.

She paused at the door, expecting the inevitable—the bruising flight of one of her colleagues toward the hallway connecting the New Headquarters Building with the Old—and was rewarded with a sharp jolt in the rib cage as Sandy Coutts careened past her.

"Sorry," he muttered. And never looked up from the cable he was reading.

Sandy was a small, fussy, white-haired man with a correct British accent. His wire-rimmed spectacles were clouded with thumbprints. He disapproved of Caroline—Sandy disapproved of all young people on principle, and particularly female ones—and yet she regarded him with affection. He was a character straight out of George Smiley's Circus. And he knew everything there was to know about Beirut and Lebanon. If, while crossing the street in his distracted fashion, Sandy Coutts were to be hit by a bus one day, the collective memory of Middle East analysis would be wiped out in an instant.

Where partitions divided the room, a particular branch held sway: the Hizballah people, the Bin Laden people, the ones who followed the PFLP-GC. Caroline turned right on Bin Laden Lane and made her way to Via Krucevic. It was the place she called home in the CTC—the branch that watched the 30 April Organization. Its members were an elusive band of international killers—madmen, probably; psychotics and sadists and all-around bad boys, certainly—but disciplined and deadly. Their agenda was simple. They wanted a Europe cleansed of the non-Aryan races; they waged terror in order to achieve it.

Thirty months earlier, they had blown up Eric's plane.

"Hey, Mad Dog." Cuddy Wilmot was already standing by Caroline's desk. He was one of the few people allowed to call her that—the name Eric had given her after a reckless display of courage during her paramilitary training—but then, Cuddy had been Eric's friend. Now he was Caroline's. He was also her branch chief.

"The afternoon briefing at State is canceled," he told her. "Scottie's called a staff meeting for nine A.M."

"Any news of the Veep? What hospital she's in?"

Something about Cuddy's face—the half-apologetic way he shoved the bridge of his glasses upward with one finger—warned Caroline that bad news was coming. Cuddy never apologized.

"Have you seen the footage?" he asked.

"Didn't have time." She glanced at a television monitor suspended from the ceiling; a few people were gathered in a tight knot under it. She started to walk toward Scottie Sorensen, the Center's director, but Cuddy grabbed her elbow.

"Come into my office."

They serpentined through the huddle of desks, past fat piles of paper balancing rotary fans and coffee mugs tattooed with lipstick, past bookshelves bulging with academic journals and videotapes and yellowing scraps of newsprint. Other than the people watching the news, everybody in the place was bent over their terminals, intent on scanning the traffic that had been dumped overnight. Searching for the spoor that presaged a terrorist kill—the threat phoned in to an embassy, the report of a suspicious briefcase—anything that might scream culpability in the Berlin bombing.

"What is it?" she asked Cuddy, feeling her heart accelerate.

He closed his office door behind her. Not that it mattered; the walls were made of glass.

"I think you ought to see this in what passes for privacy." He bent over the VCR and stabbed at a button.

"Why?"

He didn't answer. Everything about Cuddy—the sleeves of his yellow oxford cloth shirt rolled up to the elbows, the ugly polyester tie he kept in a desk drawer and knotted around his neck as an afterthought—was as it should be. But in the small room Caroline could feel his tension humming.

"You think this was done by our boys." She said it quietly. "That they hit the Gate. You think 30 April tried to kill the Vice President."

"I don't know what to think. That I'm going insane, maybe. Have a seat, Caroline."

The footage was German, pulled off the Agency's massive satellite dishes. She ignored the network voice-over and focused on the screen. A wide-angle shot of the new embassy, the crowd milling around Pariser Platz. A surprisingly nice day for Berlin in November.

"Who's the guy at the mike?" Cuddy asked.

"Dietrich, Graf von Orbsdorff," she replied. "Foreign minister. Former Christian Democrat turned Social Conservative. He fought with Helmut Kohl for two decades, then switched parties when Fritz Voekl and his fascist buddies moved into town."

"He's dead," Cuddy said without emotion.

Caroline took a deep breath and expelled it slowly. As a leadership analyst in the Office of Russian and European Analysis (a place known by the unfortunate acronym of DI/OREA), she had followed von Orbsdorff for nearly six years, before Scottie Sorenson had persuaded her to join the CTC. She knew everything about the German foreign minister—where he bought his suits and how much he paid, the address of the apartment where he kept his mistress, why his father had committed suicide before the Nuremberg trials.

"There's Payne," Cuddy said. "Watch closely."

"Meine Damen und Herren . . ."

The Vice President looked so very small, Caroline thought, as she stood poised behind the podium. Her black hair, cut in a smooth bob to the chin, fluttered in the breeze. She wore a dark red suit—well tailored, the color of blood.

"Interesting speech." Caroline folded her arms across her chest, as though they might protect her from the coming blast. "Probably not the one she was supposed to give."

Cuddy did not reply.

And then Sophie Payne lifted her head, distracted by something off camera. A second later, the image rocked, then careened wildly out of focus.

"Veep's down," Caroline said, eyes on the screen.

The television camera wheeled to face the Brandenburg Gate. The lens caught a mad stampede of bodies, the opened mouths screaming. Cuddy lowered the volume. "Now watch."

The film went blank. A pause, and then a helicopter filled the camera, wavering against a slate gray sky. A stretcher swung gracefully upward into its belly.

"That's Payne?" Caroline leaned forward, frowning. "What exactly happened to her?"

"German liaison is claiming she was shot by a Turkish sniper. They found the guy with a slug in his head from a dead Secret Service agent's gun."

"The agent's dead? Shit."

"Twenty-eight people are dead, Carrie." Cuddy said it savagely. "Forget the Veep. Look at the belly of that chopper."

He picked up the remote and rewound the tape. Again, the helicopter filled the screen.

"Look at the guy at the winch. Everyone's so focused on the goddamn stretcher they haven't even noticed."

Caroline looked. She saw a man with unruly blond hair curling over his black leather jacket. Aviator sunglasses. Powerful shoulders. A thin blade of a nose. Wide lips pinched together in concentration. His hands reached out to steady the swaying stretcher, and with one glimpse of his strong, blunt fingers Caroline knew the truth.

She stumbled out of her chair and fell on her knees by the monitor. Splayed her hands across the screen as though that might bring him home.

The man in the chopper was Eric.

THREE

Langley, 8:23 A.M.

O kay. so she's probably not in a hospital."

Caroline was pacing like a leopard on a short leash, five feet in one direction, five feet in the other. She wanted to run out of the Center, run madly down the hall, run to wherever Eric was at that moment. *He's alive, he's alive. The bastard is alive.*

"Sit down, Caroline," Cuddy told her. "Someone will notice. We don't want that to happen."

She started to speak, started to hurl the anger of wasted years in his face—then sat down abruptly.

"You didn't know," he said.

She looked up. "Did you?"

"I wasn't married to him."

His bitterness was like a sharp blow. "Do you think I could pretend that he was dead? For *two years*? Or that Eric would trust me to do it?"

"Eric loved you, Mad Dog." Cuddy studied a brown stain—coffee, probably—on the carpet at his feet. Unable, now, to meet her eyes. "He trusted you with a lot."

"Not with his life," she retorted. "Eric trusted nobody with that."

They were both silent a moment, the thought of Eric like another person in the room.

"It'd be one hell of a way for a terrorist to get information," Cuddy said distantly. "To have a wife in the middle of the most sensitive counterterrorism network in the world."

"You know me better than that."

"I thought I knew Eric."

"Stand in line," she whispered.

"Don't cry, Mad Dog. It doesn't suit you."

He was wrong; she wasn't going to cry. "Who else knows?" she asked.

Cuddy shrugged. "Can't say. He looks different. There's the sunglasses, the longer hair."

And most of the CTC personnel were fairly new. Their rotations through the Center were at the most two years old. They thought of Eric as a dead hero, one of the stars chiseled sharply on the Agency memorial. There was a good chance he had gone unrecognized.

"Scottie?" she asked.

"We'd have to tell Scottie in any case."

"He'll go to Atwood. He'll have to."

Cuddy shoved at his glasses impatiently. "What do you want, Caroline? Your husband screwed the entire U.S. government this morning, okay?"

She tore open the door and sped toward the CTC director's office. Stumbled once on her high heels and swore out loud. It was a testament to the madness of the day that nobody even looked at her.

———

Scottie's door was open, but he'd turned off the fluorescent lights. He sat behind his desk in the unnatural

gloom—white-haired, hollow-eyed, host to more para-
sites than medical science had isolated. His face bore a
look that Caroline recognized. The look of a case officer alone in the field who knows he has been betrayed.

He was a private man who kept most people at a distance. He had graduated from Yale at a time when
Intelligence was still glamorous, and he wore the code
of silence like a good English suit—unobtrusive, yet tailored to the man. A string of ex-wives would argue that
he was charming—too charming for his own good—
and charm had made his career. Scottie's recruitments
were like an exercise in seduction, and the rush of it
all—of taking a soul into the dark side of Intelligence—
kept him hungry for the field. He loved running agents,
loved the dead drops in the deserted parking lots, the
midnight surveillance, the unexpected takedowns.

Caroline thought that he had loved Eric.

It was Scottie who had pulled her husband off his first
tour—in Kabul, in the middle of the Soviet-Afghan
war—and sent him to Beirut. After Beirut it was
Athens, where Scottie was Chief of Station. Then
Nicosia. Then back to the CTC, where Scottie got the
director's slot and made Eric his deputy. Only to send
him to Budapest twenty months later, a decision that
Caroline could barely forgive.

Scottie would not be deceived by long hair and sunglasses.

She tapped twice and waited.

His eyes slid over to hers, slid away. "Come in and
shut the door."

She positioned herself squarely between the chief and
the vague middle distance he was studying and said,
"What are you going to do?"

"You've seen the tape?"

"I've seen Eric."

He smiled grimly. Unlike Cuddy, Scottie didn't bother to question her loyalties. Thirty years in the buttholes of the world, Scottie would have said, had taught him all he needed to know about loyalty. Either Caroline Carmichael was a terrorist mole or she was a victim like the rest of them. That was a question for the Agency polygraphers to answer.

"How fortunate that you never remarried. Any idea, Mrs. Carmichael, what our fair-haired boy is up to?"

"None whatsoever. Did you set this up, Scottie?"

A faint smile. "Now *that* would have been magnificent. But even I cannot come up with a good reason to snatch Sophie Payne. She's too short and too intelligent for my taste."

"Never mind that. Let's talk about Eric. Why pretend to be dead for more than two years? Why lie to all of us?"

"I don't know." He pushed himself away from his desk and stood up. "Only Eric can answer those questions, Caroline, and unfortunately he's incommunicado at the moment. Our first duty is to find the Vice President. Everything else is homework."

He was right, of course; Payne's life hung in the balance. The small matter of a dead man's resurrection would have to be ignored for a time.

"It seems fairly obvious that she's not in a German hospital," Caroline said.

Scottie shrugged himself into his suit jacket. He favored glen plaid, like a latter-day Duke of Windsor; he must own twenty variations on the theme. "The White House is beginning to realize that, too. None of the Berlin facilities has admitted her. President Bigelow is screaming for information, and the Germans are giving him squat."

"Did you hear Payne's speech?"

"I imagine we'll hear it ad nauseam before the day is out. It was impolitic, under the circumstances, but hardly enough to spark a kidnapping. I've watched the footage over and over, Caroline. The bombing, the confusion, the medevac chopper—it all took about nine minutes. That argues a fair amount of sophistication and planning. We're dealing with professionals."

"Of course," she replied. "But which ones?"

He held her gaze. "If you don't know, then I'm certainly not going to guess."

"What is that supposed to mean?"

"Well, Caroline, you were married to him. You tell me. Of all the terrorist groups Eric worked, whom did he want to screw the most? Because he's obviously jumped into bed with somebody."

"Christ," she muttered. "I hope to God it's not 30 April."

"I doubt he'd still be alive if it were." The statement was hard. "Krucevic and his kind taste betrayal in their mother's milk. They'd have blown Eric's cover inside of three minutes and killed him in three and a half."

"He's our only lead, Scottie. To the Vice President. You realize what that means?"

"He's a killer, Caroline, and he's out in the cold. Dare Atwood has asked for a briefing. I'm due right now on the seventh floor."

"You have to tell her about Eric." It was half statement, half question; Caroline dreaded the answer.

"I was hoping you might do that," Scottie said.

FOUR
Langley, 8:40 A.M.

SO WHAT AM I SUPPOSED TO BELIEVE, ERIC? Tell me that.

Caroline follows Scottie's elegant back through the broad corridors connecting New Headquarters with Old. The walls here are mostly glass. The space is arranged as a museum. She inventories pieces of the Berlin Wall and OSS radio transmitters without seeing them. *What am I supposed to think? That you're a hero, or a traitor to the cause? A madman or a savior? What's the story this time, Eric?*

She has been here before. She knows this tight place between reason and heartache as well as she knows the contours of her bed. Words of caution clamor in her brain, and once—for Eric—she would have flung them to the four winds. But now there is her training to think of. Her position within the Intelligence community. All the professionalism that is expected of her. And what the hell does she owe the bastard, anyway? *Two and a half years, Eric.* Alive. And not one word.

Their heels echo on the scarred linoleum, then are swallowed in the rush of other feet thudding from corridor to corridor. The halls of espionage are awash with bureaucrats, with Case Officers and Managers, Technicians and Administrators. Caroline is an Analyst, and has been for years. Well before the word was a job title.

When she considers her life—when she attempts to picture it—she sees a loop of unbroken thought, coiled like a strand of DNA. She is comfortable in her head. She observes and judges from a distance. It is a talent she was born with, one that earns her a living. Now work reinforces nature—or perhaps it is nature alone that determines the structure of her days, the cubicle in which she sits, the green light of the Intelligence cables flickering softly in the filtered air. Her Agency job is somehow inevitable, a genetic predestination.

Every day she slips off the George Washington Parkway and slides behind the safe shelter of her desk. She flips on her computer. She downloads the truth. She follows an account, which means she tracks 30 April through the wilderness of news flashes, clandestine reports, transcripts of illicit conversation beamed down from satellites orbiting in space. She follows the shadow of a beast unseen and attempts to describe its height and color. She briefs the Policy-makers—she tells them what has been and what might be—and they trust her enough to listen. Caroline has earned a reputation for reliability. And when the Policy-makers award her their respectful silence—when they gaze at her steadily, hanging on every word—Caroline glows with a sense of triumph. What the Policy-makers do with her information is their own affair. Her job is *beyond* policy. She is the High Priestess of Reason, she lives in Objective Thought. It is the deepest safety she has ever known.

Reason can be trusted, reason doesn't let you down.

Reason won't leave you grieving without so much as a postcard.

In Caroline's life, betrayal has always come from what she cannot control.

"You have a very high analytic," her Agency interviewer had said as he flipped through her application all those years ago, "and the introversion is practically off the charts."

"High analytic?" Caroline repeated. "Is that good?"

He looked up from the file, dark eyes accusing. He was in his late thirties and might possibly have been attractive once, but was running now to fat. His wedding band was smudged, his tie soiled; he smelled mustily of failure. He told her his name, and she assumed that he lied. She decided to call him George.

"Find the company of strangers utterly draining? Parties exhausting? Do you often stay home, in fact, at the last minute?"

"Sometimes. What has that got to do with the job?"

The office had been part of a square and featureless building on the outskirts of Vienna, Virginia. She sat before George's desk, her skirt suddenly too short for comfort, uncertain what to do with her knees. She was waiting for the bus to the polygraph center, where it was rumored that three applicants were dismissed for every one who survived. In the past ten months, the FBI had unearthed every drama of her college years, every friend she could claim, every joint she might regret. She was twenty-three and on the verge of security clearance. Only the box and the wire, the unconscious guilt that might trip her up, lay between her and the job.

"You're an INTJ, Ms. Bisby," said George.

This was well before Eric and the name she assumed

like an official alias; well before Mad Dog came howling from the underbrush.

"Only four percent of the general population fall into that category. But it's heavily represented among Agency analysts. Almost thirty percent, in fact. You've found your way home. Congratulations."

"INTJ?"

"Just a classification. In the Myers–Briggs Type Indicator. It means you're rational rather than emotional; that you make swift judgments; that you prefer to work in quiet and solitude." The murky eyes slid away from her own. "More comfortable, perhaps, with *ideas* than *people,* Ms. Bisby. It's not a criticism. Just the classic description of an Intelligence analyst. Your ticket to the job."

"I see," Caroline replied. "So that's a good thing, right?"

———

Now Scottie is pushing the button for the elevator and Caroline is trying not to replay in her mind that piece of German videotape, Eric's head emerging from the chopper like a fox from its den. Beside her, Cuddy Wilmot rocks on his worn heels, his hands shoved into his pockets. He has retrieved his polyester tie from his desk drawer and scrounged a suit jacket from a friend. It hangs unevenly above his wrinkled khaki pants. Caroline is aware of Cuddy's unspoken sympathy; it clings to him like sweat. But he says nothing. She folds her hands over her stomach and studies the panel of lights above the elevator, tracking the descent.

What hooks everybody is the information, the vanished George confides in her ear. *Satellite intercepts, foreign news translations, classified reports from controlled agents—more pieces of the puzzle than you ever knew existed, delivered to*

*your desktop with the tap of a finger. Access, Ms. Bisby. Access
gets the High Analytics every time.*

There is such a thing, Caroline might reply, as knowing too much. As drowning in all the data the world
flings at you.

Eric, she thinks, *how the fuck could you do this to me?*

————

When they entered the room, Darien Atwood was gazing through the rain-spattered window at the belt of
trees dividing the Agency campus from the George
Washington Parkway. Caroline registered beeches and
maples, a preponderance of pin oak. The branches wavered and dissolved in sheets of chilling rain. The DCI
ignored the three of them, as though concluding some
kind of mental conversation; and so they approached
her desk in silence, lowly supplicants before an altar.
Scottie reached a furtive hand to his perfectly knotted
tie.

Caroline had known Dare Atwood for eleven years.
Well before she was DCI, Dare had managed the re-
gional office in which Caroline cut her analytic teeth.
Despite the gap in their ages, they were fellow travelers:
smart women impatient with mediocrity, demanding of
themselves and everyone around them. Dare's progress
through the bureaucratic ranks—her ascension to the
Senior Intelligence Service and, eventually, to the post
of Director of Central Intelligence—had placed a natu-
ral distance between them; but if Caroline possessed a
mentor in the clandestine world, it was Dare.

She was familiar, through long association, with the
small personal tics that betrayed Dare's feelings. She
studied the DCI's rigid back and saw that she was
enraged.

Dare was a tall woman with a face as lined as a wind-fallen apple. Her black wool dress could have graced a Shaker; her smooth gray hair resembled Joan of Arc's. Her heels were never more than two inches high. She fairly screamed a capable practicality; in another century, she would have commanded a boarding school for young ladies, or ruled a kingdom through the convenience of a husband. The DCI permitted herself two luxuries: a wardrobe of brilliantly colored Hermès scarves purchased through the years in Paris, and a deep topaz stone, cut in a cabochon, that she wore on her middle finger. They seemed revelations of an interior life far richer than her appearance inferred.

Like Caroline, Dare was born an analyst. She, too, was a High Priestess of Reason. Caroline realized she was depending upon that fact this November morning. Dare would find a way out of Eric's labyrinth. It was just a question of time.

"It's three o'clock in the afternoon in Central Europe," Dare said to the rain beyond her window. "Berlin was hit at twelve. They've had three hours to get out of the country."

"In a helicopter," Cuddy Wilmot amended. "That means they could be anywhere."

"If they're intelligent, they'll have ditched the chopper within minutes and switched to cars." Scottie's voice was dismissive; they all knew that Eric was intelligent. "They'll assume a few hours' lead time while the dust settles and we're confused about the Vice President's whereabouts. But at this point, the chopper's a dead end."

"Assume they're in a car, then," Dare said impatiently. "Headed where? Toward Switzerland or Poland?"

She was looking now at Scottie, her back to the

streaming trees, her arms folded tightly across her chest. Rage, still, in every line of her body; rage completely contained. Toward Eric? The situation? Or Caroline?

"They could've gone to ground in Germany," Scottie told her. "Even in Berlin, there are a thousand places they might be hidden."

"Not with the entire Voekl security force on the loose." The impatience was scathing now, a personal slap. Dare despised easy answers. "You've seen CNN. The men in black are turning Berlin upside-down."

"If I'd gone to the trouble to stage that medevac rescue," Caroline said, "it'd be for one reason—to divert attention, and buy time. Then I'd get the hell out of Dodge before the borders closed."

"So you're betting on Eastern Europe." Dare could have added, *Where Eric knows the roads.* The thought, unspoken, hovered over all their heads.

"We have no way of knowing where they've gone," Scottie objected, "until we know who they are."

"Then let's hear an educated guess," the Director snapped. "It's what we're paid for."

"The German police are claiming that the bomb was set by *gastarbeiters*," Cuddy said tentatively, "the legal aliens Chancellor Voekl wants to send back to Turkey."

"I've seen that report. It's bullshit." Dare gripped the edge of her desk and eyed the three of them. "Sophie Payne was not kidnapped by a bunch of disaffected *gastarbeiters*. At this point, the U.S. is the only friend those people have. They'd be mad to strike against us."

"The Turks make a convenient scapegoat for the Voekl regime," Caroline pointed out. "So convenient, I'd almost believe Fritz Voekl ordered the hit himself."

"Then he should have done it before Payne opened

her mouth." Scottie frowned. "That speech can only have been an embarrassment to him."

"Incitement to riot, in fact," Dare agreed. "Next, the Germans will say the Veep brought this whole mess on herself. Then they'll send us a bill for the Brandenburg." She twisted the topaz on her finger. "So what are we left with?"

"A presumed-dead case officer on the wrong side of the law." Scottie, Caroline noticed, was avoiding her eye. The man possessed depths of sensitivity long untapped.

"And with whom is the case officer cavorting?" Dare asked. "Any ideas, Caroline?"

Too many, in fact. I am drowning in Access. The plane disintegrating, the children like candy wrappers in the updrafts over Turkey—*Eric, how the fuck could you do this to me?* Access, Ms. Bisby. Gets the High Analytics every time. *Never mind the man like a fox in his den.* Assemble the facts. Marshal your arguments. *Analyze.*

"Eric worked a number of terrorist targets over the years," she told Dare. "The PFLP–GC. Abu Nidal. And right at the end, Bin Laden. But he was obsessed with only one—the 30 April Organization."

"Thirty April." The DCI traced an intricate pattern on her dark green blotter. "An East European terrorist group with acknowledged hostilities toward the United States. Neo-fascists, reactionary extremists, the type who hate to see women in power."

"Sophie Payne and her liberal agenda would push all their buttons."

"Not my first choice for the Vice President, Caroline." Dare's voice was harsh. "They're certifiable."

"And perfectly capable of pulling off this morning's hit. Ever since the NATO intervention in Kosovo, they've been looking for a way to hurt us."

"Scottie, what account was Eric working in Budapest?" Dare asked.

"At the time of his death—or what we thought was his death—he was Chief of Station."

"In other words," Caroline said, "he wasn't supposed to be working *anything*."

"Serving more in the role of grand coordinator of everyone else's targeting, is that it?"

"Eric never really took to management," Scottie admitted apologetically. "He couldn't give up the field, Dare. He thought 30 April was too difficult a target for junior CO's. So he tried to recruit within the organization himself."

"And did he succeed?"

The Counterterrorism chief hesitated. "I believe he was closer to penetrating them than we'd ever been before."

Dare took a turn around the room, thinking it through. "Thirty April bombed a plane that Eric Carmichael was supposed to be on. Is that why the plane went down? Because Eric was on the passenger list? It seems a bit excessive, killing two hundred and fifty–plus people in order to get one man—but we know that Krucevic's boys are a law unto themselves."

"Or . . ." Scottie said delicately.

"Or Eric Carmichael was working with 30 April well before MedAir 901, and got the bomb on that plane himself. Again, a bit over the top as a means of declaring oneself dead—but who's to argue with the irrational?"

Involuntarily, Caroline shook her head.

"You don't think so?" the DCI challenged. "How much did you know about your husband's work in Budapest, Carrie?"

I knew about silence. I knew withdrawal. The shrouded figure in the bed each morning, the retching over the porcelain bowl.

"Very little," she replied evenly. "Eric was always discreet about operational matters."

"Even with his *wife*?" The DCI was incredulous.

It was what they all expected, Caroline thought, this collusion of marriage. No possible way to excuse her ignorance. She watched them thinking: *What kind of wife were you, anyway?*

"Eric always protected me," she attempted. "He told me nothing. I was the person most at risk besides himself."

Dare snorted. "Risk! You knew what you were getting into when you married him, Carrie. There were always several Eric Carmichaels. It was a crapshoot which would surface on any given day."

"Of course." Caroline bit down on the edge of anger, managed to suggest calm. "Eric was trained to live a lie. That's what case officers do. And if you're good at your job—if you work the hard targets—the lies start to seem like the only truth you've got."

"Hear, hear," Scottie murmured ironically.

Caroline ignored him. "Thirty April operates out of Central Europe. It was clear Eric and I had been sent to Budapest for that reason. Of course I put two and two together. But I never knew how close Eric had gotten to them. And when he was killed, I thought he'd failed."

"And rather spectacularly, at that." Dare's tone was brisk. "How encouraging to learn instead that he succeeded in penetrating the bastards. Now if we only knew *why.*"

"He wasn't on MedAir 901 when it blew up, obviously. I can't tell you why. *I don't know.*" Her voice rose—was she defending Eric? Or herself? "I don't know how he came to be in Berlin this morning. But I do know that Eric Carmichael had a visceral hatred for terrorists and for 30 April in particular. He would never adopt their methods."

"We saw him today in that chopper, Mad Dog, kidnapping the Vice President of the United States."

It was unlike Cuddy to lash her so brutally; he was an analyst, too, he lived by his objectivity. But the anger in his voice was entirely personal. Eric's defection had rocked Cuddy's world.

"Isn't it just possible that once Eric discovered his plane was hit—that he was officially dead—he decided to stay that way? That he infiltrated 30 April in order to nail them for MedAir 901?"

"Caroline," Scottie said quietly.

But she persisted. "For all we know, he showed himself to us deliberately this morning. What if it was the clearest message he could send? *You've got a guy on the inside.*"

"Whom we wouldn't need if he'd done his job in the first place!" Cuddy again, brittle with exasperation.

"We can't know what Eric is doing," Scottie declared, "or what he might have done two years ago. Whether he thinks he's operating under deep cover or not, the truth is, he's gone completely AWOL. He's committed an act of terrorism against the U.S. government. Twenty-eight people died this morning. Seven more are in critical condition. Our Veep is missing. We can't cover him on this one, Carrie."

"A guy on the inside," Dare repeated thoughtfully. "Have you considered what President Bigelow is going to say when he learns there was a CIA case officer on that chopper?"

Caroline looked at Scottie. The Terrorism chief did not immediately reply. He merely studied his Director with a frank expression of bemusement, the one he reserved for particularly boring dinner partners. It was obvious that the President would have all their asses in a sling.

"We'll be stripped to our shorts and whipped out of town," Dare informed them succinctly. "We'll be hauled before a Congressional investigation to explain something none of us understands. We'll be—"

"Ridiculed and pissed on by every son of a bitch inside the Beltway," Scottie concluded.

"And we'll be shut out of the Payne investigation." Caroline's voice was tight. "When, at the moment, we're the only ones with a lead."

"We've got no choice," Cuddy Wilmot protested.

"Haven't we?" Dare shot back. "Think what you're saying, Wilmot. None of us will be immune when the press gets their knives out. Everything will be distorted: Eric's history, our investigation of MedAir 901, all your work for the past two and a half bloody years. All our efforts to save lives and put these psychos behind bars. Crucified before a television audience of two hundred million."

"And meanwhile," Caroline said, "Sophie Payne is still out there. Trying to get home."

"That German footage?" Dare asked. "Is it being shown on CNN?"

"Yes." Scottie reached into his breast pocket for cigarettes, although he had quit smoking months ago. "And probably the other networks as well."

Dare's dark blue eyes locked on to Caroline's. "How recognizable is your Eric?"

As a fox in a den, as a shroud among the living. The scent of lemons in the unquiet dark—

She did not quite answer the question. "When the FBI realizes that Payne has been kidnapped, they'll shove that tape under a microscope."

"They won't be looking for a dead man." The DCI spoke with decision; she had weighed the options and jumped. "We have no choice but to stand behind Eric Carmichael. He's our curse and our gift. We blow his cover and we blow our own. But if we let him run for a bit—and follow where he leads—maybe we can salvage something from this travesty."

"You're suggesting . . . a cover-up." The lack of emotion in Scottie's voice betrayed his shock.

"I'm suggesting we admit the truth," Dare replied. "With the quality of the videotape and the chaos in the square, which of us can be certain what we saw? Eric Carmichael—or a man who simply looks like him? It would be foolhardy in the extreme to say anything to anyone—much less the President—without more proof."

"And foolhardy not to follow every lead," Caroline added.

Dare nodded once. "Right."

Cuddy Wilmot shifted uneasily in his chair and studied his hands. Caroline kept her face expressionless and her hope tamped down. *Hope for what, exactly? Eric's redemption? He wouldn't thank me.*

Scottie steepled his graceful fingers and affected an air of candor. "Forgive me, Director, but I must object. Anything short of Eric Carmichael's immediate disavowal is far too dangerous, for ourselves and the Intelligence community."

"We live in a dangerous world, friend."

"Do you realize what you're asking?" Scottie straightened in his chair and assumed the look of wounded dignity he usually reserved for Congressional Oversight. "You're asking us to *lie*."

"I am asking you to do exactly what you pledge to

do every day of your lives," Dare told him crisply. "Disclose information on a need-to-know basis. Right now, Scottie, nobody needs to know about Eric Carmichael."

He opened his mouth; she raised one hand, as if under oath.

"I may think entirely differently in a few days. Events may so order themselves that a rapid disclosure is inevitable. But I see no reason to rush to judgment now. In fact, I think such a course would prove injurious to the kidnapping investigation and, ultimately, to the survival of the Vice President."

"You're serious."

"Never more so." She held his gaze. "But I need your commitment, Scottie."

"Or my resignation. Jesus!"

"You won't resign. You wouldn't throw that woman to the dogs and walk away."

"But neither do I intend to go to prison. Not for you, Director Atwood, and certainly not for Eric Carmichael!"

"I wouldn't expect you to." There was a trace of amusement in Dare's voice. "Give me three days, Scottie. No more. Seventy-two hours of effort behind the scenes. State and FBI will head up the investigation, of course—and we'll be expected to scour the world for information. We'll try our damnedest to figure out where the Veep is and how to reach her. And we'll support the President in every possible way—short of full disclosure. Full disclosure gets us all screwed. And Payne *dead*."

Dare had deliberately raised the ante. No one wanted to be responsible for the Vice President's death. Caroline felt a spark of admiration for the DCI; Scottie was silenced, Cuddy Wilmot overwhelmed. Dare had the guts to manipulate them all. But Caroline clung to her line like a drowning woman.

"For the moment," the DCI concluded, "we keep all knowledge of Eric Carmichael's survival completely to ourselves. *Not one word* of what has passed here is to leave this office. End of discussion."

FIVE

Langley, 9:30 A.M.

WHEN THE THREE OF THEM had left her, Dare sat
still for a moment and stared at her hands. The
fingers had once been beautiful; now they were crabbed
with age and misuse. She touched her cabochon topaz
and remembered the man who had given it to her.
Then she put her head down on her desk and closed her
eyes. She was fifty-three years old—young to command
such power, too old to conceive of doing anything else.
If the Agency's peril in the present situation was great,
so was her own. Never mind that Eric Carmichael had
walked on her predecessor's watch. If he was found and
exposed, Dare would have to resign.

She was the first woman ever to command the comfortable suite apportioned to the Director of Central
Intelligence. They were all behind her, the shadow men,
their portraits ranked on the headquarters walls: pipe-
smoking Allen Dulles, jaunty unto death; slick-haired
Richard Helms, with all the self-possession of an under-
taker; gentleman Bill Colby, the perfect dinner partner;
and ruthless Bill Casey, whom she'd battled and served.

A preponderance of Bills, now that she thought of it—and these men had other things in common. All were entrenched in the old-boy net, the cozy club of prep schools and Ivy League, of wartime service in the OSS, of an age when espionage was sanctified by David Niven in a blue blazer. All would have looked on Darien Joan Atwood as an outrage—a competent secretary, perhaps, but not to be trusted with a table in the executive dining room.

They had bequeathed her this office, a bed and full bath available for use in twenty-four-hour crisis, a conference area with a massive cherry table, an adjoining suite for her personal assistant, and a bevy of secretaries. She had a C-141 Starlifter at her disposal, and an Air Force colonel to fly it. A navy blue armored sedan chauffered by a bodyguard. Even a personal elevator—with a secret access code—that carried her directly from the seventh floor to her private garage.

But what Darien Atwood really commanded was an intricate hierarchy of power. The CIA was only the most obvious borough of her realm, the neighborhood she called home. As Director of Central Intelligence, she held the reins of the entire Intelligence community: the eavesdroppers and decoders at the National Security Agency, the overhead reconnaissance satellite teams, the military-minded missile counters plugging away at the Pentagon. They all reported to their chain of command, of course; but their agency chiefs were in thrall to Dare.

To be a woman in such a position was to invite flak. Dare survived her Senate confirmation hearings on the strength of her record—she had spent twenty-three years as an analyst at the CIA, rising steadily through the bureaucracy, and done two tours of duty on the staff of the National Security Council—but many of the doubts were voiced in private. Was she tough enough? Could she adequately assess the nature of security threats? Would she be snowed by hostile Intelligence forces (the Russians came to mind) posing as newfound friends? Did she, in short, have the balls to do a man's job?

And now, Dare thought, Eric Carmichael would answer that question for all of them. Carmichael's fate, and that of the woman he held captive, would make or destroy Dare's career. She smiled derisively. Either way, there'd be a *Newsweek* cover in it.

Eric she had already dismissed; there was no road back from the place he had gone. She was taking a terrible risk by suppressing his identity; some would call it criminal. There would be no defense if she failed—only a Congressional hearing and a plea bargain for immunity. But Eric alone might lead them to Payne, and in the Vice President's salvation, Dare read the future of the CIA. What had Abraham Lincoln said? "I must bury the Constitution in order to save it"? Her present position was precisely like that.

The telephone on her desk shrilled a summons. She allowed it to ring once, then picked up the receiver. Jack Bigelow wanted her in the Oval Office.

SIX

On the Czech–German Border, 3 P.M.

SOPHIE PAYNE AWOKE TO THE SOUND of a woman's sobbing.

The weeping went on and on, inconsolable, repetitious, maddening beyond belief. She wanted to scream for silence, but, too weak and too detached to part her lips, she submitted to the monotony. At some point she would be forced to open her eyes—forced to take up again the questions she knew were hovering—but for now, it was enough to float in velvet and ask nothing at all.

Until the moment she realized that the sobbing was her own.

They had stuck a needle in her arm. She was coming out of a drugged sleep.

She sat up sharply and slammed her head against a flat surface. *I'm under a table,* she thought. *They left me under a table. But why is it so dark? I can't get the blanket off.*

She tried to reach for her face. No good; her hands were tied behind her back. She struggled to open her mouth, but her lips were sealed shut, probably with tape. The blanket muffling her head was some sort of hood. But she could still hear—the sobbing was proof of that. However blind and mute they had made her, they could not stop her ears.

Sophie eased herself to the right, cautiously, and felt another slope of wall. The same thing to the left. She was confined in a box about three feet wide and five feet long.

A coffin. She was in a coffin, buried alive.

The horror of it made her panic. Her wrists strained against each other, the tape cutting cruelly into them; the tape held firm. Between the gag over her mouth and the hood over her head, she was suddenly suffocating. She gasped for air, stars exploding before her eyes. Then she sank back, whimpering with self-pity, and tried to breathe through her nose.

And in the silence, she felt it.

The box was moving.

It crept sideways, then ground to a halt. Something—an axle? A brake pad?—squealed faintly. The box slid sideways again. Shuddered to a halt. The squeal of the brake.

She was in the trunk of a vehicle that was barely moving. A car? Were they approaching an intersection? Or just caught in heavy traffic?

Either way, there might be people around.

She sat up and butted her head hard against the trunk lid. Did it again and again, braying through her bonds like a crazed animal, until pain forced her to stop.

No one delivered her.

The car eased forward, slid to a halt. Eased forward again. Perhaps it was a freeway, snarled by an accident, and in the general frustration the rocking trunk went unnoticed. Or maybe the car was filing through a toll-booth.

Then comprehension came like a piercing ray of sun, and in her mind's eye Sophie saw it clearly: a snaking ribbon of stalled traffic tiny as Matchbox cars, the German border crossing far below. She had glimpsed a similar scene the previous day from the privilege of an Air Force chopper, on her way into Berlin.

Or was it two days ago, now? A week?

Terror washed over her again. How long had she been in the trunk? How long had she been missing?

The car eased forward, braked. There was a pause, and then a man's voice said quite distinctly, "Thanks. Have a good day."

He had retrieved his passport from the border control and hailed them in Boston-accented English. *She was being kidnapped by an American*. What the hell was going on?

Sophie Payne slammed her head against the trunk roof and screamed.

The car gained speed and plunged into another country.

SEVEN

Langley, 11 A.M.

I'M GOING TO COUNT TO THREE," Eric says, "*then I want you to jump.*"

Caroline is sitting alone in the fourth-floor bathroom of the Old Headquarters Building, safely concealed within a locked stall. Somewhere beyond the bathroom door, Sophie Payne is still missing and the work of the CTC continues; but Caroline's mind has fled backward a decade or more, to the heat of a Tidewater spring, the black cloud of no-see-ums hovering before her face, the peculiar smell of sweat when it is generated by fear.

She is crouching in the open doorway of the jump tower. A canvas harness bites into her chest. The white paint of the old wooden struts is flaking away under her moist palms. Forty feet below is a blur of grass and dirt bisected by the rope line she is expected to trust. To her back, unseen but felt, is the mass of others—braver than she, quieter in their panic, knees poised for ascent along the three flights of stairs. She has no choice but to jump.

Eric's hand in the small of her back. The cool pressure of it through the dampness of her fatigues.

"Don't push me," she mutters.

"I won't. One, two, three—"

He sweeps his left arm forward, as though that might release her. She doesn't budge.

"Let's try it again."

"Would you stop touching me?"

"One, two, three—"

"I said don't push me!"

Eric glances over his shoulder at the waiting line of trainees, looks back at her profile. She will not meet his gaze. "It's the perfect distance, Caroline," he says conversationally, into her ear. "Forty feet. That's why they built the tower this high. To make you sweat, to show you the power of your fear. Anything less, and you think you'll survive; anything higher, and you're too remote to care. Nobody knows why. Forty feet. It terrifies us all."

She swallows, nods.

"Trust the line. Trust me."

"Just let me jump by myself."

"It's a little like sex," he continues, in the same tone. "Some of us need a push now and then. To get over the edge."

She pivots and stares at him, amazed at his recklessness; but his expression is perfectly neutral. Only a watchfulness in the blue eyes, a shrewd calculation of her response. She glances away, feels the heat flood her face.

She is exactly twenty-five years old. Eric is maybe thirty, a lean and agile man she barely knows. He belongs to the Agency's Special Activities Service, SAS, a paramilitary force designed to be sent at a moment's notice anywhere in the world. He has ruled Caroline's life for the past month, demanding what she once thought impossible. And for Eric, she has tried to do it. She has navigated alone across ten thousand acres, dodging armed Chinooks hunting her by air; she has rappelled off a helicopter skid with an M-16 strapped to her back. The desire for his respect, his grudging acceptance of a woman in a man's world, is like a junkie's need for a drug.

He has begun to invade her dreams with a desire so complete that she awakens wet and shaking in the predawn darkness, crying out for his touch. Sleep for Caroline has become both seduction and purgatory. She will return soon to Langley. Eric will stay in deepest Tidewater. It is unlikely she will ever see him again. The vital thing, the essential thing, is never to let him know the extent of his power.

She crouches once more in the tower doorway, knees bent, eyes fixed on the line. "Give me the count."

"One, two—"

And then she feels his hand shove her ruthlessly off the platform, and she is sailing down the line with her mouth open in a full-throttled yell, half terror, half outrage, the anger surging up with the force of the ground. She rolls and tumbles. Tears off the harness. And turns to shout up at him. "You asshole! You *pushed* me!"

But he is already urging the next trainee to jump.

So much, Caroline thinks, *for trust.*

———

She begins to feel him watching her, blue stare averted as soon as she looks at him. In the base club he bends low over a pool cue, blond hair grazing his brow. The click of the balls, the crowing as a shot goes home—

they resonate through the clamor of voices like bullets singing across an empty range. He ignores her deliberately, flirts with her friends, waits to see if she has noticed. In the manner of men who toy with desire, afraid of what they want.

Caroline begins to hate him. When she speaks to Eric at all, it is with something like contempt.

The last evening of her paramilitary training, the class holds a farewell dinner. Caroline endures the speeches, the increasing inebriation, only so long. Then she slips outside to walk the trail along the river, alone in the cooling dark. She considers leaving early, a drive north in silence. Preferable to predawn hangovers and awkward farewells.

There is a footfall behind her, noiseless as a cougar's. A sigh that might be the wind stirs last year's cattails, although the night is windless. She stops short, keenly aware of her isolation, sensing the menace of a predator. To the right, the densest woods. To the left, the blackest water. Somewhere ahead, the Yorktown Bridge twinkles, remote as Brooklyn. A scream would be lost here; to run is suicidal. And she has been trained, after all, in self-defense. She has been taught to kill with a single sharp jab of her cupped hand to the windpipe, although even now she does not believe it.

She turns. Sees the watchful blue eyes, unaverted for the first time. He is poised to spring or run, she is uncertain which.

"You," she says.

He takes a step toward her. She retreats, and halts him in his tracks.

"I know it seems safe," he says. "The safest place in the world. Guards at the gate and grenade launchers in every corner. But you shouldn't walk alone in the dark by the river."

"I have never wanted very much to be safe."

"No." A flash of teeth in the darkness. "It's a type of cowardice in your book. You look for risk instead. Why is that, Caroline?"

That's not who I am, she thinks. *That's what you've made me.* "You don't join the CIA for job security, Eric."

"No. You join to sit at a desk and analyze cables all day. To write up your opinions as fact and generate more reports. A numbing dose of computer screens and low-level briefings, day in and day out. The life of reason. Is that what you want, Caroline?"

Reason is safe, she wants to say; *reason can't cut the heart out of your body.*

He is within inches of her now. She catches the scent of his skin—sunlight and underbrush, a secretive life lived out-of-doors. "I think you'd die a slow death, like a diver cut off from air. I think you're made for better things."

"Are you recruiting me?" she asks in disbelief. "The SAS has no use for women."

"I'm no longer in the SAS." His voice is exultant, the voice of conquest. "As of tomorrow, I belong to the Directorate of Operations. Case officer training. It's what I've wanted for years."

"And what does that have to do with me?"

He studies her for a few seconds, saying nothing. Then his finger traces the skin of her shoulder, bare tonight in her party dress. Gooseflesh under his touch: The demons of sleep come to life.

"What does this have to do with me, Eric?"

"I've been poised on the edge a long time, Caroline. Afraid to step out into nothing. Some of us need a little push."

The hand curves to find her shoulder blade, circles the sudden tautness of a breast. She arches away from him, unreconciled, even as her pelvis melts toward his. And then his mouth is at the base of her throat and her fingers are raking through his hair. The grip of wanting so fierce it robs her of breath.

"I know who you are," he whispers. "I know what you crave and what you fear, what you pretend and what you hide. I know the depth of your strength and your doubt. I even know what you think of *me*, Caroline."

She wants to run, she wants to sink down into the grass and take him deep inside her, she wants never to see him again.

The urgency of his mouth is a kind of whip. She feels his hand trace the flesh of her inner thigh, find the heat at its core—and then he releases her so abruptly she nearly falls. In the sudden quiet there is only his breathing, the sound of river water slipping through the weeds. She considers telling him to go to hell. But nothing he has said—nothing he knows—is untrue. And he is staring at her as though she could decide his life with a word.

"What does this have to do with me?" she repeats.

"You're the one woman I could trust in the depths of hell, the woman who would believe regardless of everything. You're what I need, Caroline. And I've never needed much."

She closes her eyes, takes a shuddering breath.

"Let's leave tonight," she says. And steps off some inner tower.

––––––––

The one woman I could trust in the depths of hell, the woman who would believe regardless of everything.

Caroline paces the bathroom floor and considers her options. Had Eric left her behind deliberately in Frankfurt airport, ignorant and faithful and trusting and stupid, while he set off to remake the world? Had she been his ultimate cover, the grieving widow no one would blame? Or was today's bomb at the Brandenburg an impossible accident, his face in a helicopter a bizarre coincidence, that defied her attempts at rational explanation?

What was she supposed to believe, exactly, in this particular hell?

Belief, like trust, isn't rational, she thought. Belief is blind, a wash of black in a room full of light, a breath suspended at the end of a diving board. She had loved Eric, but she never trusted him with much. There were parts of his life forever closed to her, regions of his soul she could not navigate. She had gone with her gut when she married him, ignored the advice of family and friends, giddy with all she was not considering.

But the High Priestess of Reason is not easily silenced. Voices had persisted in Caroline's brain. There were the questions she asked, and answers he tried to give; terms they negotiated like peacemakers at parley.

Until the final silence of the Frankfurt airport, and the final explosion.

––––––––

What are you thinking? Eric asks.

His body is perfectly still in the cratered grass. All

around them the Virginia night is thick with pine pollen, with midges, with the musky smell of spent sex; but his skin, where her fingertip traces a rib, is marble cool. Stillness is one of his talents. He keeps the world at bay, he opts out of action, he retreats inside his head where the best secrets always are. Six months at the Farm, in case officer training. *And so it begins,* Caroline thinks—the life he cannot share. He has traded his fatigues for chinos and oxford cloth, in the classroom he rolls up his sleeves and loosens his tie, he looks like a wolf sleeping by a primeval fire, partly tamed but never domesticated. What do they have to teach him, really, these retired CO's pensioned off into training? Six months, and he knows what he has always known: how to watch without being seen.

She feels him watching even while she sits alone in Arlington, a hundred miles away—that silent surveillance like a stroke on her neck. The sense of him burns in her throat as warm as whiskey, and she thinks, *He is watching me.* Eric's love, Eric's too-intent and narrow-eyed passion, her breath catching thick at his touch.

"What are you thinking?" he asks her again.

"Have I given you that right, too? The inside of my head? You've never given it to me."

She sounds deliberately amused. Her way of keeping the world at bay.

"That's important, isn't it? What I give and don't give."

"Only when you want something in return," she says.

"You try very hard. To love me without conditions. You think that's what I need."

"Isn't it?"

"You're afraid of losing me. If you build me a cage." His voice is remote.

She sits up, pulls her bare knees to her chest, the sticky wetness between her legs nothing more than a mess. She reaches for her clothes.

"All right," she says. "I'm thinking about loyalty. Whether it's possible to give without thought, without conditions. Blind loyalty."

His hand closes on her wrist. She stops pulling up her jeans. Slides into the crevice between his side and his arm and lies there, her cheek against the marble skin.

"Blind loyalty is always possible. And it's always a mistake."

She lets out a little sigh of despair. "Where are *your* loyalties, Eric? I'm not talking about love or sex or even myself. I'm curious. About you. What claims your soul?"

A snort. "You think I've got one?"

She turns away from him. Shoves her foot into a shoe.

He watches in silence. Another man would be smoking now, but Eric gave up cigarettes when he gave up the streets of Boston, gave up his foster family's name, gave up the idea of fairness. He is watching her trying not to notice him watching her.

"You can't do this job without some kind of loyalty," he says. "You can't be a marine, a Green Beret, or an Intelligence operative—not unless you decide that something matters beyond yourself."

"Your country?" She tugs a sweater over her head and mutters, "Bullshit. *Country* is an excuse for wanting to die."

He thrusts her back into the grass with such unexpected force that she's winded for an instant. She lies there, Eric's weight on her chest, his eyes inches from her own, and stares into the blue.

"Okay. One loyalty drives me, one thing I won't betray. Call it a pact with myself, Caroline, if you're tired of *country.* A long time ago I said I'd never close my eyes on deliberate evil. That sounds pretty broad, and pretty simple. But it's my brand of integrity. Of keeping the faith. Of an inner standard I walk every day. I may hurt the people around me, I may fail them in ways they never expected—but I will not do less than the best job I can with the work in life I've chosen."

"Which is?"

"Making the world a safer place."

She moves under him restlessly, an objection forming. He ignores her.

"You think that sounds stupid. Or grandiose. Fine. I'm not like other people, Caroline, who dream of a perfect world and try to create it, even if it's just in their own backyards. I pace off the property and find out why it's for sale. I test the broken board in the fence where the fox creeps in, I poke spikes in the rat holes. I name every weed and mark where it grows. It's all I've got, Caroline—this permanent fixer-upper. You stop work for a day, and the place falls down around you."

―――――

Caroline stares at herself now in the fourth-floor bathroom mirror. There are lines scrawled at the corners of her eyes, dark blotches under the skin. Her lips are thin and dry. She closes her eyes, waiting for a whiskey rush, for the sense of Eric watching her—but nothing comes across the miles that separate them, no sense of love or loyalty.

You stop work for a day, and the place falls down around

you. Only she hadn't stopped. She'd been working for years, plugging holes and nailing up fences. And he'd never bothered to tell her he was alive.

Where were you going from Frankfurt, Eric? And why are you hiding in those weeds you marked so carefully?

What exactly am I supposed to believe?

EIGHT

Langley, 11:53 A.M.

CAROLINE'S STRONGEST IMPULSE upon quitting the women's room was to leave the Old Headquarters Building. She could retrieve her car from the acres of asphalt that lapped the campus like a modern-day moat, and drive through the back roads of McLean, the high banks of horse fields and elm. In a car, however, she would have no buffer from her raging thoughts. No work to consume her, no colleagues to force the daily pleasantries from her mouth. She turned back into the CTC and strode toward the ranks of gray metal shelves that rose at one end of the room. She had researched the lives of the men—and they were all men—who made up 30 April. Their stories were presented almost clinically in the Agency's biographic profiles.

These one-page reports were intended for use as briefing aids for government officials. The bios were chatty and informative, riddled with small detail and the occasional sweeping judgment. Text was punctuated with Intelligence controls—*U* for Unclassified, *C* for Confidential, *S* for Secret. The most heated debates flared over the use of ORCON information—Originator-Controlled—which signaled that the source was a foreign national, an asset on the payroll of the Directorate of Operations.

A secret agent, in the more romantic language of a vanished age.

Caroline pulled out a heavy green file and sat awkwardly on the carpet, high-heeled legs folded as discreetly as her slim skirt would allow. She would start with the apprentice in the group, the youngest of Mlan Krucevic's recruits: thirty-year-old Antonio Fioretto.

Fioretto was a computer genius, twice incarcerated for fraud in Italy, where no one is imprisoned for fraud. The funds he'd illegally transferred out of a variety of Swiss bank accounts had never been recovered. He now served as 30 April's main accountant and electronics whiz. The photograph in his biographic profile had been taken from a police mug shot—grainy, unsmiling, curly-headed, and weak-jawed. The hair was blond; he was *Milanese*. What the photo failed to show was the healed scars of three suicide attempts. Antonio's wrists were hacked to shreds.

She slid his file back into the stack.

Otto Weber. Native of Zurich, recovered heroin addict, an obsessive bodybuilder and martial arts practitioner. He had grown up on the streets, quit school at thirteen, worked episodically as a male prostitute. Weber was rumored to be a confirmed sadist. The 30 April member who enjoyed killing.

Vaclav Slivik. A retired captain in the former Czechoslovak Army, Slivik could fly anything with wings and served as 30 April's explosives and weapons expert. A mild-looking man, from his photograph; cyn-

ical eyes, a humorous mouth. In 1972, at the Munich
Olympics, he had won a gold medal in the pentathlon.
He allegedly played cello in his spare time, although
public performances were rare of late.

Caroline pulled the fourth file and opened it with
unsteady fingers. This one she would read in its entirety.

Mlan Krucevic. Leader, 30 April Organization.

No picture for the bio she had written three years
before, and updated every six months. Krucevic had
never been captured on film.

*Perhaps the most ruthless terrorist to emerge from the
breakup of Yugoslavia, Mlan Krucevic is thought to reside
in Germany, although his present whereabouts are unknown. A trained geneticist with advanced degrees from
two European universities, Krucevic served as director of a
Croat prison camp in Bosnia-Herzegovina from 1990 to
1993. He is alleged to have approved the torture and
murder of over three thousand Muslim and Serb men
during his tenure at the prison camp, where he is believed
to have used biological agents in human experimentation. He has been indicted by the International War
Crimes Tribunal on nineteen counts of crimes against
humanity and is currently a fugitive from justice.
(C NF NC)*

*In 1993, Krucevic announced the formation of the
30 April Organization, a neo-Nazi militarist group,
with the simultaneous firebombing of seven Turkish
guest-worker hostels throughout Germany; sixteen people
died in the acts of arson. According to a reliable source
with limited access, 30 April is also responsible for the
death of Anneke Schmidt, Germany's former Green
Party leader, and the kidnapping and murder of Dagmar
Hammecher, granddaughter of the German federal court*

judge Ernst Hammecher. The terrorist group is also suspected of orchestrating last year's assassination of Germany's popular Socialist chancellor, Gerhard Schroeder. (S NF NC OC)

In the 30 April Organization, Krucevic has assembled and trained an elite group of mercenary fighters hailing from several European countries, who are united by their adherence to his ideology. Although Krucevic has allegedly professed anti-Semitic views, his deepest hatred is reserved for adherents to the faith of Islam, which he has declared is on the verge of destroying Christianity. An untested source with good access reports that Krucevic's ultimate goal is the ethnic cleansing of Central Europe. (S NF NC OC)

According to a reliable source with limited access, Krucevic fled Bosnia-Herzegovina in 1993 and lived under a series of assumed names in Scandinavia and eastern Germany. He is reported to have set up a black-market network for the production and distribution of deadly biological agents. Krucevic may secure considerable income from a series of legitimate front companies to which he has been tied, but the chief source of 30 April's funding remains unknown. As an avowed enemy of Islam, Krucevic has spurned the usual Middle Eastern patrons of terrorism. The bulk of his funding probably comes from private sources within Europe who support his ideological goals. (S NF NC OC)

We believe that Krucevic is highly intelligent, disciplined, and dedicated. Although an extremist in his political views and the methods he employs to further them, he is not, in our view, mentally ill. When he kills, it is for strategic or philosophic reasons, rather than as arbitrary acts of sadism. (S NF NC OC)

Krucevic demands unquestioned loyalty from others, but is incapable of trust. He does not tolerate dissent *within the 30 April Organization; according to an untested source with good access, Krucevic personally shot two of his senior deputies last year in an internal purge. (S NF NC OC)*

Krucevic, fifty-eight, is the son of a Croat who committed suicide after World War II. He is estranged from his wife of thirteen years, Mirjana Tarcic, but is believed to have custody of their twelve-year-old son, Jozsef. He reportedly speaks Croatian, Serbian, German, and some English. (C)

What the bio did not mention, Caroline thought, was that Krucevic's father was rumored to have been an Ustashe concentration camp commander. The place he might have governed from 1942 to 1945 bore one of the ugliest names in Yugoslav history: Živ Zakopan, "Living Grave." But no one had ever found the camp after the war; no witnesses survived to describe its horrors. Only whispers and imprecations remained, the furtive sign against the evil eye, among the children and grandchildren of those who had died.

The CIA was not in the practice of printing rumors.

Four grainy black-and-white photographs were tucked into Krucevic's file. Caroline studied the first, dated seven years before: a shot of a tenement house in flames, a Turkish woman raising her hands in anguish, keening. At her feet was the blanketed corpse of her small son. The next photo was now famous the world over: a Mercedes limousine creased in its midsection like a metallic boomerang. Gerhard Schroeder's body lay at a bizarre angle across the backseat, his right hand dangling from the open passenger door. The chancellor had been an attractive man before Krucevic crushed his armored car like a soda can.

Caroline's fingers hesitated over the final two pictures. She hated seeing them. They had been taken in a police morgue, as exhibits in a trial that would never be held. Krucevic's trial for inhuman cruelty, for utter lack of heart.

Dagmar Hammecher was three and a half when she was snatched from her nanny at gunpoint. She had bright gold hair that cascaded down her back, and she loved to pose in ballet shoes. Her mother taught in a Hamburg medical school, her father was a banker. But it was Dagmar's grandpa whom Krucevic intended to destroy. Ernst Hammecher was a federal court judge charged with considering the constitutionality of Germany's new alien-repatriation laws. He had survived the Nazi era, and was no friend to bigots. He was expected to reverse the legislation. Ernst Hammecher received his granddaughter's hand in the mail two days after she had been kidnapped.

Caroline forced herself to look at the police photograph. The childish fingers still curled upward, as they must have done a thousand times in Dagmar's short life—reaching for her mother, her favorite stuffed toy, the curved handle of a juice cup. But the edge of the severed wrist was ragged and black with blood. They had not attempted to spare her pain.

"*Otto,*" Caroline whispered. The 30 April member who enjoyed killing.

The final shot was of Dagmar's corpse, dropped on her grandfather's doorstep six days after the child's abduction. The small features were gaunt and pale, too drawn with suffering to be those of the little girl who loved ballet tutus and chocolate ice cream. Krucevic had shaved her head. The wounds of electrodes placed in the child's skull were obvious even in reproduction.

Her throat tightening, Caroline thrust the vicious image facedown against the file folder and read through Krucevic's bio again.

One of the sources she had used in the report—a DO source—had been characterized as untested, with good access. She flipped quickly through the documents attached to the left-hand flap of Krucevic's file. A translated piece from the German newsmagazine *Das Bild;* another from a Sarajevo newspaper; five State Department cables out of Frankfurt, Bonn, and Belgrade; and three TD's—the classified and sifted reports disseminated by the Directorate of Operations. These were what she sought.

When the DO released clandestine reporting for an Intelligence analyst's use, it always withheld the foreign agent's code name. As an act of kindness, however, the directorate characterized the sourcing. A reliable source was one whose information had proved accurate over time; an untested one offered intelligence that couldn't easily be verified or that was too recently reported to assess. But any source with good access was inherently more valuable than one without.

Unless that access was used to sell false information. Krucevic was certainly clever enough to plant a mole in the CIA's turf; but what had this one actually reported? That the good doctor had shot two of his people in an internal purge. That he was driven to wipe Islam out of Central Europe. Nothing particularly earthshaking, and hardly worth Krucevic's brilliant effort at deception. A 30 April mole would have been put to better use.

And yet Caroline felt an almost sickening surge of

excitement at the thought: A source with good access to 30 April *existed*. A source who might know where Eric was. A source who could lead them to Vice President Sophie Payne.

His code name and history could be found in one of the DO's asset files, to which Caroline was routinely denied access. She was an analyst, not a case officer; she had no clearance for information that linked a source to his identity, a code name to an address. But Scottie Sorensen and Cuddy Wilmot did.

She checked the report's date and origination. The TD had been disseminated the previous February from the DO's Hungarian branch. Which meant the asset was probably handled by Buda station.

"Hey, Mad Dog, could I see you in my office for a minute?"

She gasped involuntarily, clutching the file to her chest. "Cuddy, you scared the hell out of me. What's up?"

He grimaced. "Nothing major. Just an evaluation I'd like you to sign."

It was a deliberate lie, and Caroline saw with mild shock that they had become a cell within a cell, collaborators in a subterfuge.

"Okay," she said neutrally, and tucked the Krucevic file under her arm.

"Interesting reading?" Cuddy inquired as they walked toward his office.

"Nothing you haven't seen before. They like to say that leadership analysis is the *People* magazine of Intelligence, but I don't think *People* will be running this stuff anytime soon."

"Let's pray for that, shall we?" He shut the door firmly behind her. He had abandoned his glasses, and the hazel eyes were bloodshot from hours of scrolling through text on a computer screen. The look on his face—self-absorbed, absent, as though he pursued a line of thought only remotely connected to the scene before him—was one Caroline knew well. Cuddy was in the grip of the chase. Until he nailed Sophie Payne's kidnappers, he would abuse his body, his brain, and the people around him.

"You need a cigarette," she said, dropping into the seat before his desk. "Or a good long run."

"And what do you need? A leave of absence?"

"Answers to a lot of questions would be just fine. Or a shoulder to cry on."

"Why don't you call Hank?"

"Hank's shoulders are a little too well tailored for tears. Besides, I haven't talked to him in nearly a year."

"Then I'd say it's high time."

"He never liked Eric, Cud. And what could I tell him? It's all a close hold anyway."

Hank. His silver-haired profile rose in Caroline's mind, shimmered there like the outline of a perfect knight, an old-world cavalier. The acute gaze, the measured speech. Hank never swerved from the path of reason. He'd taught her everything she knew, and most of what she'd forgotten.

"The DCI would advise me not to talk to my lawyer," she added. "Even one in my family."

"Not all Hank's counsel is professional."

Caroline shrugged in discomfort, and Cuddy dropped the subject. They stared at each other for a few seconds in silence, uncertain what to say. Every topic seemed forbidden.

"Feeling betrayed?" Caroline asked finally.

"Feeling stupid," Cuddy replied.

"Sometimes they're the same thing."

"Scottie's asked me to head up the Berlin Task Force. I got the impression I had no choice."

"This is where I say, 'That's why they pay you the big bucks.' Right?"

"Not if you want to survive." His eyes were unreadable. "I've had just about as much as I can take, Carrie. I've spent thirty months investigating a crash that didn't kill my best friend, and I've just been told by the DCI herself to suppress information critical to the recovery of the Vice President. I don't know why I'm still here."

"Maybe," she suggested, "because you think you can fix it. Big mistake, Cud."

He laughed harshly and looked away.

She felt a sudden rush of sympathy for the man. He was a good person, a faultlessly honest person, who didn't deserve this kind of painful ambiguity. Never mind that ambiguity was the human condition: Cuddy lived in a happy mess of absolutes. He refused to eat meat, but his fingertips were permanently stained with nicotine. He stood in the rain-filled doorways at the end of the Agency's corridors ten times a day, burning his death ration and hoping to save his lungs later with a three-mile run. He fought the last good fight in the U.S. government—tracking terrorists—but believed Amnesty International was a front for Communist insurgency. He spoke five languages, all of them well, which was something that most people did not know. Cuddy never advertised.

Each morning, he drove down the Maryland side of the Potomac while Caroline drove up the Virginia. He wore jeans and carried his work clothes in a backpack. He parked his car on Canal Road and canoed across the

Potomac to the Agency's foot. Those last few moments, Caroline thought—Cuddy gliding alone through an arrowhead of water—were all he could really claim of his day.

"Who's working the task force with you?" she asked him.

"Dave Tarnovsky. Lisa Hughes. Fatima, in case there's a Middle East connection."

But not Eric's wife. Caroline would be kept at bay, an unknown quantity. There was nothing wrong with Cuddy's team—Tarnovsky was an ex-SEAL, an expert on explosives; Lisa Hughes had just completed her doctorate in Middle Eastern studies; and Fatima Bowen was a native Lebanese, one of the dark-skinned, silk-clad, black-haired women who served the CTC as a translator and general cultural referent. She'd married Mike Bowen twenty years earlier, during his last tour in Beirut. When he died in the 1983 car bomb attack on the U.S. embassy, Headquarters had given Fatima a job. Lebanese women with a thirst for revenge were to be prized above rubies.

"Sounds like Scottie is focusing on the Palestinians," Caroline said neutrally. "To buy time, I suppose?"

"To divert attention from Eric. Per Atwood's instructions."

"That might work . . . until 30 April makes contact."

"And won't we look like idiots if they do." He glanced at her sidelong. "What was Eric really like in Budapest, Carrie?"

"You visited us in Nicosia," she said tiredly. "Multiply that by ten. On good days, he was jumping out of his skin. On bad days, he was comatose."

"Was he close?"

A sudden, sharp memory of Eric's hands roaming

over her body. The Mediterranean heat, black olives and lemon. How long had it been since he had touched her?

"Close? Not to me. I suppose it makes sense that he walked away without a backward glance in the Frankfurt airport. I don't know what happened, Cuddy. How he managed to drift so far."

"Not close to *you*," he corrected impatiently. "To penetrating 30 April. Was he jumping out of his skin because of the danger? Or because he'd already turned on all of us?"

"I don't know." Her throat was tightening despite her best efforts. "I just do not know, Cuddy. He stopped talking."

"Even to you." A flat statement.

What kind of wife were you, anyway?

She could not trust herself to reply.

"That's strange," he muttered. "Even the polygraphers recognize a case officer's right to pillow talk. They've practically canonized it."

Pillow talk. From a man who had walked the streets at night, while she tossed alone and restless? Cuddy, Caroline thought, would make a damn good polygrapher himself. He had a genius for posing the brutal question.

"Maybe he wanted to protect me——" She bit off the words. A more credulous woman could go on believing that Eric was protecting her—that the whole elaborate lie of the past thirty months had been designed to shield her from terror. But Caroline refused to be credulous any longer. The credulous impaled themselves on swords of their own making.

"Scottie tells me Atwood wants you polygraphed."

She laughed at the abrupt change of subject. "I suppose it's inevitable. She has to know whether I'm telling the truth about believing Eric was dead. Let's hope the polygraphers keep their questions confined to MedAir 901."

"I think we can assume they will. Atwood is unlikely to share the fact of Eric's existence with Security. Just keep your mind on the plane crash and forget about Sophie Payne. You'll be fine."

"Scottie likes to add a column of numbers when he's hooked up to the machine." Caroline spoke with an effort at lightheartedness she was far from feeling. "He swears it keeps him from reacting to the questions. But I'm lousy at math."

"Then try spelling. Anything is preferable to nerves. Nerves can look like guilt to the box, and guilt might register as deception."

"Thanks. You've no idea how comforting that is."

He studied her, then said, "I wish I could go with you."

"But some things, as my grandma told me during potty training, we are forced to do alone." Caroline unclipped the clandestine report from Krucevic's file and slid it across the desk. "Take a look at this, Cuddy. There's a DO asset who's close to 30 April."

"Hungarian desk." Cuddy flipped to the second page, brows knit, instantly absorbed. "This guy could be in Buda. Hell, by this time Sophie *Payne* could be in Buda."

"Exactly. We've got to send out a tasking cable."

"And how do we phrase that cable, Carrie? 'Hey, guys, the official Task Force line is that the Palestinians are responsible for the Berlin bombing, but chat up your 30 April asset and ask whether he's ever heard of Sophie Payne'?"

Caroline frowned. "I've read weirder tasking cables, thank you very much. Case officers are used to working blind. And with the Veep snatched, Scottie will have every terrorist expert the Agency owns sniffing the ground—the reports will come flooding in. This is a *lead*, Cuddy—"

Cuddy tossed her the DO report. "We don't know diddly about this guy, Mad Dog. He's untested. What if he's one of Eric's recruits?"

He was closer to penetrating 30 April than ever before.

"I wouldn't be surprised if he was," she replied.

"Then think about that. The source would be tainted, wouldn't he?"

"Tainted," she repeated. "Because he knew Eric?"

"For Christ's sake, Carrie! As of this morning Eric's whole career is suspect. We don't know when he betrayed us or how completely. We don't know what's true and what's crap. Every report, every recruitment— they're compromised. And that goes for everybody Eric ever handled."

"We could find out who recruited this one," she shot back, tapping the TD. "The Hungarian desk could tell us."

"If I called in some favors, maybe. But I'm not sure that'd be a good idea."

"The TD is barely six months old," she argued. "This source is still out there, Cud—still on our payroll."

"And you think he could lead us to Eric and, by extension, Payne. Forget it. It's a nonstarter. Don't let Eric screw you again, Carrie, just because you want to believe."

There was a short and painful silence.

"I think you ought to see something," Cuddy said.

He walked out of the office. After a second, she followed.

He led her to a computer terminal that Scottie kept reserved for one use only—the terrorism database, DESIST.

It was the pride of the CTC, a compilation of over a thousand terrorist groups and organizations. Raw data—phone numbers, bank accounts, airline manifests, business cards—could be fed into the computer and analyzed for patterns too slight and seemingly random to attract attention. When DESIST went to work, the most amazing connections between utter strangers appeared as if by magic. DESIST could tell you when one man in Belgrade carried the address of another in Zurich, or whose phone number rang in which safe house. It could match passports to false pictures, bring up a myriad of aliases, connect the dots between terrorist groups that the world believed to be enemies: members of the IRA who were friendly with Hizballah; bankers who laundered money for both the Kurdish PKK and the Algerian Jihad. An entire world of uneasy relationships existed in the DESIST data banks, a labyrinth of obligations and mortal mistrust.

"Sit down," Cuddy said, "and plug in Eric's alias."

"Which one?" she asked.

He raised an eyebrow. "I only *knew* one."

"In Budapest, he was using 'Michael O'Shaughnessy.' "

"Try it."

"But you know there are no Americans listed in this database," she protested. "It's illegal for the CIA to track U.S. citizens."

Cuddy shrugged. "Does a dead man have citizenship? Try it, Mad Dog."

She typed in the name. The computer thought about it for a split second. And then it spat out two words, *Mahmoud Sharif,* and a phone number. She wrote down the number and plugged it into the database. Nothing. She glanced at Cuddy.

"Try just 'Sharif.' "

Obediently, she ran the name through the system. An extensive file reeled out. " 'Hizballah bomb maker,' " she read, " 'legally resident in Berlin.' "

"Sharif is believed responsible for that series of bombs the BKA found last March," Cuddy told her. The BKA—the Bundeskriminalamt—was the German equivalent of the FBI. "He'd wired them into electronics—television sets, stereo components, laptop computers—and stored them in an abandoned apartment in Frankfurt."

"I remember that," Caroline said. The BKA had confiscated seven of the bombs safely; an eighth had exploded in the act of being defused. Two men had died. "Why didn't he go down for it?"

"Sympathetic judge. Circumstantial evidence."

"I see."

"German Intelligence is convinced Sharif made twelve bombs. So where are the other four?"

"Underneath the Brandenburg?"

Cuddy shrugged. "Ask Sharif, he'll say he knows nothing about electronics. He's just a carpenter with a German wife and a kid named Moammar."

"Aren't they all. I guess the phone number wasn't his, or it'd be in the file."

"The phone is disconnected. I walked down to the Exxon station on Chain Bridge Road twenty minutes ago and dialed it."

"So if it's not Sharif's . . ."

"It's Michael O'Shaughnessy's. Got it in one." He

pulled up a chair next to her. "Last August, Sharif was shaken down by Israeli airport security when he tried to fly from Frankfurt to Malta. They pulled his address book, Xeroxed it, and sent the contents here. Somebody—a Career Trainee, probably, who never heard of Michael O'Shaughnessy and couldn't have known it was an Agency alias—entered the name into the database."

"We don't know how old this information is," Caroline hedged. "People keep numbers in their black books for years. Maybe Eric made legitimate contact with Sharif years ago. Maybe he targeted him for recruitment."

"It was a datebook, Caroline. Sharif bought it last January. Nothing in there is less than current. He talked to Eric sometime this year. And that disconnected phone was in Berlin."

"You think they planned this," she said. "That Eric was in Berlin and recruited Sharif to build the device that took out the Gate. Why, Cuddy? Why would a Palestinian do anything for a neo-Nazi like Krucevic?"

"Who said it was Krucevic? All I saw was Eric in a helicopter. Anyone could have been flying it, Caroline. You know that."

"But, Cuddy—"

"It could have been anybody," he interrupted. "We won't know who snatched the Veep until they make contact. And once they do—whether it's Osama bin Laden or Hizballah or, yes, 30 April—the FBI will be in charge of the investigation."

"You just want this whole thing to go away, don't you?" Her voice was brittle with frustration.

"Of course!" he burst out. "Isn't that what any sane person would want? Or have you had the time of your life today, Carrie, hiding in the women's bath-room?"

"I'm sorry," she said inadequately.

"Don't hope for good things, Mad Dog. They're just not thick on the ground."

NINE

Prague, 5:52 P.M.

"MRS. PAYNE."

A harsh voice, faintly mocking. Sophie turned her hooded head and groped vainly for a face. A piercing light penetrated the cloth masking her eyes; nothing else did.

"Help the lady out, Michael."

A firm pair of hands under her armpits, and she was hoisted free of the box in which she had traveled now for unreckoned hours. She groaned at the bruising pain of it; her tethered wrists, pulled obscenely behind her back, had gone numb.

The unseen Michael half thrust, half carried her along a smooth surface, probably concrete. A pathway—toward what, exactly?—cold and pitted under her stockinged feet. She was still wearing the suit she had chosen for the embassy inaugural.

It must be spattered with Nell Forsyte's blood. Sophie's throat tightened, torn between the desire to retch and the need to sob. Nell was dead. She, Sophie, was alive. That should have been comforting—but

Sophie was no fool. The men who had abducted her would attempt to bargain for her life. And much as he liked and respected her, the President would never negotiate with terrorists.

The air was sharp and chill. She felt the weak sunlight fade, had a palpable sense of passing indoors. A short, stumbling flight of stairs, a stubbed toe. Her son Peter's laugh rang suddenly in her ears—infectious, still young, the faintest edge of her dead husband in its timbre. What did Peter know of her fate? Was he frantically calling the White House, demanding information—leaving New Haven on an afternoon train, with just an ATM card in his pocket?

She was thrust abruptly into a straight-backed chair; they left her that way for an instant. Then the hood was pulled off, charging her hair with static electricity. She looked around, blinking in the ruthless light of bare bulbs. A windowless room, probably a cellar of some sort, with carpeting and a few pieces of functional furniture. Doorways led to who-knew-where—but one of them, certainly, to the outside.

Four men, ranged around the room, gazed at her impassively.

"Mrs. Payne."

The voice came from behind. She turned and looked into a face she knew could never be Michael's. Michael was the American who had driven the car. This man was not an American.

Black hair, close-cropped as a marine's and balding in the center. A harshly beaked nose, small brown eyes under curved brows. Sallow skin. A frankly sensual mouth. His body was compact and powerful, his hands too large for his wrists. He wore gray flannel trousers and a sweater; without touching it, she knew it was cashmere.

She had expected a black turtleneck. Something to go with the handgun he slung casually in his shoulder holster.

He squatted down before her chair. A faint odor of aftershave—sandalwood and lime—and cigarette smoke. A scar like an arrow in the short hairs at his temple. Not a knife wound—a bullet, perhaps? She lacked the experience to say.

"You look relatively unscathed."

She resisted the impulse to answer. The tape over her mouth could only make her ridiculous. But she kicked upward sharply and without warning, landing a foot directly in his crotch; he fell backward with a cry of pain. Before Michael or one of the others could react, he had rolled to his feet and whipped the gun from its sheath. The barrel bit into Sophie's forehead.

"Mlan," one of the men said in warning.

He stared into Sophie's eyes, completely composed. Then he slid the gun back into its holster. "Tape, Vaclav."

A middle-aged man with a cherub's face silently produced a roll of black electrical tape.

With infinite care, the man named Mlan crouched once more at Sophie's feet. He held her gaze deliberately, daring her to kick him again, while he slid the hem of her narrow skirt up to her thighs. Then he lashed one ankle to the right chair leg with tape, the other to the left.

That quickly, she was exposed, knees sprawled wide, helpless to cover herself. He had chosen his retaliation well; mere physical violence would have strengthened her. This was a humiliation so casual and calculated it almost made her weep.

"I should have explained something," he said. "I am

difficult to provoke." He reached for the tape covering her mouth and tore it off. Sophie cried out—then looked away, ashamed.

"I should also have introduced myself," he added, wadding the tape into a compact ball and handing it without a word to Vaclav. "My name is Mlan Krucevic. That will probably mean nothing to you."

"On the contrary," she said clearly, "I know a great deal about you, Mr. Krucevic. It's hard to follow the Balkans or terrorism without running into your name. But then, neo-Nazism and its psychotics are particular concerns of mine."

He rose, still poised between her knees. "A Vice President who can read. How intriguing."

Sophie looked up at him coolly. "You didn't know? And I thought you did your homework."

"Oh, I have, Mrs. Payne. More than was conceivably necessary. One might say I know everything about you. But then, democracy and its decline are particular concerns of mine."

"Then you must know that I, too, am difficult to provoke."

"Perhaps. But I didn't destroy the Brandenburg Gate and kill a number of innocent people merely to provoke *you,* Mrs. Payne."

"If you're thinking this will have the slightest impact on Jack Bigelow," she said, "you're mistaken."

He raised an eyebrow. "Then it will be the first time in a long life."

"There is always a first time, Mr. Krucevic."

"Of course," he said thoughtfully. "But what was *your* mistake, Mrs. Payne? Coming to Berlin? Or running for public office? Who are you, really, but the sum of your errors and lies?"

He began to pace before her, a professor in front of a half-filled lecture hall. The four men stationed around the room stood at attention, their eyes following Krucevic.

"We should start, I suppose, with the official dossier. You are forty-three years old, the daughter of German intellectuals. Your parents emigrated to the United States in 1933. Your father was a journalist—a clever man with words, educated for a time at Oxford, comfortable in English as well as German. Your mother was the daughter of a wealthy German porcelain manufacturer who lost most of his money after World War One. She was raised, regardless, in an atmosphere of privilege.

"We both know that your father was a Jew who renounced his faith and pretended to adopt your mother's beliefs. He even changed his name from Friedman to Freeman once he got to the United States. But that sort of posturing would never have saved his life, Mrs. Payne, or even your mother's. Had your parents remained in Berlin in 1933, you would not have been born."

"You're out of your mind." Whatever Sophie had expected from Krucevic—threats, intimidation, even physical harm—it had not been this. "My parents were Lutherans. They had friends who died in the Resistance. For years they struggled with guilt—thinking they should have stayed in Germany and fought Hitler to the end."

"That may be what they told you," Krucevic retorted, "but they lied. Your father was a Jew. His people died in Bergen-Belsen and he did absolutely nothing to save them. I have seen the records, Mrs. Payne."

"Bullshit," Sophie spat out.

Krucevic thrust his face mere inches from her own.

There was a new malevolence in his eyes, naked pleasure at her subjugation. "Let's just call that your first mistake."

He began to pace again. "After four years at Radcliffe, you did the expected thing: You married a graduate of Harvard Business School, one Curtis Payne, the son of an old Philadelphia family, what your people call 'Main Line.' How amusing it must have been to trip down the aisle in Episcopal splendor, a mongrel brat! And when poor Curtis died of cancer during his first term in Congress, you took over his seat and parlayed it into a term in the Senate." He ticked off the points on his fingertips. "You have never remarried. You have a son named Peter at Yale. How have you managed it so long, Mrs. Payne—suppressing the truth of your past?"

"I suppressed nothing," Sophie said.

"Liar!"

"It's the tendency of the madman to see his obsession wherever he looks, Krucevic. You know nothing about me."

He threw back his head and laughed. "Really! Then what if I tell you your shoe size is 7AA? Your preference in takeout, Thai soft-shell crabs—from a restaurant on Dupont Circle? That you mismanage your money and are chronically late in paying your credit card bills, that you've gone through three lovers in the past eighteen months? I know their names and the ways they made love to you. I know which were sincere and which were interested in fame. I know that one—the Republican senator—wanted to marry you. You declined gently, in part because of politics, and in part from consideration for the feelings of the senator's wife. I should imagine your heart is not easily touched, Mrs. Payne, however available the rest of you."

He stared pointedly at her spread knees. The stripping sense of exposure. She stared back, hating him.

"There is nothing to tracking a woman like you," he said softly, "a woman who lives in the public eye. My watchers were simply lost in the crowd. But even in your shower at the Naval Observatory, Mrs. Payne, you were never truly alone."

A frisson of fear, like a spider crossing her neck. "So you chose me to kidnap," Sophie said briskly, as though some sort of deal had been struck. "You spent the money and the time. I suppose this is about revenge for the NATO air strikes against Belgrade. Am I right?"

But Krucevic was staring at his watch; he had already dismissed her. "Otto—bring in the boy. It's time for his shot."

One of the silent men—bald, muscular—disappeared through a door behind Sophie. So he was not Michael, either. That left two possibilities: the curly-haired weasel with the nervous face, or the lean blond with the day-old growth of beard. The latter had kept his eyes trained upon her through most of the interview, and curiously, his watchful stillness had given her strength. He was Michael, she was sure of it. She smiled faintly at him; his gaze shifted to Krucevic.

The door behind Sophie opened again. A child's voice, sharp and high-pitched with fear. "Please, Papa! Not the needle! I promise I'll be good—I *promise*."

Sophie craned her neck around and saw them: the powerful bodyguard, and the boy rigid with apprehension. Unruly dark hair fell like a protective screen over his wide gray eyes; from the frailness of his body, Sophie thought he might be about ten. He had called Krucevic his father, and now the man was reaching for a syringe.

Involuntarily, Sophie strained against her bonds.

"Now, Jozsef—we talked about this before," Krucevic said soothingly. With one hand he stroked the boy's pale cheek; the other held the hypodermic. "For the good of the cause, remember? You want to make me proud. The thigh, Otto, I think."

In one deft movement, Otto thrust the boy face downward on the floor and pinned him there. Krucevic sank the needle into the flesh of his son's leg.

Jozsef cried out.

"You bastard," Sophie hissed. "What have you done to him?"

Krucevic twisted his fingers in her hair and pulled her face close to his own. "Nothing I wouldn't do to you, Mrs. Payne. Given time."

TEN

Washington, 2:31 P.M.

J ACK BIGELOW'S COWBOY-BOOTED FEET were propped
on his broad mahogany desk. Like many men who had
come late in life to Texas, he made a point of embracing its
eccentricities. But then, Texas had given him the presidency.

"I've got the director of our Federal Bureau of
Investigation here, Fritz," he said, "and a few other folks
who'd like to hear what you have to say. So I'm
going to put you on the speakerphone. That okay
with you?"

"Of course, Jack." The German chancellor's voice
sounded remote and disembodied.

Dare Atwood immediately discounted anything the
man might say. Someone comfortable with an audience
of unknowns, in a room he couldn't see, was hardly
planning to bare his soul.

"I have to tell you, Fritz, I'm just sorrier'n I can spit
about the mess you've got over there in Berlin,"
Bigelow drawled.

"A tragedy," Voekl replied, "for both Berlin and the

German nation. It is our Oklahoma City." He spoke English too carefully, caressing each syllable before releasing it with regret.

"Any word of Vice President Payne?" Bigelow asked.

"Jack, I regret to tell you that I have no news to offer. None of the hospitals in Berlin has admitted Mrs. Payne as a patient, and the medical helicopter itself has not yet been located. We are doing everything in our power, of course."

"Sure you are." Bigelow's shrewd eyes, utterly devoid of their usual warmth, slid over to Dare. "And you're still goin' with the notion of these Turks, Fritz? As the responsible parties, I mean?"

"Every indication at the bomb site would lead me to believe that the Turks are responsible, yes. We are confident of an arrest very soon."

"Once our FBI boys get over there—excuse me, boys and *girls,* Fritz, don't want to be sexist if I can help it—maybe we'll get a better handle on what's goin' on. We're sendin' out a team tonight, should be there by dawn tomorrow."

"That is excellent news, Jack." Voekl said it woodenly. "You must know, however, that we are very well equipped to manage the crisis. We have been expecting some reprisal from the Turks for some time. They are unhappy with the stringency of our program of repatriation."

"Naturally," Bigelow tossed back, as though he had never trashed the German repatriation program on television worldwide, "and when folks are unhappy, Fritz, no tellin' what they'll do. Now let's us just suppose for a minute that we've got a *different* group of unhappy people runnin' around Berlin. Turks'd make real good

whipping boys, wouldn't you say, for anybody else operating in the region?"

"Perhaps. But whether we are talking about the
Palestinians or the Islamic fundamentalists or even the
Kosovo Liberation Army, Jack, we both know that
we are talking about the same thing. Third-world
extremists who bring their battles right to the door-
steps of Europe and the United States. We have got
to start cutting the ground from beneath their feet.
Denying them a platform from which to launch their
attacks."

"Sending 'em back home, eh, Fritz? Well, as we like
to say around here, that's just openin' a whole 'nuther
can of whup-ass, now i'n'it?"

"Pardon?"

It was as well, Dare thought, that Voekl couldn't see
the joyful malice on the President's face.

"Just an expression," Bigelow said.

"You know how much I deplore the use of terrorism, Jack."

"Don't we all."

"But you will agree, I am sure, that a nation without hope may naturally turn to violence to achieve its
ends."

"That's the story of America, Fritz."

"Yes, well . . . you have publicly stated that the fight
to end terrorism will be this century's greatest challenge.
I agree—I have always agreed—and I am ready to help
you in your fight. For fifty-five years the German
people have stood on the front line of Western civilization. Beyond us, and the protection of our culture,
lies all the anarchy of the East. We have already begun
to see the destructive tide of Muslim immigrants
from Yugoslavia and the disintegrating Central Asian

republics. They all end up in Germany eventually, ripe for violence."

"Not to mention the Palestinians you folks've been harboring for decades," Bigelow added.

"The policies of my predecessors were lamentably lax. But I know that terrorism will be the twenty-first century's Cold War, Jack—and I remember the Cold War better than most."

"It was the making of you, Fritz, as I recall."

Before he had founded the Social Conservatives in the former East Germany, Fritz Voekl had been a rising star of the Communist Party. He'd begun public life as the young director of the most efficient munitions complex in Thuringia; he'd parlayed that success into a berth in the Party hierarchy. By 1988, however, it was clear that Voekl found the Party too confining. He publicly denounced Communism and was imprisoned for his pains. That act of defiance instantly made him a local hero. Not to mention a political phoenix. When the Party structure collapsed like faulty scaffolding a year later, bringing the Wall and everyone down with it, Voekl was set free to enjoy the show. He opened champagne amidst the barbed wire, he swung a pickax at Checkpoint Charlie. He had always possessed an exquisite sense of timing and a shrewd ability to read the people's mood.

"So it was," he said to Jack Bigelow now. "I learned many lessons from my life behind the Iron Curtain. Chief among them is this: The nation that denies a people hope will never win the war. A nation that *gives* its people hope, Jack, gives them a reason to fight."

"And you see hope as . . . ?"

"Money, Jack. Money. If I can pour deutsche marks

into the developing economies of my buffer states—
Slovakia, Hungary, the Czech Republic, even Poland—
with time, I will turn despair into hope. I will deny
the terrorists a foothold for their anarchy. And protect those who fall within the German sphere of influence."

Dare frowned slightly at the phrase "German sphere
of influence." But Bigelow was tired of chatter. He
made a lewd gesture in the speakerphone's direction—
something suggestive of a giant hand job—and prepared
to sign off.

"Listen, Fritz, we're always glad to know you fellas in
the Federal Republic are fightin' the good fight. You get
any news of Sophie Payne, you call me right away,
y'hear? I'll be sendin' those Bureau boys over to Berlin
ASAP."

"Thank you, Jack."

"You give that pretty little daughter of yours my best,
okay? Bye, now."

Bigelow snapped off the speakerphone, then glanced
around the faces assembled in the Oval Office. There
was Matthew Finch, the National Security Advisor, a
quiet, bespectacled, kindhearted man with an absolute
intolerance for bullshit; Gerard O'Neill, Bigelow's
Secretary of State, who was drumming his fingers
impatiently on the arm of his chair; Al Tomlinson, the
FBI director; and General Clayton Phillips, chairman of
the Joint Chiefs. Phillips frowned as he studied his
notes.

"Hope, my ass," Bigelow drawled. "Somebody better
tell my friend Fritz about Osama bin Laden, terrorist
billionaire. Now *that's* the kind of money gives people
hope. Wouldn't you say so, Dare?"

"A chicken and an AK-47 in every pot," she replied.

"One can hardly blame Voekl, Mr. President. He has to be feeling rather stupid right now."

"He may sound that way, Dare, but problem is, Fritz is no dummy." Bigelow lifted his boots off the desk and thrust himself out of his chair. "So what's he tryin' to pull, anyway? I call him about Sophie, and I get a stump speech about investment opportunities in Central Europe."

"Trying to change the subject?" suggested Al Tomlinson, the FBI director.

"Then he's doing a lousy job of it," said O'Neill, the Secretary of State. "No bunch of disaffected *gastarbeiters* kidnapped the Vice President. A bomb in Berlin gets them nothing but bad press."

"I agree." Dare glanced down at her notes, feverishly thrown together in the past forty minutes by a senior analyst in DI/OREA. "But the Berlin police have issued a curfew for all Turkish aliens resident in the city and placed a cordon of riot police around guest-worker neighborhoods to deter reprisals. They're also conducting a house-to-house search for the Vice President and her captors. We don't believe they'll find a trace of them in Germany. In our opinion, the terrorists are long gone."

"I can see Turkish extremists bombing the Gate," the President said thoughtfully, "but not snatching Sophie in a stolen chopper."

"They'd be more likely to kill her outright, just to make the German government look bad," agreed Matthew Finch. "Or target a German they hate, like Voekl."

"Who, instead of being dead, now has the ideal excuse to hit the Turks harder. Do me a favor, Dare." Bigelow wheeled suddenly toward her. "Start snoopin' in Fritz Voekl's backyard, okay? I want to know what time his daughter Kiki's curfew is, who Fritz calls for phone sex late at night, whether he puts whole milk or two percent on his Wheaties in the morning."

"Done."

"Fritz Voekl wasn't flying that chopper," objected Gerard O'Neill.

"No. But he wasn't in the square to take the blast, either, now was he, Gerry?" Bigelow pinned him with a look. "Any of your cookie-pushers over in the Bottom of the Fog get a better idea, you be sure an' send 'em to me."

O'Neill smiled nervously.

"I think we can usefully speculate about the parties responsible," Dare interjected. "The resident Turks are probably a scapegoat. Both the Voekl regime and possibly several other groups operating in the region would kill to discredit them publicly."

"Could be Kurdish separatists," Al Tomlinson said abruptly. "They love it when Turks get egg on their faces."

"But the PKK has been in disarray in recent months," Dare pointed out, "since Turkish forces captured their leader."

"Who snatched all those guys from Beirut in the eighties?" The President glanced around inquiringly. "Terry Anderson. Bill Buckley. That whole bunch. Who grabbed them?"

"Hizballah." Dare had spent most of the eighties on the National Security Council, frantically trying to get the CIA's Beirut station chief, William Buckley, home before he died of torture. She had failed. Jack Bigelow, on the other hand, had spent the eighties reinventing himself from corporate raider to the most trusted man in America.

"If the rag heads were behind it," snapped Gerard O'Neill, "we'd have heard from ten different terrorist groups by now, all claiming responsibility."

"Probably true," Dare conceded. "And Hizballah has never kidnapped a woman."

"So who do we blame, Dare?" Bigelow demanded.

The real question, after all the perambulation. She drew a deep breath. "We believe the sophistication and timing of this particular hit rule out the lesser Middle Eastern organizations. In our opinion, three groups could be responsible: a German cell trained by the Saudi-in-exile, Osama bin Laden; one dispatched by the Palestinians—Ahmad Jabril or the PFLP-GC; or a group operating under the 30 April Organization."

"Germany's always been lousy with terrorists," muttered General Phillips. "They send in kids with student visas, marry them to fräuleins, wait for a convenient moment to activate."

Bigelow sighed. "Sort it out for me, Dare."

"As I'm sure you're aware, Mr. President, Osama bin Laden has been able to strike the U.S. significantly in the past, despite our constant efforts to monitor his terrorist network worldwide. He's independently wealthy and he works through a variety of front organizations, some legitimate, some less so."

"I thought he liked to operate outta the third world," the President said.

"But he may well have established a foothold in the new German capital years ago. You'll remember that bin Laden's father made his fortune in construction. Building contractors of every description have been the most visible commercial enterprise in Berlin for the past decade."

"And he sure loves taking out U.S. embassies," muttered Gerard O'Neill. The memory of rubble in Tanzania and Kenya still had the power to enrage him.

Bigelow glanced at his watch. "I know enough about bin Laden. Go on."

"Ahmad Jabril, head of the PFLP-GC," Dare said. "An old PLO hand who broke with Yasir Arafat decades ago. Jabril styles himself as an ideologue, a man who offers no quarter while Israel exists. But he likes hits with a lot of public relations value. His men bombed our troop trains in Germany in 1991."

"Then I'd say blowing the Brandenburg Gate is tame by comparison." Bigelow's eyelids flickered. "Why Sophie?"

Dare shrugged. "Jabril's lieutenant is serving a life term in a German prison. Maybe he wants him released."

"It's after nine o'clock in the evening over there," Bigelow said impatiently. "Why the *hell* don't they give us a call?"

Because Sophie Payne is already dead, and they've got nothing to bargain with now. Dare could have voiced the unspoken thought poisoning the room. Instead, she waited, briefing papers at the ready.

"And the last group, Director?" the President asked.

She felt a flutter of disquiet in her stomach. "The 30 April Organization."

Bigelow frowned. "Neo-Nazis, right? The ones you think assassinated Schroeder?"

"We suspect they murdered Schroeder because he championed NATO air strikes against Belgrade. Mrs. Payne might very well have been next on their list."

The President stretched painfully. A ruptured disk in his lower vertebrae caused chronic back pain. "The guy who runs that organization is a war criminal."

"Mlan Krucevic. A Croat biologist. We believe he's operating out of Germany. Here's his bio."

Bigelow reached for his reading glasses and scanned the document swiftly. Then he thrust it at Matthew Finch. "I'll have to ask my pal Fritz why he isn't cutting the ground from under *this* joker's feet."

"Too much money in pharmaceuticals," Matthew Finch murmured.

"The German police have tried to snare Krucevic for years," Dare said, "but 30 April is an organization that leaves few tracks. Rather like our own right-wing militia groups."

"Who's funding them? Or is this nut case an independent operator?"

"Krucevic never lacks for funds," Dare told Bigelow. "He shifts money through a variety of numbered Swiss accounts. We think he channels most of it through a front company in Berlin called VaccuGen. It produces and exports legitimate livestock vaccines, although there is strong evidence to suggest it also does a healthy trade in illegal biological agents. Krucevic has a reputation in the gray arms world for concocting deadly bugs. I've placed the company on the NSA's target list. We should have everything that goes in or out of the place fairly soon."

"Do you have anybody inside?"

She repressed a sharp breath, although Bigelow's question seemed innocent enough. "Not really, but we've been targeting them for some time."

Clayton Phillips glanced up from his doodling. He was a kind-looking grandfather of a man, despite the rows of brass gleaming on his uniform. He had raised three girls himself and had a soft spot for the Vice President. Dare detected the marks of strain around the general's eyes; he was chafing at inactivity, at his own sense of uselessness. The word *target*, however, had caught his attention.

"Could we send in some cruise missiles against their operational base?"

"We'd have to locate it first," Dare answered. "Krucevic has a genius for self-protection. His identity and movements are so closely held, we've never even seen a picture of him."

Matthew Finch fluttered the bio. "This is picture enough. Krucevic is ruthless, he's efficient, and he's got no compunction about butchering Germans. He's nuts. But why snatch Sophie Payne? If revenge was the point, why not just shoot her in the square?"

"Then we should expect a demand," the President said sharply. "Krucevic's agenda for Sophie's release. Tit for tat. So what exactly will this asshole want?"

"A Europe cleansed of the non-Aryan races," Dare replied. "And that, Mr. President, you will never give him."

There was silence as everyone in the room considered the implications of what she had said.

"They killed Nell Forsyte," Bigelow said quietly. "Shot her in the head. It would take that—a direct hit—to stop Nell in her tracks. She had a four-year-old daughter."

"I'm sorry, Mr. President." Dare folded her hands over her briefing book. The topaz winked and was swiftly covered. "For Ms. Forsyte and all the others."

"Mr. President?"

Maybelle Williams, his executive secretary, peered apprehensively around the Oval Office door.

Bigelow folded his reading glasses and smiled at her as though nothing really bad could ever happen. "Yes, darlin'?"

"The Situation Room just called. Embassy Prague has got a videotape of the Vice President."

ELEVEN
Prague, 8:15 P.M.

THE MAN SOPHIE THOUGHT WAS MICHAEL sliced the bonds at her ankles and wrists and hauled her down a corridor to the bathroom. Windowless, like everything in the subterranean compound, it offered no chance for escape. Michael stood in the doorway with a gun poised while she used the toilet. She tried to ignore him, knowing that Krucevic would use this sort of humiliation to wear her down. When at last she stole a look at Michael, she detected only boredom.

He threw a pair of sweatpants, a sweatshirt, and some socks at her feet. "Put those on."

"Why?"

"Because your clothes are starting to stink."

She turned her back and stripped off her ruined suit. A red line across her thighs showed where Krucevic had pulled the skirt taut, and a dark blot like the map of Europe stained the fabric. Nell's blood.

Wordlessly, Michael handed her a comb.

For the first time in that extraordinary day, Sophie

felt an overwhelming desire to cry. Her hands were shaking.

She dragged the comb through her short black hair and splashed water on her cheeks. Then she dried herself with the front of her sweatshirt, a technique recalled from Adirondack camp days. There was no mirror in the room; perhaps they were afraid she would smash the glass and cut them all to pieces. She probably looked like shit anyway.

"What in God's name are you doing here? You're American, aren't you?"

The look on his face was half amusement, half contempt. "I have orders to beat you if you try to talk to me, Mrs. Payne," he answered in German. "We all do. Don't push your luck."

He seized her by the arm and pulled her along the passageway, back to the room she already thought of as prison. Halogen lights now hung from the ceiling's steel beams; they flooded Mlan Krucevic's face and that of the cherubic Vaclav, who held a video camera. Beyond him stood a gurney.

"Ah, Mrs. Payne. A vision in black." Krucevic's mood had altered subtly, she noticed; he seemed in the grip of subdued excitement, his movements jerky and tense. He nodded to Otto. "The gurney."

Before she had time to react, Otto seized Sophie in a fireman's carry and dumped her unceremoniously on the stretcher. She lunged upward. But like young Jozsef, she lost. Otto snapped a belt over wrist and ankle, immediately restraining her. She thought of the needle, the desperate child, and felt a sickness in the pit of her stomach.

"Is this really necessary? I'm not likely to kick you again."

"No," Krucevic said slowly as he settled a newspaper next to her right ear, "I don't think you are. Vaclav?"

He stepped toward them, video camera dangling in one hand.

"Start with a close-up of Mrs. Payne's face, will you? Focus on the newspaper's date. Then pan back until they can see how she's lying. On no account are you to focus on me."

Strapped down and stripped of her elegant suiting, Sophie was no longer a person to Krucevic. She had become the merest prop, a faceless bundle in black sweats. She struggled uselessly against the gurney straps, then realized she only looked weaker. As though she was afraid. Panicking. How to seize control of the situation?

She refused to admit that control was completely beyond her. Refusal might sustain her for several days—if she survived the next few minutes.

The camera lens came within a foot of her face. If this tape was going anywhere near the United States—if there was a chance that Peter might see it—she had a duty to remain calm.

"Good evening, Mr. President." Krucevic's voice came from somewhere in the darkness beyond the floodlights. "Let us state for the record that we have in our keeping one Sophie Friedman Payne, Vice President of the United States and apostate Jew. It is Tuesday, November ninth, somewhere in Central Europe. Observe the copy of the *International Herald Tribune* you see on your screen; it bears today's date. We are the 30 April Organization, and as Mrs. Payne is familiar with us, I must assume we need no introduction."

The camera lens retreated several feet, took in the gurney and Sophie's shackled body.

"Do you know, Mrs. Payne, why you are here?"

"Because you murdered my bodyguard and kidnapped me," Sophie said without hesitation.

"You are here as a token of faith," Krucevic amended patiently. "Of faith and commitment on both our parts to an enlightened course of action. Have we harmed you, Mrs. Payne?"

"No. You've terrorized and humiliated me. But it takes a great deal more than that to harm me, Krucevic."

He had walked around the perimeter of the room until he could see her face, although he remained carefully off camera. His arms were folded across his chest, his dark eyes fixed on her own. "I'm afraid it does," he said. "Otto? The hypodermic, please."

Sophie flinched involuntarily as the man approached. His face was now concealed behind a black hood, but his eyes were unmistakable—dull with malice and anticipation. In his right hand he held a needle. She jerked convulsively in her bonds.

"It is to Jack Bigelow that I am speaking now," she heard Krucevic say. "I hope I may call you Jack, Mr. President. I am about to conduct a demonstration. I know you will watch very carefully."

He nodded. With a sudden, sharp movement Otto plunged the hypodermic into Sophie's thigh. She cried out at the shock of it, the gratuitous pain; behind his mask, Otto smiled.

———

Eight people were assembled in the White House secure videoteleconferencing center, or VTC—a smallish space with an oblong table, twelve chairs, a wide-screen monitor, and a million-dollar array of telecommunications equipment. With its vaulted door and security panel, the room resembled a steel diving chamber; it might almost survive ground zero. Like all secure facilities, it was Tempest-tested: Any electronic or magnetic signals emanating from the space could be neither intercepted nor recorded by an outside party. There was a secure VTC room now in every major government agency; recently, they had been installed in the principal embassies worldwide. A multiparty network of secure voice, image, and data communication could thus be established within seconds.

Thirty April was aware of that.

At 9:07 that evening in Prague, the driver of a passing car threw a package toward the U.S. embassy guardhouse on Trziste Street. The marine guards wasted half an hour assembling a technical bomb team before discovering the package held nothing more than clothing, a used hypodermic, and a videotape. The clothes were later determined to belong to the kidnapped Vice President. And the tape—

The tape was screened by the ambassador, the CIA Chief of Station, and each of their deputies. Four people called from diplomatic dinners, clandestine surveillance, and one very inviting bed. At 10:12 Prague time, the ambassador contacted the White House.

Now they were all watching—Bigelow, Finch, Tomlinson, O'Neill, Phillips, and Dare. They were joined by the President's Chief of Staff and the White House Situation Room's chief Intelligence officer. Bigelow was restless; he sat barely two feet from the screen, beating a tattoo on his right knee with a presidential pen.

As Otto's hand slashed down with the hypodermic, everyone jumped. And then glanced surreptitiously at one another. The air in the VTC room was stale with tension; Dare was sweating in her black wool dress. Mlan Krucevic was famous for one thing—biological agents. As everyone in the VTC room was fully aware.

"Mrs. Payne has just been injected with a bacillus your Intelligence people will want to research," said Krucevic's voice. "I call it Anthrax 3A. My own hybrid of the common sheep ailment, quite deadly in humans. Where the disease normally takes three days to kill, mine can achieve death in three hours. Mrs. Payne should begin to exhibit the symptoms in about thirty minutes. Fever, blood in the stomach and lungs, a systemic infection. If the disease is allowed to progress unchecked, she will hemorrhage and die.

"It is an immensely unpleasant death, Jack. I've tested Anthrax 3A extensively among the Muslim population of Bosnia-Herzegovina."

Bigelow shifted in his chair.

Sophie Payne's eyes, caught in the video lens, widened slightly. "I don't believe you," she said to the man off camera. "You're bluffing. There was nothing in that needle."

"Why?" Krucevic's voice retorted. "Because you're a woman? Because you're the Vice President of the United States? Neither fact is of the slightest importance to me. To me, Mrs. Payne, you are just another Jew. One who should never have been born."

"Killing me gets you nothing," she shot back. "If I die, so does your bargaining power."

"Exactly," Krucevic replied evenly. "Which brings us to hypodermic number two. Otto?"

The audience in the VTC room had time to notice Sophie Payne's labored breathing, the increasing ruddiness of her cheeks. Fear? Or something more deadly?

And then a hooded figure appeared on camera, a fragile child in his arms.

"You have a son, Mrs. Payne," said Krucevic's voice.

"You know I do. You probably know his shoe size."

"You love him dearly, I believe?"

Sophie did not answer.

"I, too, have a son. This is my boy, my Jozsef."

Bigelow scraped his chair closer to the screen, stared at it intently.

The boy lay limp in Otto's grasp, head thrown back, thin legs slack. Beads of sweat glittered on his forehead. His lips, Dare saw, were flecked with blood.

"Jozsef means everything to me," Krucevic said. "But for my cause, like Abraham and his Isaac, I would sacrifice even my son. A half hour ago I injected Jozsef with Anthrax 3A. In two hours, his lungs will fill with fluid. In three hours, he will drown in his own blood.

"Do you believe me now, Mrs. Payne?"

"Jesus," Bigelow hissed. "This guy's one taco short of a combo platter. Does he really have a son?"

"Yes." Dare's eyes stayed on the screen. "Whether it's that poor kid or not, who can say?"

"Sophie seems to think so," Matthew Finch observed quietly. "She looks like hell."

But the camera lens had shifted to the hooded figure. He laid the boy on the floor. Something flashed in his hand—

"Otto is holding the one thing that can save Sophie Payne's life," Krucevic told them. "An antibiotic developed in my own laboratory specifically to combat Anthrax 3A. This antibiotic will save my Jozsef. But whether it can save Mrs. Payne . . . that depends entirely upon you, Jack."

The needle slipped into the boy's vein. The plunger went home.

"Dare," Bigelow snarled over his shoulder. "You got anybody out at the Agency who knows about this sort of shit?"

"Yes," she said, "although we need that hypodermic to determine what he's really injected her with."

Bigelow nodded. His eyes were still locked on the video.

"You know what we stand for," Krucevic said reasonably. "A single Central Europe, rid at last of mongrel races and their degeneracies. A Central Europe free to pursue the highest goals of mind and body without the interference of the United States, a Central Europe founded on a genetically pure population. You, Mr. President, and your democratic policies stand in the way of that dream. You foster miscegenation and export its ideals. It's a clever policy, of course—it allows you to divide and conquer. The United States as world policeman, isn't that the goal? First you create the conditions for civil war, then you fly in and establish martial rule. And it all begins so gently. With gestures of good faith, a McDonald's franchise in Red Square."

Bigelow snorted.

"Over the course of the next five days, a series of events will occur throughout Central Europe that might normally trigger an aggressive response from the United States. However, in deference to Mrs. Payne, you, Jack, shall not lift a finger to intervene. You will refrain from mobilizing NATO forces. You will placate your allies. You will turn a deaf ear to any appeals for help.

"If you do otherwise, Sophie Payne will die an unpleasant death. But if you behave, Jack, we will eventually release Mrs. Payne unharmed. Inform the U.S. embassy in Prague of your decision immediately. If you decide to abandon Mrs. Payne to the needle, raise the flag in the embassy garden only to half-mast. If you accede to our demands, raise the flag to the top of the mast. At that point, Mrs. Payne receives my antibiotic. Should you go back on your promise, however . . . there is always another needle."

The camera lens crept closer to the Vice President's face. As the image focused, the watchers assembled in the White House VTC room saw Sophie Payne's lips form three words.

No, Jack. No.

Washington, 3:30 P.M.

J ACK BIGELOW CRUMPLED THE FRONT PAGE of the *Washington Post* and tossed it toward a wastepaper basket. The Oval Office was considerably cooler than the VTC room, but everyone looked uncomfortable. Except the President. From his expression, Matthew Finch thought, Bigelow might be facing a round of golf rather than an international threat.

In twenty-three years, Finch had won cases with Jack, faced bankruptcy with Jack, survived a vicious campaign for the presidency with Jack. The two men had fly-fished Montana, endured Finch's divorce, and attempted Everest together—their least successful undertaking to date. It was popular among the press to describe the President as a genial bear of a man; they played up his good ol' boy manners the way they celebrated Julia Roberts's teeth. But Finch's long apprenticeship in the art of Jack gave him a privileged understanding, an ability to read volumes in the slightest sign. Most men betrayed their stress in their bodies. They fidgeted. They ran their fingers through their hair.

They might even take a swing at somebody when the situation deteriorated. Jack Bigelow, on the contrary, became more contained. He throve on adrenaline.

Everything Mlan Krucevic had spit at the video camera had whetted Bigelow's appetite for battle. Sophie Payne was a proxy for both men; from this moment on, their argument was with each other.

"What the hell does he mean, a series of events in Central Europe?" Bigelow demanded.

"Since he went to the trouble to bomb Berlin and kidnap the Vice President of the United States," Finch replied, "I imagine we can expect fairly serious episodes of terror. Krucevic wants to bring the U.S. to its knees. He specifically instructed us to restrain our allies. That means his moves in the next five days will be bold, destabilizing, and played for high stakes. Sophie's too significant a chip to waste on trivialities."

Bigelow nodded. "But where exactly will he land? And what can we do to spike the damage without sacrificing Sophie?"

"May I suggest, Mr. President, that I task the Agency's key country analysts to search for signs of instability in their accounts?" Since viewing the video, Dare Atwood looked older and grimmer, as though the skin of her face had turned from flesh to stamped metal. She was self-possessed as always; she sat in her chair awaiting the President's pleasure; but Matthew Finch felt the sparks of urgency crackling off her frame. "I could establish a Central European Task Force. Staff it on a twenty-four-hour basis."

"I s'pose it can't hurt, Dare. And get the NSA to process traffic for those countries on the highest-priority basis."

Al Tomlinson cleared his throat and glanced uneasily around the room. "What did he mean, calling Mrs. Payne an apostate Jew?"

No one replied.

"The Bureau did her security clearance," Tomlinson persisted. "She was raised Lutheran, married Episcopalian."

Bigelow shrugged. "He's a neo-Nazi, Al. He sees what he hates everywhere he goes. And Sophie's parents were German."

"But they emigrated well before the war." Tomlinson sounded aggrieved, as though his Bureau's background checkers would be held responsible. "Mrs. Payne was born in the U.S. Jake Freeman knew Roosevelt. He wrote columns for the Washington *Star*."

"It's irrelevant what Sophie might be," Finch said flatly. "The important thing is what Krucevic believes. He believes she's Jewish. That gives a fascist like him the right to treat her like dirt. He's telling us loud and clear that he has no reason to spare her life."

"Think he's in Prague?" Bigelow asked abruptly.

"For at least as long as it takes to raise the flag in the embassy garden," Dare Atwood replied. "Give it an hour. Then they're gone."

"And you're thinkin' the flag should be raised." He crumpled another sheet of newsprint, tossed it, missed. "Regardless of the cost. I can't give this guy a blank check, Dare. Who knows what he might do? Blow up a plane. Or the Hungarian parliament."

"Or sprinkle Anthrax 3A on all the salad bars in the free world," finished Matthew Finch. "Besides which, we have a policy of non-negotiation with terrorist groups."

"I know what our policy is, thank you very much."

Finch grimaced; being slammed in public was one of the privileges of a First Friend. "On the other hand, it doesn't look very presidential to sit on your hands and leave a woman hanging out to dry. Especially one as popular as Sophie."

"Well, don't that just drop the turd in the punch bowl, Matt," Bigelow snarled. "You're supposed to *advise,* remember? Not *confuse.*"

"I'd suggest you pursue two courses of action at once." Finch jotted something on a legal pad and glanced coldly at Bigelow over his glasses. "Publicly, you state that you do not negotiate with terrorists. Privately, you buy time. At least until Sophie gets that antibiotic."

"Time." Bigelow glanced at his watch. "At least two hours have passed since they made the video. Jesus F. Christ."

He didn't have to elaborate. If Sophie Payne had actually been injected with Anthrax 3A, she would be in agony right now.

Finch passed Bigelow a sheet of paper. It was the biographic profile of Mlan Krucevic that Dare had offered him earlier. He had scrawled at the bottom, *Find out who wrote this.*

Bigelow looked up. "Dare, who's handling the 30 April account?"

"A number of people, Mr. President. But that bio was written by a leadership analyst named Caroline Carmichael. She's working the MedAir 901 investigation in the Counterterrorism Center."

"She seems to have a handle on this guy," Bigelow said. "Once you've read this, nothing he said or did today is much of a surprise. Although I'm not sure I'd call him *sane.*"

"Perhaps," Finch suggested, "Ms. Carmichael should be sent to Berlin."

"These jokers aren't *in* Berlin, Matt." The President

was impatient. "After that flag goes up, they may not even be in Prague."

"But they staged a brilliant hit in the heart of the new capital," Finch persisted. "*Somebody* in Berlin knows the 30 April operation. Krucevic must have a network there, something that could be identified and exploited. Where else do we start if not in that square?"

"Caroline is no case officer, Matt," Dare protested.

He dismissed this with a wave. "You've got case officers on the ground. Carmichael understands the terrorists' thinking. She knows how to deal with Krucevic. She might even be able to predict where he'll go. Hell, if it ever comes down to negotiation, she'll be invaluable. We need her in Berlin."

"But she's not accustomed—"

"Then let's call it a go," Bigelow interrupted. "Get the girl on the plane."

―――――

In a previous incarnation, Dare Atwood had run the Office of Russian and European Analysis. She had trained Caroline Carmichael and followed her progress through the bureaucratic ranks as an eagle follows the flight of its young. When MedAir 901 exploded thirty-three minutes after takeoff, it was Dare who met Caroline's plane from Frankfurt and broke the news of Eric's death. A cord of unspoken affection ran between the two women that made the present disaster all the more painful.

But as she stared through her office windows at the dismal autumn night, Dare felt something like heartache. Her affection for Caroline was irrelevant now. She had only one course of action open to her; she would take out the cost in nightmares if necessary.

Alerted by something—a footfall, a shift in atmosphere—she turned an instant before the tap came on her office door. Ginny, her executive secretary, peered around it. "Ms. Carmichael to see you."

"Hello, Dare," Caroline said as she crossed the DCI's carpet for the second time that day. She was one of the few subordinates who still called Dare by her first name. "Am I allowed to ask how it went at the White House?"

"You are. As well as could be expected. Thirty April has made contact."

Caroline came to a dead halt midway between Dare's desk and her easy chairs. Her pallor was suddenly dreadful.

"You were hoping, somewhere in your mind, that it wasn't Krucevic," the DCI said softly. "So much for hope. Take a seat."

The younger woman did as she was told. After an instant, she managed the look of fixed calm Dare remembered from the morning's conference. She doubted it had been evident for most of the afternoon. Caroline had spent the past four hours off campus, in the polygraphers' relentless hands. Four hours of questions and seismic bar graphs, of emotions wildly fluctuating. At one point, the Security report noted, the subject had looked close to tearing the wires from her fingers and walking out. But the infernal machine had eventually given her a clean bill of health.

"I'm sorry to call you back here at this time of night," Dare told her. It was seven-thirty, late by government standards.

"I'd have come anyway, if only to hold Cuddy's hand. What sort of contact?"

"They dropped a video and the Vice President's clothes at Embassy Prague."

"Payne is on the video?"

"I'm afraid so."

Caroline's eyes narrowed. "She's not—"

"Not dead." Dare twisted the topaz on her finger. "By now, with any luck, she might even be resting comfortably. But if she's left for long in 30 April's hands, I wouldn't vouch for her chances."

Caroline nodded, her lips compressed. "I'd hoped her status would shield her."

"Status didn't do much for Gerhard Schroeder." Dare, too, had seen photographs of the Socialist chancellor's blasted limo. The mortar that had killed Schroeder was triggered when the car crossed an infrared beam. No smoking gun, no fingerprints, only a crater where a man had once been.

"What I heard today convinced me that Mrs. Payne is in extreme peril," Dare said. "Which makes me question whether 30 April has any intention of returning her at all."

The implication hung in the air between them.

Caroline took a deep breath, a swimmer about to plunge. "Did you see . . . Eric?"

"No. It was impossible to see anyone. Krucevic was never visible on camera—just a voice. The rest of them, maybe three or four men, wore hoods. Krucevic referred to a few by name. Otto, I think—"

"Weber," Caroline said automatically. "Did he call anyone Michael? Cuddy thinks it's possible Eric is still using his Agency alias. He found something in DESIST."

Dare shook her head. "But there was a boy. Jozsef. Krucevic claimed he was his son."

She watched Caroline consider this fact like a cut stone under a spotlight.

"And he offered the kid up to the world of television? I wonder why. He kidnapped Jozsef, you know, from his mother. If we could find her—" She stood and began to turn restlessly before the DCI's desk.

"We could use her," Dare concluded quietly. "You think like a case officer."

Caroline laughed. "I wish. That's what we need— a cowboy with a cause. Only whom do we trust?"

"I've always preferred straight thinkers to straight shooters. So think out loud. Krucevic and company were in Prague a few hours ago. Where are they headed?"

"Prague is probably a diversion," Caroline replied, "but they'll want to stay fairly close to an urban center, in order to use our embassies for contact. Bratislava is an easy jump from Prague. So is Budapest or Vienna. Poland is the wrong direction. If they'd wanted Poland, they'd have started there from Berlin."

"*If* they're operating in a linear fashion," Dare countered. "Don't rule out Poland. These people are byzantine."

"Serbs are Byzantine," Caroline corrected her. "Krucevic is a Croat. He would *not* consider that a compliment."

"Caroline, I'm sending you to Berlin on the Bureau's plane."

The younger woman stopped pacing.

Dare said, "You're traveling at the request of the President."

"I am? Gee. Maybe he'll give me one of those nifty little stickpins with the presidential seal on it."

"Support the Bureau investigation, Carrie, in any

way you can. It'll be headed up by the Berlin Legal Attaché, but our station chief—a fellow named Walter Aronson—should be grateful to have you."

"I know Wally."

Of course Caroline knew Wally. He had replaced her husband in Budapest two and a half years ago. "You're going under State cover," Dare continued. "Ambassador Dalton has been informed you're coming. Embassy communications are down, and the staff is mainly operating out of Dalton's residence. You'll make the best of it, I know."

"I always do," Caroline said.

"Travel Section has your itinerary and funds. You can pick them up on your way out of the building. Your dip passport is in order, I hope?"

"Last time I looked."

Dare glanced in a file. "And you have a backstopped identity. A Jane Hathaway, resident in London. Still clean?"

"I suppose so. I haven't used her since Nicosia."

"Will you be carrying a personal weapon?"

"Yes."

The DCI snapped the folder closed.

"Dare, how much time do I have?"

"The plane leaves Dulles at midnight."

"Why Berlin? Why not Prague, since that's where the video surfaced?"

"By the time you fly into Central Europe, they'll have left Prague behind. We can't chase a moving target. But if you're on the ground in the midst of the investigation, Carrie, you may figure out where they're headed."

"I want to go to Budapest."

Dare went very still. "Because it was Eric's last posting?"

"Partly." Caroline hesitated, then shrugged. "*Any-thing* can be hidden in Budapest."

It was not, Dare thought, the real reason. But sometimes we conceal the real reasons even from our-selves. She decided to let it go. "We both know there are two investigations under way, Carrie, and two types of manhunt. If you can make a case for track-ing 30 April in Budapest or Vienna or Krakow, then make it. But start with Berlin. It's what we're expected to do."

"Yes." The professionalism had descended again; nothing of Caroline's emotion was visible in her face. "I'd like to see that tape."

"Not possible. It's a very close hold."

"What do you really expect me to do in Berlin?"

"Whatever the situation requires, my dear. I don't expect you to single-handedly assault the strongholds of 30 April, but short of that . . ."

"I'm not a fool, Dare. I know very well I'm being sent out as bait."

"You're being sent at the President's request," Dare said quietly, "and believe me, he has no thought of bait-ing anyone. He merely admired your competent analysis."

"Which you very thoughtfully provided. You manip-ulated him into asking for me. Don't deny it. I've worked with you long enough to respect the subtlety of your mind. You think I'll draw Eric out of hid-ing. And then betray him for the good of Agency and country. But I can promise you, Dare, that wher-ever Eric is—and it's not going to be Berlin—he doesn't care a rat's ass about me. I've known that since this morning."

"We know nothing whatsoever of Eric's mind." Dare's voice hardened. "Much less his heart." She did not bother to argue with Caroline about her motives or methods; they had both been schooled in the ways of Intelligence. To attempt to deceive each other was childish.

"Even if he did give a shit about me, Dare, he'd never place me in danger by contacting me now. He'll head in the opposite direction."

"That may be true, but we have to try." She stood up abruptly, signaling that the interview was at an end. "You'll report back through station channels wherever you are. Use my private slug for routing, and throw in a special channel classification. What would be appropriate? Nothing that might be confused with the Task Force."

"Who will have access?"

"No one but me."

Caroline took a scrap of paper from Dare's desk and scrawled a word on it swiftly.

"Cutout," Dare said. "How appropriate."

It was the Intelligence term for a go-between. Or a pawn. Somebody used by both sides, for reasons she was never intended to know. Dare folded the slip of paper in precise fourths, then tossed it in her burn bag. It would be incinerated that evening, along with every other compromising detail of that turbulent day.

"You can still walk away, Carrie. You could refuse to go."

"Not if I want a future." Her tone was matter-of-fact. "I have no option but to attempt to find Eric and, through him, Mrs. Payne. But don't expect much, Dare. Eric was trained by the best."

"And Eric trained you." Dare reached for Caroline's hand; it was shockingly cold.

The younger woman smiled faintly. "I'm not angry,

Dare. I'm not confused. I know what I have to do. But I go with few illusions."

"Then may I say—go with God, Caroline."

"God blew up at thirty thousand feet, Dare, somewhere over the Aegean."

THIRTEEN

Dulles International Airport, 10:15 P.M.

CAROLINE HAD FOUND IT DIFFICULT to fly lately. The chartered Boeing 777 was scheduled to depart for Frankfurt at midnight. The plane normally held around two hundred and fifty people. Tonight it would carry thirty-eight, most of them employed by the FBI—forensic technicians, bomb experts, people who understood the stress patterns of explosives on metal and concrete. In counterterrorism work, it was common to find Intelligence operatives alongside Special Agents, the one adept at working the networks, the other at clamping on cuffs. Caroline was comfortable with the Bureau people she knew and with joint CIA-FBI operations. But she had never actually flown to the site of a bombing before. The men and women sharing her airspace tonight were experts of a sort unfamiliar to her.

On the ground in Berlin, they would search for the axle of an obliterated car and hope that it bore a serial number; they would probe the crater at the Brandenburg's foot, shifting stones made ancient by blood and grief. They would sample the soil for chemical residues and put a name to the force that had shattered the Hotel Adlon's fine plate-glass windows. And in a barren hall set aside for the purpose—a school cafeteria or a deserted beer garden—they would pick at the sleeves of the victims' coats with exacting and callous tweezers.

In about eight hours' time they would swing into action, Caroline thought, without pausing for sleep or acknowledging jet lag. They would jostle for position with the local police, yell louder in English when they misplaced their translators, and somehow, in the middle of the devastated square, produce a forensic miracle. Forgetting, if they had ever known, that the Brandenburg Gate had once been beautiful.

She nursed her gin and tonic in the VIP lounge, one of the offhand perks of crisis travel, her eyes fixed on a rerun of *Friends*. She had already presented her handgun—a Walther TPH—to airport security, along with the multiple forms required for international clearance. Her photograph, along with her seat assignment, was now posted in the cockpit of the plane, and every member of the flight crew was aware that Caroline Carmichael carried a gun. She imagined she was not alone in this; among the various Bureau personnel represented on the Berlin flight, a handful must be armed. But it was unusual for an Agency analyst. Most employees of the CIA never carried a gun. Dare had generously offered a duplicate set of weapons clearance forms made out in the name of Jane Hathaway—her backstopped alias—but Caroline had refused. Jane was supposed to be a banker living in London. She would never pack a Walther in her Kate Spade purse.

She took another sip of gin. The butterflies were starting to hum and sing in the pit of her stomach. Takeoff was the worst. Takeoff was a shove from a forty-foot platform, the harness in free fall around your waist;

takeoff was acceleration without a brake mechanism at hand.

A metaphor for the process of explosion.

She should have told the psychiatrist about her fear of flying. He might have found her ramblings illustrative. But she had been in no mood to illustrate much for Dr. Agnelli this afternoon.

"Let's talk about the period before the crash, Mrs. Carmichael. How much did you know about your husband's past?"

"His past? You mean, like . . . his childhood?"

"If you will. Parents, friends, early influences. That sort of thing."

"The man's dead, Doctor. The question of influence is rather moot, wouldn't you agree?"

Had Dare ordered this session in a comfortable chair, the lighting as dim as a bordello's? She must have. An assessment of Caroline's sanity, once her ignorance had been proved by the box with wires. And how much, exactly, did Agnelli know about Eric? The psychiatrist seemed like a gentle man, persuasive, his face scarred indelibly by acne. He held a pen suspended between the tips of his index fingers and stared at her in a fashion that was not unkind. She mistrusted him implicitly.

"My husband rarely talked about his childhood, Doctor. It was not a happy time."

"Really. Did he ever say *why*?"

A buff-colored file lay closed on his right knee. Hers? Or Eric's? In either case, Agnelli possessed more information than he intended to admit. She had worked with psychiatrists before. She recognized the method. He would not influence her testimony; he would prefer that she indict Eric herself. But to what end? How much had he been told?

She shifted in the chair, tweed upholstery sticking testily to her stockings. "I'm sure you've seen his personnel file."

"Mmmm." Noncommittal.

"He was a foster child," she elaborated. "You must know that."

"I see. And his foster parents were . . . less than ideal?"

"Much less." She attempted neutrality, as though she were conducting a high-level briefing. Nothing in her voice of the violence that had shaped him.

"The father was eventually imprisoned on a charge of manslaughter, I understand."

"Yes."

Agnelli waited, eyes steady. Caroline stared back. If he knew about the prison time, he knew what it was for.

"And did that . . . episode . . . affect your husband, Mrs. Carmichael?"

"It must have. In some way." She folded her arms over her chest. "What exactly are you looking for, Doctor? My husband's been gone for years."

Gone. The word she would use henceforth, conveniently inexact.

On the television screen, Monica and her brother were arguing about breast size. Commercials interceded. Caroline finished her gin and tonic. And then, suddenly, Jack Bigelow's face filled the screen.

"We have confirmed beyond a doubt that terrorists abducted Vice President Sophie Payne from the site of the Berlin bombing this morning." Bigelow's suit jacket was on, the bags under his eyes accentuated by the press room's glare of lights. He looked cold and rather deadly, Caroline thought. As though the scripted lines were processed by one part of his brain, while the other—the more calculating—had Sophie Payne's captors pinned against the wall. She wondered if, somewhere, Eric was watching.

"Everything that can be done to locate the Vice President will be done," Bigelow continued, "and her kidnappers will be punished to the full extent of the law. But the United States will never be held hostage to the goals or threats of a band of thugs, regardless of the cost. Mrs. Payne knows that. When she consented to serve this country, she accepted that burden of sacrifice. Our hearts and thoughts are with you, Sophie."

In the split second of silence that fell between the President's final word and the storm of questions hurled at him from the assembled reporters, Caroline distinctly saw his fingers tremble. It was a slight movement that came as he gripped the sides of his podium and focused on the TelePrompTer, but it was betrayal of something, all the same. Fear? The rush of crisis? Or simple exhaustion?

Agnelli would have loved it.

"Gone, but hardly forgotten," the psychiatrist had said this afternoon. "It must have been extremely difficult for you to come to terms with your husband's . . . loss."

"I'm not sure that I really have," Caroline had replied, with the suggestion of frankness. "But you know the old saying, Doctor. 'Those who live by the sword die by the sword.' Eric understood that Intelligence work posed some risks."

"You were married . . . how long?"

"Ten years." Here she was on safer ground. "Is that what this is all about? My grief? How well I'll handle another terrorist bombing?"

Agnelli thumbed the manila file balanced on his knee. "It says here that Eric knew the man his father killed. Clarence Jackson."

Back to that. The interest in her a blind. "He was a history teacher at Eric's high school."

"A teacher. I see." The pen was slipped into a breast pocket, the fingertips steepled. Agnelli was warming to his subject. "Would you describe Mr. Jackson as a mentor?"

Caroline shrugged. "I don't know whether Eric would have used that word or not. He liked the guy."

"And yet his father murdered him."

"*Foster* father, Doctor. Eric never knew his own."

The psychiatrist twitched impatiently, as though her objection were trivial. "Clarence Jackson was of African-American extraction?"

Caroline gazed at him wearily. "You're the one with the file."

"Killed in what amounted to a mob lynching?"

"It was 1972 in South Boston, Doctor. The level of violence was rather high."

"Mmmm." He glanced down at his neat pages, no longer feigning indifference. Who had put him on to this? "I see that your husband was also sentenced in juvenile court, Mrs. Carmichael, and spent several months in a detention center."

"For vandalism. Not murder."

"That sort of thing is probably a prerequisite for the Green Berets." He smiled thinly.

"Not to mention the DO," she shot back. "I hear they're recruiting in the JDC's these days."

Agnelli hadn't enjoyed her little joke.

She supposed there was a picture, for anyone who cared to paint it, of Eric as a trained survivor—a man who from birth had learned to trust no one. Eric was too intelligent, of course, for the casual brutality of his foster home; he was charming, he drew people to him even as a boy—people like Clarence Jackson, who saw something in the scrappy white kid with the obnoxious parents and had been beaten to death for his trouble. Eric could win hearts, he could manipulate and exploit. It was a different kind of violence.

It was possible to see that particular Eric, the one who lived only in his statistics and files, hovering over Pariser Platz in a stolen helicopter. *That* Eric had absorbed the viciousness of his childhood. *That* Eric was fascinated by the people he had been trained to destroy. It was something no analyst worth her paycheck would fail to consider; Dare Atwood certainly had. Caroline had no choice but to consider it herself. The Eric she had loved must be a mirage. Why shouldn't Agnelli's be real?

She asked for another lime and received a second tiny bottle of gin to go with it. The butterflies in her stomach were settling down to sleep, the tension that had knit her joints relaxing inexorably. Takeoff, at this rate, might be nothing more than falling off a log.

There was her boarding call, at last. She rose and felt the blood pound suddenly into her temples. She would regret the gin in what passed for morning.

She gathered up her magazines and paperbacks, her laptop computer and her briefcase. She gave one last glance at the television screen. Chancellor Voekl filled it, his arm around the shoulders of the Czech prime minister. An announcement of German technical assistance and antiterrorism aid, the CNN newscaster said, following the explosion of three pipe bombs in historic areas of Prague.

Bombs in Prague. Where 30 April certainly had been only hours ago. She walked slowly toward the screen, straining for the sound of Voekl's voice above the babble of departure.

He was speaking in German, his words sonorous and deliberate before the translator's text took over. The transfer of Volksturm militia to the Czech Republic underlined the common cultural past and mutual security concerns of the two Central European countries; it heralded a joint commitment to combating the destabilizing influence of outside forces in their societies, and gave notice to those who would threaten peace. . . .

Caroline fought down her frustration. What time had the bombs exploded? And where exactly had they been? Did the Prague police have any idea who was responsible?

The image shifted suddenly from Fritz Voekl's face to that of a suffering child. Enormous eyes, dark with pain. A hectic flush in the cheeks. With her wispy red hair and her tattered party dress, she was nonetheless an angel. The child thrust her thumb in her mouth and turned her face weakly toward her mother's shoulder. Caroline's heart surged upward in her chest, a prick of unexpected tears under her lids. To hold a child like that—the soft floss of her hair, the warm weight—

"Sixty-three more children died of mumps today in the ethnic Albanian squatters' village on the outskirts of Pristina, in Kosovo," the newscaster said implacably. "Thousands of former refugees, who returned to find their villages and housing destroyed by Serb forces during the 1998 Kosovo war, have taken up residence in the makeshift housing constructed from the remnants of bombed buildings. But World Health Organization officials say the strain of mumps virus that struck last week is unlike any on record. Producing severe glandular swelling and excessively high fever, the disease has already claimed the lives of two hundred and thirteen children, a mortality rate that is both unusual and alarming. More ethnic Albanians are sickening daily. Thus far, the deadly mumps virus appears to be confined to the squatter area, but local leaders warn the infection could spread despite stringent efforts at quarantine."

Caroline turned away from the screen. One more voiceless tragedy in a part of the world that had already given up hope, one more small angel dead by morning in her mother's arms. Disease followed war like morning followed night; it lurked in the ruptured water mains, in the rat-infested rubble. It riddled the dirt where the children played. But the weight of grief in Yugoslavia was impossible to comprehend. The Kosovars had lost their homes, their livelihoods, and now their children—the one thing they had fought so desperately to save.

Caroline walked toward the flight attendant, her boarding pass extended, then stopped dead as the German translator's voice picked up where the newscaster had left off. Fritz Voekl was sending German medical teams into Kosovo armed with an experimental new mumps vaccine. Fritz Voekl—who had fought NATO involvement in the Yugoslav civil war, who thought the Kosovars were just another bunch of poor-mouthed Muslims looking for a handout. So what if their children were dying? That left fewer to feed.

The teams would begin inoculating ethnic Albanian children throughout the province as soon as they arrived.

Caroline stared at the screen in disbelief as Voekl

smiled for the flashbulbs. She would never have called the chancellor a humanitarian. But refugees stay home, when home is safe and healthy. Maybe Fritz had figured that out at last.

It was unlikely he'd learned to care.

Part II
WEDNESDAY, NOVEMBER 10

ONE

Pristina, 3:45 A.M.

SIMONE AMIOT FOLLOWED THE ORANGE GLOW of the man's cigarette as he crossed the rutted dirt road and made for her tent—a bobbing spark in the darkness of the wee hours, like a june bug uncertain of its flight. His figure was backlit by a single flaring torch the police guard had thrust into the mud—a bulky, formless sil-houette, hands shoved into the pockets of a battered down jacket. His chin was lowered over his chest, as though he were lost in thought or intent upon watching where he put each foot. There was an air of assurance about him, even at this distance; of relaxed accommoda-tion with his squalid surroundings, the uniformed men patrolling at his back. He could not, Simone decided, be a parent.

She removed the earpiece of her stethoscope and folded it briskly in three—then spared a second to lay her cool, smooth fingers on the bare chest of the four-year-old boy lying inert on the cot before her. She did not need her stethoscope for this one anymore. She drew the sheet over his head very gently and allowed her hand to rest on the brown hair, still damp with sweat. Drago Pavlovic. Three days ago he had been playing in the street with a combat fighter made of paper and sticks. He had grinned at her as she walked by, and roared the sound of his engine. Drago was sturdy for his age, with brown eyes and freckles on his nose. He was about to lose his right front tooth.

Drago was number three hundred and twenty-seven. Or was it twenty-eight? At least Simone was spared the job of breaking the news to his mother. The woman had been murdered the previous year.

She rubbed wearily at her forehead, as though she could push aside the burning sensation of tears and futility. Pristina was her third stint with Médecins sans Frontières—Doctors Without Borders—but it was by far the most difficult. Last year, and the year before that, there had been bullet wounds. Burn victims. Broken limbs. Dehydration. Horrible in themselves—but things Simone could treat. In Pristina, she was brought face-to-face with the limits of her own power. She had no tools to fight the mumps ravaging the squatter population. And nothing to keep it from spreading.

In the past five days, she had personally held vigil over more than two hundred children. Most were buried now in hastily dug graves on the edge of the squatters' camp, their delicate features dusted with lime. Her years of schooling, her years of practical knowledge, the drugs she had flown in from Toronto—none of them did any good. She might as well have been a woman of the Middle Ages, showering incantations and powdered bat wing.

A handful of Simone's more than two hundred stricken children had actually survived the mumps scourge. One of them, a little girl with bright red hair, was sleeping soundly on a cot in the far corner. Although still weak and far from well, Dania gave them all hope. When the fever took her, she plunged like the others into delirium and dehydration, but in Dania's case the IV feeds and ice compresses actually seemed to work. Her mother, whom Simone knew only as Ragusa, sat stoically by the child's bedside for three full days. She sponged her daughter's forehead with a damp cloth, exchanged her soiled nightdress for a clean T-shirt, whispered relentlessly to a mind that wandered far in hectic dreams. She said little; she spoke almost no English. Her husband and brother had been shot by the Serb militia. Her eldest child, a son, was hiding out in the hills with a band of Albanian guerillas. One daughter had been lost on the road and never recovered. A blind grandmother and little Dania were all that Ragusa had left.

At three o'clock in the morning two days before, when the child's fever at last had peaked and broken, settling back down to double digits—when Simone could tentatively declare that the danger was past and the child would *live*—Ragusa had stared at her, unbelieving. Then she had thrown herself across Dania's sleeping form, her shoulders shaking with sobs of terror and relief. She had cried aloud in thanks to a God that was not Simone's, a God that had taken other sons and daughters without hesitation or mercy. Simone touched the woman's shoulder, and she turned to seize the doctor's hand. Ragusa had managed to call her child back from the Valley of Death, but she believed it was Simone who had saved her.

Later, as she crossed the muddy tracks that separated the hospital tent from the rest of the camp, Simone saw the woman waiting shyly by the mess tent door.

"Coffee, Ragusa?" she asked, hoping that these words at least were comprehensible. *"Un peu du café?"*

Ragusa shook her head. She was clutching something close to her frayed coat. Simone hesitated, uncertain how to bridge the gulf of language, but then the woman seized her hand and pressed her burden into it.

"For you," she said haltingly. "Dania. My thanks. Is all . . ."

It is all that I have, all that I can give you, who have given me back my life.

Ragusa hurried past her. Simone looked down into her palm. The woman had parted with the last few things she possessed: three tampons, their paper covers torn and grubby. Simone placed them carefully in her white lab coat pocket and watched Ragusa retreat across the rutted mire. She could have laughed aloud, or cried. But all she felt was unworthy.

The flap of the medical tent was swept aside, and the orange glow of a cigarette arced to the dirt like a dead-headed flower. The man she had glimpsed in silhouette a moment ago. He had the decency to stamp his tobacco out, in deference to the ailing children.

"May I help you?" she said in English.

"I don't know," he answered in the same language, surprising her. "It's the middle of the night. But I thought somebody might be here. Could I borrow a thermometer?"

Simone rose from the dead child's bedside and moved toward him. "Is someone ill?"

He hesitated. The air of assurance faltered a little. In the half-light thrown by her propane lantern, she saw him for what he was: a man torn from sleep, eyes bleary with worry, but determined not to panic. "It's Alexis. My oldest girl. She's rather . . . hot."

"I see. I'd better come."

Simone delayed only long enough to inform one of the nurses about Drago Pavlovic's death. Then she pulled on a jacket over her white coat and jeans, gathered up her medical kit, and followed the man out into the darkness. People were already stirring all over the camp; she heard the clang of coffeepots, caught the flare of fires, the guttural hawking of an old man's throat. A wave of fatigue so powerful it was akin to vertigo nearly knocked her off her feet. She was not the only doctor in Pristina—there were at least fourteen volunteers from North America and Western Europe— but the epidemic had strained them to their limits. And today would bring a fresh wave of sick and dying.

"I'm Enver," he said, holding out his hand. "Enver Gordievic. You're the doctor from Canada."

"Toronto, yes. Simone Amiot." He had surprised her again. But she was accustomed enough to camps by this time to know that gossip is every refugee's lifeblood. She kept her hands in her pockets and smiled at him; the casual gesture of shaking his hand was just one more way of passing sickness. "Do you know Canada?"

He shook his head. "I've only been to D.C."

Not "Washington," not "the United States"—but "D.C." Simone decided to assume nothing about Enver Gordievic.

He led her to a shelter built out of scraps of lumber, a windowless box the size of a doll's house. It was canted unsteadily on a cinder-block foundation; but it had a door that swung on rope hinges, and when Simone ducked through the opening and stepped inside, she found the interior fairly warm and dry. He had built bunk beds for the children. There were two of them, both girls.

"Alexis," he said softly—and then, in a language Simone could not understand, added a few more sentences. His hand smoothed the child's golden hair. She raised her head weakly, then let it fall back on the pillow. Even at a distance of five feet, Simone recognized the glassy eyes and flushed cheeks of fever. She drew a quick breath of rage and frustration, then crossed to the little girl's bedside.

"She's burning up! Why didn't you bring her straight to the clinic?"

"Because the kids who walk in there never walk out," Enver said bluntly. "She has the mumps?"

"Of course. I can tell just by looking at her. The swelling hasn't come out yet, but it will in a matter of hours. It's the dehydration that concerns me. She needs an IV feed, and quickly."

"No." He reached for Simone's arm and steered her firmly toward the hovel's door. "Thank you very much for your time, Dr. Amiot, but all I needed was the diagnosis. I'll take it from here."

"Are you nuts?" Simone swung on him furiously, then her eyes widened. "You're planning to get her out of the camp. I can assure you, Mr.—" His last name escaped her. "—Enver, that the care your daughter will find elsewhere in Pristina is no better than what we can offer her here. If you move her, she'll die."

"That may be true. But there aren't a hundred other kids lying in beds next to her, competing for attention, elsewhere in Pristina. I'm taking her to my mother." He bent down and gathered the little girl up in his arms. His face, when he looked at Simone, was deliberately calm; he was a man who knew what he needed and how to get it.

"Will you do me a favor?" he asked her.

"Please, Enver. Don't move the child."

"Would you watch Krystle for me? The little one? It'll take me an hour to get to my mother's and back."

Simone turned away from the two-year-old slumbering in her bunk and pulled open the door. "I can't. I'm sorry. I've got to find Dr. Marx. Perhaps he can convince you to bring Alexis to the tent—"

"Don't waste your time."

"I don't," Simone said abruptly. "I use every spare minute to save these lives. Your daughter *can't* leave. She can't set foot outside this camp. As of midnight we were put under strictest quarantine. Surely you've seen the police patrol? The epidemic cannot be allowed to spread throughout the rest of the city, or the province. Try to leave, and the police will beat you silly. Try harder, and they'll shoot."

"I've got to go to work in the morning! I've got clients!"

"They'll have to wait."

"How long?"

"I don't know." Her fingers spasmed on the doorknob. "Until this is . . . over."

He stood there, his daughter in his arms, and Simone watched as his expression changed. The easy assurance fled. What replaced it was a look she had come to know: hunted, desperate, defiant of the odds.

The look of a cornered animal.

TWO

Georgetown, 4:13 A.M.

DARE ATWOOD WAS DREAMING OF TREES: spectral branches writhing like the architraves of a cathedral when one stares at them too long, neck craned backward, the self diminished by an inhuman height. The light under the leaves was cathedral-like, too; dim as clouded glass, smothered with incense. She began to walk through the tunnel of tangled limbs, but the branches were keening, they screamed for sunlight and air. She had never known a tree could grieve—and with her knowledge came an unreasoning fear, so that she turned abruptly in her sleep and repressed a whimper. She must run, must find the road again and the car she had abandoned—but the trees had closed and shut off her path.

I need an ax, she thought, and looked down at her hands. All she held was her Waterman pen.

The shrill cry of a bird in her ear—primeval, ravenous. She jumped, and the trees shattered as though they were painted on glass. The phone was ringing.

The phone.

She struggled upward, heaved back the bedclothes, and groped into the darkness for her secure line.

"Dare Atwood."

"Director," came the apologetic voice in her ear, more cordial than primeval birds. "I'm sorry to disturb you." It was like Scottie Sorensen to sound collected and urbane at 4:13 A.M. The wee small hours were Scottie's native element; it was the time when hunting was best. "We've just heard from the CDC—and you had asked to be called."

"Go ahead," Dare said tersely. The CDC was the Centers for Disease Control in Atlanta. The hypodermic dropped with Sophie Payne's clothing on the steps of the Prague embassy had been flown there by jet for analysis. Dick Estridge—a twenty-three-year veteran of the CIA's Directorate of Science and Technology, an authority on chemical and biological weapons—had been dispatched to meet the plane. Presumably he and a CDC epidemiologist had worked for most of the night.

"It looks, walks, and talks like anthrax," Scottie told her.

"So Krucevic wasn't bluffing."

"No. If this is really the needle that inoculated the Vice President."

"That's an assumption we have to make." Dare considered the point, as she had considered it a thousand times since Payne's abduction. The needle and its contents represented a worst-case scenario. If they were merely a bluff, so much the better. If they weren't, then the President and the Agency should be prepared. "Or don't you agree?" she asked Scottie. "Does the CDC think the needle is a fake?"

"No. From what Estridge tells me, the anthrax bacillus is particularly hardy. It can survive exposure to sunlight for days, and it can live in soil and water for years. The trip to Atlanta in a used hypodermic was nothing. And then there's the blood."

"Blood," Dare repeated.

"The President authorized transmittal of Mrs. Payne's medical records from Bethesda Naval to the CDC. Her blood type matches residue found in the hypodermic."

He was holding something back, Dare knew. Offering her the security of facts before venturing into the unknown.

"What else, Scottie?"

"It's the fact of the hypodermic that has these people concerned. Apparently anthrax is an airborne infection. It's a germ we inhale. Or a spore, as Estridge calls it. It invades the lungs and causes symptoms similar to a chest cold, followed by respiratory shock and death. But Krucevic injected his bug directly into the Veep's bloodstream."

"Go on," Dare said.

"So the infection is systemic."

She frowned into the darkness. "But he also injected her with an antidote. Or so we hope. That would be systemic, too—wouldn't it?"

"Yes and no. The normal treatment of an unvaccinated patient exposed to anthrax *inhalation* is a four-week cycle of antibiotics, along with a three-part program of follow-up vaccination. It's damned persistent in the human body. Krucevic claimed that this particular bug is about ten times as virulent. He also claimed to have an effective antibiotic. Something specific to his engineered anthrax strain. But the CDC is highly skeptical. If Krucevic can knock out that deadly a bacillus in one shot, they say, then he's making medical history. They'd like to meet the guy."

Dare's heart sank. "They think she's still sick."

"They think she's going to die in a matter of days," Scottie said.

"Can we save her? If we get to her soon?"

It was an unfair question, Dare knew—one Scottie could never answer. He avoided it with predictable grace.

"What worries the CDC is the bacillus's tendency to cause ulcers. There's a form of anthrax infection common to livestock workers—they get it from infected sheep—that leaves open sores on the hands and arms. Estridge says the CDC is afraid that a bloodborne infection like Mrs. Payne's could result in secondary ulceration of her major organs. Heart, liver, the lining of the stomach, you name it. . . ."

Dare winced. "She could be bleeding inside."

"And completely shut down over the next forty-eight hours. The woman should be in an intensive-care unit."

"But surely Krucevic would have considered that. He's a biologist himself."

"Maybe he doesn't care. Maybe he never intended for Sophie Payne to survive."

"But he injected his own son with the stuff!"

"He *said* that he did," Scottie cautioned. "But what do we really know, Director?"

"Nothing," she retorted, "and we don't have to know. All we have to do is assume. We have to project every possible scenario for the Vice President; we have to be prepared to offer solutions. That's why we exist, remember?"

Scottie was silent.

"Get somebody at the CDC working on this bug," Dare ordered, "because when the Vice President comes home—and I mean *when*, Scottie—she'll need a treatment regimen already in place."

"Got it," he replied, and hung up.

Dare pressed her hands against her eyes and considered making coffee. Something about trees and an ax fluttered on the edge of her consciousness. She brushed it aside and called the President.

THREE

The Night Sky, 3:47 A.M.

CAROLINE CARMICHAEL IS SOARING across the Atlantic at thirty-nine thousand feet, an arrow shot straight at the heart of Central Europe; but in her fitful dreams, she crouches low in her grandfather's dew-drenched furrows and waits, tensed, for pursuit.

The smell of damp Salinas earth rises from the morning fields and mingles with the dense musk of artichoke leaves, with the flare of garlic flowers from across three hectares, with creosote and diesel fumes from the black ribbon of highway. It is August 7, 1969, and she is exactly five years old. Her father has been gone for most of her life, gone somewhere in Asia without being dead, in a plane that failed him when he least expected it. She knows his face and name by heart, she knows the outline of his story as another child might know Santa Claus—Bill Bisby, Salinas hero, with the fields of artichoke and garlic in his blood; Bill Bisby, a flyboy at twenty-two, with his finger on the after-burner; Bisby the careless warrior, her daddy. A kind of elf, with his short, dark hair and his open grin, one

hand waving forever before the cockpit shield comes
down. Bill Bisby, who might just slide down her chimney come Christmas.

Your daddy was a hero, Grandpa whispers in her ear.
*Your daddy died for his country. Your daddy might be coming
back, someday. It'd be just like him to fool us all. You've got to
make your daddy proud.*

A screen door slams. Caroline cocks her head and
watches as Grandma shakes the crumbs from Grandpa's
napkin, then turns back into the house without a glance
for the warming day, without a hint of Caroline crouching secret in the acrid furrows. Grandma's lips are folded
in a line as straight as an ironed napkin edge; her eyelids
are red. Caroline bites hard at a hangnail trailing from
her thumb.

Her knees are dirty, and one of them bleeds. Her
hair has not been combed. She has been up for four
hours, up since the last hour of darkness and the irriga-
tion machines rolling like giant spiders across the landscape. She is waiting there among the green leaves, the
scent of garlic and artichoke, for a last glimpse of her
mother.

Brakes squeal as a truck slows at the crossroads, turning toward Gilroy, its outline shimmering like a mirage
in the morning heat. Caroline ignores it. She has heard
such things from birth, as common as birdsong and the
whisper of surf when the wind blows from the west.
Her ankles ache from crouching and she needs to pee,
but she stares unblinking at the farmhouse's front door.

And there, thrusting carelessly through it in her worn
jeans, blond hair flying, a pack already slung over her
back, is Jackie. She clatters down the sagging wood
steps. She shoves open the VW van's battered door and
hurls her heavy rucksack—army green, probably from a

surplus place, the irony of it lost on her—into the back.
Then turns and waits for Jeremy. Or is it Dave? Last year
it was Phil.

Caroline rubs at her streaming nose with a dirty hand,
then wipes it on the skirt of her dress. Grandma would
purse her lips and frown; she would think, inevitably, *Just
like her mother.* When Jackie is gone, Caroline will creep
into the house and stand furtively before the washbasin,
before anyone sees. Have they missed her yet? Are they
worried? Do they remember that it is her birthday?

The man with the beard and the long hair, the
leather vest and the bell-bottom jeans with heart-shaped
patches and peace signs scrawled in ink, avoids the door
altogether. He shuffles around the far corner of the
house from the direction of the privy, his thin frame
curled in an eternal question mark. He stares at his own
shoes as he walks. A mongrel dog lopes at his heels,
tongue dangling. Its breath reeks of raw meat and decay,
the good-natured slobber left in Caroline's lap.

"Carrie!" her mother calls. She cups her hands to her
mouth and bellows again. "*Carrie!* Shit! Where the *fuck*
did that kid go?"

Caroline crouches closer to the earth and tries not to
breathe.

Jackie turns, impotent and furious, her gaze roaming
over the morning fields. Her daughter kneads the soiled
cotton of her dress between hot and damp fingers.
There was yelling last night, too, when she was supposed to be asleep; shouts and demands and a bitter sobbing that might have been her grandmother's. They
would not let Jackie take her away, Grandpa said, cutting off the tears; they owed that much to Bill. And to
the child. It was no life for a five-year-old, in the back
of a van. It was no life for Jackie.

"Don't tell me how to raise my kid, old man," Jackie had said.

"Seems to me you ain't raising her," Grandpa had replied.

And then, much later, the scent of pot and her mother's hand in the darkness, smoothing Caroline's hair back from her face. Caroline squeezed her eyes shut and pretended to sleep; she prayed that Jackie would stay all night, while the moon shifted across the face of the clapboard house and the cicadas died down to a murmur. But Jackie rose after a moment and shuffled back up the hall, the tip of her joint a wandering flare.

Now the man who may be Jeremy or Dave or even possibly Phil orders the dog into the back of the van. He slides the door shut with a rumble. Grandma is standing on the front porch, her fingers gripping the rail, her face wiped clean of emotion.

"Where's my kid?" Jackie snarls. "Where've you put her, Ellie?"

Grandma allows herself to blink. "Nobody *puts* Caroline anywhere. The child has a way of hiding herself."

"Right. Convenient. Isn't that *fucking* convenient, Dave? *Christ.* Well, let's find her. Carrie!"

Caroline's heart is suddenly pounding in her rib cage; she buries her face in the leaves. She is one second away from racing toward the woman with the blond hair, one second from hurling herself into her mother's arms. She so wants to be wanted. But she remembers, with the sharpness of a child's memory, what it was like being Jackie's girl. She can still smell the stench of her own unchanged diapers, the hunger of forgotten lunch and dinner and then breakfast again, the nights she slept hiding under a blanket in the back of a thousand cars, terrified that Joe or Zane or Eddie might remember she was there.

"Carrie!" The voice hoarse with smoke and rage.

Her grandfather's broken shotgun snaps suddenly to attention. The sound is small in the morning air, almost an indifference, but Caroline's head comes up and her eyes move unerringly to the man standing silent on the front porch, his gun leveled at Jackie. Bill Bisby's dad. The hero's father.

Jackie freezes where she stands, outlined against the waving artichokes, the van at her back. Caroline watches the anger drain from her face, sees her eyes close in bitterness.

"It's time to go," Grandpa says quietly. "You go on, girl, and get in that van."

The blond hair writhes as she turns. She gives him the finger. But she goes.

———

When the minibus stops for an instant at the end of the dirt drive and hesitates, then lumbers with the pain of hard old age in the direction of Santa Cruz, Caroline rises from the ground. She is suddenly sobbing. She has wet her pants. Her mother is gone, as she has gone every year of Caroline's life. But Grandpa is sauntering slowly through the field, the shotgun barrel broken over his forearm. He is whistling a tuneless little song that might be "Happy Birthday." He knows exactly where Caroline is; he has found her there before. In his other hand is a present tied in blue ribbon.

They do not hear from Jackie for another three years.

———

Caroline stirs in the airless dark of a hurtling plane. The gin has left her cotton-mouthed. She is flying toward Eric, who fell off her radar like vanished Bill Bisby—only this time the hero came sliding back down the chimney. It is Christmas in midair, and Caroline is supposed to believe in miracles now, however improvident. What would her grandfather say to all this? What would he think of Caroline's Eric?

He would wonder how she came to be so far from Salinas.

———

"My condolences, Mrs. Bisby," says the man at the edge of the cemetery as the rain spatters down around them and their pumps sink into the mud. "Your husband was a good man. He died too young."

Grandma weeps into her handkerchief. Caroline grips her elbow with one hand and an umbrella with the other. It is February, and Caroline is barely eleven years old—February, and whole sections of the coastline are falling into the sea, Highway 1 is closed. The artichoke fields and the expanse of garlic are drowned in mud. She tries not to stare at the crumbling edge of her grandfather's grave, the way the loamy earth is sliding downward. She tries not to think of him at all.

The rain swept over Caroline's grandfather while he drove south from San Jose in the dark; it dogged him down the curves of the Santa Cruz mountains; it filled his headlights and obliterated his windshield. He steered blindly into the grille of another truck, arms flung up before his face—and so he ended, the hero's father, still believing his boy was coming home.

The silver-haired man standing before them in the Salinas cemetery pries the umbrella from Caroline's hand. He clasps her chilled fingers in his enormous palm. She sighs deeply and, without thinking about it much, buries her face in his black raincoat. He strokes her hair while Grandma weeps.

"I'm Hank Armstrong," he says. "Jackie's uncle. I've come to take you home, Caroline."

———

"Home" turned out to be a duplex on Park Avenue, a house on Long Island, a woman named Mrs. Marsalis who presided over the kitchen in a starched uniform. Home was home for only a few months of the year, because Hank was wise and would never make Grandma an enemy; Caroline's real life was in Salinas, he knew, among the sodden fields. Hank sent Grandma money that year, "to help out with Caroline's upkeep," and took the child to Paris. He made plans for the following summer; he told Mrs. Marsalis to redecorate a bedroom in Southampton. He rejoiced in this gift of a child to light the winter of his life. He altered his will.

For the first time, Caroline flew in a jet plane and tried not to think of falling.

Grandma sold off the fields of artichoke and garlic; she took a pittance for the house her husband had built. She moved north to the city and accepted elevators. She stood over her sink, where there was no longer a window, and stared unseeing at the wall.

Caroline returned from her travels with Hank. She talked of Manhattan and of the Eiffel Tower. She practiced French. Large boxes of books arrived from New York each week, and Caroline read them aloud to her grandmother in the evenings. She read in bed long after the rest of the lights were doused. Hank paid for her private schooling. She wore a plaid jumper, a white blouse with a Peter Pan collar, a navy blue tie. Hank wrote to her on thick, cream-colored paper, in an elegant blue hand—or perhaps he dictated, and the hand was Mrs. Marsalis's. The news from Park Avenue.

Nothing unfit for Grandma's ears. But Caroline did not read his letters aloud. She tied them with ribbon and buried them in drawers.

He was a quiet man, Hank Armstrong, who marshaled his thoughts and chose his words with precision. He loved Caroline without understanding the point of expressing it. When she cried for her grandmother or fell into moping silence on days of relentless rain, Hank invariably offered her a book. It was the only comfort he knew.

He had married and been abandoned by at least three wives. He had no children of his own—just Jackie, his sister's girl, who only called when she was broke.

It was on one of those occasions that Jackie had offered up Caroline, the prize chip in her floating crap game. And Hank had taken the gamble.

"I never understood your mother," Hank told Caroline once, under the influence of gin and the Hamptons sunset. "But then, I never tried."

———

She was supposed to go to law school and join Hank's firm. That was always the plan, from the time she was fifteen—*Caroline will go to law school,* Hank said, and make him proud. Her intelligence should not be wasted. Her flashes of brilliance, her cunning with words, her shy smile above the private-school uniform—all offerings on the altar of good fortune.

What Hank wanted, Caroline knew, was *safety.* He wanted her life to be free from violence—the rage of feeling, the tragedy of wandering, the upheaval of passion and loss. And for the most part Caroline agreed. After all, emotion had never done much for Jackie. But in the end she turned her back on Harvard Law and chose Langley instead.

Hank toured the CIA campus on Family Day. He boned up on foreign policy. He talked of law school as something she had merely deferred. Until Eric Carmichael burst out of the Tidewater and confounded them both completely.

"Caroline is no trouble," Hank had said proudly when she was seventeen; "Caroline follows her head, not her heart." It was inevitable, she thought as her plane descended into German airspace, that the rebellion would come when Hank least expected it. There was something in her blood that was wholly un-Armstrong—a hint of Bill Bisby and his wild contrail, a fascination for free fall.

What if she were to call Hank now, to pick up the cabin phone and say, *Hank, I need you, I'm scared and I'm lost*?

People had a way of betraying you. They died; they dropped off the face of the earth. Or worse, they traded their souls and came back down the chimney like vicious Christmas elves: a familiar face, a stranger's heart, and a load of baggage on his back.

The trick was not to let them see you still cared.

Berlin, 8:30 A.M.

GRETA OPPENHEIMER DID NOT LOOK LIKE the
sort of person who should be manning the phones
in a stylish front office. Greta wore heavy shoes with
thick soles and the sort of stockings that were intended
to suggest a glossy tan but merely cast a brown pall over
instep and leg. Her face was crinkled. She applied a
heavy concealer to the dark circles under her eyes each
morning, but by ten A.M. the camouflage had worn off,
and the smudged sockets peered out at the world with
undisguised exhaustion. Greta's clothes were sage green
or charcoal gray. They conformed to the fashion of ten
years previous, and might even have dated from that ancient period. Her dull blond hair was shot through with
silver, unkempt, like a bird's nest abandoned high in a
leafless tree. She was a woman formed by hardship; she
expected to disappoint. Greta lived alone, and festered
in her loneliness. She was thirty-four years old.

Fred Leicester, who worked in the new U.S. embassy on
Pariser Platz and contrived to ride the number 8 U–Bahn
from Wittenau every morning, although he really lived

clear across the city in Dahlem, had a pretty good sense of who Greta Oppenheimer was. He knew that her parents had been poorly educated, that she had grown up in a small village in Thuringia and reported to the local factory at seventeen. He knew that her parents had died playing chicken on a single-lane highway when she was almost twenty, and that she had married and divorced before she was twenty-four. He thought she might be religious, in a private and stricken way. In another era she might have turned ecstatic and raised stigmatized hands in praise of a punishing Lord. But the latest millennium preferred the prosaic. Greta forgot to speak in tongues. She turned receptionist instead.

The convulsive end of the German Democratic Republic in 1989 had carried Greta along like a Popsicle stick in a storm drain; history bewildered and drowned her. Ten years in unified Berlin had failed to improve her lot. Greta lived with one foot on the threshold of the present and her entire body leaning back into the past; she lived in ignorance and suspicion and a moral rectitude as lifeless as dust. She scrupulously saved every spare pfennig, without the slightest notion of what she would ever spend it on.

She was, Fred thought, a perfect target for recruitment. What Greta craved was a new dream, an ambition within her reach. And he was the man to give it to her.

Like most men of his training and background, Fred Leicester believed that women who live alone and who are unhappy should be grateful for male attention. The notion of grateful women and all that they might tell was hallowed in the annals of espionage. Grateful women talk. They make room on their seat in the U-Bahn, sliding heavy buttocks toward the smoke-fogged windows. Their hearts thud painfully beneath their drab sweaters at the prospect of another commute, of Fred Leicester ducking through the train's sliding doorways, his morning newspaper in one hand and a cooling cup of coffee in the other. Grateful women sell out the last man to neglect them without a moment's hesitation, and feel better for the betrayal. It was Fred's hope that with keen eye contact, a few warm smiles, a request for assistance with his stumbling German, Greta would begin to talk. She was his developmental in the middle of Mlan Krucevic's empire, his sole prospect for Sophie Payne's salvation. For Greta, Fred had taken the S-Bahn north from Dahlem that morning, switched stations twice, and waited with innumerable cups of coffee for the hour to be ripe.

He stood now on the underground platform and looked toward the approaching Wittenau train. She always chose the third car from the front, always sat on the far side of the aisle. It would be easy to raise the subject of yesterday's horror: the rail lines were shattered at Pariser Platz, all the trains were running late. She might express sympathy, perhaps, in view of his nationality; if the car was quite full, they might be forced to hang by the ceiling straps together, jostled by Fate and haphazard politics. The train would go nowhere with great difficulty. Fred would suggest they get off and share a taxi. Or stop for coffee until the crowds subsided. She would agree after an instant's hesitation, an anxious look half cast over her shoulder. It was one of Greta's mannerisms. By this time, he knew them all.

Grit swirled up from the platform, and Fred narrowed his eyes. The train creaked alongside. Fred tossed his half-empty cup in the trash and threw himself into the scrum. A human wall of bodies, of rigid limbs denying entry, the doors closing at last behind his back. A mad rush from the waiting commuters; an unseemly jostle at the doors. Were they so desperate for work this morning, these Berliners, for the normalcy of routine after yesterday's bloody violence? Impossible to know whether Greta was sitting next to a window, her gaze fixed on the middle distance. Fred strained upward on tiptoe, glanced left and right, the length of the carriage. Then he made the survey again.

Greta Oppenheimer was not there.

———

She had gone to work early that morning, but the call she expected never came. Greta fixed her eyes on a slight defect in the weave of the industrial carpeting—a pull in the nylon that tufted up like a human eyelash—and knew that the door to the office would not open that day. She would sit in her chair while the clock hand moved with the invisible sun. Other people, their concerns far different, might gather in corridors above and below her; they might stand clustered at their coffee stations or lavatory mirrors, chatting aimlessly. Greta would be paralyzed with duty. Waiting for the call that meant He needed her.

Even to herself, she could not pronounce His name. It was too powerful and immense, like the Old Testament God. He knew nothing of the way he affected her, how she hoarded the few words He spoke, turning them over in the dusk of her apartment later like scavenged treasure. He did not know that she had kept a scrap of paper merely because it bore His handwriting, that she could close her eyes and bury her face in the desk chair because He had sat in it once. He did not know that she would die for Him.

He did not know she was alive.

A crackle of static from the speakerphone on the

desk, and Greta jerked in her chair, the blood throbbing painfully in her temples. What to do? What was required of her? There was no one else to answer. She must not fail.

Another burst of static. Someone was buzzing for access at the street. This was unusual and thus frightening. She reached a trembling finger to the phone's bank of buttons. *"Ja?"*

"I have business with VaccuGen," said a woman's voice in German.

Greta glanced upward at the small television screen that hung in one corner. The woman turned her head. She wore a nondescript coat that looked dark gray and might, in fact, have been any color. Her black hair was shoulder length. Heavy glasses masked her features.

"The offices are closed," Greta said firmly, and clicked the button off.

More static, insistent, blaring—and Greta wished, suddenly, that she had never come into work at all, that she had stayed at home like so many good Berliners, terrified of the Turks. "What?" she snapped.

"My business is with the lab."

"Your name?"

"I'm from the Health Ministry. It's about the mumps vaccines. The humanitarian relief."

Greta's brow cleared. Of course—she had known of the vaccine consignment for Pristina; it was the one matter of legitimate business she could expect all week. It was a large shipment—ten thousand ampules at least, the first of several scheduled for the refugee population. "You are familiar with the loading dock?" she asked.

"No."

"Where is your truck?"

"I was told nothing about a truck," the woman outside retorted. "I have come for the health minister's personal supply. The minister is to carry it to Kosovo himself tomorrow as a goodwill gesture."

Greta hesitated. "I was not told," she said.

"Is there anyone with more authority in the office?" The woman was fumbling in her handbag, searching for her official identification; through the surveillance monitor Greta could sense her impatience. "Anyone who might be able to help me? Greta Oppenheimer, for instance?"

"I am Greta Oppenheimer." Surprise brought her upright.

"Mlan told me to ask for you," the woman said, and stared directly into the surveillance camera's lens.

Greta's breath snagged in her throat. How could this creature utter the word with such a casual air? As though it were a name like any other? A name you might toss over a dinner table: *Pass the cabbage, Mlan.* No one knew His name, no one but the handful of faithful admitted to His presence. Certainly not this bitch, who had never laid eyes on Him, who could not possibly *know* Him. Heat surged through Greta's veins and burst in a wave at her cheeks. *He had told this woman her name.*

"I am Greta," she repeated.

"Then open the door, you crucifier of Jesus, before I freeze my tits off," the woman spat out contemptuously.

And Greta obeyed.

"I haven't got much time," she said briskly, and tugged at the fingertips of her gloves.

Her voice, freed of the speakerphone's distortion, was heavy and coarse. German was not, Greta thought, her first language; but what was? She might be Russian or some other type of Slav. A woman from the East. From His homeland.

"The minister has requested twelve dozen ampules."

"That's our normal crating quantity. . . ."

"Good. Fetch it."

Greta glanced over her shoulder. She swallowed nervously. "I have no access to that vaccine."

"What?"

The sunglasses were swept off, and a pair of black eyes, heavily rimmed in kohl, stared at her implacably.

"The laboratory is closed," Greta said. Such a vague word for the battery of electronics that encircled His kingdom, that ensured the unworthy were barred. "I have no access to the storerooms."

The woman's brows came sharply together. "But this is nonsense! It was expressly approved by Mlan himself! What am I to tell the minister?"

Greta stared at her helplessly.

The woman fished a second time in her capacious handbag. Like her clothes, it was black. She might have been dressed for mourning, Greta thought, or an avant-garde play. The only spot of color was at her throat, a white scarf wound tight as a tourniquet.

She held up a piece of paper and began to read from it. " 'Vaccine No. 413. A box of twelve dozen ampules. To be personally called for on November tenth.' I *am* at VaccuGen, yes? And you *are* Greta Oppenheimer?"

"Yes." Who never called Him by His name.

The woman slapped her gloves on the reception desk. "Then what am I to do? Tell the minister that Mlan failed him again? Is the entire *shipment* locked away somewhere? Because if it is, young woman, I can assure you that the minister will have Krucevic's balls for breakfast. The minister is expected in Pristina tomorrow, and Ernst Schuler is not a man to look ridiculous. Do I make myself clear?"

"The shipment is in the loading bay."

"And do you have access to *that*?"

Greta nodded.

"Then for the love of the Savior, take me to it," the woman snapped, "before I call Mlan myself. No one will notice a carton more or less, and it's as much as my life is worth to return to the ministry empty-handed."

———

When the woman had scrawled some initials on a notepad and left with the box under her arm, Greta went slowly back to her desk. It was a brief excitement; it had afforded her the sound of a human voice. She was not likely to hear one again that day.

But in this she was wrong. She had not been reseated in the reception area twenty minutes when the static burst out again. She glanced up at the street monitor and saw the figure of a balding, middle-aged man, the collar of his good cloth coat turned up against the cold November day.

"May I speak with Greta Oppenheimer?" he asked.

"I am Greta," she replied. And was suddenly filled with foreboding. Never had she been requested by name. And now twice in one day—

"I have come for the mumps vaccine," the man said.

"Your colleague has already been here," Greta replied.

"What colleague?"

"From the Health Ministry. For the vaccines. The minister himself sent her."

"My dear young lady," said the man, amused,

"someone has been having a joke with you. Do you know who I am?"

He turned his face fully into the range of the camera positioned above his head. Greta stared intently at the monitor; a sickness rose in her throat.

"Ernst Schuler," she whispered.

The Minister of Health.

FIVE

Bratislava, 10:15 A.M.

As DARE ATWOOD HAD PREDICTED, Sophie Payne was no longer in Prague.

Her captors had tried to take her to Hungary, driving out of the city at one o'clock in the morning, after the American flag in the embassy garden had been raised to full mast and the President was known to be cooperating. They had injected her with the Anthrax 3A antibiotic and bundled her into the trunk of Michael's car, heading first east through the night and then, abruptly, when it became clear the Czech border guards were searching everything that approached the Hungarian border, south. They skirted the Tatras Mountains and ended, after many hours, in Bratislava, which had once been called Pressburg and known the glory of the Austrian empire. Now the city was famed for recidivist Communism and thuggish politics, for the Semtex explosives manufactured on its outskirts, for dispirited pottery and rudimentary wine. The ancient vines trailed through the hills like bony fingers, scrabbling for a purchase in the dust.

They had intended to reach Budapest but chose Bratislava by default, because Vaclav Slivik knew a woman in the Slovak State Orchestra. Many years ago, when Olga Teciak was a young woman of twenty-four whose sloe eyes and graceful limbs were utterly bewitching against the prop of her cello, Vaclav had pursued her violently, and she was enough in the thrall of the past to accord him some kindness now. When he knocked on the door at 4:33 A.M., unheralded and unapologetic, she was so disoriented as to let him in.

It was only after the guns appeared that Olga understood what she had done. But by then, her doom was sealed.

Sophie lay now on the woman's cracked tile floor, her hands and feet bound, her mouth gagged. The bathroom smelled faintly septic, an odor of decay unsuccessfully masked with ammonia. Olga's apartment was one of a series of similar faceless cubicles in one of the mass of faceless Soviet-built concrete towers strung across the Danube from the historic heart of old Bratislava. The complex as a whole could boast the highest suicide rate in the country. It looked like an architect's embodiment of despair. And at the moment, Sophie found the mood to be catching. She had crossed yet another border. No one, it seemed, was following.

They had carried her into Olga's home in the early-morning darkness with a hood over her head. Olga was not permitted to glimpse her face. Any ministrations required by the captive were offered through the proxy of young Jozsef, who, like Sophie, had suffered the indignities of Anthrax 3A and thus possessed some inkling of how to remedy them. The first thing the boy was permitted to do was to remove the gag from her mouth; the second was to offer her coffee, the very smell of which turned her sour stomach. He was sitting by her now, knees hunched up under his chin, eyes blazing darkly in his frail white face. He was staring at her, as though struggling to frame her meaning in words he could understand. Sophie was conscious of his gaze, but she kept her eyes fixed on a patch of damp that had stained Olga's ceiling the color of weak tea.

"You should drink something," Jozsef said at last. "Water, maybe?" He said it in German, which was the language his father preferred him to speak. It was also, by happenstance, the language of Sophie Payne's childhood, and she answered him almost without thinking.

"Where is your mother?"

He was silent for the space of several heartbeats. Then, fearful, he hunched himself tighter and whispered, "Belgrade. I think she is still in Belgrade."

"Does she know where you are?"

He did not answer.

Sophie reconsidered the patch of damp. The iron taste of blood was in her mouth and in her nostrils. Conversation was difficult. Her brain balked at the effort to concentrate. But the issue of Jozsef's mother recurred, as though it might be important.

"Did you want to leave her?"

"He took me. In the night. He held my mother's throat to the knife. He said terrible things to her, terrible. She was weeping. I could not even say good-bye."

"How long ago?"

"I think it was before Christmas. But we never had Christmas, so I do not really know."

"It's still November, right? It must be. So you've been gone almost a year."

Again, he did not answer. The knees stayed hunched

under his chin, as though all that kept him alive was the tight grip of hand on wrist.

"You should drink something," he said again.

"A little water."

Watching him sway and then recover as he stood up, Sophie remembered that Jozsef, too, had been injected with the bacillus. He would be feeling the same persistent ache in every joint, the pounding at the temples. And looking at the little-boy knees (he wore thin cotton shorts, no socks on his crabbed feet), she remembered Peter at eight, his bare feet filthy from running through the long grass around the Vineyard house, screen door banging in his wake. The sound of his voice, high-pitched as a bobwhite's at dawn, calling across the meadows that ran down to the sea. The memory suffused her with peace and longing; longing not so much for Peter—who had become a singing wire, taut with strain and the life of his own ideas—but for the simple things Sophie had once held like water in the palm of her hand.

"Here," Jozsef said. He placed the rim of the glass against her lips. She stared into the dark wells of his eyes. This child was as much a prisoner as she was. But no power and no government would bargain for his release.

"What time is it?" she asked.

"Around ten o'clock in the morning."

He tugged her upright, supporting her with an unexpectedly wiry strength. She drank the tepid water, too thirsty to argue with its taste, and felt the boy's rapid pulse fluttering against her like a bird.

When she escaped Krucevic, Sophie decided, Jozsef must leave with her.

The bathroom door slammed open, the edge jamming painfully against Sophie's leg. She grunted and spurted water on Jozsef's fingers.

"Mrs. Payne," Michael said. "You're awake."

"Yes."

Jozsef dabbed at her wet face with a wad of toilet paper.

Michael nodded toward the boy. "Is he treating you right?"

"What a question."

He slid into the room. With Sophie prone on the floor and Jozsef hunkering by her, there was scarcely space for the man's feet. Michael bent down and untied her hands; when she tried to bring them forward, every nerve ending from shoulder to wrist screamed in protest.

"Okay, Joe, your dad has some breakfast for Mrs. Payne." Michael, too, spoke in German; it seemed to be the terrorists' lingua franca. "Go get it for us, would you?"

The boy vanished through the doorway.

"I've been instructed to let you use the facilities," Michael told Sophie. "If you scream or attempt to leave by the window"—this was a mere mail slot of a metal frame, incapable of accommodating a three-month-old baby—"you will be shot."

"Fine," she said wearily. "That sounds like heaven right now."

"Good girl," he muttered under his breath in English. "If you can joke about it, you're still alive. And I will not let you die at this man's hands, do you understand?"

Arrested, she stared at him. He stared back. She did not know what to read in his eyes.

Then he raised his handgun to shoulder height, muzzle pointed at the ceiling. "I'll be just outside," he said impersonally.

Sophie hobbled to the toilet. She felt suddenly stronger.

———

Mlan Krucevic had miscalculated. Or rather, he had found that circumstances were different from his expectations, and he was forced to improvise. He mistrusted improvisation. He had never known anyone—including himself—to improvise without error. The key to his entire method of warfare was meticulous preparation. And so of course he had a fallback plan.

He had always loathed Slovakia. In the present instance he loathed it even more.

In Olga Teciak's living room there was a laminated plywood coffee table, an olive green couch with worn upholstery, two lamps, and a carved chair that had probably belonged to Olga's grandmother. There was also a very good television. Krucevic sat in front of the blank screen and considered his options. The Hungarian border was watched. He refused to risk a crossing by car. Therefore, he would have to find a plane. That meant a predawn trip to the Bratislava airport and a break-in at the private aircraft hangar. He hoped to God there *were* some private aircraft in this miserable country.

He searched his mind for the flaw, the unseen error that could destroy him. He detected nothing, and that in itself was unsettling. Perfection was against the laws of Nature; perfection's appearance was always something to mistrust.

He glanced at his watch: 10:53 A.M. And at that instant his cellular phone trilled. He stiffened. The cell phone was solely for emergencies, the last extreme of need. And then only *he* would make the calls. No one was ever to call *him*.

He could let it ring—could ignore the caller entirely. But what if disaster overcame him as a consequence? He picked up the phone on the fourth trill and said, *"Ja?"*

"Mein Herr. I am sorry to disturb you—I know it is against the rules—" Her voice was abject with terror.

Greta. He frowned at the phone. "Is something wrong?"

"A woman—a woman came. Not who she said she was. She took the virus."

"What virus?"

"The vaccine," she amended. "No. 413. For mumps. The one for humanitarian relief. She said that she was from the Health Ministry, she had a paper, she was so very angry—oh, Herr Krucevic, I am so terribly sorry—"

"No names!" he barked, more loudly than he had intended. "No names," he repeated. "Who was she?"

"She did not say."

"And you *allowed* her to take the vaccine?"

"She was from the Health Ministry," Greta bleated pathetically. "She signed her initials to the dock manifest. I cannot make them out. And then the health minister, Herr Schuler, arrived, and he said it must be a joke. A joke!"

She sounded as though she was nearly peeing with terror, on the verge of tears. *You stupid cow,* he cursed her silently. *You hopeless and sodden piece of human shit.* Gently now, gently, before she fainted.

"What did this woman look like?"

"Dark. Black hair, black eyes, black clothes. She spoke with an accent like—"

She had been about to say, *like yours.*

"—Like someone from your country."

"Anything else?"

"A white scarf. Around her neck."

Anger flared like bile and flooded his mouth. *Žalba! Fucking mother of a whore. She—! She had taken it! Then by the bloody cross of King Tomisav, I will find her. And when I do, I will slit her throat as a traitor and a Serb.*

"What am I to do?" Greta begged in a whisper.

She was already stupid, but fear would make her dangerous. He must give her something to do, a purpose, before she destroyed them all. Krucevic's mind leapt forward, considered and discarded options. "Close the office and get to Budapest," he told her. "I have a job only you can manage."

"I shall not fail you, *mein Herr.*" She was sickening in her gratitude. He could do with her what he chose. He cut the connection.

His enemies were trying to destroy him. But God was on his side. He had discovered the treachery before it was too late. If only he were in Budapest now! But all movement was impossible before dark. He had roughly one hundred kilometers to travel—three hours by road, twenty minutes by air—and time was slipping through his fingers. He must be patient. He must not allow rage to make him careless.

A white scarf around her neck.

The error of improvisation.

Krucevic cursed the Czech border guards, cursed Slovakia, cursed Vaclav Slivik and all the women he had ever known. He cursed Olga Teciak with particular virulence. She was the most available object of his hatred.

Olga was a stranger. He distrusted her simply because she was unknown and because she was a woman. She was huddled now in her bedroom with her young daughter cradled in a blanket. Both of them were terrified. Olga had probably figured out who Sophie Payne was; it was no secret any longer that the American Vice

President had been kidnapped. Word had gotten out, by newspaper and television broadcast. He had been a fool to follow Vaclav's advice. Teciak could not possibly be trusted.

He required some sort of insurance.

"Mlan," Michael said behind him. "Mrs. Payne is awake and eating."

It was one of Krucevic's rules that they refer to the woman with courtesy. Courtesy was another form of cruelty. He dismissed his anger, the shadow of fear, and moved on to the next step.

"Good," he said briskly. "She'll need her strength. It's time to take a picture for the President."

———

Jozsef was chewing companionably with Sophie on the bathroom floor, although the meal was quite dreadful: canned orange juice, stale white bread, some sort of processed cheese. She choked on the food and the persistent taste of blood. It must be something to do with the anthrax, she decided. Not everything had an antidote.

"Do you know where we are?" she asked the boy.

"Bratislava, I think. But you should not ask me any questions. About the operation, I mean."

Sophie smiled faintly. "Is that what I am? An operation?"

"That is how my father calls it."

"I see. But we were in Prague a few hours ago. Your father said so, when he was filming me."

"Yes." Jozsef's voice dropped apprehensively. "We were not supposed to come here, I think. We changed our route quite suddenly last night, because the guards were searching people. Michael got you through the first crossing—from Germany to the Czech Republic—with his American passport, but Papa did not think it would work this time. And so we turned back."

Hope stirred in Sophie's heart. "So it was the Czech guards your father was afraid of. But crossing into where?"

"If you ask me questions, lady, and I talk to you, there will be trouble."

"My name is Sophie," she said.

Jozsef turned this over in his mind. "My mother's name is Mirjana."

"Do you miss her?"

The fringe of lashes lowered over his eyes. He was rolling something rapidly between his fingers.

"What is that?" Sophie asked.

The fingers stilled, then were thrust into his pocket. "Nothing. Do you want that piece of cheese?"

She shook her head. He seized the cheese immediately. She waited while he ate.

"There is a woman here," Sophie said.

"And a child. The woman's name is Olga, but I do not know the girl's."

"A girl? How old?"

"She is sucking her thumb still, and she is very frightened by all of us. The woman is frightened, too, although she tries not to show it."

"So the woman is not one of you?"

"I told you. We were not supposed to come here. The woman is a friend of Vaclav's. That is dangerous for her and probably for Vaclav, too," he added.

"Dangerous how?"

The boy drew his finger across his throat. The gesture was all the more appalling for its casualness.

"But she's helped you!" Sophie protested.

"She had no choice. And now she will say anything

to protect her little girl. Those who are afraid, lady, are like snakes under the heel. They strike as soon as you move."

Sophie was about to argue with him—about to utter stupidities about the impossibility of hurting the innocent—but the words died in her mouth.

"When I was young," Jozsef continued, "I had two friends. Brothers. They lived on the street where I lived, and our mothers used to push us along the pavement together in our prams. Our mothers liked to talk. They shared things from their kitchens; they sewed together and drank coffee. When I had a ball or a toy, I shared it with the brothers, and they with me."

"That's good," Sophie said encouragingly when he stopped. "It's good to have friends, Jozsef. Have you lived all your life in Belgrade?"

"No," he said doubtfully, "I do not think I have ever lived in Belgrade, or if I did, it was very long ago. My mother is there now. She is Serb. That is why my father took me from her. We are Croats. And at the time I am speaking of—when I was a young boy—we lived in Sarajevo."

"And do you still have friends there? In Sarajevo?"

He shrugged.

"What happened to the boys? The brothers?"

"They were Muslim dogs." His beautiful eyes met hers. "When the war came, my father knew that their father would kill us if he did not kill him first, and so Papa went in the night and cut his throat. Then he killed the boys one after the other as they lay in their beds, and showed their mother what he had done. He dropped their bodies at her feet."

Sophie forced herself to speak. "No one who had a boy of his own could do such a thing. No one."

Jozsef's black brows came down, puzzled. "But they were Muslims and we are Croats. If my father had allowed them to live, they would have grown up to avenge *their* father's death. I would do the same."

"I cannot believe that."

"Then you are very foolish, lady. Or you have not seen enough of the world."

Sophie thought of the endless trips on Air Force Two, the succession of state visits and briefings and prepared speeches. "Perhaps you're right, Jozsef. And your father? He told you that he had killed your friends?"

"He took me with him that night. I watched what he did."

The boy's fingers were worrying the object in his pocket again. He drew it out, and she saw that it was a rabbit's foot—a triangular bit of dirty white fur, pathetic.

"When she saw them lying dead, lady, their mother fell on her knees and tore at her hair."

"I suppose your father killed her, too?"

Jozsef tossed his good-luck charm over his shoulder and caught it behind his back in one deft movement. "A woman suffers more when she is allowed to live, lady. But Drusa—that was her name—was afraid of the suffering, I think. She twisted her skirt into a rope and hanged herself from the kitchen window."

Sophie squeezed her eyes shut. When she opened them, Mlan Krucevic stood in the doorway, staring down at her. His son's face was white as a bone.

"Get out," Krucevic said.

Jozsef scrambled to his feet and darted around him.

"Mrs. Payne."

She lifted her face and stared back at him. He handed her a newspaper. The headline screamed her own name.

"I require your assistance, Mrs. Payne."

"Then you will have to unbind my feet."

"That will not be necessary. Please hold the newspaper below your chin. Vaclav?"

Krucevic stepped back, and a camera lens took his place. Unconsciously, Sophie raised a hand to smooth her hair, and then—caught out in a vanity so misplaced it was painful—dropped it to her lap.

"This will be sent to your friends at the White House, Mrs. Payne, so I suggest you consider what you say. For the record I would like to state that you are still the prisoner of the 30 April Organization and that, true to our word, we have administered the Anthrax 3A antidote since our last communication. Would you describe your experience, please?"

"I'm still alive."

"But unfortunately, we have no guarantee that you will remain so."

"Most of us have to live with that uncertainty," she said.

This seemed to give him pause. But only for an instant.

"Jack, Jack," Krucevic said, with all the sorrow of a disappointed parent. "What were you thinking of? Alerting the Czech border guards? For shame. Under the terms of our agreement, you were to refrain from attempting to rescue Mrs. Payne. And yet, mere hours after the flag went up in your embassy garden, you've gone back on your word. Don't let it happen again, Jack. I require free passage throughout the region. I want that message sent to every head of state in Central Europe. And I do not want to be thwarted again."

It was only a matter of moments, Sophie thought,

before he produced another needle. But instead the camera lens zoomed in on her face.

"I won't use a hypodermic this time, Jack. If you fail me again, I will put a bullet in this woman's brain. Even the most powerful nation on earth cannot bring people back from the dead."

SIX
Berlin, 12:06 P.M.

CAROLINE CARMICHAEL REACHED BERLIN at ten-thirty Wednesday morning, twenty-two hours after Sophie Payne's kidnapping.

Almost nothing was left of the city she remembered.

She had visited twice during her posting to Budapest, when reunification was just a word and the movement of the capital from Bonn still years away. Bulldozers and cranes had taken root everywhere in the vacant lots, profuse as mushrooms after rainfall, and a trip across the city was an exercise in strategy, a meticulous ground campaign waged with map and mental compass. Equipment the color of sulfuric acid, pits that yawned a football field's depth into the earth, the halogen-lit midnights and clouds of exhaust—these were all that one knew of Berlin in the mid-nineties. The West had decided the past must be regained, and if not regained, then rewritten. A political process, on the face of it; but emotional in its force, perhaps because it was so obvious and so physical. The Wall had divided families and consigned the most glittering of Berlin's neighborhoods—the haunts of kaisers and courtesans, seditionists and strippers—to the shabbiness of memory. The Wall had left places like Potsdamer Platz, once the bustling heart of Berlin, to silence and weeds, its paving stones aching for a footfall.

But Berliners, over time, had grown used to the change. New life had sprung up along the internal border like ground cover after fire. And then the cranes had come, in soaring ranks of red and blue and gold, their arms outstretched to the east.

Caroline drew wide the curtains of her window. The plane full of technicians from Washington had flown into the bomb site so quickly that the embassy, its communications arrays shattered, had received no cable of their coming. The Secretary of State had phoned the ambassador's residence; a harried first-tour officer had spent most of the night finding accommodation for nearly forty people in a frightened city already inundated with visitors. Caroline had drawn the Hyatt, a spanking-new hotel in the middle of the reborn Potsdamer Platz, where the towers of the Sony Center jostled for position and waves of raw mud still lapped at the foundations. It was rather, she thought, like being the first resident of a space station, one of civilization's outriders. She would have preferred a converted old palace off Kurfürstendamm, where the whoosh of tires on the rain-wet streets was as soporific as surf; but the Hyatt probably offered a good government rate. Even in crisis, economy ranked high among a first-tour officer's considerations.

And if she leaned forward now and glanced left, her nose pressed against the window, she could just make out the shattered glass dome of the Reichstag. An ill-fated building, she thought—burned by Hitler, and now racked by damage from his neo-Nazi followers in the blast that had swept Sophie Payne away. Politics had a way of turning violent in Berlin. Whole streets were obliterated, then recast with a different face. This was something Berliners understood: They lived on a volcano. The cranes could do only so much before history would have its way again.

She kicked off her shoes and fell back on the bed. Solid polyester beneath her hair, nothing like the eiderdown smelling faintly of the farmyard in a small hotel off Kurfürstendamm. She felt a sharp pang of nostalgia for old Berlin. Here at the Hyatt, she might have been anywhere, the trappings of Central Europe consigned to the last century.

Except that Eric was within range. He breathed the same coal-laden air. Caroline closed her eyes and for an instant felt terrified. She wanted to draw the pillow over her head and smother in darkness. It was unlikely that even a single member of 30 April was still in Germany. Eric must be miles away by now. But she felt the force of his presence play over her like a tracking beam.

Was she mad even to *try* to draw him in?

That was what Dare Atwood wanted. A trap—for Eric, and ultimately for his master.

Caroline, the lure.

Dare had no fucking idea what a marriage was like. How you could love a person without even knowing him. How he could own a piece of you, despite nearly three years of absence and betrayal—how he could command some shred of loyalty and give nothing in return. Was it something about the marriage vow? That glancing blow of the sacred?

And in her heart of hearts, Caroline knew that she couldn't summon Eric anymore. He had no desire to see her. He had chosen, after all, to *leave*. A trap was not a trap without a lure.

She felt relief flood over her like a kind of peace. Eric might betray *her* abominably, but she would not be required to betray *him*.

Absurd.

She was too tired to resolve the questions of love and loyalty, the war between reason and heart. She had a job to do. A Vice President to find, the Agency to protect— that vast, imperfect sum of too many parts, that humming hive of secrets, most of them not worth knowing. What did she owe Eric Carmichael, anyway? She had paid enough debts during a decade of marriage.

What would she say if they actually came face-to-face? What would he say if he knew that she was hunting him?

Don't even ask, Mad Dog. If I told you, I'd have to kill you.

The oldest joke in the Intelligence book.

He would have to be hunted, all the same.

She glanced at her watch. Wally Aronson, the Berlin station chief, expected her at the ambassador's residence in an hour. But the Brandenburg Gate lay straight down Ebertstrasse from her hotel in Potsdamer Platz, a brisk walk in the cold afternoon air. She just had time.

———

A police barrier wrapped Pariser Platz like a package, turning the chaos into an apparition of order, the reflexive German impulse. Caroline stood in her jeans and sweater, a bright plaid blazer open to the raw wind, and snapped pictures from the edge of Strasse des 17 Juni, the broad boulevard running straight through the heart of the Tiergarten to the Brandenburg Gate. Beyond

Pariser Platz, 17 Juni became Unter den Linden, the most beautiful boulevard in all of Berlin, with its royal palaces and museums and meandering river Spree. A decade ago, Unter den Linden was closed to the West and Strasse des 17 Juni led only to the Wall—a dead end rather than a gate.

The Brandenburg had been a neoclassical dream, modeled on the Acropolis's Propylaea: six Doric columns surmounted by a plinth and frieze, the figure of Peace drawn by a chariot. *Ironic,* Caroline thought as she photographed the torso of a shattered horse in the rubble of the Gate. In Berlin, Peace was driven by the engine of war, Peace came at the cost of constant bloodshed. Napoleon had marched his Grande Armée beneath the Gate not long after it was built; Prussia had trained her cavalry in the square; Hitler's *Übermenschen* had goose-stepped down Unter den Linden; and East German guards had patrolled within spitting distance of the prancing horses. But it had taken terrorists to topple the chariot to the ground.

She ignored the barriers and the cones and the police and walked insouciantly forward, to the very edge of the bomb crater. The FBI technicians were already there, some of them kneeling on plastic sheets at the edge of the torn earth, others in conversation with what Caroline supposed were German investigators.

One man stood apart, arms folded over a creased tan raincoat. Its very ordinariness screamed Government Official. He was stony-faced and hollow-eyed from lack of sleep, but there was something arresting in the stillness of his pose. If he had not been standing inside the official barriers, Caroline would have taken him for a mourner. His face had the self-absorbed potency of grief. As she looked at him, he turned his head and stared straight at her. No hint of friendliness or curiosity; the look was frankly hostile. He took her for a disaster junkie.

She raised her camera and ignored him.

There were television crews, too—an embarrassment of television crews, from every major American network, from the Berlin and Frankfurt and Hamburg stations, from Italy and France and the U.K. and Poland.

This was going to be easy.

Caroline took pictures of chaos: chunks of macadam, twisted cables, the intestines of the city thrown obscenely outward. The construction of the square's new U-Bahn station had taken years; now its subterranean walls caved inward. Broken glass shimmered everywhere.

She panned across the square to the embassy door. The shattered platform on which Sophie Payne had stood twenty-four hours ago was still there, one end pitched skyward. Yesterday, pennants had snapped in the breeze. Then bullets, screaming and blood, a gurney wheeled madly to the platform's edge. *Eric.*

She lowered her camera and studied the building. It was a large embassy, and most of the windows in the facade were smashed, but the walls themselves had held. The blast, then, had been strong enough to destroy the Brandenburg Gate while leaving much of the surrounding structures intact. A surgical bomb, if such a thing could truly be said to exist. A diversion, while the real victim disappeared into the blue.

"Ausgehen Sie, bitte."

A police guard, voice harsh with contempt, was advancing upon her, his face obscured by a riot helmet. The federal eagle screamed red and gold across his black shirt—he was one of Fritz Voekl's special troops, the

Volksturm. Caroline raised her camera, focused on his face, and snapped.

Taking office on the heels of assassination, the new chancellor had made fighting crime a priority of his first year. Crime, Voekl declared, sprang from the conflict between Western European values and Eastern ones, between Christian and Muslim ways of life. Crime was the product of the Turkish population, in fact; until the Turks were sent back to their own country, all that decent Germans could do was to stand firm against their demands. And the Turks were just the tip of the Muslim iceberg: The trickle of Albanians and Montenegrins, of Kurds and Kazakhs and Georgians and Uzbeks from the east, was alarming in the extreme. Tolerance was a mistake. Acceptance was insanity. Germans, even liberal Germans such as Voekl's murdered predecessor Gerhard Schroeder, were dying in the streets.

The message had played superbly at the polls, particularly among Ossies, the former citizens of the defunct German Democratic Republic, where crime officially had never existed. Now the Ossies were joining Voekl's Volksturm, his national militia, in droves. And as she stared at the policeman's spread-eagle insignia, Caroline had to admit the chancellor's savvy. Voekl had killed one problem—persistent unemployment in the east—while brilliantly furthering his anti-Turk agenda. And he'd placed throughout the country an army loyal only to him.

"Hinaus!" The truncheon was raised, the black shirt close enough to graze with her fingertips. She felt the man's animosity wash over her like a strong smell.

"Speak English?"

He shook his head aggressively. She stood her ground, focusing her lens, and saw a British television crew pivot to film the encounter. In a minute the cop would take her camera and dash it to the pavement. Deliberately, she leaned around him, pointed her lens at the embassy, and clicked the shutter.

The gurney, it was believed, had come from within—a bogus rescue operation staged from the roof. Caroline had watched the videotape of Eric so many times she had the sequence embedded in her mind. The period from explosion to kidnapping had been slight—about nine minutes. Therefore, 30 April must have known how to navigate the new building before they'd ever landed the chopper. That, in itself, was suggestive.

"Halt!" He grabbed her arm and thrust her back from the barrier. Caroline tensed. Then she screamed.

Two American camera crews joined the British one already filming her. The Italians looked interested and started to move.

"Let go of me, you asshole!" She broke free of the policeman's grasp and held her camera behind her back. "Jesus! Isn't this a free country?"

The guard raised his truncheon obligingly. The film crews filmed. And then a raincoat-clad arm was thrust between them, and someone said, "It's okay."

It was the man she'd seen earlier, staring at the wreckage. She had time to register sandy hair, a beak of a nose. He said something in German to the Volksturm guard, and the truncheon was abruptly lowered. Then he turned to Caroline. Sharp hazel eyes simmered with anger. And something else. Contempt?

"This isn't the best place for sightseeing, ma'am. We'd appreciate it if you'd move on."

"Okay, okay," she said, deliberately rude. "I'm going. *Jesus.*"

With luck, she'd make the evening news.

With luck, Eric and his friends would be watching.

SEVEN

Berlin, 1 P.M.

THE WOMAN WHO HAD STOLEN Mlan Krucevic's vaccine No. 413—the mumps vaccine that would soon be injected into the bodies of thousands of Kosovo's children—had wasted little time in getting the box of ampules out of the country. At the main counter of Malev Air in Berlin's Tegel Airport, she presented a signed letter typed on the official stationery of the Hungarian Ministry of Health and an equally impressive packet of documentation from a Hungarian lab. She managed the same air of officious irritation that had carried her through her encounter with Greta in the VaccuGen offices, and after one Malev Air attendant pressed her too closely about her mission, she embarked on a furious lecture in geopolitics. Hungary, Mirjana Tarcic reminded the attendant, shared a border with Yugoslavia. Tens of thousands of ethnic Hungarians inhabited the autonomous Yugoslav province of Vojvodina, just across that border. And since Hungary was now a member of NATO, which had pummeled Serbia from the air for months, tensions in the autonomous province were running high. Who knew when floods of refugees might start spilling into southern Hungary? And what diseases and vaccines might be necessary then? The Hungarian Ministry of Health had determined it should be prepared. If the Malev Air attendant wished to discuss the matter further, she could refer him to her ministry superior.

A tedious twenty-three minutes and seventeen seconds later, Mirjana Tarcic carried the sealed carton containing her estranged husband's mumps vaccine onto the Budapest flight. Malev Air magnanimously dispensed with the requirement of security X ray. Radiation might harm the vaccines, and that was the last thing anyone wanted. The cause, as Mirjana reminded them, was a humanitarian one.

She placed the box between her booted feet, halfway under the seat in front of her, and remembered a similar box of vaccines on another flight. She had just copied Mlan Krucevic's method for getting a bomb onto a plane. But this time the vaccines were real, and potentially more explosive than the package that had blasted MedAir 901 out of the sky. She hugged her arms across her chest and stared through the window at an approaching baggage train, overwhelmed for an instant by what she had done. If Mlan found out, he would hunt her down and kill her.

And she knew him well enough to believe that he would find out.

She read no magazines, she made no conversation with the elderly Hungarian woman seated next to her during the two-hour flight. She kept her sunglasses on. Mlan, Mirjana knew, had spies everywhere. To beat him at his game, she must be more vigilant than he, more far-sighted, more paranoid. There was nothing like thirteen years of marriage to a psychopath to teach you about survival.

———

In Frankfurt, Germany, at Headquarters NSA Europe, Patti DePalma sat at a desk in a windowless room that was utterly silent except for a Muzak version of Paul Simon's "Bridge over Troubled Water." The Muzak was piped throughout the sprawling government complex in the IG Farben building; it was intended to mask office conversation in the event anyone was listening. Patti frankly loathed the tinned tracks—"Memory," "What I Did for Love," even the Clash's "Rock the Casbah." They made her feel like a character in a book by George Orwell. And life as an intercept translator was Orwellian enough.

This morning, however, only an hour into her shift, Patti was spared the bastardized Paul Simon. Her earphones were on. She was listening intently to a conversation in German pulled directly from a rhombic antenna array designed to intercept a wide range of very specific communications. Since Dare Atwood's first conversation with President Bigelow regarding the 30 April Organization eighteen hours earlier, this particular array, made up of diamond-shaped wires scattered over several hundred acres, had been intercepting communications at VaccuGen in Berlin.

And so Patti listened as Greta Oppenheimer sobbed out the story of vaccine No. 413 to Mlan Krucevic. From there, it was merely a matter of locating the phone Krucevic had used. And within two hours, Olga Teciak's Bratislava apartment complex was circled in red on a large-scale map of the city pasted on the White House Situation Room's wall.

———————

"Mad Dog! Come on in."

One of Wally Aronson's hands grasped the ambassador's glossy black door. The other beckoned Caroline almost surreptitiously, as though his password to the clubhouse might expire without notice. A marine guard stood at attention in the hall, his eyes riveted on thin air.

"He's expecting you, but we haven't much time," Wally told her. "He's due at the chancellor's for cocktails."

The ambassador's residence was a grand old place in Charlottenburg, with nine-foot windows and chestnut trees that threw heavy shade in summer. A world removed from Pariser Platz. Caroline had taken a few minutes at the Hyatt to dress in business clothes, and was suddenly glad.

"You look great, Caroline." Wally touched her lightly on the shoulder, a gesture halfway between a salute and an embrace, and that quickly Caroline was back in boot camp, Wally swinging from a chin-up bar with his boot laces dangling.

He was short and lithe with a perpetual smile hovering around his eyes. The goatee had grayed since Caroline had last seen him, two years before. They were old friends from the Career Trainee program and Budapest; now he was Chief of Station, Berlin. It was a plum he'd pulled relatively early in his career—but then, Wally had been born with the soul of a spy. He had probably rifled his mother's love letters as soon as he could read, Caroline suspected, and worn gloves to do it.

He led her past a formal drawing room hung with miles of gray-blue silk, its atmosphere thick with the suspended breath of public spaces. Caroline looked at the purposeful chairs, all elegant line and backache, and imagined the parties—a crush of black velvet and white satin, the haze of cigarette smoke that always amazed Americans and was inescapable in Europe. Wally crossed the wide hall—here there were ceiling frescoes of Venus rising, an abandon of putti—to a set of double doors. The ambassador's study.

But the room, when Wally threw open the doors, was empty.

He crossed the worn Aubusson carpet to the French windows. Beyond them was an expanse of browning grass, lime trees bereft of leaves. A smudge of afternoon sky. A white-haired man lounged in a canvas chair below the terrace, one elbow resting on a card table, thin legs extended before him. He wore a navy blue windbreaker, khaki pants, Top-Siders without socks. A faint breeze stirred a sparse lock of hair, and as he reached back to smooth it, the veins on his hand pulsed blue. Two men, strangers to Caroline, sat at his right and left. In their wool suits and trimmed hair, they resembled models imported for a photo shoot.

"Ah, there you are, Wally." The ambassador spoke with relish, as though the COS had just brought round the drinks cart. "Good man."

"Our guest from Washington, Mr. Ambassador. Caroline Carmichael of the CIA's Counterterrorism Center. Ambassador Dalton."

Ambrose Dalton stood up. His hand, when Caroline shook it, was dry as vellum. He was a member of an old Connecticut family, a political appointee who had made a fortune in merchant banking. His wife's name was Sunny. She had found her life mission after the Daltons' son broke his neck in a rugby game; now she educated the insensitive about the rights of the physically challenged. The Daltons gave generously to a variety of causes, some of them political. As a couple, they were two of President Bigelow's oldest friends.

They were quite well acquainted with Sophie Payne.

"I'm so very sorry, Mr. Ambassador, about the damage to the embassy," Caroline told him. "You and your staff are well, I hope?"

Dalton took her hand between both of his and patted it, more in sympathy than salutation. "We lost two of our marine guards. Mere boys. But you know that, I expect."

She nodded wordlessly.

He studied her face, a calculation flickering in his eyes. "I understand you're an expert, Ms. Carmichael, on this Krucevic character. Any expertise is, of course, a comfort, but I'm afraid you've come to the wrong place. Sophie cannot be anywhere in Berlin."

"Is that what the German police are saying, sir?"

"They say that no Turks could possibly have slipped past their borders, and that the extremists, when identified, will be summarily shot." Dalton's voice was as dry as his hand.

"Never mind that none of the men filmed with the helicopter was even remotely Turkish," Wally added, "or that the video dropped in Prague identifies the kidnappers as the 30 April Organization."

"Our German friends have not been privileged to view the terrorist video," the ambassador reminded him. "For that matter, neither have I. I merely read the gisted transcript we received in the diplomatic pouch this morning. You may assume, Ms. Carmichael, that everyone at this table has also read that summary. May I introduce my Chief of Mission?"

"T. Hunter Price." One of the imported models half

rose and nodded, then sank languidly into his seat. Caroline put him down immediately as a cookie-pusher with an attitude. Price would regard the embassy bombing as a State Department affair: He would resent the Agency's involvement.

"And this is Paul Dougherty," Wally said, his hand on Caroline's elbow. "Paul's in the consular section. You owe him your hotel room."

"Hey, Caroline," Dougherty said, jumping up and smiling broadly, "I read your stuff last night. Really cool."

A first-tour Agency officer, no doubt, fresh from the University of Kansas or Georgetown's foreign-service program. Dougherty looked about thirteen. She wondered where Wally's more experienced people were, and then answered the question herself. They were meeting with counterparts in German Intelligence. Or were dressed in white overalls and canvas caps, trolling the streets in plumber's vans, with listening equipment trained on a variety of buildings. Hoping against hope for a sound that might lead them to Sophie Payne.

"There's Tom!" Dougherty chirped, his gaze going beyond Caroline. She turned and saw a rangy man in tweeds loping across the terrace, his hands shoved into his pockets. The newcomer had abandoned the government-issue trench coat for a rumpled oxford cloth shirt, suede bucks, and an old rep tie. One of his shoelaces had broken and been summarily knotted into place. His nose appeared to have suffered a similar fate. And from the appearance of his right cheek—which bore a red crease from eye to lip—he had recently fallen asleep on someone's sofa with a copy of the newspaper folded under him. *Der Zeitung*, perhaps. It was shoved into his pocket along with his hands.

"LegAtt," Wally Aronson muttered under his breath, and then, more audibly, "Caroline, meet Tom Shephard, the FBI's Legal Attaché in Berlin. Tom's co-ordinating our investigation on the ground."

"We've met," Shephard said. "At the crater."

"I walked over to the Brandenburg to take a look around," she explained to Wally.

"You took more than that." Shephard continued to study her, as though she were a rare form of plant life he had only just discovered. The hazel eyes were still sharp, but the earlier simmering anger had vanished. "Do you always put your foot in it like that?"

"No," she replied tersely. "And I usually don't have to be reminded of it, either."

"Was there some problem?" Hunter Price was the sort, Caroline suspected, who loved to recycle his neighbors' affairs each morning over embassy coffee.

"Mud," she replied. "Mud was the problem. The Tiergarten is churned to mush, and I definitely put my foot in it. See, Mr. Shephard? I even changed my shoes before this meeting."

"Let's get started, shall we?" The ambassador slid back into his seat. Caroline set her laptop on the ground unopened; she had brought it with the intention of typing her meeting notes, but the computer's battery had run down and there did not appear to be an electrical outlet in the embassy garden. She drew out a yellow legal pad instead.

"I think we've all read Ms. Carmichael's material and found it quite compelling," Dalton observed. "Should we ever locate the Vice President and her attendant thugs, we shall be in the proverbial clover with Ms. Carmichael here on board. I hope you will excuse our impromptu picnic, my dear. We cannot entirely trust the acoustics within the residence."

Caroline frowned. "You think you're being bugged? In *Germany*?"

"We sweep the place every week," Wally broke in, "and we haven't actually found anything. But there have been . . . incidents. Or should I say coincidences?"

"Within six weeks of taking up my post, Ms. Carmichael, I discovered to my astonishment that whenever I presented my objectives to Mr. Voekl's late, unfortunate foreign minister—you were familiar with Graf von Orbsdorff, I presume?—he invariably knew what to expect. Either Orbsdorff was a clairvoyant, or he was cheating at the international game. Personally, I plump for the notion of cheating." Dalton scowled, an honorable schoolboy. "And so I adopted the habit of taking my conferences *en plein air*. A fresh breeze focuses the mind wonderfully, don't you agree?"

She smiled at him. "Can anyone summarize for me what we know of the bombing to date?"

"For that, I defer to Wally and Mr. Shephard," Dalton said briskly. "Gentlemen?"

"We know that the embassy blueprints were sold to the highest bidder," Wally began, "probably by the project architect long before construction was completed. Worse, we know that 30 April knew precisely where to hit the internal surveillance equipment. Agency techs have already gone through the building. Every camera and fiber-optic insert along the gurney's path was shot to hell."

Eric, Caroline thought. He could have looked at the embassy's blueprints and predicted with certainty where the security equipment would be placed. The realization came to her with a sick sense of disbelief—that Eric could have betrayed a U.S. installation so easily to someone like Krucevic. She closed her eyes to shut out the image of the tilted platform, the twenty-eight dead. And thought of something else: If Eric had told his 30 April cronies where to find the cameras and fiber optics, he'd as much as told them about his Agency past. Which meant that they knew everything that mattered.

Did they even know about *her*?

She felt chilled to the bone. "So your VTC room is out, as well as cable channels."

"They'll be up and running in another twenty-two hours."

"It'll take at least a week to get the building completely secure and operational," Tom Shephard said. He ran his fingers distractedly through his hair. "It's like these guys had a three-D map of the building downloaded off the Internet, or something."

So much for her cutout channel. And the ambassador's residence was bugged. Caroline would have to call Headquarters from a corner pay phone and speak in riddles.

"They certainly hit the embassy fast," she commented. "From the news coverage, it looks like nine minutes from explosion to kidnapping."

"Which means they practiced." Paul Dougherty's eyes were alight, as though he'd awakened this morning to find himself cast in a techno thriller.

With the faintest suggestion of indulging the children, T. Hunter Price drawled, "This is infinitely fascinating, but it has nothing to do with the problem at hand. That being the location of Vice President Payne."

"Go ahead, Hunter," said Shephard with studied politeness. "If you know where she is, we'd love to hear."

"I wouldn't dream of stealing your moment, Tom," Price replied. "I merely attempted to focus. The ambassador's time is short."

"Mr. Shephard has clearly profited from the fresh

air," Dalton declared placidly, "and may be allowed to proceed. Tom, tell us what you've learned from the crater."

"We think the bomb was in a television broadcast van parked right next to the Gate," Shephard said immediately. "We'll know more once Forensics has cataloged and thoroughly tested the wreckage, but the truck axle has already surfaced—and been ID'd."

"That was quick," Wally observed.

"Luck." Shephard shrugged. He was studying the path made by his forefinger as it trailed across the surface of the ambassador's card table. "The truck belonged to Berlin's TV Channel Four. The two cameramen and the reporter who were supposed to be in it were found floating in the Spree last night. They'd been assigned to cover the Veep's speech. They never arrived."

"So instead of renting a van to park under the Gate, 30 April stole one and killed its occupants. These guys weren't about to leave a paper trail."

Shephard's eyes flicked over to Caroline. "Multiple murder increased their risks considerably. But it also covered their tracks more effectively. No rental documents, as in the Oklahoma City bombing or the hit on the World Trade Center. And being a real broadcast van, the truck looked far more plausible in place."

"What about the medevac chopper?" Caroline asked. "Has anyone located that?"

"Possibly." Shephard focused on his finger again. "Somebody parked a helicopter near the rail lines south of Templehof yesterday—that's the old East Berlin airport—and set it on fire."

"Destroying any traces of prints or fibers," Caroline said.

"Most of them. Yes."

"Have any of the local hospitals reported a missing medevac pilot?" Wally asked.

"A young woman by the name of Karin Markhof," Tom Shephard told him. "Still no trace of her. Either Markhof was paid to turn over the bird to 30 April and got out of town fast once the Brandenburg blew—or she's lying dead somewhere."

"She's dead." Caroline said it without hesitation. "Krucevic leaves nothing to chance."

"Then let's hope he screws up somewhere down the line. Because that's all we've got."

Wally stroked his goatee, eyebrows furled like question marks. T. Hunter Price adjusted his tie. Dougherty looked from face to face like an eager puppy.

"Does the station here have any 30 April assets, Wally?" the ambassador inquired.

"A few, sir."

"What's 'a few,' Wally? Exactly?"

"Two," the Chief of Station conceded. "In the developmental stage."

"Which means you've got squat," muttered T. Hunter Price.

"We've got a woman who works in the Berlin office of VaccuGen, Krucevic's main front company," Wally shot back. "She's not on the payroll, which means she hasn't been vetted, and I'm not at liberty to discuss her particulars. But one of my officers has been developing her for months."

"And?"

"Fred is still trying to make contact."

Price threw up his hands in mute eloquence.

"What about the other recruit?" Caroline asked.

"He's a different kettle of fish. Brilliant, oddball, and an unreconciled Communist. Krucevic wants to own him, but our guy thinks Krucevic is poison. He cracks security systems for a living."

"So how'd he come to us?" Caroline asked.

"He applied for an embassy job. As a security expert."

"Fascinating," burbled T. Hunter Price. "You just brought this crook in, I suppose, to discuss your mutually shady pursuits over a glass of Schultheiss. And in the process, you probably gave away the embassy's fiber optics and security installations, Wally, to no less a personage than 30 April's chief safecracker. I congratulate you, friend. I really do."

"Horse pucky," the station chief said. "I didn't interview him at the embassy." But he had flushed an angry red.

"Have you talked to him since the bombing?" Tom Shephard was rigid with interest.

"Last night. I didn't tell him why we wanted Krucevic." Wally glanced around the table. "Nobody in Berlin knows for a fact that 30 April did the Brandenburg, much less the Vice President, so I made it a fairly general query. But my guy thinks Mlan is headed for Hungary. Krucevic told him to get to Budapest and await instructions. I asked him nicely to keep us informed."

Budapest, Caroline thought. *I'm wasting my time here in Berlin.*

"So this asset of yours is working for the terrorists." Shephard was scowling.

"He's not an asset. He's a developmental."

"Which means you're not paying him."

"Not formally. No."

"But you're considering placing him on your payroll. A borderline criminal who consorts with terrorists."

"You want a terrorist asset, Tom, you've got to get your hands dirty."

It was the oldest debate in the counterterrorism game: how to penetrate the organizations you pursued without adopting their methods. Most of the people at the CTC, Caroline thought, would agree that it was impossible. You could trace a terrorist's funds. You could blow up his training camps and operational bases. But you could not learn his most private thoughts, his most diabolical schemes, without an ear in his private councils. That meant controlling one of his own. Paying for terrorist treason. And that single fact almost guaranteed that someday, somebody—in the halls of Congress or the pages of the *Washington Post*—would accuse you of bankrolling a monster.

"Hungary," the ambassador said thoughtfully. "It's a big place. But this is good, Wally. It's a start. I suggest you get on the horn to your opposite number in Pest and direct him to work his assets."

"Yes, sir," Wally said briefly. He did not remind Dalton that the secure phones were down.

"There must be a 30 April body somewhere in that city," the ambassador said. "We must get to him before Krucevic does."

"Isn't there some way to prevent 30 April from entering Hungary?" Shephard asked. "The borders should have been closed as soon as the bomb went off yesterday."

"They haven't been, and they won't be," Dalton told him. "The President undertook to give Krucevic his freedom until Sophie Payne is recovered. Any sign of an international manhunt, we jeopardize her safety."

"That can't go on indefinitely."

"As far as our German friends are concerned, I imagine it could. It serves their ends to admiration. Why close the borders, when the enemy is within? You of all people must know, Tom, that the enemy is the infidel Turk. He lives among us. He is to be punished for 30 April's crimes, while 30 April gets away with murder."

"Which raises a few questions about Fritz Voekl," Caroline observed, "and his commitment to fighting international terrorism."

Dalton smiled at her regretfully. "There are so many questions about Fritz Voekl, my dear. Questions that even I shall not put to him, I'm afraid. We need more information—the kind of information that can be used to pressure him—if we are to proceed from a position of strength. And now, if you'll excuse me," the ambassador said with a general nod, "I must present my respects to the chancellor and his daughter. It is young Kiki's sixteenth birthday, and *le tout Berlin* will be raising a glass."

EIGHT
Pristina, 2:13 P.M.

ENVER GORDIEVIC WAS STARTLED AWAKE at the first knock on his shanty's door. His heart pounded. He glanced first at Krystle, the baby, who was napping in the lower bunk; she stirred drowsily and began to wail. Then he looked toward the door. No windows in the hut, no way to know who stood there. But it must be faced. Even if it was Simone.

He took the three steps at a run and pulled open the flimsy piece of wood. The Canadian doctor was framed in the doorway, her face lined with weariness, all her heart in her eyes. *Alexis—*

"You'd better come," she said. And he didn't ask any questions, just gathered up the little one in her blanket and raced across the churned mud to the medical tent. Simone was there before him, by the side of the cot where his daughter had lain through the early hours of morning, an IV taped into her small wrist. Her hand was on Alexis's forehead, her stethoscope was searching the little girl's chest. His daughter looked spent; her eyes were closed. She was not, Enver thought, even moving.

He waited, holding his breath, for Simone to shake her head, to draw the sheet up over his daughter's golden hair—for his world to crack apart like a shattered glass.

He'd spent eight hours pacing the hospital tent floor, running his hands through his hair and talking, talking, to the woman with the French name, while friends watched his baby and Alexis spiraled downward into death.

"How will I tell her mother?" he had asked Simone once in despair, and she had looked at him in surprise.

"You're married?"

"*Was* married. She was killed in a fire. During the civil war." *I was supposed to take care of the girls.* "She'd always wanted a little girl. Someone to dress up, like a doll. I wanted boys, you know? Kids I could play soccer with."

"Girls play soccer, too."

He'd nodded distractedly. "It doesn't matter. I wouldn't trade my girls now. They're all I have left of Ludmila—she was only twenty-eight when she died. And I loved her."

He had paused, embarrassed to be talking so freely to this woman, who had hundreds of other children to care for, other parents to hear. But Simone was sitting quite still, her eyes on his face; his confessions hadn't bored her.

"Your wife must have been beautiful," she had told him. "Your girls certainly are."

"She named them after movie stars. From an American television show. *Dynasty*—you know it? She wanted everything for Alexis. Everything she never had. And for a while, we were doing so well. I had my practice, she had her apartment house—she inherited it from her father. Six apartments, six families. None of them survived the fire."

He had spoken without emotion; he had told this story too many times to feel it anymore.

Simone had risen and gone to a small boy turning restlessly in the cot next to his daughter's. "How did you escape?"

"I was in Budapest. Attending a constitutional-reform seminar sponsored by the U.S. Justice Department. My mother brought the girls to me for a holiday—she had never been to Hungary herself—but Ludmila couldn't get away. When war broke out, she called and begged me to stay. She wanted the girls to be safe." He had looked directly at Simone, his eyes bright as if with fever. "I never saw her again."

"But you and your daughters survived."

"So we could die *here*?" he had retorted. It was the first sign of real bitterness he'd allowed himself to feel.

Simone had ignored it. She pressed a cold cloth against Alexis's forehead. "You're a lawyer, then."

"That doesn't mean much in Kosovo. Law has nothing to do with survival."

"But someday, you'll use what you learned in that seminar. Don't give up hope, Enver."

Alexis had whimpered in the cot, and Simone felt for her pulse. There were so many children now. One hundred and fifty-three more had arrived at daybreak. They lay in the tent with barely eight inches between their cots, some on pallets on the dirt floor. They moved into beds when another child died—

"Why aren't you getting it?" he had asked her abruptly. "This disease. Why is it just the kids?"

"I don't know. Maybe it doesn't strike adults. Or maybe, if you've had the more common forms of the disease or been inoculated against them, you're immune. We know so little about this strain—we don't even know how the epidemic started. Or why the disease strikes boys far more savagely than girls—every gland in the boys' bodies is swollen. But a German lab has been studying the virus intensively and has come up with a new vaccine. We expect some German medical teams to fly in any day and begin inoculation."

"A vaccine? Specifically for this strain? How did they make it so fast?"

"I don't know." Her eyes met his, and the agony in them was like a lash. "Enver, I'd urge you to have your youngest vaccinated."

"Do you think it's safe?"

"I think it can't be worse than what we've got."

He had thought about it all morning, while Alexis worsened; he had carried the idea of a vaccine back to his shelter when Krystle needed a nap. He had fallen asleep despite his best intentions in the quiet of that room, thinking of mumps, of killing strains. And while he slept, his elder daughter's time had run out.

He took a step now toward Alexis's cot and reached for her hand. It was cold—colder than his own, which was clammy with fear and raw weather. If only she would open her eyes one last time and look at him—if only he could hear her say his name—

Simone shook her head and removed her stethoscope from Alexis's chest.

He would not look at Simone. He would not let the glass shatter, and with it, all the world—

"I'm so sorry, Ludmila," he whispered to his dead wife. And buried his face in their daughter's sweat-soaked curls.

NINE

Bratislava, 3 P.M.

IN OLGA TECIAK'S APARTMENT, the air grew stale and the hours dragged. Once the videotape was made, Krucevic sent Michael out in a car with Otto as caretaker. The two men drove across the Danube and into the center of Bratislava, where the U.S. embassy sat next to a massive old hotel in the Soviet mode, a former casino for party apparatchiks. The embassy had once been a consulate; when Slovakia declared independence from the Czech Republic in 1992, its status was upgraded, but an air of unhappiness lingered. Bratislava would never carry the prestige or romance of a Prague posting, and even the buildings knew it.

Michael was behind the wheel. The American embassy was coming up on the right, a block and a half away; early-afternoon traffic snarled the lanes ahead. The key was to crawl along in the right-hand lane, as though intent upon finding a parking space, until the red light ahead changed and the traffic moved freely. They had gone around the corner twice before this, circling the embassy's position, in an effort to time the signal's changes. Thirty seconds, Michael thought, before red phased into flashing yellow and then blue-green. He was nearly abreast of the embassy door, maybe two yards still to go, when Otto rolled down his window and fired his gun at the lens of the nearest surveillance camera. The lens shattered. The far camera went next, just as it pivoted electronically to sweep the embassy's street front. Two deliberate pops, mundane as a car's backfiring, and the marine guards were suddenly shouting.

The light changed.

Otto hurled the bubble-wrapped videotape at the embassy steps. It skittered across the sidewalk directly in the path of a woman walking an overweight schnauzer; the dog hiccuped hysterically and lunged. One marine leapt forward and shoved the woman to the ground. The other kicked the package back into the street and then fell to the pavement, roaring, "Fire in the hole!"

Michael floored the gas pedal and spun sharply around the corner, rocketing down the side street that ran alongside the embassy building. He dodged one car to the left, careened into the opposite lane, jogged around an oncoming van, and turned left at the next intersection, the flow of traffic being blessedly with him. It was a simple thing now to head for the river.

"Fucking broad daylight." Otto had rolled up the window and was staring back over his shoulder, intent upon a possible tail. "What the fuck's he thinking, huh? That we'll fucking die for him? Just one of those joes saw our plates—"

"They didn't see the plates," Michael said. "What are you saying? That Mlan made a mistake? That he's losing it? I wouldn't let him hear that."

"What do *you* know, you useless piece of meat? You got shit for brains. Peas for balls. Next time, I throw *you* out the window."

On the pavement in front of the American embassy, nothing exploded. One of the marines got to his feet and studied the package. The schnauzer broke free of its screaming mistress and sank its teeth into the marine's ankle.

"You did well."

Stoop-shouldered, with a bald spot as decisive as a Franciscan's on the crown of his head, Béla Horváth was peering into a microscope ocular at a sample of vaccine No. 413—Mlan Krucevic's answer to the mumps epidemic. No one else was in the laboratory. Except for the dark-haired woman with the white scarf wrapped like a bandage around her neck.

"Can you tell anything?" Mirjana Tarcic asked him.

"For that, we need time. Trials with mice. DNA scans. Assessment and analysis. But this is a start. The best we could possibly have."

Béla took off his glasses, leaned toward her as she sat on the lab stool in a pool of light from a Tensor lamp, and kissed her cheek. "You're very brave, you know."

She flinched as though the praise stung her. "And then? When you have your analysis? What will you do with it?"

"Tell Michael. He's the one who wants to know."

She shook her head. "It's not enough. We have to tell the world."

"Tell them what?" Horváth smiled at her indulgently. "That the latest Yugoslav terrorist is quite possibly insane? The world will not be surprised."

"I did not go to Berlin for Michael," Mirjana said tautly.

"No. And I do not flatter myself that you went for me. Why exactly did you go, Mirjana?"

Wordlessly, she reached her hands to her throat and unwound the scarf. It was as much a part of this woman as her sharp nose, her writhing dark hair. Béla had not seen her throat in at least five years.

The final length of silk trailed away. Her hand dropped to her side, clenched. He drew a deep breath, steadied himself, and reached trembling fingers to her cheek. She reared back, as though he might strike her.

"Mirjana," he whispered in horror. "Who did this to you?"

The wound had healed long ago. But the vicious edge, torn and rewoven like the bride of Frankenstein, stared out accusingly from the pale expanse of her neck. She had been savaged. It was as though a wild animal had gnawed at her flesh, and what remained was carrion for birds.

"Mlan?" he asked.

She began to wind the scarf once more around her throat. "You remember the Krajina?"

The Krajina. A bloodbath in Bosnia, Serb killing Croat, Croat killing Serb. Thousands died.

"We had gone there, Zoran and I, with the boy."

"Zoran?"

"My brother. Mlan had been missing for weeks. We believed he was dead." Her dark eyes were flat and unreadable, a look Béla knew of old. "Sarajevo was in ruins, our building had been hit. Zoran was mad to join the Serb forces—he was twenty-three, Béla, filled with rage and hatred. I went with him to the Krajina because I had nowhere else to go. Our parents were dead. There was the boy. I thought we might find protection."

Protection.

"They came in the night, the Croat killers. They tore us from our beds and set fire to the houses, they shot some where they lay. They took the men in a group to the edge of town, and there they butchered them. And I—I hid my Jozsef in a cellar with some women and their babies; he was only seven, Béla, but they would have killed him—and I went after Zoran and the Croats."

She pointed to her neck. "This is how they killed my brother, Béla. With a chain saw."

"Mlan?" Béla whispered.

"He kept them from killing me," she replied, "when they had started. But he did not stop them from raping me four, ten, sixteen times. And he did not save my brother. I watched Zoran die. He screamed, Béla, all the hatred that was in him—*useless*. It did not save him. But perhaps it kept him from being afraid.

"You call me brave. But you are a fool, Béla. I am afraid every day and night of my life. Afraid of *him*."

"I know. That is *why* I call you brave. Fear does not stop you. You take the plane to Berlin—"

"He wanted Jozsef, you see," she went on, as though he had not spoken. "Mlan thought I had left the boy with friends in Sarajevo. He thought the pain and fear would make me tell him, that I would buy my life with my Jozsef's blood. But I told him nothing. He had no choice but to let me live. If I died, he would never find his son again."

"And he did," Béla said.

"Four years later, in Belgrade. By that time, The Hague had branded Mlan a criminal. No one thought he would show his face in Serb territory again. But it was a mistake to think we were safe. Mlan came and stole my boy in the night."

Béla reached over and snapped off the Tensor lamp. "You went to Berlin for Jozsef."

She shook her head. "I will never see Jozsef again. I went to Berlin for revenge."

———

Sophie could feel Michael's presence beyond the bathroom door. He stood guard there, ostensibly to keep her within, and yet she felt as though he really kept Krucevic out. This was absurd, of course; in her circumstances, it was a piece of self-delusion so pitiful it was dangerous. It set up a false sympathy. Michael had done nothing to prevent her infection with Anthrax 3A. He had done nothing, if it came to that, to prevent her kidnapping in the first place. So what was his game? Why was he a member of 30 April at all? And what did he truly mean by those muttered words, *I will not let you die at this man's hands?*

She almost wished he had said nothing. He had created the illusion of hope, and she needed to fight hope as much as despair. In her mind she had erected a wall of vigilance, one that permitted no hint of the fate that awaited her to penetrate inside. The wall assumed her end would be painful and that her only choice was to meet it with dignity. She burned, nonetheless, with questions.

"What do you do all day?" she asked Jozsef. "When you're not standing vigil over the operation, I mean?"

"Sometimes I read books. Sometimes he lets me watch the television. It depends."

What had Peter done at twelve? He skateboarded. He rode his bike. He spent a lot of time outdoors on baseball and soccer fields. He played Nintendo and computer games and he bragged to his friends and he never, never spent an entire day hunched in the corner of a dank bathroom in a stranger's house.

"Do you ever play games on a computer?"

His head came up at that. "You saw it? Tonio's computer?"

"No. Does he have one?"

Jozsef nodded. "Tonio is a genius."

"I suppose he told you that himself."

"My father says it. It is why he allows Tonio near him, although Tonio sings American music and is not to be trusted when the liquor is in him. When Tonio is drunk, he sings louder, and my father orders Otto to beat him. But Papa needs Tonio for his genius."

"Really," Sophie said, growing more interested. "And what does Tonio do for your father?"

"He can find his way into any computer system anywhere in the world." Jozsef was proud. "He once found his way into most of the banks in Switzerland, and into the Italian treasury, but for that he went to prison."

"Not much of a genius, then, if he got caught."

"Tonio hated prison so much that he tried to kill himself with a razor. He swears he will not go back again. It is why he fights for my father. To get back at all of them."

"The Swiss banks?"

"And the West. The West is very evil."

"I thought the West was your father's only hope. He hates the East, right?"

Jozsef frowned. "It is complicated, I think. Papa hates the East, certainly, because all evil comes from the East; but the West is evil, too. It must be . . . *cistiti*. What is the word? *Washed?* . . . before it is good again."

"Cleansed," Sophie murmured, and thought of the mass graves in Bosnia and Kosovo.

"Cleansed." Jozsef tested the word on his tongue.

"And so Tonio will cleanse the West with his computer. What bank will he break into next?"

But this, it seemed, was far too direct a question. The boy retreated into himself, once more the guardian of the operation, his fingers worrying the fur of his good-luck charm.

"Who gave you the rabbit's foot?" Sophie asked.

A swift look, pregnant with apprehension.

"It's never out of your hands."

"I found it."

"That's probably what you tell your father. It's not the truth."

He glanced over his shoulder, then leaned toward her. "My mother gave it to me. For luck during the war, when she was afraid that a sniper's bullet would take me."

"My son has a good-luck charm," Sophie lied. "Not a rabbit's foot, but a ring from our naval academy. His father gave it to him before he died. Peter wears it on a chain around his neck, and it never leaves him."

"His father was a naval person?"

"Curt was a jet pilot a long time ago. In the American navy."

"Ah." Jozsef's eyes darkened. Too late, Sophie remembered what American jets had done to Belgrade. "The ring. It has brought your son good luck?"

Peter's face—so much a blend of Curt's and her own that she could no longer see where one began and the other left off—flashed briefly before her eyes, then was gone. She felt a pain so sharp she could not speak for several seconds, and then said, "Yes. I think it has brought him luck. Except for his father's death, of course."

"His father was shot?"

A commonplace question for a terrorist's son.

"He died of cancer."

"Then perhaps your son forgot to wear his ring that day," Jozsef said with unconscious cruelty. "I have never lost my rabbit's foot, and until I do, I shall be safe. I know that with certainty, so help me God."

"Is that why you keep it secret? So that the luck won't fade?"

He hesitated and again looked over his shoulder. She knew then that the reason was Mlan Krucevic.

"It is all that I have left of my mother," the boy whispered. "If my father knew where it came from, he would take away. And what would happen to Mama then?"

"You have to keep her safe, too," Sophie said with sudden comprehension.

There was a knock on the door and it opened. "Jozsef," Michael said. "You're wanted."

The boy's hand clenched on the scrap of dirty white fur. Then, looking at Sophie, he held his finger to his lips in the age-old gesture for silence. She lifted her finger in return.

TEN

Berlin, 5:07 P.M.

CAROLINE WOULD HAVE LOVED to raise a glass with *le tout Berlin* herself. Or a bowl of steaming lentil soup at Café Adler, the small bar that still sat opposite what had once been Checkpoint Charlie. Years earlier John le Carré, a mere David Cornwell employed by the British secret service, had watched the Cold War begin from one of the café's ringside seats. Checkpoint Charlie had been replaced now by something the Germans called an office park; but the Adler was unchanged, smoky with the romance of mitteleuropa. It was time, she thought, to retreat into yellow lamplight and scattered tables, to nurse her jet lag with tea and silence. And consider her next move.

Wally refused to let Caroline wander off, however, and he had no intention of returning her to the Hyatt unfed. They drove through the barricaded streets in his brand-new Volvo, zigzagging around the yawning pits of construction that bisected every boulevard. The early darkness of Berlin's autumn had fallen like a theater scrim over the city; rain lashed against the windshield.

Caroline's jet lag was so profound she had begun to shake.

"God, it's good to see you, Mad Dog," Wally said. "What's it been—two years?"

"More. How did you like Budapest?"

"Nice town. But not my best work. It's a thankless job to replace Eric Carmichael. You *can't* replace him. You just show up and exit stage left as soon as possible."

He was trying to make her feel good. The truth was, few people in the Agency could recruit or handle agents as effectively as Wally. He was everybody's hometown buddy—the boy who'd never had a date to the prom, the one who held your hand late at night in a thousand seedy bars. With his worn wool suits and his graying goatee, Wally was genuine, Wally was sympathetic, Wally was a stand-up kind of guy; and before you knew it, Wally had slipped you some money and a contract and you were spilling your guts to the CIA.

"So I suppose they gave you Berlin as a way of easing you down gently, right? You're one step away from a Bronze Intelligence Star and a comfortable retirement in upstate New York."

He grimaced at the windshield. "I look plausible and I can bullshit up the wazoo, Carrie, but I'm not Eric. What he wouldn't do with this mess, huh? Wouldn't he be in his element right now? A rescue plan for the Vice President of the United States. The ultimate cowboy operation. Of course, if Eric had been around, the hit would've never happened. He'd have rolled up 30 April long ago."

"Except that they rolled him up first," Caroline said. And added Wally to the list of people Eric had betrayed.

He glanced at her. "You any closer to pinning these guys for MedAir 901?"

"No. And that investigation is now on the back burner. Sophie Payne has to take precedence."

"We'll get 'em," Wally said positively. "We always do. Even if it takes ten years."

Caroline had breathed, drunk, and slept MedAir 901 for the past thirty months. Now the mere mention of the plane made her skin crawl. If the investigation continued—if Cuddy Wilmot delved deeper into the truth, like a child picking at a scab—what exactly would they learn? That Eric had deliberately killed two hundred and fifty-eight people in order to fake his own death? That as far back as the Frankfurt airport—a farewell kiss in a crowded concourse—she had not the slightest idea who her husband really was?

"There's something I have to ask you, Wally."

"Yeah?"

"Eric's handling of the 30 April account. In Budapest. Before he died. You must have walked into a nightmare when you took over."

"How so?" Wally swerved to avoid a jaywalker suddenly illuminated in the headlights, and cursed into the darkness.

"From what I remember, Eric was pretty close to penetrating the organization. He had a recruit in Krucevic's inner circle. Or so I thought."

"In Budapest?"

Wally wasn't trying to stonewall her. He was simply searching his memory for operational matters that belonged to another posting he'd left six months ago. Then his eyelids flickered and he downshifted for a turn.

"That'd be DBTOXIN," he said.

Caroline's breath nearly caught in her throat. A code name to attach to her untested source, a piece of the denied DO file. Wally was trusting her with operational Intelligence. She had better take it in stride. "DBTOXIN?"

"The last fish Eric reeled in. A biologist in Buda. Trained with Krucevic at the university in Leipzig during the old Cold War days. They're pals from way back."

"Think they're pals still?"

Wally considered. "Maybe I should get on the horn to Buda and set up some tasking. See whether TOXIN knows where Krucevic is headed."

"I sure as hell would."

"Wonder if the guy's still on the payroll."

"So he wasn't blown when Eric died?"

"TOXIN? No way." Wally glanced at her. "Is that what you've been thinking? That Eric's last recruit betrayed him? And that's why Krucevic blew up his plane? Disaster's not that personal, Carrie, even in this business."

Time to change the subject.

"Speaking of personal," she said, "how's Brenda?"

Brenda was Wally's wife. She was a California native, a vegetarian, and a massage therapist. He had met her during language training in Monterey. She was the last person anybody expected to fall in love with Wally, but the hometown-buddy routine had apparently worked.

"Brenda left Berlin about a month ago, right after Voekl came to power. Her grandparents were Holocaust survivors, Caroline. She's not sticking around to see whether Fritz is sane."

"He's never been overtly anti-Semitic, Wally."

"No German politician can be and survive. Voekl says the right things. But the language is a sort of code, Caroline. Attack the outsider—even if it's the Muslims this time—and sooner or later, you'll catch up with the Jews."

Caroline winced. "Did she take your kids?"

He nodded, gaze fixed on the wet asphalt rippling in the headlights. "The apartment's like a mausoleum."

Brenda was important to Wally, but his two boys were his reasons to live. "That must be tough," Caroline said.

He shrugged. "We call each other a lot. And my tour's up in eighteen months. Look, I'm starving. Why don't we grab something and head back to my place?"

"Something" turned out to be wurst from a kosher deli in the Scheunenviertel, the old Jewish quarter of Berlin where Wally had an apartment in a converted nineteenth-century town house. They ate brown bread, dense and nutty, and soft German cheese with the wurst. Wally drank dark beer. They sat on a faded velvet sofa in his high-ceilinged living room and talked of inconsequential things—people they knew and hadn't seen in months, recipes for a true Hungarian *gulyás*, Brenda's practice in the Maryland suburbs. And when the insistent edge of Caroline's hunger had been muted, she wiped her fingers on a paper napkin and sat back to enjoy Wally's wine.

"So do you sweep this place?" she asked, casting her eyes up to the ceiling.

"Every day, with the best possible broom," he replied. "It's clean. As far as I can tell."

"No coincidences?"

"None that are more than coincidences. You can talk, Mad Dog."

"Where do I start, Wally?"

He held her gaze impassively. "First, tell me why you're here."

Her pulse throbbed. *Don't look like you've got something to hide,* she thought. *Wally always knows. Wally was born a spy.* She forced a rueful smile.

"I'm here because Jack Bigelow is desperate and I happened to write a bio he actually read. The President seems to think a mere analyst can pull Sophie Payne out of a hat. I can't begin to tell you what I'm expected to do. I don't know myself."

"Then I propose you sit back and watch Tom Shephard."

"The LegAtt?"

"He's in charge on the ground. You monitor his moves and wait for information. That seems to be what analysts are most comfortable with. Watching and waiting."

Caroline's smile deepened. "How you cowboys despise us!"

"Not me," Wally protested. "I've got nothing but respect for the Headquarters wonks. It's just not who I am. I need . . . to make decisions faster. I need to *act.* Even if what I do turns out to be wrong. You analysts demand so much certainty, you know? Before you're willing to move off a dime."

Certainty, Caroline thought. It had nothing to do with the shadow world of Intelligence. Intelligence was predictive. Intelligence was fact spurred by instinct, a wing flying on a prayer. Wally was right. Analysts were too damn obsessed with their own security. Too concerned with getting it *right* to say anything at all.

But time and facts were two things she lacked in the

midst of Eric's disaster. She'd have to clutch at the puzzle pieces before they materialized, trust her gut as well as her brain.

"Not that I mean *you,* Caroline," Wally amended. "I remember Mad Dog. I know what you're capable of. A threat and a grenade, right when it counts. Now *that's* moving off a dime."

Mad Dog. A trickle of adrenaline, recalled from the past, floated down Caroline's spine. Had she ever been quite so reckless, so determined, so *insane* as her nickname would suggest?

She had. She had never forgotten what drove her during the months of counterterrorism training, nor how the momentary madness had felt. That knowledge was like an uneasy knife pricking at her brain. The force she could not control. Her demon.

She shook off Wally's words and said, "Who've you got working the terrorist account?"

"In the station? Fred Leicester. You know Fred?"

"The name. We've never crossed paths."

"He was out trolling the streets today in the hope of turning up a lead."

In a plumber's van full of electronics, probably. Leicester had gone through six months of tradecraft training at the Farm with Eric, tailing unsuspecting tourists through the streets of Williamsburg, Virginia. What she knew of Fred took about twenty words to say: He was a well-meaning putz. He believed the CIA was the free world's last, best hope. And his tradecraft was shit. Fred was persona non grata waiting to happen, the worst fate that could be visited on a case officer's career. When you were PNG'd, the world took notice. Your diplomatic immunity was stripped and you were exposed as a spy in your host country's newspapers. You went home in disgrace, your cover permanently blown. And in most cases, you never worked abroad again.

"Fred is the one developing our girl in the VaccuGen office," Wally said. "And he follows the local Palestinians. There's always a floating crap game where the rag heads are concerned. Paul—the kid you met today—does a few jobs now and then. Dead drops, brush passes . . . It'll never be Berlin in the Cold War, but it's good experience."

"So you've got some terrorist assets here."

"Not a whole lot to speak of." Even with Caroline, Wally operated on a need-to-know basis. "Most of that stuff, frankly, has been handled out of Bonn and the Frankfurt base up until now. Mad Dog, what are you looking for?"

"Mahmoud Sharif."

"Sharif?"

"Yeah. Palestinian. Bomb tech. Internationally known criminal. He wouldn't happen to be a volunteer, would he?"

"A controlled asset? *Sharif?* Are you crazy?"

"Just curious."

He shook his head. "Not that it wouldn't be the coup of coups to recruit him, don't get me wrong. But Sharif'd probably slit his own throat before he'd betray Allah."

"A true believer, huh?"

"Well, there are true believers and then there are fanatics. Mahmoud's not dumb enough to blow himself up for the glory of the jihad, Mad Dog. He just makes the bombs and lets the fanatics smuggle 'em on the planes."

"How unsporting. By karmic law, every bomb maker should be required to self-destruct with one of his own devices."

"Sharif's been on pretty good behavior lately. Works his carpentry business during the day, runs a sculpture gallery over in the Tacheles by night."

"The what?"

"Tacheles." Wally said it with relish. "Isn't that a great word? Yiddish, for 'let's get down to business.'"

"Mahmoud Sharif works in a place with a Yiddish name? Jesus."

"It's the abandoned building on Oranienburger Strasse. You've seen it—size of a shopping mall, derelict ever since the war. Cafés, experimental art, nightclubs— *très nouveau, très* hip, even for hip Berlin. The concerts in summertime practically blow this whole quarter away."

"And he owns a sculpture gallery. That's got to be a front. I bet he's running arms or drugs out of there."

"He's a reformed individual, our Mahmoud. He's got kids to consider." Wally's voice was heavy with sarcasm. "But why the interest in Sharif, Carrie? He can't be involved with the Payne kidnapping. No Palestinian would do a job for Mlan Krucevic."

"His name turned up in DESIST."

Wally set down his beer bottle. "Turned up how?"

"I don't know. Cuddy Wilmot said his Berlin phone number tracked with 30 April."

Wally whistled. "Hizballah and the neo-Nazis. I don't believe it, Caroline. Sharif *did not* take out the Brandenburg."

"Some link must be there. The computer found it."

"Then the computer's wrong. It's happened before."

"But somebody with knowledge and skill made the Gate's device, Wally. This was a surgical hit. Most of the surrounding buildings are intact. You don't get that with a barrel of fertilizer and kerosene."

"No. You don't. But neither do you walk up to Mahmoud and say, 'Hey, brother, done any jobs for the infidel lately?' "

"There are subtler ways of gathering information."

"Maybe you should run this by Shephard. He's got good ties to the BKA—the Bundeskriminalamt, the German federal police. Maybe they could tap Sharif's phones. They can do it legally now, did you know that?"

Caroline nodded. For five decades the German constitution had forbidden wiretaps, a reaction to the Gestapo persecution of the Nazi era. That had changed a few years ago, when German prosecutors voiced their frustration at being denied the routine evidence a hundred other countries collected on suspected criminals.

Wiretaps.

With a surge of vertigo, Caroline felt the broad plank floor of Wally's living room careen upward. She'd just handed Wally Mahmoud Sharif—whose phone lines might lead directly to Eric. *Stupid, stupid.*

Dare would never forgive her. She pressed a hand to her forehead, willing the exhaustion of jet lag to recede. "Are you sure you want to share this stuff with the BKA?" she asked.

"You mean DESIST? We probably won't. We can offer up Sharif for other reasons. But I'll let Tom handle that. He's pretty used to working liaison. Which reminds me. You'll see Tom tomorrow at the Interior Ministry. Bombing meeting. I'll pick you up at the Hyatt at ten-thirty."

"You might want to check with Scottie Sorensen first," Caroline suggested feebly. "About the wiretapping, I mean. Just to be sure. I wouldn't want to end-run Scottie's authority."

"Okay." From the sound of Wally's voice, he was humoring her and trying not to feel annoyed. It was rare for an analyst to second-guess the station chief. "What exactly is worrying you, Mad Dog? The BKA are pretty good at intercepts, believe me. Makes you wonder how often they practiced under the old law."

The floorboards steadied, her vertigo receded. "Who are they tapping these days? *Gastarbeiters?*"

He laughed brusquely. "Don't need wiretaps for them. Guest workers have no citizenship rights. Under the Voekl program of repatriation, you just frame 'em and deport 'em as fast as you can."

"You really don't like the chancellor, do you, Wally?"

"What can I say, Carrie? I don't trust Voekl's politics. And he's a dangerous man."

"Dangerous how?"

Wally took a pull on his beer. "You're the leadership analyst."

"I follow terrorists, not mainstream politicians."

"Well, then maybe you should broaden your scope."

She studied him over the rim of her wineglass. "What are you saying?"

"Sometimes the boundaries between the state and the fringe aren't so clear. Look at Arafat. One day he's a guerilla hero, next he's a virtual head of state. Or Syria's Assad. How many nutsos with a gun did that guy fund from the presidential palace, huh? I won't even *mention* Qaddafi."

"You think Voekl is funding terrorists?"

"Maybe not terrorists. I would never go so far as to suggest he's behind 30 April. He's not that stupid, Carrie. But there's been a rash of hate crimes throughout Central Europe. We think that Uncle Fritz's party is bankrolling some of them."

"You *think*?"

Wally tossed his bottle in the trash. "I know, I know—I need the evidence. All that certainty you analysts love. I'm working on it."

"What kind of hate crimes? Guest workers? Petty stuff?"

"Not entirely." Wally suddenly looked uneasy. "If it were domestic incidents alone, we'd be inclined to sit back and bide our time. Chancellors come and go. But this stuff is bleeding into other people's backyards. Take the Café Avram, for instance."

"Café Avram."

"Jewish revival place in old Krakow. Ever been to Krakow?"

Caroline shook her head.

"It's about three and a half hours due east as the crow flies. Eleven hours, if you're lucky, by the Polish roads. I drove over right after we landed here, back in early August. I wanted to see Auschwitz, or rather Brenda did. Some of her people died there." He leaned forward, hands clasped idly between his knees. "The camp and the rail yards are sitting right there in the middle of this gorgeous farmland, Carrie. Rolling hills, gnarled old trees, a man walking behind a horse-drawn plow, straight out of *War and Peace*. Some of the farmers were burning leaves. The essence of autumn, right? Only you draw it in with your breath and you can't help but think, *the smell of burning. Ashes and burning.* Everybody in that countryside must have smelled the ovens, and they went right on plowing." He paused abruptly.

Caroline prompted, "Café Avram."

"Right. The old Jewish quarter of Krakow is beautiful. Spielberg filmed *Schindler's List* there, you know?

Café Avram had become a sort of cultural center. Jewish music, kosher food. A tourist mecca. Anyway, three months ago, somebody torched it. The owners slept over the shop. Both were killed by the fire. And their three kids."

"And you think Voekl's party was behind the arson?"

"The Warsaw station is looking into it. They cabled us for information."

Caroline frowned. "But you said that no German politician can afford to be anti-Semitic. And why would a German party be operating beyond its borders?"

"All politics is local, Caroline. It's just the money that's international."

"You actually suspect that the Social Conservatives are funding hate crimes in neighboring countries? But Wally, the potential for blowback is immense!"

"The Social Conservatives are funding local chapters of their own German party in small towns throughout the region," Wally said tensely. "The SC is in Poland, it's in Slovakia, it's even showing up in poorer sections of the Czech Republic and Hungary. It's a party that feeds on economic disaffection, Caroline, and there's plenty of disaffection in Central Europe. Communism destroyed their industry; now democracy is destroying their markets. Nothing's easier for these poor bastards than to pick a leader who will blame the outcast of the moment—and voilà, everyone has a target for their anger." He glanced at her. "And there's a lot of anger, Carrie. I'm telling you, it scares the hell out of me."

"So in Krakow, the outcasts were eating at Café Avram?"

"Sure. It takes one to know one. Jews have been the *gastarbeiters* of Poland for four hundred years."

Caroline set down her wine. The alcohol was blurring her senses. "Nobody likes Voekl, nobody trusts him . . . and yet here he is. Running the damn country. How did that happen, Wally?"

"There was a convenient death."

Gerhard Schroeder. And 30 April had murdered him. "Voekl was there to take advantage of it," she said. "He'd amassed a considerable amount of power first."

"Which means that your premise is wrong, Caroline. *Somebody* likes Voekl very much indeed. And they voted en masse."

"More economic disaffection?"

"Maybe. Among the Ossies. Voekl comes from the east, you know. His claim to fame was running the best explosives plant in the GDR. He was an old Party hack before he was the face of the New European Union. But it's more than that. He's charming. He's plausible. He's telegenic in a media age."

"If you like your men in jackboots."

Wally laughed. "Come on, Carrie! The man's a wet dream of Aryan motherhood! Silver hair, blue eyes. The Italian suits, the flashing white teeth. You've got to look beyond the furious rhetoric. Germans like their rhetoric delivered in a fist-pounding fashion."

"He's been married three times."

"So he gets out the women's vote. And that kid of his—Kiki—is like a poster child for family values. She's cute, she's sweet, she's as blond as they come. Go into any hausfrau's kitchen, from Kiel to Schleswig-Holstein, and Fritz Voekl's picture is hanging somewhere near the stove. Half of Germany is in love with him."

"Half of Germany was in love with Hitler."

"Then we've got to place our hope—and our covert funding—with the other half," Wally said bluntly. "A remarkable Resistance sprang up here during the Nazi years. It got zero help from outside, and it was brutally suppressed. But there was no CIA then."

The CIA: Last, Best Hope for the Free World. *Right.* There were still some people in Operations who believed it. Caroline considered Wally and all those nights of sympathy wasted in a thousand badly lit bars, his hometown-boy routine threadbare and compromised, and felt a surge of affectionate pity. Thank God there were still people like Wally around to do the Agency's shit work—people with integrity. Otherwise, how would the world know what to betray?

Wally knew. He had figured out right and wrong years ago and chosen his side. Caroline only hoped he'd chosen well.

"The world has changed," she told him. "Voekl could never be as obvious as Hitler. Europe won't let him."

"Voekl's not interested in Europe." Wally flicked away her objections as though they were gnats. "He's interested in power at home. And to shore it up, he needs a new enemy."

"The Turks?"

"The entire Islamic world, Mad Dog. According to Voekl, Islam has torn apart the Balkans, the Central Asian republics, North Africa, the Middle East. And who's to argue? It's pretty tough to find an Arab apologist these days."

"Some campaign platform," she muttered.

"Listen." Wally raised a forefinger and shook it under her nose. "People said that about the National Socialists in 1930. By 1933, the Nazis had their hands around Germany's neck. Never underestimate the lure of the Big Lie."

The Big Lie.

Like the one she was living herself.

ELEVEN

Bratislava, 6:37 P.M.

OTTO WAS SNORING on Olga Teciak's couch. Vaclav was scrounging for food in the kitchen. Tonio was bent over a laptop computer, absorbed in the numbers he was crunching; Michael stood guard before the bathroom door. Mlan Krucevic pulled the carved antique chair close to the television screen and watched the evening news. A restless anger fretted at his entrails.

The lead story was Vice President Payne's disappearance. The White House refused to release any information about her captors or their demands, citing the sensitivity of the issue, but media speculation was rife. Most of the world's terrorism experts had deconstructed the Brandenburg hit and concluded it was entirely engineered to mask the political abduction. The FBI was analyzing footage of the helicopter's occupants to determine their identity, but the German police maintained that the terrorists were Turkish. An intensive interrogation of Berlin's resident alien population was under way. A curfew had been imposed on Turkish neighborhoods. The image shifted to the Brandenburg Gate, where police guards in black and red and gold surrounded the bomb crater. Tourists crowded to the international lens, and the Volksturm looked hostile.

"Michael," Krucevic said over his shoulder. "Bring Jozsef. He should see this. Hurry, before the footage ends."

It was important that the boy understand the effects of violence—the political as well as the actual. What Krucevic had caused to be done in Berlin was a direct challenge to every Berliner's comfort. Krucevic had brought fear into all their lives; he had returned them to the state of nature, when every day survived must be considered a form of victory. Jozsef should be made to understand what power truly was.

"Look at that," he said, sensing the boy behind him.

No response.

He looked around and saw his son's white face, Michael's hand on his shoulder. Both were staring at a blond woman whose camera was pointed at a Volksturm guard; the guard was screaming at her in German. In another instant the uniformed man might snatch the camera away.

"Americans," Krucevic said bitterly. "They behave like children wherever they go." He moved to turn off the set, but Michael said, "Wait."

It sounded oddly like an order. There was a set expression on his ashen face, an expression Krucevic had seen only once before, when Michael was on the verge of killing a man. Looking at him, Krucevic forgot to be insulted and said quickly, "What?"

"Bombs in Prague. There were bombs in Prague after we left." The fixed look wavered and vanished. "The Czechs called for German assistance. Could be why the border was tight."

Krucevic considered this. It would be beyond Fritz Voekl's control, of course, what the Czechs actually did. But a miscalculation nonetheless.

"Would you like to fly tonight, Jozsef?" he asked the boy playfully. "A small plane, something Vaclav can manage? If you're very good, I'll let you take the controls."

His son gave him a look so dark and glassy with fever that he was appalled. Krucevic rose to his feet, hand outstretched, but the boy's eyes rolled back in his head and he crumpled to the floor.

"Get him to the woman's bed," Krucevic snapped at Michael. "He's sick. Can't you see that he's sick?"

Without a word, Michael scooped up the child and carried him away.

Fear jangled in Krucevic's brain. He bit back a curse and went in search of his antibiotics.

———

The little girl named Annicka was huddled in a corner of the bedroom with a blanket, murmuring to a doll. Olga hovered in the doorway, one hand clutching the neck of her robe tightly, as though the men might rape her. It was ludicrous, Krucevic thought as he bent over his unconscious son. Whatever beauty the woman had once possessed, whatever had attracted Vaclav Slivik, was long since gone. She was too thin, too tired. Too beaten in spirit to be anything but abysmally depressing. He slid the needle into Jozsef's vein and sent a small prayer with it.

Olga came to stand silently beside him.

"What do you want?"

She swallowed nervously. Jozsef moaned and his head turned once on the pillow. He was still unconscious. If the anthrax had resurged . . . if the antibiotic wasn't working . . . But it must be working. He, Krucevic, had designed it himself.

"Well?" he asked Olga.

"I want to send my daughter to my sister's."

"No."

"But Annicka goes there whenever I work!"

"You're not working tonight."

Her head drooped like a condemned woman's.

"Mlan," said Vaclav from somewhere behind her. "There will be talk. Olga has a concert tonight. If she does not appear, the phone will start ringing. There will be knocks on the door, explanations—"

"Yes, yes," Krucevic snapped. "When is the performance?"

Hope flared in her eyes. "Eight o'clock. I usually leave at six-thirty."

He rose from the bedside and studied her face. Olga's fingers clutched at the robe convulsively. He reached out, irritated by the terror, and took her icy hand in his.

"Then go," he said. "Do everything you normally would. Except for the child. She stays here until you return. Understand?"

"But my sister—"

"Tell her Annicka is sick. Tell her you have asked a neighbor to sit with her. Tell her anything but the truth." His grip tightened on Olga's wrist. "If you tell the truth—to your sister or anyone—your little girl dies."

Olga's eyes dilated, then shifted imploringly to Vaclav's face. Krucevic released her hand.

"Get dressed," he said.

———

Sophie lay alone on the tile floor of the bathroom and stared at the ceiling. The patch of damp she had seen upon first waking had darkened with the failing light. It seemed to have grown, too—it was growing still, as she watched, like a visible manifestation of some inward cancer, the edges creeping remorselessly into the dull gray plaster.

A wave of heat rolled over her. Was her mind betraying her? Was she getting delirious? The point was to focus on something other than herself, something beyond her fever, beyond the room. She searched her brain for a safe fingerhold, a pit in the rock she might cling to.

> *That time of year thou mayst in me behold*
> *When yellow leaves, or none, or few, do hang*
> *Upon those boughs which shake against the cold*
> *Bare ruin'd choirs, where late the sweet birds sang.*

Then something, something—twilight and black night . . .

> *In me thou see'st the glowing of such fire*
> *That on the ashes of his youth doth lie*
> *As the death-bed whereon it must expire*
> *Consumed with that which it was nourished by.*

She shuddered, coughed. And tasted blood.

The door opened.

"Mrs. Payne." Krucevic's face bobbed and swam in the dim light; the door frame he leaned against wavered like a snake.

"Where is Jozsef?" she asked.

"Jozsef is ill." Did she imagine it, or was his voice less in command? He held aloft a hypodermic needle. "And so, I imagine, are you."

"Don't touch me!"

"I have no choice." There it was, the strain behind

the words, faint as a ghost. The man was afraid. "This is medicine, Mrs. Payne. You require it."

She began to struggle, but a great weight had pinned her legs, her arms were like lead, her sight was reeling. *Krucevic is afraid.* He grasped her wrist and thrust the sweatshirt sleeve upward.

He is afraid.

The pinprick of a needle in her vein.

He had not expected this, then. The fallibility of modern science. The spiking of his own power. Not just Sophie Payne was at risk now—not just the hated hostage—but his own son.

This thou perceivest, which makes thy love more strong
To love that well which thou must leave ere long.

TWELVE

Bratislava, 6:45 P.M.

OLGA TECIAK FLED FROM HER APARTMENT with her cello case dragging behind her like a corpse. She fled with her blood pounding in her veins and tears welling in her eyes. In all the years of her life, years when Slovakia was a police state and years when it was a democracy in name only, she had never felt the depth of terror that animated her at this instant. The police state had never threatened her child.

She tossed the cello into the back of her car and drove out into the night, through the chasms of ugly concrete buildings, all of them alike. Rain lashed down, and a dark gray service van—electricity? plumbing?—blundered heavily into a puddle ten feet away and sent a sheet of water slapping against her windshield. She jerked backward, as though the dirty brown stream had struck her in the face. The van shouldered past. It went on, the driver glancing neither to right nor left.

Olga sped over the bridge that spanned the Danube. She did not spare a glance for the houseboats pulled up along its banks. She ignored the floodlit ramparts of Bratislava Castle; the fortress had never saved her from anything. She drove toward the city's heart, debating within her mind what exactly she should do.

———

"Mlan," said Vaclav Slivik quietly. He was positioned at the window, staring through a slit in the drawn drapes. A pair of high-powered binoculars hung around his neck. Behind him, the lights were doused. With the coming of night and Olga's release had also come caution; they would post a guard until she had returned, until they could leave.

"What is it?"

Vaclav held a finger to his lips and with his other hand motioned Krucevic to his side. The two men stared down at the darkened parking lot. Vaclav pointed. On the curb opposite the building's main drive, the dark gray van was almost invisible in the night; Krucevic could make out nothing but a broad, square hump. An apparently deserted hump. The hairs rose along the back of his neck.

The listeners had arrived. They had tracked him through Greta Oppenheimer's phone call; soon they would be searching the building with electronic ears for the voice that matched their profile. *Criminal stupidity*. Why had he waited for darkness? He should have gone when he had the chance.

They would not find him immediately. But in a matter of minutes, the building would be surrounded. The roof, a landing pad for commandos. And he had let Olga Teciak go.

"The fire escape," Krucevic murmured in Vaclav's ear. "There must be one. Take the car and find that woman while you still can. Then meet us tomorrow in Budapest. Go!"

The Slovak State Orchestra was performing that evening in the opera house, not far from the U.S. embassy, where even now, the CIA station chief was in communication with the team in the dark gray van. Olga Teciak looked at her watch. She had twenty-seven minutes until curtain time, which was in fact no time at all. At this very moment, she should be pulling into her parking space, unloading the cello, and tuning her strings amidst the gabble of her section's voices.

She drove past the opera and the Carlsbad Hotel (where the Soviet-era casino lights gleamed red and white in the darkness), past the U.S. embassy building with its invisible guards. Rain pelted her windshield, rain that held the promise of snow, and she mopped frantically with her bare hand at the steam clouding the underside of the glass. Unable to come to a decision.

They did not simply let you walk into the embassy, of that she was certain. It was United States territory, after all, and no one could merely walk into the United States. You required powerful friends, influence, a great deal of money or the proper kind of blackmail. Olga's life was too ordinary for these.

She drove aimlessly, her vision clouded by the fog on her windshield. Then she swerved abruptly and brought the car to a halt at the curb. She fumbled in her purse for a token.

A dash through the rain in her high heels and long dress, the coat pulled willy-nilly around her, no protection at all. The icy rain streamed through her chignon and down her neck as she reached the pay phone. Her hair would be ruined now, the hem of her formal gown splashed with mud. Impossible to appear onstage even if she threw down the receiver and drove back like a maniac. She willed her numbed fingers to thrust the token through the slot. Her die was cast. She asked for the number of the U.S. embassy.

The operator gave it to her in a neutered voice. The operator had no conception of what it was like to leave a terrified little girl in a house full of violent men, to leave your only child because you had no choice. The operator did not know what this phone call would cost.

"Embassy of the United States," said a woman in abominable Slovak.

"Please," Olga said, the tears suddenly crowding her throat, "you have got to help me and I have not much time. I must speak to your ambassador."

"The ambassador is engaged this evening."

"But the woman you are looking for is in my house, and they are going to kill her. They are going to kill my daughter, they are going to kill me—"

A hand slammed down abruptly on the phone's cradle, cutting the connection. The line went dead.

Olga gasped.

Vaclav Slivik stood behind her, a quizzical smile on his face. She must look wild, and pathetic, Olga thought: wet snarls of hair about her forehead, mascara streaming.

"You're soaked, my dear," he said. "That will never do for the performance. What are you thinking of?"

"I—I needed to call a friend," Olga said.

She replaced the useless receiver, her fingers clenched as though she could not bear to relinquish hope.

Vaclav grasped her arm. "You're in no condition to drive. It has been a long day."

"Yes," she said.

"Then perhaps I should take you to the opera."

His fingers tightened around her coat sleeve; she was a rabbit in a snare. She stumbled at the curb. Rainwater drenched her shoes. Vaclav pulled her upright without a word and steered her toward his car.

It was parked a few feet behind her own, and in his haste to reach her, Vaclav had left the headlights on. They flooded the backseat of Olga's car and the cello case huddled there like a third person. Vaclav didn't bother to fetch the instrument. They both knew she would never need it again.

———

Otto Weber ignored the fire escape—no one who intended to appear innocent before the eyes of a dark gray van would consider climbing by stealth down the back of the building. Otto walked out the front door, in a drab old raincoat borrowed from Olga's closet, with a serviceable black nylon briefcase slung over his shoulder. He wore a knit cap on his shaved head. And for the first time in a long time, he looked possessed of a certain decency.

He strolled casually down the drive, head bowed in the rain, his eyes on the puddles forming at his feet. His gloved hands swung idly at his sides. He seemed oblivious to gray vans and their questionable occupants, although he was making directly for their position at the curb.

He went up to the blue car sitting two spaces behind the van and groped in his pockets for keys. They would be studying him in the rearview mirror now, ready to drive on at a moment's notice. He let his eyes drift indifferently over the bulky old vehicle, its lettering scratched and the bumper eaten with rust, and then his expression changed to one of joyful interest. He had need of an electrician himself. He had been meaning to call one today. He sauntered up to the driver's window and tapped on the glass with one large knuckle, grinning foolishly at the guy behind the wheel.

They were polite to a fault, these Americans.

When the window slid down, Otto put a bullet in the driver's brain. His companion died reaching for a gun.

THIRTEEN
Berlin, 9:17 P.M.

WALLY CALLED A TAXI FOR CAROLINE and gave the driver instructions to take her directly to the Hyatt. But the moment the lights of Sophienstrasse dwindled in the distance, she tapped on the man's window and told him in passable German to pull over. She handed him some marks and set off alone, on foot, into the darkness of the Jewish Quarter. She was looking for Oranienburger Strasse and Mahmoud Sharif.

The abandoned building that Wally had called the Tacheles was really the remnant of a much larger structure that had been mostly destroyed by Allied bombs. It rose five stories above the street and consumed most of a city block. Neon lights and clouds of steam punctuated the Berlin darkness. She stopped in front of Obst und Gemüse, a restaurant across the street, and studied the wreck of a building from a safe distance. It was the sort of structure a giant might assemble as a play toy, all tumbled blocks of concrete, jagged frames where there had once been windows, a few massive Art Nouveau figures still poised on the ends of columns. Arches that trailed away into nothing. An elevator shaft exposed to sky. Most of the windows were boarded up or bricked over; the scorch marks of intense heat still flickered up the walls. Derelict pipes and the remains of a refrigerator were scattered on the ground, found art. And from within came the sounds of laughter, a racking cough, the current of voices.

The helmeted Volksturm guards were there, of course, pacing along the broken sidewalk with machine guns raised. But the policemen seemed less menacing against a backdrop of smoky light and laughter. It was remarkable, Caroline thought, that they even allowed the Tacheles to exist. It looked like the kind of building the Fritz Voekls of the world tore down.

There were several entrances punched in the building's side. She chose one, hitched her purse higher on her shoulder, and dashed across Oranienburger Strasse.

A rusted iron door, standing ajar. She slid inside and paused an instant, allowing her eyes to adjust. Before her, a corridor tunneled into the Tacheles, bare bulbs swinging from an outlet in the ceiling. She followed it until it dove right and presented her with a flight of stairs; then she went up, heels clattering on the bare iron treads.

The second floor was less claustrophobic. A gallery ran around the open stairwell, with doorways opening off it. Some were dark, some glaringly lit. A jangle of guitar chords floated through one yawning entry; Caroline peered inside.

A man stood before a table, blowtorch raised. He wore a steelworker's metal helmet and canvas overalls, but his arms were bare; a hammer and sickle was tattooed on his right bicep. Before him on the table was a mass of metal; beyond it, entirely nude, a woman posed

in a chair. A boom box played at maximum volume—
German techno rave—and the man was shouting his
own lyrics, enthusiastically off-key. A window was open
to the night, cold enough to raise gooseflesh on the
model's thigh; her teeth, when she glanced at Caroline,
were chattering.

Caroline turned to go, but the woman in the chair
barked an unintelligible word, and the man wheeled,
thrusting his visor skyward, and shouted in her direction. Caroline stopped in the doorway. The blowtorch
was switched off. Another word in broken German, and
his bloodshot eyes were staring at Caroline from a face
streaming with sweat.

She managed a few sentences. She was looking for an
artist—a man who worked in wood. Did he know
someone named Mahmoud?

He jerked one thumb over his shoulder, toward the
other end of the building, and then pointed at the floor.
Downstairs.

The naked woman in the chair lit a cigarette, as
though it might keep her warm.

Caroline followed the thread of a Billie Holiday song
filtering into the corridor, followed it down another
flight of steps, the darkness viscous like fog against her
face. *Bye, bye, blackbird,* Holiday sang, her voice as plain-
tive as midnight rain. And then Caroline glimpsed the
door to the café.

It was named, incongruously, America.

A yawning hole, a *boîte de nuit,* dense with conversation and smoke. The ceiling was very high and painted
black. So were the walls. Against them, canvases of massive figures sprang to life, more vivid than the people
ranged around tables below. A woman with red hair
and blue fingernails tapped cigar ash into her wineglass.

Caroline was sharply aware of loneliness. Of herself, poised on the threshold of a place not her own. And of the pulse in her head, beating faster now.

There was an empty stool near the corner of the bar. She made her way through the tables, her shoes sticking to the spilled beer on the floor.

"What can I get you?" the bartender asked in German.

"Radeburger," she replied. A Dresden beer she remembered Eric ordering.

He nodded and slapped a glass on the counter. Poured the beer with precision, as only a German can, until the head was two inches thick. She was afraid to lift the glass, afraid of making a fool of herself, and so she smiled at him and laid some money on the counter. He took it without a word and punched some buttons on the register, his eyes scanning the room beyond. All his movements were quick and thoughtless; he was a man who knew his own mind. He was also a careful man. The cash register faced outward and there was a mirror over the bar, so that on the rare occasions when he had to turn his back, he could see what needed to be seen. Was the fear of crime so universal in Berlin—despite the Volksturm parading on the sidewalk, despite the heedless woman sitting naked upstairs—or was the caution habitual, something to do with this man's life?

"Do you speak English?" she asked.

He shook his head, unsmiling.

"You're from the States," he said, in German again. "American girl."

Caroline nodded.

He whistled tunelessly under his breath, eyes roving. As she followed his gaze in the mirror over the bar, she realized he was watching the helmeted police.

"Do you know a man named Mahmoud Sharif?"

The whistling died away, and his eyes slid back to her face. "Mahmoud? Why do you want Mahmoud?"

"You know him?"

He turned away from her without a word and disappeared through a doorway to the left of the bar. Caroline found the courage to lift her beer. After her first sip, she gained confidence. After the second, an older and much larger man was standing where the bartender had been.

"You're the lady who asked about Mahmoud."

This time, the words were in English.

"Yes. Do you know him?"

"Do you?" The man was white-haired, with an enormous mustache curling up at the tips and muddy brown eyes swimming in false tears. *"I weep for you," the walrus said: "I deeply sympathize."* He wore a dingy shirt with a soiled collar. A brown apron spattered with grease. Was he a short-order cook or the café owner?

Caroline sat a little straighter and set the beer glass down in front of her. "Mahmoud and I have a friend in common. This friend asked to be remembered to Mahmoud."

The man regarded her steadily, as though her next words were preordained. And so she said them.

"Could I leave a message?"

"A note, perhaps?"

"That would be fine."

Without taking his eyes from her face, the Walrus pulled a pad of paper from the pocket of his apron and a pen from behind his ear. "There. You write it, I'll see that he gets it."

"When?"

He shrugged.

"If time were unimportant, I could find Mahmoud myself tomorrow."

"When time is important, it is also very expensive," the Walrus said.

She handed him a five-hundred-mark note.

He pocketed it without a glance. "I will deliver your message tonight."

Caroline wrote:

I am Michael O'Shaughnessy's cousin from London. I have come in search of him on urgent family business. Michael has told me that you know where he may be found. I will be waiting in Alexanderplatz by the base of the television tower tomorrow morning at 8:00.

She signed the name *Jane Hathaway*. Her backstopped Agency identity.

She folded the piece of paper precisely in two and handed it to the Walrus. He tucked it without comment into the capacious apron pocket and vanished through the darkened doorway. In an instant, the younger man had reappeared, his face impassive, his eyes still roaming over the café.

She left the Radeburger unfinished on the counter.

Part III

THURSDAY, NOVEMBER 11

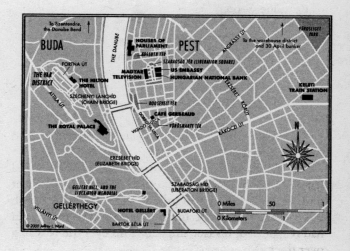

ONE

Budapest, 3:14 A.M.

THE AMERICAN VICE PRESIDENT had seen enough of 30 April's hangouts to recognize a legitimate operational base. The one in Budapest was no improvised effort, no apartment borrowed from a cast-off lover. This was a nerve center, Sophie knew, entirely windowless, possibly underground. It had a private garage with cameras and infrared detection devices mounted almost invisibly above the doors; it had comfortable furniture, beds, showers, a sound system, a supply of food and clothing, a weapons arsenal, and an impenetrable security cordon ensuring that a klaxon would sound throughout the complex if she attempted escape.

With the prison came a certain amount of freedom. She was allowed to move about her bedroom and bath—nothing in either room could be used to effect escape or suicide. She lay on the bed and stretched her hands toward the ceiling. And felt the surface pressing down. In such a place it was impossible to guess the hour of day. Whether it was raining out or not. Whether the world believed she was already dead.

"You will be comfortable?" Jozsef asked her anxiously. The bruises under his eyes were painful to see. Sophie's fever had abated; she was weak, she ached for sleep, but her thoughts no longer rippled like silk through a liquid brain.

"Comfortable enough," she answered.

He smiled—the swift, tentative look she'd come to recognize—and turned away. "I will bring you breakfast in a little while. Not like in Bratislava. Real food. And coffee."

There was the sound of running water, an oddity in the muffled underground atmosphere; it seemed to come from within the wall. And something else: a voice. She turned.

"Michael," Jozsef explained simply. "He talks to himself in the shower. Your bathroom is next to his."

Sophie nodded. "I think I may shower myself." How long had it been? Two, three days? How long since the explosion in the square? Was anyone in the United States doing *anything*?

"If you need me, press the button." Jozsef pointed to a panel near the bed. "The black one, not the red. The black is an intercom, and you can ask for help. Or for a book. Whatever you need."

"A newspaper would be nice."

The boy hesitated. "That is a little difficult."

Because it would tell her too much? Or because one of the men would have to leave the compound to buy it?

Jozsef took a remote control from his pocket. The door to her room slid back, then slid shut behind him. She was entombed.

She forced herself to move and went into the bathroom. Michael was still talking. She sat down on the toilet seat and leaned her head against the tiled wall.

It was never possible that we would let her go, Jozsef's voice whispered in her brain.

The woman named Olga and her child were dead. With them had died Sophie's final hope.

She had seen my father's face.

Sophie, too, had seen Krucevic. She could describe him and his men. Whatever the dance of negotiation that went on above her head—whatever Jack Bigelow was prepared to do or say—she would never be released.

And so the knot of grief like a clenched fist. Grief for the unknown woman and her daughter, of course, but grief, too, for the stupid hope that had sustained her.

She had fabricated a dream—that Michael could be trusted, that he was a traitor buried deep in the Krucevic camp. She knew now that he was as brutal as the man he served.

He was still talking to himself on the other side of the bathroom wall. Sophie closed her eyes and listened.

———

Caroline awoke, as she always did when adjusting to European time, in the middle of the night. She lay in the sterile darkness of the hotel room and listened to the whoosh of an elevator shaft, the rumble of ice from a machine in the corridor. She was twenty-three floors above the streets of Berlin; she might have been anywhere. She had laid down the first planks in a trap meant for her husband, without knowing exactly what to do if he happened to fall into it. She had exhibited herself to television networks; she had asked the Walrus to contact Mahmoud Sharif. She had set a process in motion; and for an instant, alone in the hotel room dark, she felt a shaft of panic. What if that process spun out of control? What if Eric came headlong when she least expected him?

As though she had willed it, the telephone rang at her bedside.

She groped for the receiver.

"You're a difficult woman to find."

She could not speak. Then her pulse, which seemed to have stopped for an instant, throbbed wickedly through her veins.

"This is the fifth hotel I've called," Eric said, "and it's not easy for me to use a phone."

She sat up. "Jesus God, where are you?"

"In the bathroom. Hear the water?" He must have held the cell phone up to a shower head; she had the dizzying sensation of being run through the wash. "I have a habit of humming to myself in here. It masks a host of ills. Monologues, tirades, illicit phone calls. Particularly at three A.M., when everyone else is asleep."

"Eric, where the *hell* have you been for the past two years?"

"Two years, six months, and thirteen days, Mad Dog. I think you know. I've been with him. The guy you're looking for. And he's been all over the map."

"Christ," she breathed. "You sure do take this shit in stride."

"I killed a child today, Mad Dog."

Caroline tightened her grip on the receiver.

"She was six years old. Her name was Annicka. She was frightened and alone and I took her into the back room and comforted her. I rocked her in my arms and sang a song in English she could never have understood."

"Where's Sophie Payne, Eric?"

"I told her that everything was going to be all right, that she would see her mama soon."

"Don't tell me this. I don't want to *hear* this."

"And while she buried her face in my shoulder and sobbed, I put a silencer to her temple and I pulled the trigger."

"You should have put it to your own head first."

"I considered that."

Anguish and love and rage welled up in Caroline's throat, choking the words she might have said.

"Welcome to Berlin, Mad Dog." He sounded faintly amused—affectionate, even—but it was the voice of a stranger in Eric's mouth. Dare Atwood had miscalculated. She had sent Caroline out to bring the rogue agent home—but Caroline could not tempt Eric any longer.

"How did this happen to us?" she whispered.

"I imagine we chose it."

"Bullshit," she retorted. "*You* chose, and the rest of us trailed along—me, Sophie Payne, that little girl you shot to death. Why, Eric? Why not be a hero for once and turn the gun on Krucevic?"

"Because getting him for the kidnapping of Sophie Payne isn't enough, Mad Dog." His voice had dropped to a whisper, difficult to pick out against the background of rushing water. "I want to get him for everything. I want the plans, the network, the proof of complicity at the highest levels. I want Fritz Voekl's balls in a sling."

Fritz Voekl?

"And how many more children will you kill?" For an instant, she expected him to hang up. Nothing but the sluice of water pouring over the damned.

"Her mother was already dead," he told her. "And Annicka could describe Krucevic if anyone asked. He could not allow her to live."

"Then let him pull the fucking trigger."

"It was me or Otto. I couldn't put Annicka into Otto's hands."

"Eric, tell me where you are."

"Get out of this, Mad Dog. While you still can."

"Eric—"

But he was gone.

———

After that, she didn't pretend to sleep. She turned on all the lights, even the ones in the bathroom, and sat propped in bed with the covers pulled up to her armpits, shivering uncontrollably.

How many people had Eric murdered? Not terrorists, whom she could dismiss as so many bodies in a war—but how many men and women? How many little girls? She'd thought of the dead in Pariser Platz as blood on Mlan Krucevic's hands, not her husband's. She knew now that she had been comforting herself with a lie.

She reached for the phone at her bedside and punched in an Agency number. He answered on the first ring.

She imagined him sitting there, silk tie loosened, hand to his salt-and-pepper brow. There would be beads of sweat breaking out on his forehead, the result of malaria endemic in his bloodstream. It would be dinnertime in Virginia. He'd be thinking of Kentucky bourbon, neat. She closed her eyes in relief.

"Hey, Scottie."

"Caroline." A glance at his Rolex, swiftly calculating the time difference.

"I just heard from our fair-haired boy."

"How?" He was instantly alert.

"Phone call."

"Change your hotel, Carrie, and watch your back. Did you get his location?"

"Are you kidding? He wasn't calling on business. He'd just killed a child and needed to justify it."

"If he calls back—"

"*Scottie,*" she interrupted, as though he couldn't possibly have understood the terrible thing she had just said. "Scottie, have you ever killed anyone?"

"Aside from Athens, I've never even carried a gun. Caroline, did you ask him how our missing friend was doing? Did he say anything that might help us find her?"

"No. He shot the breeze and told me to go home."

There was a creak as Scottie shifted in his desk chair. "He gave you nothing."

"Squat," Caroline agreed. "But he'll make contact again. He'll have to. I'll make myself a nuisance."

"The call was a warning, Caroline. Your next contact could be a bullet in the brain."

"Scottie," she cried. "How did this man we both love turn out to be someone we never even knew? Can you tell me that? Have you got a *clue*?"

"Carrie, remember the open line," Scottie urged her softly.

She drew a shuddering breath and raked her fingers through her hair.

"This isn't your fault," he said. "It's not my fault. Neither of us can fix it. So concentrate on what you *can* fix. Okay?"

"It's part of the training," she said through her teeth. "You tell these guys that working for the enemy is the ultimate betrayal—of their friends, their country, themselves. And at the same time, their *job* is to convince *other* people to do exactly that: to sell out everything that matters."

"The line, Caroline," Scottie repeated.

"Who can live with that kind of paradox? No wonder people go nuts."

"It's the nature of the game." His reproof was like a slap. "Do as we say, not as we do. Cynics handle it best—or idealists. People who can live with an inherent contradiction. The others quit after their second tours. Or drink heavily and stay."

"So which was our fair-haired boy? Cynic? Or idealist?"

"He's out there murdering children, Caroline."

The truth, inexorable. But she tried one last time.

"Let's say he wants the Big Man. And all the marbles. To do that, he'd have to close his eyes to a certain amount of evil. But that wouldn't necessarily mean that he was evil *himself,* would it?"

"The ends justify the means? I have heard that sentiment so many times in my life, Caroline, and it still sounds infinitely attractive. And false. We saw the means in Berlin two days ago. No ends justify so much spilling of blood."

Now who had forgotten the open line?

"He *wants* you to feel sorry for him. He'll use that against you. *He has no right,* Carrie. He cut you out of his life, remember? He cut both of us out. And I for one don't give a shit about his reasons."

But Caroline *did.* Caroline wanted to know *why,* more than anything in the world. As though knowing the reasons for deception and betrayal might negate the horror of what had happened, might put her life back into the neat little box in which she had lived. Bitterness flooded her mouth.

"Are you telling me to avoid all contact with him?"

"Have all the contact you like. Do drinks. Do dinner. Take a walk among the autumn leaves. But if our golden boy refuses to give up the goods—our missing friend, in perfect condition—then shut him down, Caroline. Everything else is just crap. Understood?"

All too well.

"Now get some sleep."

"Thanks, Scottie," she told the dead line. Then she cradled the receiver and sank back against her pillows. Somewhere in Central Europe, Eric was stepping out of a shower. Cynic or idealist? Did the answer matter anymore?

She thrust back the covers. To find Sophie Payne, she would first have to find Eric. And if luck was with her, Mahmoud Sharif would know exactly where he was.

TWO

Berlin, 7:30 A.M.

CAROLINE WORE BLACK KNIT LEGGINGS and a black tunic for the Palestinian bomb maker. A black swing coat that skimmed above her knees. Black cashmere gloves and a red beret perched on her bobbed dark hair. The hair was a wig and it went with her back-stopped identity, the passport in the name of Jane Hathaway she had brought from Langley. She wore red lipstick to match the beret, and a pair of black Chanel sunglasses.

Eric's voice murmured with the sound of tap water in her ear, relentless, caressing, the voice of conscience and nightmare. All that he had said looped endlessly in her mind, a refrain she could not banish. He stood behind her as she drew on her clothes; he lifted her hair from the nape of her neck. She moved now under the glare of his gaze—and wondered briefly who had set the trap for whom.

He called me in the night. He knows where I am. Because Sharif already got to him? Because he saw my face on a newscaster's screen? Eric. That little girl. Jesus, Eric.

Her fingers trembled as she applied her makeup; trembled with anger and longing. At this rate, she'd jump sky-high when Sharif tapped on her shoulder.

She briefly considered carrying her snub-nosed Walther TPH in a thigh holster concealed by the swing coat, then rejected the idea. Palestinian bomb makers might consent to meet with the anxious cousin of an underworld acquaintance, but they would be certain to search her thoroughly first. Jane Hathaway spent her days banking in London; she was unlikely to carry a piece with her on holiday.

The concierge at the front desk looked at her blankly as she passed. Caroline pushed jauntily through the revolving door, as though she had nothing more than shopping on her mind.

She purchased the *Herald Tribune* at a sidewalk kiosk and scanned the headlines as she walked. Sophie Payne had not been found. The U-Bahn in Potsdamer Platz was tempting—she could read as she rode—but the distance was short and the morning air, the *Berliner luft*, a gift to the sleep-deprived. She strode east along Leipzigerstrasse and then north along Grunerstrasse, marveling at the new life springing up amid the careworn avenues of the Mitte district. And rising before her as she walked, more alien with every step, was the Communist television tower's steel needle, like a hypodermic piercing the sky. *A hypodermic.* Everything reminded her of Sophie Payne.

Alexanderplatz, where Prussian and Russian troops had once drilled to defeat Napoleon; where the streetcar lines of the Bismarck era converged in raucous confusion; where prostitutes and lorry drivers and clerks convened in a hundred different bars, until the Allied bombs of 1943 leveled the square and, two years later, the Soviets marched in to "liberate" the city. It was a

vast and chilly emptiness still, several football fields in
size. Grunerstrasse plunged beneath it, to emerge on the
other side as Neue Königstrasse; there were very few
approaches by car. He would have to walk up to her, or
drive by to the northeast, on Karl-Marx-Allee. She took
up a position at the television tower's base, facing the
Allee, and proceeded to study her newspaper. It was
hard on eight o'clock.

Standing there in the middle of the drab morning,
Caroline fought back a persistent sense of the ridiculous.
If Mahmoud Sharif could even remember the name of
Michael O'Shaughnessy from a telephone call made
months before, he was unlikely to risk his neck because
of it. Why drive out early in the morning for the sake of
a woman he had never seen? She turned over the front
section of the *Herald Tribune* (the same edition Mlan
Krucevic had placed under Sophie Payne's chin the previous day) and found a picture of herself, snapped in
Pariser Platz by an enterprising news photographer. The
Volksturm guard she had confronted was holding his
truncheon high, and Caroline's mouth was open in a
scream. She stared at the image, fascinated. She had
never seen herself in newsprint before. Was it this,
rather than the television footage, that had triggered
Eric's phone call?

At the thought of him, her mind winced and leapt
away.

A dirty white Trabant—a pitiful putt-putt the size of a
golf cart—drove slowly past on Karl-Marx-Allee. Caroline's
eyes flicked up, considered it, then looked down at her paper. It was for Sharif to broach the question.

Eight-fourteen. More cars passed. She'd read the
news that mattered, and was killing time with feature
stories. The white Trabant again, traveling in the oppo-

site direction. Only one person behind the wheel, too distant to be clearly seen.

"I think that perhaps you are Ms. Jane Hathaway," said a quiet voice at her shoulder.

Caroline did not jump. She folded her newspaper deliberately and tucked it under her arm.

He was a compact and neat person in a black leather jacket and tweed pants. Dark skin, eyes the color of espresso, black brows and mustache.

"I am," she said. "Are you Mahmoud Sharif?"

"Please come with me," he said by way of answer.

When she hesitated, a second man materialized behind her. He placed a persuasive hand on her elbow.

"Very well," she said coolly, and went without a backward glance.

They bundled her into a steel gray Mercedes, Caroline in the middle of the backseat with a man on either side. A third man drove. She felt a moment of panic, a wave of claustrophobia. She subdued it with effort. It would not do to betray a fit of nerves. She was merely a friend's cousin.

The first man who had approached her drew a length of white cloth from his pocket.

"It is not permitted to see where you are going. I must beg to cover your eyes."

If they were kidnapping her, Caroline thought, they would hardly have been so polite. They would have shoved a wad of cotton in her mouth and forced her head down to her knees—if they hadn't stowed her in the trunk first.

She removed her sunglasses and placed them in her purse. Then she inclined her beret toward her escort, praying that her wig was secure. The hands came up behind her head, a ceremonial gesture. And he covered her eyes.

At first they drove at what seemed a normal pace, darting in and out of Berlin traffic with the occasional pause for a right or left turn. Then Caroline heard a few words flung back from the front seat, something brief and explosive in Arabic. The driver was swearing. Her companion's fingers tightened on her arm.

"Who should be following, Jane Hathaway?"

"Following *me*? No one. I know no one in Berlin."

The Mercedes lurched forward, picking up speed, and swerved violently to the left. Caroline slid against the man beside her, and he grunted.

"There is a white Trabant behind us. My friend who is driving is certain it has been behind us some time. Who do you know with a white Trabant?"

"No one. I'm a stranger here. But if it's a Trabant, it won't be behind you long. They've got no power."

"That is not the point," the man said sternly. "We cannot take you to Sharif if we do not know who is following. You are with the police, perhaps?"

"Of course not! I told you. I'm from London. I don't know anybody in Germany. Maybe it's one of *your* friends."

He did not reply. The car swerved again, accelerated, made a series of abrupt turns.

Wally. Plausible, sympathetic, endearing Wally. Had he set her up with the story about Sharif at the Tacheles and then watched to see what she'd do?

Or was it someone else from the station—someone deputed by Dare Atwood, perhaps, to keep tabs on her?

Dare knew what Jane Hathaway looked like.

When you're under surveillance, Mad Dog, said Eric's voice in her mind, *never, never let your tail know you see him. If you do, he'll suspect you're worth following.*

But Sharif's men had never learned Eric's lessons.

Bore him to tears. Change your plans if necessary. Abort the meeting or the dead drop or the safe-house visit. And when you lose him, do it so casually he never sees it coming. Never with a high-speed car chase through a crowded city, where the cops might decide to get involved.

As the Palestinians were doing now.

But no cops were interested in a gray Mercedes careening through eastern Berlin. All the cops in the city, it seemed, were standing guard around the rubble of the Brandenburg Gate.

—————

Fingers fumbled at the cloth around her eyes. "You may get out now, Jane Hathaway."

He was already standing at the open car door, one hand politely extended. She placed her own within it and allowed him to help her out of the car. Arab courtesy, she thought. There would probably be a plate of dates and figs in the room beyond.

What she found, however, was a space as deliberately innocuous as an Agency safe house. Whatever their problem with mobile surveillance, the Palestinians had absorbed some form of tradecraft.

Three windows, blinds drawn. One couch, quite characterless, and two armchairs at correct angles beside it. A coffee table with an ashtray in the event that she smoked. Beyond this, a small cubicle that was probably a bathroom.

No family photographs, no magazines with address labels, no books that might reveal a personal taste. No telephone. No television. She was certain she would find the windows and front door locked.

She took off her coat and threw it over a chair. "Which of you is Sharif?"

The tidy man in the leather jacket smiled slightly. "None of us, Jane Hathaway. You may call me Akbar."

The names of the other two were not for her keeping, it seemed.

"How did you hear of this . . . Mahmoud Sharif?" Akbar asked her.

She frowned, as though puzzled. "From my cousin Michael, of course. Michael O'Shaughnessy. He's done some favors for Sharif in the past."

"Sharif is beholden only to Allah," he replied.

"Then perhaps the obligation was my cousin's," Caroline suggested graciously. "But Michael told me that if I ever needed to reach him, Mahmoud was the one man in Europe who would know where he was."

Akbar perched on the arm of the sofa and studied Caroline. She continued to stand, her back to the wall and her eyes on the door.

"Why is this Michael so difficult to find?" he asked.

"Aren't most of Mahmoud's friends?"

"But no." He spread his arms out wide to include the silent pair ranged behind him. "We are as you see. Present when you required us. Without even the demand of a proof or a demonstration of good faith."

"Other than the little matter of a blindfold," Caroline pointed out.

His expression did not change. "Why do you wish to see Mahmoud?"

"I told you. I need to find my cousin. His father has just died. There was no way to contact Michael, and I need to speak to him about the family."

"Perhaps a message could be passed."

"Perhaps. But I don't think that's for you to say, Akbar. Unless you really are Sharif."

Mirth flooded the dark eyes. It was gone before Caroline had a chance to interpret it.

"And now I must beg to examine the contents of your purse, Jane Hathaway."

It was a large black leather shoulder bag in the shape of a backpack. It fairly screamed Knightsbridge. She handed it to him wordlessly and sank down onto the couch.

He carried the purse to the bare table and shook out its contents. Caroline could have recited them in her sleep.

The sunglasses, on top.

A red leather wallet, with about one hundred and fifty-three marks in bills and small change, a Visa card, a Harrods credit card, a British driver's license, and a long-distance calling card.

A picture of Eric from Nicosia.

A U.S. passport with the usual navy blue cover, bearing the name of Jane Hathaway and an address in London. The picture had been taken at the Agency; it was a good likeness, despite the wig.

Three Chanel lipsticks, all of them well used.

A pen and pencil in a case.

A matchbook from last night's bar at the Tacheles.

A cell phone.

A small hairbrush, with several black hairs from the wig wound around its bristles.

A few phone numbers (London exchange) and jottings on crinkled slips of paper, some of them receipts from Jane's favorite pub in Hampstead.

"And what is this?" Akbar inquired, his index finger thrust through an olive green metal ring. He held it up and twirled it slightly around his knuckle. A single rod about an inch long swung from its middle.

"Don't you know?" Caroline asked him blandly. "It's a grenade pin."

The black brows lifted. "A curious item for a lady's purse, surely?"

Caroline smiled. "My cousin Michael gave it to me years ago. He was a Green Beret."

Akbar twirled the pin once more around his finger, thoughtfully this time, then set it down beside the lipsticks. "Saleh will remain with you, Jane Hathaway. I shall go for a time and return. You must be patient. Sharif is a busy man."

He thrust her things back into the bag and, with a curt bow, turned for the door.

THREE

Budapest, 9 A.M.

"HOW ARE YOU FEELING THIS MORNING, Mrs. Payne?"

He always spoke to her in English, although the others used German. Sophie suspected that he thought her unworthy of his adored tongue. The electronic door had slid back so noiselessly that she had had no warning. He leaned there against the jamb with a newspaper in his hand. She sat up in bed and stared at him.

Sophie had not been sleeping. She had been studying the ceiling in an effort to detect whether it had any stains on its surface, and if so, whether they would start to move. This might, she thought, be an indication of the recurrence of her illness. But for all her vigilance, the effects of anthrax would probably surprise her. As had Krucevic.

"Considering the past twelve hours," she said in answer to his question, "I'm fine." It was a patent lie, but she had no intention of rewarding him with the truth.

The mad surge for the door, her head bound in a blanket, her mouth stuffed with somebody's socks, her mind screaming with vivid, shaming panic. An arm belted around her waist. The jolting dash down echoing stairs. No one speaking, the sensation of cold and wet in the pelting rain. The child lying murdered on her mother's bed.

Sophie was placed on the floor of a truck between Otto and Michael, sightless and mute, with a raging desire to weep burning in her nostrils. She suppressed it viciously, willing the grief to turn to hatred, a passion that would sustain rather than destroy her.

"You have remarkable resilience," Krucevic said now.

"It's one of the great American secrets. We endure. Jack Bigelow has resilience, too. I wonder if he has more than you."

Krucevic smiled. "If you're suggesting this is a test of wills, Mrs. Payne, I'm afraid you romanticize the matter. This is not an affair of honor between two gentlemen, with yourself as the prize. Neither of us values you that much."

"I'm not concerned about myself. Except inasmuch as my life or death affects the fate of my nation."

"How admirable. And how difficult to believe. Do I detect a trace of hypocrisy, Mrs. Payne? Is it so important to consider yourself a martyr? I suppose it lends a certain style to death. If one cares about such things."

He threw her the phrases the way another man might toss potato chips to a dog, his mind entirely on other matters. The tension that had turned him rigid in Bratislava was gone; he seemed at ease, at home with himself, impervious to concern. Sophie fought with despair. If Krucevic could stand in her door without a care in the world, events must be turning his way.

"What are you really after?" she asked.

"Why should I tell you, Mrs. Payne?"

"Because when you get what you want, you'll kill me. And before I die, I'd like to know why."

He studied her. "Have you so little faith in your government? Jack should have saved his time and money. That failed raid will have cost him something in respect."

"What raid?" she asked sharply.

"The one that drove us out of Bratislava last night. Drove us, I might add, in a U.S. government–operated mobile listening post. Otto killed the agents and shot up their electronics before we loaded you in the back." He pushed himself away from the wall and walked toward her. "Your people found you, Mrs. Payne. And no doubt they meant to rescue you. But in a lamentably half-assed manner. I had expected better of Mr. Bigelow. A Huey or two, at least, on the building's roof. But no."

That accounted for his air of superiority. He had outwitted the U.S. government. Sophie bit back disappointment and thought, *They're on my trail. They'll get him soon.*

"So let's take it as a given that I won't be rescued. Tell me what you're up to. Is it revenge? For the NATO air strikes in '99?"

"The allied bombs destroyed Belgrade," Krucevic said indifferently. "I despise Belgrade as much as the United States. I'm a Croat, Mrs. Payne, although I don't expect you to comprehend the significance of that fact."

"You are far more than a Croat, Mlan Krucevic. You are an unreconstructed Ustashe fighter. You're a throwback to the fascist midnight of 1939. We'll agree that you enjoyed seeing the Serbian republic devastated by war. That you spared no tears for the Kosovar dead. A dozen mass graves here or there mean nothing to you. So what's the point? Why strike out against the U.S.?"

He sat down on the bed next to her. She refused to flinch.

"I know that you see me as a Croat nationalist, Mrs. Payne. That is an understandable mistake. I fought for my fellow people in Bosnia because if I had not, the Serbs and the Muslims would have overwhelmed them and the mass graves you speak of would have held only Croats." He lifted his hand and waved it gently, in farewell to the past. "That is done. Bosnia is a nation torn in three. The rifts will never heal. What the 30 April Organization attempts to ensure, Mrs. Payne, is that the plight of the Balkans will never become the plight of Europe."

Viewed this closely, the scar at his temple revealed itself as the work of a bullet. Someone had once tried to kill him. "You're working for *peace*?" Sophie asked sarcastically. "That's why you bombed the Brandenburg and kidnapped me?"

"I am working to eradicate a cancer," he replied impatiently. "Do you know that is the most common Serb image applied to ethnic Albanians? I would go further and apply it to the entire Islamic world. Adherents of the Muslim faith are the most ignorant and uncultured peoples in existence. They bring strife, fanaticism, darkness, and violence wherever they breed. And they breed, Mrs. Payne, as no people has ever bred before. Their children are their deadliest weapon. The numbers are against the Aryan peoples of the West, Mrs. Payne. You must know that. It is happening in your own country. The people of northern Europe have two or three children, while your blacks and Hispanics have a dozen each. In time, democracy will be overwhelmed in their cesspool."

He gazed at her piercingly, the brown eyes devoid of all emotion.

"This is the great Achilles' heel of the American elite. You invite the mongrels of the world to attend your universities and eat at your exclusive tables. Well, Mrs. Payne, the mongrels of the world will savage the hand that feeds them. I do not intend to let that happen in Europe."

"I don't understand," Sophie said. "How does holding me hostage affect the population of Europe?"

"It buys me time. A decent interval without U.S. or NATO intervention."

"Intervention in what?"

"The reconquest of an entire continent," he said baldly, "without armies, warfare, or trials in The Hague. And then I will set about the process of cleansing."

"The world will never allow another Final Solution. If the air strikes against Belgrade taught you nothing else, they should have taught you that."

He shrugged. "Milosevic lacked finesse. It was not his fault—he's a crafty manipulator, a ruthless executive, but his tools were limited. So were Adolf Hitler's, Mrs. Payne. Did you know that Hitler wasted valuable time throughout the first years of the war in an effort to perfect his nerve gas? Like all great masters of innovation, we stand on the shoulders of those who came before. We intend to do it right."

"You mean, you and the four guys in the other room?"

She had succeeded in nettling him; the dark eyes narrowed with malice.

"Do you think the strength of the Aryan nation sprang forth only at Hitler's command?" he barked. "It has always been there. It always will be. And heroes emerge from time to time to lead the fight for freedom."

It was then that Sophie finally understood the passion

behind Krucevic's careful facade, the inferno beneath his extraordinary self-possession. Like a Crusader from a vanished age, he had God and Destiny on his side. And at once she was afraid—deeply and coldly afraid—of what would eventually happen to her. She could expect no mercy from this man. To survive, she would have to destroy him on his own ground.

How? For the love of God, how?

"Do you know why the Serbs killed the Kosovars and drove them out of their kingdom?" he asked her.

" 'Their kingdom'?" Even if she could somehow seize a gun and figure out how to fire it, it was not enough to kill him. She had to put an end to whatever her abduction had unleashed. *How?*

"Because the Serbs have never forgotten that the invading Turkish hordes slaughtered their men on the Field of Black Birds at the battle of Kosovo."

"That was in the fourteenth century," Sophie said distractedly.

"In 1389, to be precise, and for more than six hundred years, that Serb defeat has been Serbia's most hallowed holiday. In the United States, you celebrate victory. You parade down your village streets on the Fourth of July wrapped in your American flag. Serbs have never known what victory is. They sanctify the hour of their worst humiliation. What happened recently in Kosovo—the Serb butchering of ethnic Albanians— was a vengeance six hundred years in the making."

"Glorify it any way you like," she retorted, "but it was still an unprovoked atrocity on a massive scale." *To fight him is useless; it'll only get me killed.* There were four men she knew of—perhaps more—in the compound alone, men who were armed and ruthless. *And then there's Jozsef . . . I can't leave Jozsef alone.* But were all four of the other terrorists against her? What if Michael could be persuaded to help?

"The Serb cleansing of Kosovo was the attempt by one people to eradicate another," Krucevic said, unperturbed, "and in my opinion, it was unforgivably crude."

"I'm glad to hear it." *Even with Michael's help—if I can get Michael's help—an escape won't put an end to Krucevic's plans. It's not enough to kill him and run. He has to be held accountable for the Brandenburg Gate. I owe Nell Forsyte that much.*

"I am trained as a biologist, Mrs. Payne," he confided with an air of frankness. "I tend to conceptualize in medical terms."

"Really," she replied noncommittally. *What is he talking about?*

And then she remembered the fear. The cold stink of anxiety, of fatal error, that she'd detected in him when her fever soared. Krucevic, the biologist, had been surprised by the recurrence. It had frightened him. *Why? My survival is immaterial to him. So he must be afraid for his son.*

She snatched at the thought, she hid it deep in a closet in her mind. She had found it. Krucevic's one vulnerability. *Jozsef.*

"If you discover that a cancer is multiplying in your body," he went on, "if you see that the sickened cells are destroying the healthy ones, you have two choices. You can cut off the limb where the cancer feeds, and bury it deep in the ground. Or you can systemically poison the cells within and negate their ability to multiply." He held up his hands like a successful magician. His own brilliance, the rabbit in his hat. "With patience and subtlety, Mrs. Payne, the sick cells will die. The healthy will prevail. Your body will be cancer free."

Mute, she stared at him. What he had just said was important, she knew. It was strategy, not just politics. He had told her exactly what he meant to do. He had handed her 30 April's operational agenda. But the sense of it eluded her, like a Rubik's Cube that failed to turn.

He reached his right hand to her cheek. Instinctively, she jerked away from him. The hand slid down to her neck and gripped it cruelly. His other palm caressed her forehead. "I am checking you for fever, Mrs. Payne."

"I'm fine." She was rigid under his hands. "Don't trouble yourself."

"You lie. Already you feel less well than you did when our conversation began. In a little while, you will feel even worse. That is exactly as it should be."

He rose and moved to the door. She followed him with her eyes. Was he bluffing? Or was her mind about to melt with fever?

"I want our friend Jack Bigelow to see the consequences of his ill-advised raid," Krucevic told her. "A videotape, I think, is in order. We'll wait a few hours while the bacillus gains in strength."

FOUR
Berlin, 9:27 A.M.

CAROLINE SPENT FORTY-TWO MINUTES in the Palestinian safe house while the smoke of Saleh's Turkish cigarettes gradually clouded the room. She was puzzled by the fact of tobacco—wasn't it blasphemous for a follower of Islam to use it?—but Arab culture wasn't her strong suit. Maybe the prohibition centered on alcohol. Or maybe a fellow dedicated to the jihad was immune from the restrictions applied to ordinary mortals. Regardless, the smoke was remarkably pungent. She would have to send her clothes to be cleaned before she checked out of the Hyatt.

If she made it back alive.

Saleh kept a curious sort of handgun on the table in front of him, with a free-floating barrel and an ergonomic handgrip. A Hammerli, Caroline guessed. It probably had electronic trigger action, variably weighted. Which meant it could fire if Saleh so much as grazed the table leg. A two-thousand-dollar gun in a world of five-hundred-dollar competition. The carpentry business had been very good to Mahmoud Sharif.

Saleh caught her assessing his piece. He held her gaze and did not blink. A garden-variety banker such as Jane Hathaway should look intimidated, Caroline thought— not as though she were calculating the speed of his draw. She folded her arms protectively across her chest and hunched slightly as she paced. No point in getting cocky.

She was expected at the Interior Ministry in less than an hour. When she failed to show up, Wally might be worried. Unless it was he who had tailed her from Alexanderplatz in the white Trabant.

What would Mahmoud Sharif do if he suspected she was not who she claimed? Was he likely to torture a woman? Or just shoot her in the back of the head and dump her body where no one would look for it?

Caroline glanced again at Saleh. He was studying her with unconcealed interest, eyes narrowed against the smoke.

The front door—the one she had supposed locked— swung back on silent hinges. Akbar stood there, his face devoid of expression. He took a step back, deferential now.

The man who entered was taller than the others by a good foot and broad in the shoulder, with glittering black eyes and a clean-shaven face. His nose was so sharply hooked it might almost have been a caricature, and an angry red scar bisected his right cheek—the trail of shrapnel, Caroline thought. He wore black jeans and black leather boots and a dress shirt of raw silk. He smelled, ever so faintly, of freshly sawn wood. She imagined his children, running to greet him at the end of the day and being lifted high on a cedar-scented shoulder. Wood chips in his hair. She looked instinctively at his hands. Fine-boned, sensitive, adept at the manipulation of small parts. Had he constructed the device that brought down MedAir 901? Made floating candy wrappers of all those children high above the Adriatic?

"Miss Jane Hathaway," he said, and inclined his head. "I am Mahmoud Sharif. You wished to speak to me."

What was the protocol? Should she extend her hand? Would he take it if she did? She nodded back at him instead. "I appreciate your willingness to see me. I know you are a busy man."

"For the cousin of my friend Michael I would do much," Sharif said impassively, and gestured toward the sofa.

Caroline sat down. Sharif took one of the armchairs; Akbar, who still stood by the door, snapped his fingers. Saleh crushed out his cigarette and joined him. And that quickly, she was alone with Mahmoud Sharif and the gun his man had left on the table before her.

It occurred to Caroline that there were at least a thousand questions Scottie Sorensen would have liked Sharif to answer, but posing a single one of them would destroy the perilous balance of this meeting.

"Your false passport is excellent, Miss Hathaway, and the details that support it rather extraordinary."

She cocked her head and studied him as though she could not quite follow his meaning.

"I particularly admired the pub receipts from Notting Hill Gate, and the British charwoman who answered the phone in what was supposed to be Hampstead," he continued. "I studied in England many years ago; I could not have told your housekeeper from a native.

But then, your organization has vast resources, does it not?"

Caroline frowned. "I'm not sure I understand. Is there a problem with my passport?"

"None at all," Sharif assured her with a gleam of amusement in his eyes. "And for that I commend you. A great number of such documents pass through my fingers, you understand, and rarely have I seen one so accomplished. Unless, perhaps, it was Michael's."

He waited for her reaction.

"This is all very entertaining," she said. "The blind-fold, the gun on the table, the cool-your-heels-in-the-back-parlor-while-I-run-your-numbers treatment. But I have an appointment in less than an hour, Mr. Sharif, and I'd appreciate some candor."

"Candor," he repeated. The gleam of amusement had vanished. "And would your appointment happen to be with the CIA?"

"If I thought *they* knew where Michael was, I wouldn't be *here*."

"I, too, had hoped for candor, Miss Hathaway. But you have not even trusted me with your true name. I have no inclination to help you. Indeed, I waste my time here." He got to his feet.

She decided to take a risk. "I don't think you even know where Michael is, Sharif."

"Michael O'Shaughnessy does not exist, Miss Hathaway. We both know that. Therefore he can never have possessed a cousin. *Now* tell me why I should help you."

"I'm here because Michael's father has died!" she burst out. "*Someone* has to tell him. I'm the only one in the family he still trusts."

"I detest this sort of subterfuge, Miss Hathaway. It is demeaning to us both."

She was suddenly at a standstill. *When you don't know what to say,* Eric whispered in her ear, *don't say anything at all.* Impulsively, she decided to ignore him.

"He's in trouble, Sharif."

The man actually laughed. "Aren't we all?"

"This time he could die."

"But then, he's done that before." Sharif's dark eyes flicked shrewdly up to her own. He took a small silver knife from his pocket and began to pare his fingernails. "Are you in love with him?" Contempt in the words.

"Not anymore."

He set the knife down. "I know the man you are looking for. I even know his real name. I also know that he was once employed by the CIA and that they fabricated the papers he is presently using. *Your* papers, Miss Hathaway, are remarkably similar." The eyes raked over her. "So if you are not in love with him—if that is not why you wish to see him—then I am forced to conclude that Michael is in difficulties with his government. And that you have been sent to me in the hope of finding him."

"Now I think it is I who waste my time." Caroline reached for the handbag he had left on the table.

Sharif gripped her wrist. "I have not the least intention of delivering him up to you."

She stared at him implacably.

"In fact, in other circumstances I might be moved to interrogate you more harshly, and for a longer period."

"I don't scare easily."

His fingers—the delicate, sensitive fingers—were suddenly around Caroline's throat.

She gasped, gulping for air, fighting the impulse to

battle back. *You must not show fear.* And yet fear
flooded her like a wash of warm water, moist between her thighs, rising hotly to her rib cage; a dull
thud of heartbeat, the blood panicking inside her. *Stupid,* she thought bitterly. *You stupid bitch. What were you
playing at?*

"I could ask you any number of questions." The
Hammerli's muzzle kissed her temple. "Over the course
of a week, or a year. I could find out whatever I needed
to know, Jane Hathaway, if I wished to spend the time.
Whether you scare easily or not is a matter of indifference. What is important is how much pain is required to
break you."

Her breathing now was nothing but a hiss. She kept
her hands clenched tightly in her lap, a pathetic attempt
at dignity. He watched her with the appearance of de-
tachment, as though he were watching TV. The gun,
hair-trigger, explicit in the hollow above her ear. Her
lungs were screaming for air, and for an instant, she believed he would throttle her—that she would die
clawing at his wrist in desperation. Anger knifed
through her.

"One thing intrigues me," he said idly. And laid
the gun down on the table. His other hand still gripped
her throat. She could not croak the question he
seemed to expect. He dangled the grenade pin before
her nose.

"This thing intrigues me. A keepsake, Akbar says.
Something you treasure of Michael's." He snorted derisively. "A *grenade* pin?"

She could no longer see for the black dots dancing
before her eyes. In a second she would pass out.
She reached up with both hands and dug her nails into
his wrist. His eyelids flickered, but otherwise, he re-

garded her steadily. The pressure of his thumb against her windpipe increased. Flames flared inside her head. Panic imploded like a screaming child. Her fingers went slack.

And then he released her.

"I confess I do not comprehend the grenade pin at all."

Caroline drew a shuddering breath. "People . . . attach importance to all kinds of things."

"Women, in my experience, attach none whatsoever to the instruments of war."

"Then you and I know very different sorts of women."

"Perhaps. But even if we allow for the differences between Western and Arab women, Miss Hathaway— even if we suppose for an instant that any number of bankers in London carry such things in their purses— even then, the grenade pin does not fit. You were sent by your organization to discover this man's whereabouts. Correct?"

Caroline did not reply.

"An organization such as yours does not think in subtle terms. It offers up the sentimental things: a high-school ring, a cherished love letter. It does not make a keepsake of a grenade pin."

"Then perhaps, praise be to Allah, your assumptions about me are false."

"My assumptions are never false," Sharif said softly. "The day that I am wrong is the day that I shall die."

The bomb maker's margin of error.

"So," he said briskly, "I must conclude that there is more to this matter than appears to the eye. You are unable or unwilling to be truthful; I cannot force you to be otherwise. But you know something more of this

Michael than merely his false name. I will not tell you
where he is. That I cannot do for anyone. But because
of this—because of the grenade pin—I shall undertake
to pass a message."

"Thank you," Caroline said faintly.

"It will not be this silliness about the dead father,"
Sharif continued. "We both know that Michael was
raised by vermin. . . . Do you stay in Berlin long?"

"In a day or two I will go to Budapest."

"Then I shall inform Michael that he may find you—
Jane Hathaway of the cunning and unlikely grenade
pin—at the Budapest Hilton. You know it?"

"Yes." She had had afternoon tea there once. The ruins of a monastery were built into the walls. The hotel,
however, was anything but ascetic, and quite beyond a
State Department stipend.

"Very well, then. We are done. Akbar! The blind-
fold!"

They drove her to the Spandau S-Bahn station
and left her at the foot of the platform stairs. They returned her purse and her belongings, so that she was
able to purchase a ticket from one of the automated
machines. The next thing, of course, was to mount the
stairs and await the train; but she knew that if she
attempted the steps, her legs would fold up beneath
her, and all her delicate subterfuge would come to an
end.

But for a grenade pin—

She had never felt so callow, so outmaneuvered. *So
goddamn stupid.*

The steps rose up before her. A man in a black felt
hat edged around her with a curious look, hastily
averted, and clattered up to the platform. She had less
than ten minutes to reach Potsdamer Platz and her hotel. She would have to change out of her clothes and

wig before meeting Wally Aronson. And yet she lacked the will to move.

It was as she was standing there, surveying her ticket, that a white Trabant pulled up to the curb a few feet away.

"Hiya, doll," said Tom Shephard. "Need a lift?"

Berlin, 10:15 A.M.

Y OU," CAROLINE SAID BRIEFLY.

"I might say the same," Shephard replied, "only I'd be lying. Who are you trying to be, anyway? Liza Minnelli does Sally Bowles?"

"You were following me."

"Right again. Boy, you Agency broads are quick."

She didn't move.

"Oh, for crying out loud, get *in*. We're due at the Interior Ministry in fifteen minutes, and unless you want to sing 'Cabaret' for all of Voekl's boys—which I don't think is politically correct, frankly—you're going to have to change your clothes. Which means we have no time at all."

Caroline got in.

Shephard peeled away from the curb, leaving tire tread in his wake. Not bad for a Trabant.

"So explain this to me." She was controlling her anger with difficulty. "You just happened to be driving by Alexanderplatz this morning and knew in an instant that the dark-haired woman reading the paper by the television tower was in fact *me*. Is that what I'm supposed to believe?"

"You're not supposed to believe anything. I'm not as devious as your employers. I'm quite happy to offer you the truth."

"You know the bartender at the Tacheles."

He shot her a glance. "The Tacheles? You do get around. The only bartender I know runs a dark little hole near my house in Dahlem."

"How, then?"

"I stopped by the Hyatt this morning to invite you to breakfast," he replied. "I thought we could talk about the Brandenburg Gate without the entire embassy listening in. I wanted to hear what you had to say about 30 April. Guesstimate where they might be headed."

Caroline studied him. "You've hit a wall, haven't you? The bomb crater isn't giving up its secrets."

"Not a wall," he corrected, "a minor plateau. Nothing we couldn't surmount given a normal pace of investigation. But normal doesn't apply to this baby. Normal is when the Veep is having breakfast in bed in D.C. instead of in somebody's trunk. The entire weight of Washington is sitting on my shoulders right now, and I need a lead worse than a drunk needs detox."

"You should write this stuff down. It's pure Hammett."

He ignored her. "It was clear from your cloak-and-dagger getup that you were already booked this morning. As I was pulling up to the hotel, you were walking out."

She glared at him.

"You can change your hair and you can change your clothes, darlin', but the walk's a dead giveaway. Some legs I don't forget."

The anger fused.

"What in the hell were you doing following me? And don't give me that bullshit about hoping for a *lead*."

"I thought I was doing you a favor," he said piously.

"A favor? You nearly got me killed. Shephard, you can't even surveil somebody discreetly. My friends spotted you the minute you pulled out behind them."

"Your *friends*, as you choose to call them, would think a day without surveillance was like a day without sunshine. They'll get over it, believe me. And I had no intention of being discreet. That would have destroyed the purpose."

"Which was?"

He swerved to avoid a furniture van parked in the middle of Grunerstrasse. "I wanted them to know you were being tailed. Maybe they'd think twice before they killed you."

"Oh, right," Caroline said dryly. "Thanks."

"Now, if you're done having a hissy fit," he continued, "it's my turn. Why the clandestine meeting with a bunch of rag heads? Does Wally Aronson know about this?"

Shephard, Caroline noticed, had yet to mention Sharif's name. He had no idea whom she had met with, or why.

She began to relax. "*Should* Wally know?"

"That's not for me to say. I'm not exactly in the Agency loop."

"How true. End of interrogation."

"Look." He pulled the Trabant over to the curb and slammed on the brakes. Now he was angry. "I enjoy the repartee, Carmichael, as much as anyone. It helps me hone my dating skills—"

"What skills?"

"But I haven't slept in thirty-six hours, and I've had

about enough of the attitude. I'm the head of this investigation." Shephard's hand was on her arm. "The Vice President is missing. You fly in as the 30 April expert. And next thing I know, you're wearing a wig and getting into a car with three men of Arab extraction. I don't think it was a social call. I think it was an agent meeting. And I'm certain you're holding out on me."

"I'll see you at the Interior Ministry," Caroline said, and shook him off. She reached for the door.

"I have their license plate number, you know," he shot back as she got out of the car. "All I have to do is call one of my friends in the Berlin police, and I've got an ID."

"Call away, Shephard." She slammed the door shut and leaned through the open window. "I'll be making a few calls myself. The Bureau might wonder why you wasted two hours trailing an Agency colleague this morning instead of supervising the crater."

"Oh, I'm *scared*," he deadpanned.

"Well, I'm not," she said, and walked away.

———

"Good morning, Mr. Aronson."

Christian Schoettler, the Interior Minister, was a trim man in his late thirties. He rose from his desk chair and offered his hand to Wally. "I see that Mr. Shephard is late, as usual."

"We were hardly on time ourselves," Wally replied apologetically. "The traffic today—"

"Yes, yes, it is because of the curfew. We have had the very devil of a time enforcing it, I'm afraid. Most of the Turks have been sensible and remained at home. But a few extremists thought to test the government's resolve."

He spoke English, Caroline noticed, with a British accent. An old Oxonian.

"May I present my colleague from Washington, Caroline Carmichael?"

"Ah, yes." Schoettler gave her a smile that failed to reach his eyes. "The Department of State's terrorism expert."

"Merely one of them, I'm afraid," she told him.

"But the one they chose to send *here,*" Schoettler pointed out. "That must mean a great deal. Please have a seat."

The door behind them burst open under the force of Schoettler's harried male secretary. "Herr Bundesminister, Herr Shephard is arrived."

"So I see," the minister said as Tom Shephard swung into the room. "How are you, Tom?"

"Just fine, Christian. Could use a little coffee, though."

"Georg, a cup for Mr. Shephard, if you would be so good."

"Did you hear the news?" Shephard asked the room in general. "We nearly found the Veep."

Schoettler looked up. It was the first sign of animation Caroline had glimpsed in him. "Where?"

"Bratislava," Wally broke in. "The raid failed. We lost two embassy officers. Bullets in the head."

"My deepest sympathies, Wally," Schoettler said.

Caroline's mind was racing. Where had Eric called from last night? Not Bratislava. He had killed the child in Bratislava before leaving for somewhere else. Had he sung a lullaby to the embassy watchers before he shot them, too?

"They traced 30 April to an apartment complex," Shephard explained, "and were trying to locate the actual place where Payne was held. But—"

"But Krucevic moved first," Wally concluded abruptly. "So we're back where we started. With the bombing. Christian?"

There was a short silence. Then Schoettler's aide appeared in the door with a coffee cup, and the minister said, "Why don't you sit down, Tom?"

Shephard took the coffee and the last available chair.

Schoettler pulled a dark blue file across his desk and opened it. "The Brandenburg bombing. One of the few cases in recent memory to be so quickly solved by the Berlin police."

"Solved." Shephard scowled and hunched forward. "That's news to me."

Schoettler tossed his file across the desk. "Four Turkish suspects seized in a raid last evening have confessed to the murders of the television crew and the theft of the van. They have confessed to loading that van with a mix of fertilizer and gasoline and parking it near the Brandenburg Gate. They have even confessed to detonating the bomb in the midst of Vice President Payne's speech. In a matter of hours, they will be charged with all three crimes."

"But that's crap," Shephard burst out. "The chemical residue found in the crater is from a batch of Semtex plastic explosive. We've isolated that much. You can't just—"

"I'm afraid you must have isolated the wrong thing, Tom," Schoettler interrupted coldly. "Whatever it is, it did not destroy the Brandenburg Gate. The suspects have confessed, you see."

"Fuck the suspects!"

"Tom—" Wally Aronson half rose from his chair and laid a restraining arm on Shephard's shoulder. Caroline noticed that the station chief's manner had altered subtly since Schoettler's speech. He was at once watchful and completely at ease, like a snake basking in the sun. "Let's have a look at the file, shall we?"

He flipped it open and studied the Berlin police report. "I see that all four Turks have previous records."

"Yes." Schoettler nodded. "Known anarchists."

"But none of them has admitted to involvement in the Vice President's kidnapping."

The Interior Minister shrugged. "I understand another terrorist group has claimed responsibility for that."

"And you think 30 April just seized the opportunity of the explosion," Shephard interjected sarcastically, "to swoop down on the embassy and snatch our Veep?"

"You know quite well, Tom, that it is irrelevant what I think." Schoettler's face hardened, and the quick brown eyes slid away. "We shall probably learn with time that the Turkish anarchists were in league with the kidnappers."

"I'm sure we will," Shephard retorted. "But you're better than this, Schoettler. How can you stand to eat this kind of shit every day?"

The Interior Minister rose. He extended his hand to Caroline. "It was a pleasure meeting you, Ms. Carmichael. I regret that you have come all this distance for nothing. Perhaps you can take the opportunity to see something of Berlin while you are here—"

"That's it?" Shephard was on his feet now, squared off across the desk from Schoettler. His face was pale with fatigue, the eye sockets ghastly. "That's the meeting? You don't even want to hear what the Bureau techs have learned from the crater?"

"That reminds me, Tom." Christian Schoettler touched his forefinger to his temple and frowned. "Now that the suspects have confessed, we no longer require the Bureau's assistance. The crater has been closed to your technicians as of ten o'clock this morning."

"The hell it has!" Shephard retorted.

"Please accept our deepest thanks for your hard work, and the work of your Bureau colleagues."

Shephard snatched the blue ministry file from Wally's hands and tossed it toward Schoettler's trash can. "You can't do this, Christian. It's a violation of international law. American citizens died at the Brandenburg, and the Bureau is required to investigate crimes against Americans anywhere in the world. You can't bar us from the bomb site."

"That is a point of law I am hardly qualified to address," Schoettler said with one of his brief smiles. "But as we at the ministry understand it, the Bureau's jurisdiction is investigatory only. All responsibility for the collection of *evidence* rests with the host country."

"Thank you for your time, Herr Bundesminister," Wally said, and extended his hand. Schoettler shook it.

"It doesn't end here, Christian." Tom Shephard's eyes blazed. "As soon as I walk out that door, I'm calling Washington."

———

It took both Caroline and Wally to steer Tom Shephard out of the Interior Ministry and into the backseat of the station chief's waiting car. The LegAtt was no longer shouting by the time they reached the street, but from the venomous look on his face, Caroline knew Shephard was unreconciled.

"What exactly is the Bureau's jurisdiction?" she asked.

"It's exactly what the good man said," Wally replied. "Investigatory only. We take what we can get in foreign crime scenes and hope for cooperation. Tom can threaten all he wants, but he's walking on thin ice."

"I get the impression he does that a lot."

"Like a Zamboni at full throttle." Wally shot Tom a glance; the LegAtt wasn't biting. "Believe it or not, Schoettler's one of the good guys. He's an SPD holdover from the Schroeder era. He's trying to work for Voekl without completely compromising his job."

"Well, he just failed today," Shephard snarled.

"Schoettler's back is to the wall," Wally mused. "I wonder what that means."

"A truckful of fertilizer didn't blow the Gate," Shephard fumed. "The device was strategic. It was *targeted*. It was plastic explosive with a battery and a timer, for God's sake, packaged in an acutely calibrated amount. Given a little time in the crater, we could have reassembled the device. Do you *know* what that could have told us?"

"Who made it," Caroline answered, and thought of Mahmoud Sharif.

"So forget Schoettler," Wally said briskly. "Forget the crater for a minute, and think. If Schoettler's stonewalling, then the Voekl government came down hard on the Ministry of Interior. Why would they do that?"

"They *despise* the Ministry of Interior," Tom retorted. "Voekl works around it entirely, through the Volksturm guards. They're Hitler's Gestapo all over again."

"That's why Schoettler has been permitted to stay." Wally returned patiently to the point. "He's wallpaper. He makes Voekl look good. But this time, Voekl needed Schoettler's ministry to shut us down."

"Which must mean," Caroline said slowly, "that the chancellor is afraid of what the FBI will find in the crater."

Tom Shephard pulled his eyes away from the window and stared at Caroline intently.

"We've already found evidence that contradicts their suspects. What else is there?"

Proof of complicity at the highest levels, Eric's voice muttered in her brain. *Fritz Voekl's balls in a sling.*

"Isn't it obvious, Tom? Something that connects *Voekl* to 30 April."

SIX

Budapest, 10:30 A.M.

ANATOLY RUBIKOV WAS A MAN of few words,
which is why he was still alive.

He crushed out the remains of his cigarette in the twist-
off cap of his bottled beer, and immediately lit another. He
smoked filtered cigarettes because Marya worried about
his lungs and wanted him to quit. The filter was a bone he
threw her, although filters meant nothing when a man
smoked as much as he did. Cigarettes were Anatoly's sol-
ace—an addiction, yes; a weakness, of course; but so much
a part of his biological imperative that to abandon them
now would be to poison himself with fresh air.

And the air of Budapest, when he thought about it,
was scarcely clean anyway.

He smoked absentmindedly, the way other people
breathed, his eyes fixed on the snowy television screen
mounted behind the bar. Everything was murk—the air
of the place, the yellow lights, the expression in the eyes
of the waitress with bright orange hair and laddered
stockings. The murk comforted him, and so he delayed
the inevitable accounting, the walk out into the raw

cold of the streets, the phone call he would have to make. It was ten-thirty in the morning.

The television broadcast was in Hungarian, a language he had never understood. He continued to stare at the screen, his beer drained to the faint tracings of foam, waiting for the face.

Could it be possible that no one had found him?

Anatoly closed his eyes and rested his forehead on the rim of the empty beer bottle. *How could no one have found him?*

The Hungarian National Bank occupied a building on the green swath of Szabadsag Ter, next to the embassy of the United States and across the way from Magyar TV headquarters. At this hour it should have been swarming with bankers and secretaries and clerks and factotums, all going about their legitimate business, and the man with the hole in his temple and the pool of blood under his neck should have been found by now. His picture should have flashed up on the television screen—not the man as he looked dead, but sleek and repellent in the full flush of power.

Perhaps they were keeping the mess under wraps, Anatoly thought. Assessing the damage. Deciding what could be told. If they waited much longer, Krucevic would take matters into his own hands.

And if I wait much longer, Krucevic will think too much about what I saw. He'll decide that a bullet keeps the best secrets.

The short, curling hairs at the back of his neck began to rise of themselves.

He crushed out the second cigarette and tossed a hundred-forint note on the counter. The orange-haired waitress followed him with her eyes as he left.

———

He placed the call in the Keleti train station, barely seven minutes before the Berlin train.

"Aronson," he said thickly when the receptionist answered.

"Mr. Aronson is not in. Would you like to leave—"

He hung up.

Aronson would want him to stay in Budapest. He would want him to shadow Krucevic, find out where he kept the woman, turn informer, and thus seal his death warrant. Aronson would want him—Anatoly Petrovich—to risk his life for someone he knew was as good as dead.

He turned, trailing smoke from his splayed fingers, and sought the protective cover of the train.

He cased it from front to back and took a seat at the very end of the last car—a smoking one, of course—folding himself into a corner near the half-open window in the six-person compartment. Otherwise, it was empty. He read his paper and pretended to ignore what he was actually studying frantically, the passage of other travelers along the corridor. Travelers who might be sent to kill him.

The train gave a lurch, compartment doors hissed shut. In a moment, the conductor would ask for his ticket. He closed his eyes again and saw the dead man's face.

Anatoly had never liked killing. He had done it when necessary—in the army, during his first tour in Afghanistan—but the mujahideen were wolves, rabid with violence. Killing them was a matter of survival. He had never watched a man consider his own death before—had never watched the knowledge come with all the inevitability of rain after a stifling day. When the pistol grazed his temple, Lajta's eyes had widened slightly, like a dog's when you pull hard on its ears. It was the only sign of fear the banker had shown.

The compartment door slid open, and a youngish woman—tired face, raincoat smelling dankly of the streets—shoved a bulky suitcase inside. Its zipper was broken, and she had been forced to tie the lid shut with string. Everything about her suggested a weary struggle against respectable poverty—her dark stockings, her thick-soled shoes. Hair as dry and tousled as an old bird's nest. She gave Anatoly a furtive glance and took the seat farthest away.

Did he look menacing? Or like a man in terror for his life?

The woman drew a paperback from her purse and opened it. Idly, Anatoly glanced at the cover: something in German. She was going home, then, as he was. Her head drooped, absorbed in words; suddenly, the platform began to slide backward. Anatoly did not trust himself to gaze out the window.

He was an expert at cracking security systems. The KGB had trained him, and he had worked all over the world, lifting the locks on office doors in Khartoum and Valletta and Santiago and Manhattan. He had defected fifteen years ago during his last tour, in Rome, when he'd been sent to bug the building directly next door to the U.S. embassy—a simple affair of attaching a remote fiber-optic device to one of the ancient pipes running between the walls of the two buildings.

Anatoly had never been a man of politics. He was not much of a man for morality, either, or for debating the finer points of loyalty. The KGB had been good to him. He had been good to the KGB. But it was time for their paths to part.

He had fallen in love with a translator at the Rome embassy, and the last few weeks of her tour were up. Anatoly was moving on to Kabul; Marya was returning to Moscow. He tried to buy time, a transfer, a change in Marya's assignment. The system proved inflexible.

And so, on that night nearly fifteen years ago, he discarded his cigarette, told his partner to take a hike, ignored the placement plan for the listening device, and instead disarmed the American embassy. Then he broke the glass in a ground-floor window at the back of the building, a window that should have been barred. He thrust himself through, grunting as his leather jacket snagged on the ledge—it was a coolish night in February, even the ubiquitous Roman cats gone to ground—until his sneakered feet touched something springy and soft. A tumbledown couch in a minor bureaucrat's office.

Anatoly stretched himself out on the cushions and went instantly to sleep.

In the morning, an extensive debriefing, the Soviet listening device like a peace offering on the table.

Forty-eight hours later, he and Marya were on a plane for Washington.

———

He spent eighteen months telling the CIA everything he knew about security installations throughout the Soviet empire, and about the hostile listening devices and fiber optics planted in the walls of a hundred U.S. installations. Then the Soviet empire began to crumble and the KGB heads themselves fled to Washington, and Anatoly decided to look for other work. Two years later he was a freelancer in Hamburg, Marya was thriving, their baby was on its way. He had four employees and a reputation for discretion. The difficult jobs—the problems of access or of imaginative design, the jobs that still made his blood race—he took on himself.

That was when he met Krucevic.

The man came to Anatoly with a bunker in mind.

Something entirely controlled by computer, with infrared detection zones, motion sensors, video surveillance inside and out. Krucevic wanted his own phone
lines monitored, he wanted cellular communications
routinely tapped, he wanted the hard drives of his computer systems armed to self-destruct at the first sign of
penetration. What he wanted, Anatoly decided, was to
live like a villain in a Dick Tracy comic strip.

Anatoly drew up plans. Krucevic paid him and took the
blueprints away. Anatoly thought that was the end of it. If
the security measures were ever installed, he was not to
know.

He had little idea then that he was dealing with the
devil. That knowledge came later. After Krucevic had
visited a third and even a fifth time, walking into the offices in Hamburg unannounced. He came, always, on
the nights Anatoly worked late over the bookkeeping.
His knowledge of Anatoly's movements was the least
disturbing thing about him.

He began to trade on loyalty. He began to assume
complicity. He began to threaten, to presume he owned
Anatoly and his office and his pretty house in the suburbs with two children growing in it.

And at last, Anatoly had gone to Berlin, as a penitent
goes humbly to confession, and had sought the good offices and advice of the man named Wally Aronson. He had
come to know Aronson years before, during the long
months of debriefing in Virginia, and while he doubted
that Aronson had brilliance or cunning or even great
courage, Anatoly believed that the man had no evil in
him. And all the power of American Intelligence at his
back.

Sitting now in the drab car of the MAV train while
the telephone wires of Hungary dipped and soared like

swallows beyond the window, Anatoly prayed that Intelligence might still mean something.

———

Aronson had told Anatoly that two options were open to him. The first was to throw himself on the mercy of old friends and allow them to relocate his family safely to the United States. He would lose most of what he had built in Hamburg; he would start over again a pauper in a land of wealth. But the Agency might offer some work.

Or, Aronson said, Anatoly could take a risk: He could play Krucevic like a fish, tell Aronson everything he learned of Krucevic's movements, and be compensated handsomely. The house in Hamburg, the office with four employees, Marya's contentment in her settled life—all could remain. And he would win the undying respect and gratitude of the United States.

Anatoly was, by nature, a taker of risk. And he liked the freedom he had won for himself; he liked meeting Wally Aronson as an equal, with something to give rather than everything to beg. It made him feel less desperate.

When Krucevic called, he was ready with his overnight bag and his ticket to Hungary.

———

His instructions were to await instructions.

They came at four A.M., with a ring of his bedside phone and the order to be on the pavement in front of his hotel in ten minutes.

He was there, a small kit of tools resting on the sidewalk at his feet, when the car pulled up. Krucevic sat alone in the back. Otto was at the wheel. Beside him sat another man Anatoly did not recognize but who he later learned was named Tonio. For an instant, he hesitated—the only

free space in the car was next to Krucevic, and he instinctively hated the proximity of the man—then slid into the
backseat. And kept his tools secure between his feet.

They drove swiftly through the empty streets, a yellow nimbus of rain in the predawn streetlights. Anatoly's
hands were sweating. Tonio chattered nervously, high-
pitched and annoying, until Otto reached out and cuffed
him, hard, across the face.

Otto drove to the rear of the central bank, to the electronically controlled entrance reserved for employees and
armored trucks. The massive steel gate was a system beautiful in its impregnability, and Anatoly would have approached the problem with delicacy and reverence had
Krucevic not been sitting silently in the rear. Anatoly
struggled to control his breathing, to defuse the set of rear
doors and then Lajta's office itself with an economy of
movement. By that time they had pulled Lajta out of the
trunk of the car, his hands bound and his mouth gagged,
and shuffled him upstairs through the dimly lit halls.

Where were the security guards? Had Krucevic
bribed them all?

The important thing, Anatoly decided, was not to
show fear. Krucevic scented fear like a dog, and Anatoly
knew that he reeked of it now.

He wanted no part of what they were planning. He
would have liked to leave then, with the doors wide open
and the deed still undone. But Krucevic expected him
there to the finish, so that the security devices could be re-
installed. By that time it was five A.M., still dark, and Tonio
was bent over the keyboard of the personal computer in
the finance minister's office, his concentration focused on
the monitor like a beam of light. Lajta huddled on the
floor, bewildered and malevolent. Slumped in a chair,
Otto yawned with boredom.

Whatever Tonio was doing took very little time—less than fifteen minutes—but the tension in the room sang through their veins like a pitch just beyond the range of hearing. Anatoly's fingers were ice cold. And then Tonio stopped clicking the keys and glanced at Krucevic with a grin.

"*Cazzo fottuto,* boss, we're in."

"Good," Mlan said easily, as though Tonio had mentioned the weather. "Now get back out and let's go."

The clicking of the keys recommenced. Anatoly expelled a breath. He avoided the eyes of the man on the floor.

Then Tonio stood up and Krucevic nodded at Otto.

Lajta was hauled to his feet. At gunpoint, Otto led him to the desk. The Minister of Finance was forced to sit down, and then his bonds were loosened. The gun was pressed in his right hand, and raised, with cruel precision, to his right temple. Otto waited an instant before he pulled the trigger—he looked directly into Lajta's eyes as they widened with terror, and smiled—and at that point, Anatoly could no longer watch.

———

He restored the security devices, praying he would not vomit.

They drove him back to his hotel and left him on the sidewalk.

"I know you will say nothing," Krucevic told him, "because you are a man who loves his wife. And those little girls—beautiful, the pair of them. I would not want Otto to know where such lovely girls live."

———

The rain would give way quite soon to snow, Anatoly thought as he stared through the train window; it was probably snowing in Moscow now, had been snowing already for weeks. The women would be shuffling through the Arbat in ill-fitting boots, their faces muffled to the eyebrows.

He lit his eighth cigarette. The woman opposite closed her paperback, and with it, her eyes. Smoke had placed a scrim between them that softened the deep weariness of her expression. He felt for her suddenly an abyss of tenderness, a desire to keep her safe. To do what he could no longer do for Marya and their children.

In Washington, it hardly snowed at all. But to get there—

Where, in God's name, could he go?

SEVEN
Berlin, 1:19 P.M.

A CONNECTION BETWEEN FRITZ VOEKL and 30 April," Tom Shephard repeated. "Do you realize what you're suggesting, Caroline? That the *chancellor of Germany* organized a terrorist hit in his own capital. A hit that killed twenty-eight people, seventeen of them *Germans*."

"You think I'm nuts," Caroline observed.

Shephard shook his head. "I think you're dangerous. I think if you said that in public, you'd get a Volksturm bullet right between the eyes."

"That doesn't mean it isn't true."

"If we can prove it," Wally said, "we'd bring down the government."

A look akin to joy—if joy could ever be so vicious—suffused Tom Shephard's face. What was incredible in Caroline's mouth was gospel in Wally's, apparently. That quickly, Tom was sold. "So what's the link? Where do we look for it? Not in the bomb. It was made of Semtex."

"The terrorist's material of choice. You assume that

means it came from Slovakia." Not for nothing had Caroline followed a bombing investigation for thirty months. She knew more than she'd ever cataloged about explosives. "But what if it's a Semtex-like material from a different source?"

"Forensics could pinpoint exactly where it came from, given some time and a bit more residue."

"Or maybe it's a problem with the device itself," she added. "A piece of broadcast equipment left in the bomber's van that carries incriminating fingerprints. Prints belonging to somebody the Voekl regime doesn't want connected to the Brandenburg Gate."

"Or maybe it's the bomb's timer," Wally threw in. "That's how we nailed the perps in Pan Am 103. The timer they used to trigger the bomb was one of only twelve made by a single Swiss firm for a single client— Moammar Qaddafi's brother-in-law."

"Or maybe it's a body." Tom Shephard sounded morose. "The famous extra leg, from Oklahoma City. Or maybe Mlan Krucevic himself was blown up in the van, with a love letter from Fritz Voekl in his breast pocket. But it doesn't matter, does it, if we can't get to the fucking crater."

"You give up too damn easily," Caroline said.

———

The scarred embassy on Pariser Platz was once again open for business. A mere two days after the bombing, the marine guards were back at the entrance, black armbands prominent on their biceps. Windows were boarded over where they had not already been replaced. A tattered flag flew at half mast, and concrete blast posts linked with chain blocked the building's exterior— or had they been hidden before, Caroline thought, by the ceremonial platform erected for the dedication?

The posts were designed to keep a vehicle filled with explosive from parking near the door; they had been powerless against commandos on the roof and shock waves traveling across the street. But perhaps they offered the illusion of safety to the people inside—people who knew, as she did, that if someone wanted to kill them enough, he would probably succeed.

Volksturm guards patrolled the streets leading into Pariser Platz, and barricades were everywhere. Wally abandoned his car on a side street and led them through a series of alleys to the embassy. The pavements were slick with the first flakes of snow.

As they turned into the square, Tom Shephard stopped short. Uniformed Volksturm surrounded the rubble of the Brandenburg Gate like a cordon of honor; but behind them, bright mustard against the blackened stone, reared the shovel of a front-loader. As the three of them watched, it swiveled and disgorged a twisted load of metal into the body of a truck.

"Fucking shit!"

Shephard took off at a run. Wally and Caroline tore after him. A few feet from the Volksturm cordon, they caught him and pulled him back.

"Fucking idiots!" He was struggling to break free and hurl himself at the nearest black shirt. "Get that fucking truck out of there!"

"You can't do anything about it." Caroline's voice was urgent, her fingers straining at his coat sleeve. "Tom—you'll only make it worse."

He shook her off. "Do you realize what they're doing?"

"Yes."

"They're destroying evidence!"

"Of course they are."

The bright front-loader bent, primal as a dinosaur, to devour a lamppost. Stone, metal, dust, and a few scraps of clothing clung to its jaws. The figure inside at work on the levers appeared to be whistling, oblivious to the spectators, the rolling news cameras, the enraged Shephard.

"Holy God," he burst out. "There could be human remains in there. What in Christ's name are they thinking?"

"Come on." Wally steered him gently around. "Let the press deal with it. They always do."

The Volksturm had massed near the consular section's door. There a long line of Berliners and tourists had assembled in hope of visas; most of them, Caroline noticed, were Turks. They stood in silence, eyes averted from the armed men in black; but there was an ugliness in the air, powerful as the stench of cordite. Wally pulled her toward the embassy's main entrance. Between the two of them, Carrie and Shephard, he looked like a policeman making an arrest.

"I've got to call the Bureau," Tom muttered as they flashed IDs at the marine guards and hurried down the main corridor. "This is un-fucking-believable. Do you realize what those bastards are doing?"

"*Yes*, Tom, I think we all realize," Wally said patiently. He took the broad central staircase two steps at a time, turned left at the second floor, and strode down a corridor. Caroline barely had time to register a team of technicians mounted on ladders, busily rewiring the embassy ceiling, when Wally stopped in front of an office.

"Mrs. Saunders!" he said gaily to the middle-aged woman behind the desk. "Meet Caroline Carmichael, otherwise known as Mad Dog."

"Mad Dog?" muttered Shephard.

Caroline extended her hand; Mrs. Saunders clasped it.

"Mrs. Saunders is the station's nerve center," Wally told them. "Although she has worked for an Intelligence organization for most of her life, none of us has ever learned her first name."

"It's Gladys, if you can believe," said the woman. "My mother was Welsh. Just call me Mrs. Saunders. Everyone does. You have an action cable from Headquarters, Wally"—she looked at him severely over her half-glasses, which were tethered to her head with a black cord—"and Vic Marinelli has been on the phone from Budapest. He wants you before COB today."

"Station chief," Wally told Caroline. "I put in a call to him this morning about DBTOXIN. So the cable system's up?"

"No. We used carrier pigeon. Also"—Mrs. Saunders glanced at her notes—"somebody throaty and Russian called. At least, I think he was Russian. Real hush-hush. A bad case of secret-agentitis, if ever I heard one. He hung up when I asked for his name."

Wally stood stock-still in front of the secretary's desk, considering this. "When?" he asked.

"Maybe ten, ten-fifteen."

"Could it have been our developmental?"

"Old what's-his-acronym? I don't know. Heavy smokers all sound the same to me. Particularly when they're foreign."

"Long-distance call?"

"Either that or our line's bugged. Lousy connection."

Wally whistled tunelessly under his breath while his fingers riffled the papers in Mrs. Saunders's In box. "Where's Fred?"

"He and Young Paul are out in the van, per your instructions." Mrs. Saunders sat back in her desk chair and smiled nastily. "It's so *nice* to see Fred working again. He managed to get rid of That Girl, you know. Gone home to see her mother."

Wally looked up. "That Girl, Mrs. Saunders, is his wife."

"She'll get him PNG'd one of these days," Mrs. Saunders predicted darkly. "Absolutely no discretion. Thinks it's a hoot that her husband's a spy. Hasn't the faintest clue spying's still a crime to the host country. How's McLean, sweetie?" This to Caroline.

"Congested," she managed.

"I've got a nice little house in Arlington. Keep it rented. *God help me* if I ever go back."

Wally disappeared through the office's inner door, a vaulted one, thrown open to Mrs. Saunders's view. Tom and Caroline followed him inside.

It might have been a gentleman's study—if the gentleman was a little paranoid. There were no windows: The Agency had long ago discovered that electronic emissions, even the tapping of fingers on a computer keyboard, bounced off glass and could be picked up by anyone remotely handy. Three workstations with computers and a motley collection of files dotted the space. The floor was carpeted in crimson pile that further deadened sound; the walls were lined with bookshelves. Within the walls, multiple layers of steel prevented electronic penetration. There was a document shredder, a combination safe, a few plants dying under fluorescent light, and a silver-framed picture of Brenda on Wally's desk.

"The developmental wouldn't be your 30 April safecracker, would it?" Caroline asked.

He raised an eyebrow at her, looking for all the world like a satanic Puck. "Do you need to know?"

"I'd *like* to know. If he's calling from Buda and hanging up in a hurry, maybe he's on to something."

"Maybe he is," Wally said smoothly. "If that *was* the developmental. But it's not like Anatoly to be spooked by Mrs. Saunders. We'll just have to wait until he calls back."

"What time is it in Washington?" Shephard demanded. He was, Caroline saw, still obsessed with stopping the destruction of evidence in the street below.

"I don't think it matters, Tom." Wally turned on his computer terminal. "You're not calling. Shut up and start thinking for once."

To Caroline's surprise, Shephard submitted to the abuse. He slumped into a chair and fixed his eyes on his shoes.

"You need a car and a good driver." Wally stuck his head into Mrs. Saunders's province. "Oh, *Gladys*?"

"Yes, *Walter*?" she replied acidly.

"Any of the FSNs report for duty?" FSNs—Foreign-Service Nationals—were local folk who served as support staff for the U.S. embassy.

"There's Ursula."

"Ursula would stick out like a sore thumb at a construction dump. Get me Tony."

"Tony was killed in the bombing, dear," said Mrs. Saunders imperturbably.

Wally was silent for a moment. "Okay. How about Old Markus?"

"Old Markus it is." She leaned on an intercom button and buzzed.

"Old Markus is perfect," Wally told them.

"You're sending him out after the dump truck," Shephard said.

"Why not? Got a better idea?"

"And then what—he sifts through the debris in the dead of night?"

"I doubt he'd know what to look for." Wally took off his suit jacket and reached for a cable. "You're the forensics nut, Tom. You've got all those Bureau teams twiddling their thumbs over at the Hyatt. Why not put 'em to work?"

"It might be considered against the law."

"German or U.S.?" Wally tore the cable in half and stuck it in a burn bag. "But I see your point. Whereas if I got involved, it'd still be against the law, but *you'd* feel better, right?"

Shephard said nothing. Wally smirked at Caroline. "There it is in a nutshell, Mad Dog. The Agency avoids evidence like the plague, because evidence is admissible in court, where sources and methods never go. But we love to help other people *find* evidence. It makes our little day. And are they grateful?"

"Once in a while," Shephard muttered.

"Not often enough."

"Okay, Wally," he said in exasperation. "I'm grateful for Old Markus. Let him follow the damn truck, and we'll decide later how to deal with whatever he finds."

And at that moment, the secure phone rang.

———

"Suicide," Wally said in disbelief. He sank down into his chair, fingers gripping the receiver. "Why commit suicide if you've just embezzled the nation?" His eyes were fixed on Caroline's face, but there was no expression in them; he might have been looking at a featureless wall. "All right, Vic. I understand. I'll get back to you tonight."

He hung up.

"What is it?" she asked.

"Vic Marinelli, from Budapest."

"And?"

"István Lajta committed suicide last night. Or early this morning."

Shephard looked up. "The Hungarian Minister of Finance?"

"Lajta killed himself?" Caroline was shocked. "But he's young—a rising star in the Liberal Party! People talked about him as a future prime minister."

"His assistant found him this morning. One bullet through the temple, gun lying on the floor." Wally grimaced. "His wife identified it as Lajta's."

"He had a doctorate in economics from the University of Chicago," Shephard protested.

"Even that, it seems, is no shield against bullets."

"They're sure it was suicide?" Caroline persisted.

"There was a note—or a confession, I guess—typed on the guy's computer screen."

She snorted. "Anybody can type, Wally. What'd Lajta confess to?"

"Embezzling the Hungarian treasury."

Shephard whistled.

"That includes at least a hundred million in IMF loans. The ministry is scrambling to sit on the news and trace the funds."

"So they called Vic Marinelli." Caroline immediately understood. The CIA's Chief of Station was usually declared to a friendly host country, and depending on the relationship, he could serve as a government's sounding board in times of crisis.

"Vic has asked for Secret Service assistance. The Treasury guys are pretty good at chasing down electronic transfers."

"But *why*?" she asked, working it out. "Why put a bullet in your brain if you've just pulled off the heist of the century?"

"Remorse?"

She groaned. "Oh, come on, Wally."

"He was murdered," Tom Shephard said brusquely.

Caroline caught his meaning and threw it back. "The only reason to kill Lajta—"

"—is if he didn't do it," Tom finished. "Whoever stole the cash left Lajta holding the bag."

"Vic seemed certain it was suicide," Wally objected, "and he's not stupid. The building hadn't been broken into—"

He stopped short and went very still.

"Your friend Anatoly," Caroline said grimly. "No wonder old what's-his-acronym hung up on Gladys."

Wally didn't reply. Instead, he reached for the phone and dialed a number. But before it rang, he slammed down the receiver. "If Lajta died sometime during the night, Anatoly won't even be back in Hamburg yet. *Shit*. I've got to get to him—"

"Before Krucevic does." Caroline picked up a silver letter opener and studied the engraving—a message of thanks from one of Wally's previous postings. "Do you seriously think Krucevic will let him go?"

"I don't know." Wally sank back into his chair, defeated.

"Why would 30 April steal from the treasury?" Tom Shephard asked. "If you're going to rob a bank, rob one in Switzerland. Not Hungary. I don't get it."

But Caroline did. "Fritz Voekl doesn't want Switzerland," she said. "Switzerland is clean and well ordered and more efficient than ten Germanys. Fritz wants a reason to clean up the wrong side of the tracks."

"What are you saying?"

"Voekl needs a cause. A crisis. He wants a plausible reason to send German troops throughout the neighboring countries. The countries that can't stop the Muslim hordes from invading the German sphere of influence. Voekl wants an invitation to take over."

"The reconquest of the Third Reich?" Shephard was dismissive.

"Yes," Caroline retorted. "What else is so risky it requires a hostage Vice President and a hamstrung U.S.?" She drove the letter opener deep into the soil of Wally's wilting plant. "The chancellor is attempting something so enormous—so barefaced—that only the most desperate measure can sustain it. Voekl wants Jack Bigelow to stand aside while he annexes Central Europe."

"First he's funding terrorists, now he's Hitler. That's *ridiculous*."

"Is it? He's already got people in Prague. A couple of bombs and a pat on the back managed that one. Now Hungary. When news of the treasury heist gets out— and it will, no matter how tightly they hold a lid on it— fortunes will be lost. The currency destabilized. We'll see blood in the streets. And I guarantee you that Voekl's Volksturm won't be far behind."

"I can't believe you're saying this. Ask anybody in Germany, they'll tell you the Reich was an aberration."

"If it happened once," Caroline argued, "it can happen again. Only more subtly this time, while nobody's looking. It'll happen with money and friendship and technical assistance—and some brilliant political maneuvering on the side."

"Not in our lifetime," Shephard insisted. "We wouldn't allow it."

"We just did," Caroline said.

EIGHT

Berlin, 2:45 P.M.

YOUNG PAUL, as Mrs. Saunders had called him, pulled his plumber's van to the curb in front of the children's playground on Kolmarer Strasse in Prenzlauerberg. It was a wonderful playground, famed throughout Berlin, filled with toy mills, large pumps, a variety of pulleys and chutes—an industrial wonderland for city children. Mahmoud Sharif's small boys, ages four and two, loved it. They lived only a hundred yards away, in an apartment building on the corner of Knaackestrasse.

Paul was driving a serviceable white van in the Agency's possession, a van whose sides proclaimed in correct German lettering that he was a plumber of distinction. He eased along Kolmarer Strasse until, from the vantage of his driver's seat, he had an unobstructed view of Sharif's building. It was five blocks and a world apart from the safe house Sharif had used that morning. Paul's sleek blond hair was covered with a white cap, and he wore canvas overalls in place of his usual Italian suiting. Behind him, in the body of the truck, sat Fred

Leicester and thirty thousand dollars' worth of electronic equipment.

Paul turned off the ignition and delved into a paper
sack of lunch. It was well after the German workman's
usual hour for eating, but perhaps the plumber of distinction had been preoccupied earlier with an emergency. He brought forth some bread and wurst and a
bottle of pilsner and proceeded to gaze enraptured at the
horde of youngsters screaming among the iron cages of
the play structure. It was a working-class neighborhood;
Prenzlauerburg had always been so, under the kaiser and
the Nazis and then the Communists and now the West.
Lately it had submitted to a rage for gentrification. But
many of the young faces were dusky and exotic, the hair
uncompromisingly black.

Paul ate slowly. Inside the van, Fred fiddled with buttons and winced at the whine in his earphones.

In the building on the corner of Knaackestrasse,
Mahmoud Sharif cleared his throat and flushed a toilet.
The four-year-old slapped his brother and stole a toy. A
woman named Dagmar—spiky blond hair, beautiful
eyes rimmed in kohl—picked up the baby and carried
him into the kitchen. She spoke to him in German, her
voice husky with smoke.

Paul took a swig of beer. Fred listened, and waited
for a call.

————————

"Wally?"

The COS looked up from the sandwich he was eating and said, "Yes, Gladys?"

She glared darkly but let it slide. "The boys just called
in. They're in position outside Sharif's apartment."

"Thank you, Gladys."

"Oh, *will* you stop?" Her head disappeared.

Caroline's nerves fluttered to life. "Would that be *Mahmoud* Sharif?"

Wally reached for a napkin. "Paul and Fred are out trolling. Just in case Sharif has anything to say." He glanced at Tom Shephard, who remained slumped in his seat. "Tom, you Bureau guys ever follow this clown?"

"Not on my watch. Palestinian bomb maker, right?"

"Hizballah's finest."

"I thought he'd reformed."

"So did I. But Carrie tells me that Headquarters picked up Sharif's name in connection with 30 April."

"Really." Tom sat up and twisted to gaze at Caroline. He was thinking, she knew, of the black wig and the gray Mercedes he had followed that morning. "A Palestinian in bed with the neo-Nazis . . . I suppose there have been stranger things. Like the reconquest of the Reich."

"They have a common cause," Wally observed. "Killing Jews."

"So you think Sharif made the bomb that blew the Gate?" Tom whistled softly. "I can see why that would make him interesting to Sally Bowles."

"Who?" Wally asked around a mouthful of ham.

"Cabaret," Caroline supplied. "Berlin in the thirties. Sally Bowles in a top hat and fishnets. Or should I say Liza Minnelli? Tom seems to think I look like her."

"But you're blond."

"And I can't sing."

Wally gave it up. Tom continued to study her coolly, but to her relief he said nothing of ragheads or Alexanderplatz. She made a mental note to request a new identity when she got back to Langley. Jane Hathaway was as good as blown. And as for Michael O'Shaughnessy . . .

In all ignorance, with haphazard luck, Wally was on Michael's trail. Sharif could lead the station right to Eric's door. And if he did? Disaster. For Sophie Payne, for the Agency, for Eric—

No, not her fault if Eric met disaster. He had brought that on himself.

All the same, anguish surged thick in her throat. She had done exactly what Cuddy Wilmot had warned her against: She had handed Eric's contact to the bombing investigation. And now Dare Atwood must be told, before events spiraled out of control.

"Can I use a secure phone, Wally?" she asked. "I'd like to call Headquarters."

Sharif surfaced about an hour after Paul parked the van in front of the playground. By that time, Paul had exhausted his wurst and finished the beer and moved on to the examination of a German soccer magazine, as though plumbers of distinction had nothing better to do than kill a Thursday afternoon. When the phone call came, he and Fred were almost caught unaware—because Mahmoud Sharif had kissed his wife and muttered something in Arabic to his children and had left the apartment on Knaackestrasse completely.

He swung into view for the briefest instant: a dark-haired, tall man in a black leather jacket, peering intently at the corner. His eyes passed over the plumber's van, the seething play structures.

Paul was absorbed in reading about a test match with Liverpool, parsing out the difficult German sports jargon he had never been taught at Langley.

Satisfied, Sharif unlocked the door of his gray Mercedes and slid behind the wheel.

Fred vaulted into the van's passenger seat, cursing, and screamed at Paul to follow the Benz.

They lost a few seconds. That was a good thing, actually, because Fred calmed down and Paul was prevented from dashing out after the gray Mercedes like the inexperienced and overeager first-tour officer he was.

Fred speed-dialed a number on his cell phone.

"Wally, we're following the subject. In case he decides to make a few calls on the road."

"Where's he headed?" Wally asked.

Fred studied the car in front of him.

"West," he said. "On Elbinger Strasse."

"Think he'll pick up the highway?"

"Don't know."

"Keep me posted."

The Mercedes abandoned Elbinger Strasse for Osloerstrasse, found Highway 100 and then Highway 110, and appeared, for all the world, to be heading for Tegel Airport. But just as Fred had decided that Mahmoud was taking off for a little R and R in that terrorist playground of choice, the island of Malta, the steel gray car shot past the airport exit. It headed north.

He led them straight to the forest in the middle of Reinickendorf. Here the Schloss Tegel rose like a neoclassical dream above the turgid waters of its lake. It had once belonged to the brothers Wilhelm and Alexander von Humboldt, one the founder of Berlin University, the other a scientist and explorer. Not the usual haunt of a Hizballah bomb maker.

"What the hell do I do now?" Paul asked desperately. He had come to a standstill, the van well back from the castle's parking lot. They were screened from their quarry's view by a well-trimmed hedge. But Sharif's black hair and leather jacket were just visible.

At this hour and this season, the castle was deserted: no schoolchildren skipping stones at the swans; no swans, for that matter. Only the avenue of lindens, a deserted gravel walk. The car park was virtually empty. Sharif let the Mercedes idle near the single other car—a long black Daimler sedan with a uniformed driver—and got out.

Fred patched in the station. "Wally? You there?"

Silence.

"Wally!"

"Yeah," said Aronson.

"We're at Schloss Tegel. God knows why. Sharif must have picked us up."

"Can you get close to him?"

"He's standing thirty yards away. There's one other car, a limo. Sharif's tapping on the window."

"Think it's a date?"

From this distance, Fred could make out nothing of the car's interior. The Daimler might hold an entire chorus of dancing girls. Then again, it might be empty. He studied the chauffeur. The man was probably in his sixties, a loyal old retainer; he looked at Mahmoud Sharif as one might assess an underbred dog.

"Shouldn't we go someplace less obvious?" Paul whispered urgently at his elbow.

As if echoing his thought, Wally's voice came over the line. "You can't hang out in the parking lot. Find a side street on Sharif's route home. Pick him up when he goes past. Okay?"

"Shit."

"You lost this one, buddy."

"Wait," Fred said urgently. "The driver's opening the limo's trunk. He's pulling something out. Sharif's helping. Jesus, it looks like . . . a *body* . . ."

The chauffeur carried the reclining woman to Sharif's Mercedes. She was too large to fit in the trunk; Sharif wedged her across the backseat instead.

"Shit! A piece of fucking sculpture," Fred burst out in disgust. "Now I've seen everything."

"Pack it up and come home," Wally ordered him. There was the faintest hint of amusement in his voice. "I guess the guy really has gone straight."

But as the limo driver turned his Daimler and drove away, past the idling plumber's van and the sighing lindens, Mahmoud Sharif pulled out his cell phone.

———

When Caroline dialed his secure line, Cuddy let it ring five times before he picked up. He was probably absorbed in reading Intelligence traffic, she thought, his mind deep in the clandestine maze.

"Your money or your wife."

"Mad Dog! What's happening?"

"Nothing good. I blew it, Cud. Berlin station is bugging Mahmoud Sharif."

"Carrie, I *told* you to drop it. Do you realize what happens if Wally picks up Eric's voice?"

"I know. I'm sorry. Maybe we'll get lucky. Maybe they've had a falling-out."

"What the hell am I supposed to do with this?"

"I thought Dare should have a heads-up." Caroline forced herself to sound calm. "So she can contain the problem if it goes public."

"Right," he said with a brittle laugh. "And I get to tell her."

Caroline was silent.

"Anything else?" he demanded harshly.

"Voekl's closed the crater."

"I know. It was on CNN."

"We think he's running scared. That he's deep-sixing evidence because it incriminates him."

"Maybe we should start a rumor in the *Washington Post*. 'Intelligence sources suggest . . .'"

"That should keep Dare occupied. Cuddy—"

"Yeah?"

"What do you know about Hungary?"

"They're dead broke. And there'll be hell to pay."

"So the news is out."

"I got it in a cable from Buda thirty minutes ago."

"Think it's possible Lajta was murdered?"

He considered this an instant. "One of a series of events in Central Europe?"

She smiled involuntarily at the phone. In Cuddy's world, the reconquest of the Third Reich was completely plausible. He knew, unlike Shephard, that she wasn't crazy.

"I'll start watching the corporate accounts," he told her.

Which meant the VaccuGen accounts. Cuddy had been tracing them for months now, through all the blinds and front companies and usual sleights of hand. He had a map of clandestine flows of cash, an electronic trail that branched like a monstrous bloodstream through DESIST's memory boards. Cuddy had pieces of operations he could grasp, microbytes of proof. If a hundred million dollars suddenly appeared on Cuddy's screen, the Hungarian treasury was as good as found.

The movement of Krucevic's money sketched a tantalizing tale. It was VaccuGen, Cuddy suspected, that broke the peace in Belfast; VaccuGen that nurtured militia camps in Montana and Khmer Rouge bases in Laos. Wherever a nationalist cause could thrive, there went Krucevic's money. Cuddy could map the flow of funds, but he lacked names for the networks and hard proof of what Krucevic bought.

"You work on the Sharif problem," he told Caroline now. "Keep the lid on Eric's existence any way you can. I'll fire up the database."

The database. Where all the dirty secrets lived.

Access, Ms. Bisby. It's what gets the high analytics every time.

Caroline felt suddenly afraid of all that Cuddy might find.

NINE
Budapest, 3:15 P.M.

M IRJANA TARCIC HEARD THE NEWS of István Lajta's death while driving over the Széchenyi Lánchíd, the Chain Bridge, one of Budapest's most beautiful landmarks. At night it was illuminated by a blaze of white lights, linking Buda and Pest, so that first-time travelers to the city on the Danube immediately thought of Paris. But today the bridge seemed ugly, a steel scrawl against the muddy brown river and the rain-washed towers of the lower city. It looked like what it was, an aging feat of engineering, its curvilinear heights a perfect platform for the launching of suicides.

Mirjana was stuck in traffic. She eased forward a few feet, braked, and closed her eyes. István Lajta had been a young man. Younger than herself. What kind of despair drove a person to fire a bullet into his own brain? Even in the deepest valleys of her shadowed life, Mirjana had never considered suicide. Death was an abyss. She could not steel herself to peer over the edge.

The constant brutality of her years with Mlan had taught her a stubborn survival, if only to disappoint him.

She'd clung to the edge of the cliff with her fingernails, and when Mlan approached to kick her hands from the edge, she'd clawed another hold.

Lajta had left two children. The fool. The self-obsessed, ambitious young fool. No one should abandon a child.

Mirjana's heart lurched, and with it the car. She had taken her foot off the clutch and the engine stalled. Behind her, a man at the wheel of a late-model blue Mercedes leaned on his horn and gestured rudely at her rearview mirror. A Mercedes. They were everywhere in Buda now, silver hood ornaments rising like latter-day coats of arms for a new governing class. She scowled at the man, at his perfect Italian suiting and his silk tie, and struggled with the ignition.

Jozsef. Had she abandoned Jozsef as utterly as István Lajta had deserted his two sons? She had lied to Béla Horváth. She *did* live in hope of seeing Jozsef again. Hope was a fever that burned deep in the heart of her silent nights, her sleepwalking days. Hope was almost as scalding as her thirst for revenge.

She drove on, diving toward the neat squares of the administrative district farther up the river. Beyond them was Béla's lab. She badly wanted to know what he had learned about vaccine No. 413.

But she had not gone four blocks before her way was barred.

People milled around the square in front of the old Hungarian Stock Exchange building; they were shouting and chanting in front of the National Bank, where Lajta's body had been found. A line of police, outfitted like astronauts uncertain of the atmosphere, presented riot shields and helmets to the crowd.

Mirjana rolled down her window and tugged at the

sleeve of a protester sprawled across her bumper. The man glared at her through the windshield.

"What's going on?" she asked.

"It's a protest. About that swine, Lajta."

"István Lajta?"

"The *szarházi senki* ripped off the treasury. And where's the money gone, I'd like to know! Where's my life savings?"

Szarházi senki. The shithouse nobody. István Lajta had fallen far from his days of glory at the University of Chicago.

The enraged protester pushed himself off Mirjana's hood and scrabbled for a paving stone.

"Forget these pissing sods," she shouted back. "Get to your bank and withdraw your money before it's too late."

"I already tried." The man ran forward to join a surging mass near a shop window. The glass strained under the pressure of too many bodies; an unseen hand hurled a beer bottle; the plate glass shattered like ice. The looting had begun.

Mirjana leaned on her horn. The car in front of her was submerged in a wave of protesters. And as she stared past its terrified driver, a slender woman in the tired uniform of the working class—cheap raincoat, cheaper shoes—clubbed a policeman with the pointed end of her bright red umbrella. The policeman raised his nightstick and slammed it down on his attacker's head. The woman crumpled, openmouthed, at his feet. There was an instant's pause in the crowd's roar—then the bodies surged forward like a herd of wildebeest on stampede. They flung themselves at the helmeted line, and the billy clubs rose and fell. Mirjana's heart thudded painfully in her chest. It would be a matter of seconds before tear gas and rubber bullets filled the square.

She threw her car into reverse and glanced over her shoulder. And what she saw sickened her.

A band of construction workers had pulled open the door of the blue Mercedes. One was smashing the windshield with a rock. Two others attempted to roll the vehicle on its side. And the rest—three men and a woman—had the driver down on the ground. He screamed as the steel-capped boots thudded brutally against his ribs. Mirjana reached over to the car's glove compartment and pulled out her handgun. She would not endure a pack of wolves.

She thrust herself out of the car, whispering a prayer that it would not be engulfed by the milling crowd, and pushed her way through the grunting workers. They had moved from kicking their victim to punching his face. It was a mask of blood. He looked, Mirjana thought, unconscious. Or perhaps he was already dead.

"Stop it, you sons of bitches, before I blow your heads off!" she screamed, and fired her gun in the air. No one looked up. She fired again.

The sound brought riot police on the run. The attackers turned to fight them, and instantly Mirjana was caught in the furious crush. She fought it, gasped, lost her gun and her footing, and went down.

———

Paul Dougherty parked the plumber's van in the garage of an Agency safe house in Spandau twenty minutes after leaving Schloss Tegel. He and Fred changed back into their suits behind the living room's drawn blinds, then left by the rear door and caught the S-Bahn into town.

Caroline, Wally, and Tom waited for them in the station vault. They pulled up chairs and prepared to listen to Mahmoud Sharif's phone call—the call he had made while smoking a cigarette in the deserted parking lot of Schloss Tegel.

"I called the head of our Berlin Task Force an hour ago," Caroline told Fred. "He has a lead on Sharif's bona fides." It was a patent lie, but Cuddy had told her to hold the lid on the Sharif problem any way she could. Bona fides, as everyone in Intelligence knew, were passwords you threw at your opposite number to test whether he was legitimate. "He may use the names Michael and Jane."

"Good," Wally said briskly. "We've got Fun with Mike and Jane. Let's roll."

Fred had attached the tape recorder to a small device that translated electronic pulses into numbers; within seconds, they would know exactly where Sharif had dialed. Fred pushed the play button. Caroline's mouth went dry.

Two rings, and then a woman's voice, prerecorded. Sharif had reached an answering machine.

"What language is that?" Shephard asked Caroline.

"Something Slavic, I think."

Sharif's amplified breathing filled the room. They waited for the beep. When it came, the bomb maker said in English, *"This is a message for Michael."*

Wally leaned closer to the box.

"Thanks for asking after the children. They're all fine, particularly our little girl."

"Bastard hasn't got a little girl," muttered Fred.

"Shush."

"She would love to visit whenever you're ready for her. Speaking of visits, I saw your friend Jane this morning. Jane Hathaway," Sharif repeated, with emphasis. Shephard scribbled the name on a legal pad.

"Jane sends her love. She will be at the Budapest Hilton if you want her, Michael—but I advise you to take extreme care. Once these women get their claws into you, it is as much as your life is worth to break free. Look at me! Go with God, brother."

And then he broke the connection.

Fred tossed a slip of paper at Wally. "The number's in Budapest. Registered to the name of Tarcic. Is that Hungarian?"

"No," Caroline said numbly, "it's Serbian."

"Tarcic," Wally repeated. "Isn't that—"

"The name of Krucevic's ex-wife? Yes."

"I thought those two hated each other. Why would Sharif use a contact number manned by Mirjana Tarcic?"

In a blaze of hope and disbelief, Caroline suddenly understood. *Because Mirjana's not working for Mlan Krucevic. She's working against him. For Eric.*

"There could be a hundred different women in Budapest with that name, Wally," she said carefully. "It may have nothing to do with the ex-wife."

"Oh, right." He rolled his eyes.

But even she didn't believe it. Of *course* the two women were the same. Forget the years of loss, the unspeakable betrayal, the pain and the anger; Caroline knew how Eric's mind worked. He was adept at manipulation. He instantly sensed weakness and turned it to advantage. If *Caroline* had seen the possibilities of Mirjana Tarcic—how the woman could be used, targeted against her husband—it was obvious that Eric would be ten steps and at least two years ahead of her.

"Maybe the breakup is false," Wally muttered. "A cover operation for something else."

"That might explain why she let Krucevic take the

kid," suggested Tom Shephard. "Because she's been seeing him all along."

"Fred," Wally said, "get Budapest on the line. We need to find this woman *now*."

A bubble of panic rose in Caroline's chest. *The net is tightening. Find Mirjana and you find Eric. But most important, you might find Vice President Payne*—and that was the job she had been sent out to do. *No choice, no possible way to save them both.* Her throat was throttled with unspoken words. She had laid the trap, and he was walking into it.

"Who the hell is Jane Hathaway?" Shephard asked. "Sharif's contact with Krucevic? Is Krucevic using the name Michael?"

"The names don't mean anything." Wally was impatient. "Sharif just worked them into the message. I'd say the point of the call was the Budapest Hilton." He took the phone Fred Leicester offered. "Vic? How're things on the ground? . . . That bad? It's what you signed up for. Listen—I've got a number you need to trace. The woman's a suspect in the Payne kidnapping. And put a team on the Hilton, okay? We think it's where 30 April is meeting—"

It was out of Caroline's hands now. The Budapest station would run with the recorded number. They would find Mirjana Tarcic's house. They would have Tarcic arrested on a trumped-up charge, a favor from the Hungarian police—or surveil her in the belief she could lead them to Krucevic.

And they would certainly find Eric. Unless Caroline got there first. Did she want to? Did she want to learn the whole truth about her marriage—the lies, the gross deceptions, the misplaced trust?

Wally cradled the receiver. "Marinelli's signaled a

meeting with DBTOXIN for the morning. News of the Hungarian bank crash has hit the street, Carrie. People are rioting."

She had no choice but to go forward, whatever she would find. "Wally, is there a night train to Budapest?"

"It's a sixteen-hour trip." He regarded her grimly. "Take a plane, Carrie, and stay at the Hilton. The President will spring for it."

TEN

Pristina, 4:30 P.M.

THE CHILDREN HAD BEEN WAITING patiently in line for seven hours now, ever since the German medical teams had arrived on the ground in Kosovo and set up their assembly-line vaccination. The trail of parents and toddlers snaked through the main street of the squatters' village, several thousand strong, and it moved with surprising efficiency. The young men and women—medical students, many of them, and all volunteers—had thrown themselves into the task. And while the children in the quarantined squatters' camp were vaccinated, another team had set up shop elsewhere in the city of Pristina. Fear of the spreading epidemic had knifed through the entire province of Kosovo.

Simone Amiot had not yet had a chance to speak to many of the German volunteers—the numbers of sick and dying exceeded a thousand now, and all her time was spent in the medical tent. She managed to snatch two or three hours of sleep each day. Never enough. She found herself nodding off in the midst of examinations; she moved through fatigue as though it were deep, deep water, and waited for some tide to turn. For the epidemic to peak, for the numbers to recede. Perhaps the vaccines would make a difference.

"They seem to know what they're doing." Stefan Marx was peering through the tent flap next to her. He was the head of their volunteer group, a veteran of Doctors Without Borders. A kind man who had left a thriving medical practice in Stuttgart to spend his time in the hellholes of the world. "Now, if only we knew what they were pumping into those kids' veins."

Simone looked up at him swiftly. "What do you mean?"

"I mean that this vaccine can't possibly have gone through clinical trials. I only hope to God it's not worse than the disease. But I ask you—" He gazed angrily around the crowded tent, the faces of the suffering children. "Do we have a choice?"

Enver Gordievic apparently thought so.

Throughout the day, Simone had looked for him among the waiting parents. She had hoped against hope that he would be there, with little Krystle on his shoulder. Because she dreaded the moment when she might look up and find him standing in the medical tent with another feverish child. Simone had learned from bitter experience that only one in twenty children survived this disease.

Stefan Marx laid his hand on her shoulder and smiled into her careworn face. "You should take a break," he said.

She opened her mouth to protest, to insist that she was just fine—but he'd already gone to help a nurse lift a boy from a pallet on the floor. Simone pulled on her jacket and stepped out into the early twilight of late fall. The medical teams would vaccinate under spotlights if they had to. No one wanted to turn these people away.

She hesitated, uncertain which direction to take—then found herself striding toward Enver's shelter. She had not seen him since his daughter's body had been carried from the medical tent for burial.

The small, crazily canted shack was silent as she approached. Simone stepped up to the door and knocked tentatively. And the flat panel of wood swung open under her hand.

At first she could pick nothing out of the shadows. Then her eyes adjusted, and Krystle's fair baby hair gleamed in the last bit of daylight. The child was lying on the floor, hands flung wide like a snow angel's. Enver's arms were around her. They might almost have been asleep.

Then Simone saw the neat round bullet holes in each of their temples and the pool of blood shining wickedly on the floor. She saw the pistol lying spent where Enver's hand had dropped it. He had found a third way, then—a path between sickness and untested vaccines. He had taken his girl home to her mother.

"Enver," Simone whispered. And her voice broke on his name.

ELEVEN

Berlin, 7:15 P.M.

CAROLINE PACED THE CONCOURSE at Tegel Airport, careful where she set her feet. She had cleared her weapon with Hungarian airport security; the forms had been filed, the flight crew notified. All that remained now was to wait. The sense of vertigo she had attributed yesterday to jet lag was back with redoubled force—but tonight, it sprang from fear. She was flying to Hungary on pure gut, she lacked most of the pieces of the puzzle, and her mind bucked and surged with panic. Was Eric really in Hungary? And was Sophie Payne with him? Or had she clutched at the wrong straw out of desperation and hope?

You analysts just demand so much certainty, Wally's voice muttered in her mind, *before you're willing to move off a dime.*

She had tried to think as Eric would: as a case officer in the field. She had tried to work from instinct. But the terrain was unfamiliar, like the interior of a house navigated by dark; she was terrified of hitting walls where corridors should be. If she was wrong, Sophie Payne could die.

The airport concourse swayed. *Vertigo*. She stopped short and took a steadying glance at a television monitor.

The evening news flickered across the screen. She understood German poorly—it was a language that had never taken, somehow—but the images were clear. Uniformed riot police, a man's bloodied, twisted face, a bottle exploding in midair. Shattered windows along the boulevards of Pest. Hungary was in turmoil.

"I guess the news got out," someone said behind her; she turned to see the battered raincoat, the five o'clock shadow along his jawline.

"Shephard," she said stupidly.

"I think I'm seated next to you." He fished in his pocket for a ticket and scowled down at it. "Ten-B. That means I'm in the middle seat, doesn't it? Damn Mrs. Saunders! I suppose the old bat gave *you* the window."

"What are you doing here?"

"Following Sally Bowles to Buda."

The implication was obvious: She had deceived him in the matter of Mahmoud Sharif, and he wasn't about to lose sight of her now. She almost snapped his head off in annoyance, but then Shephard shrugged as though nothing much mattered and said, "The investigation on this end is dead."

"What about Old Markus and the dump truck?"

"The stuff's going to a landfill," he said bleakly. "Wally's agreed to lead a Bureau forensics team in there after dark. Wanna bet they find zip?"

"With that as an alternative, I'd get out of town, too." She forced a smile.

He nodded toward the chaos on the television screen. "I hope you don't expect to use your ATM card while we're in happy Hungary. Stock market plummeted. The banks have frozen their assets."

"I've got cash. What do you expect to do there?"

The hazel eyes flicked back to her face. "The Secret Service requested me. For the Lajta embezzlement probe. I'm the Central European LegAtt, remember?"

"Of course. Sorry to be so dense. I'm a nervous flyer. I should have a drink or something."

To her surprise, he produced a flask from his coat pocket. "Here. Have a swig. Or do women sip?"

"I've never actually seen one of these." It was a dull silver, polished smooth from countless pockets. Someone had engraved his initials. "What's in it?"

"Single-malt Highland whiskey from a distillery I can't pronounce."

"Is this legal?"

"Come on. It's Berlin."

On the TV screen overhead, a woman screeched; Caroline could recall enough Hungarian from her Budapest days to understand the obscenities. *Az anyád!* Your mother. *Lofasz a Seggedbe!* A horse dick up your ass. She tipped the neck of Tom's flask into her mouth and felt the Scotch burn down her throat. *Bassza meg.* Fuck it. "Thanks. I have no idea what that actually tasted like—but thanks."

He laughed. "Why the nerves?"

There was no reason he should know, of course. "Unexpected turbulence," she lied.

————

The plane, as it happened, sat two to a row on the left side of the cabin, so that Mrs. Saunders's good sense was redeemed and Tom Shephard's long legs were thrust out into the aisle. Once they were airborne, Caroline passed him the sports section of her newspaper. She was thankful for a quarter hour of silence.

The news was rife with speculation about the Vice President's kidnapping but mentioned nothing of the economic chaos in Hungary—so there had been no hint, then, of the "series of events" in Central Europe. Nothing an analyst could point to, no sign of a chink where the dam would give way. She flipped through the front section and found a picture of Pristina. Rank upon rank of Kosovar children, lined up for German vaccines. Twenty-three hundred kids were now sick. Another thousand dead. And the numbers were climbing. *Vaccines*—

Caroline's thought was interrupted by a flight attendant with a drinks cart. She asked for a gin and tonic. Shephard got a beer. In all the business of napkins and ice, the newspaper was set aside and her time for solitary thought was done.

"Wally let me read your stuff. You seem to have a handle on Krucevic," Shephard told her.

"Whether it's the *right* handle is the question."

"How do you research your personality assessments, Carrie?" His tone was careful, but she heard a judgment lurking somewhere. He didn't buy the psychobabble.

"When I haven't got the guy on a couch, you mean? I use his date of birth and consult an astrologist. Krucevic was born in Saturn with Mercury rising. I don't have to tell you how bad that is."

He cracked a smile. "No, seriously."

"I use everything I can find, Tom. International police reports, foreign and domestic press, State Department reporting . . ."

"Psychiatric evaluation?"

"I usually collaborate with a staff psychiatrist, yes."

"And they think Krucevic is sane."

"Mlan Krucevic has never betrayed the least sign of

mental instability. You can't call a man nuts just because he kills people."

"Haven't you ever wanted to?" he asked her searchingly.

"Call Krucevic nuts, or kill people?"

"I mean, what's it like to follow this guy for years, Caroline? Knowing he murdered your husband?"

She felt a spark of anger toward Wally. Impossible to have a private life in the Intelligence community. "Are you asking whether I'm on a personal vendetta?"

"Let's just say you have a variety of motives for whatever you're doing. It didn't take all that talk of the Third Reich to tell me that. I saw your clandestine getup this morning. I doubt even Wally knows about Sally."

Caroline sipped her drink and decided to ignore that particular probe. "Tom, my personal life has undoubtedly affected my analysis. Let's take it as a given that I'm prejudiced against 30 April. We all are."

"But some of us more than others," he pointed out. "I may want to put Krucevic out of business, I may want to save the Vice President—but I'm not motivated by revenge. That has to make a difference."

Revenge. Caroline's spine tingled at the word. Was it revenge that drove Eric? Did he burn with desire to see Krucevic suffer, so that nothing—not even Sophie Payne, or the little girl he'd killed, or Caroline's pain— weighed in the balance? She could not comprehend the depth of such emotion. Even in her worst moments of rage and despair, vindictiveness was beyond her. But she knew it was within Eric's grasp. Revenge, to Eric, would look like justice.

"Revenge, if it's done right, makes you thorough," she told Shephard brutally. "It makes you own the enemy. It forces you to live inside another person's brain and think like he does. And that may be just what Sophie Payne needs right now. Nothing less than obsession will save her."

"Are you obsessed?"

She glanced away from him, toward the night beyond the plane window. The wing lights were flashing blue and white. "I dream of Krucevic, Tom, and I don't even know what he looks like. I feel him like a violence in my sleep."

He nodded wordlessly. "Tell me about Eric. If it's not too painful."

She almost laughed. Since Eric's phone call the previous night—that ruthless shot in the dark—Caroline had been tortured by every moment of loss and confusion endured in the past thirty months. But his voice had aroused her sleeping love—the love that had persisted, beyond terror and a false grave.

She had flown to Berlin on rage. Rage was gone now; but she could not define what had taken its place.

"Eric was a cowboy," she told Tom Shephard. "An ex–Green Beret with a lot of physical courage, the kind of person you'd want at your back when things got rough. The CIA used to be full of them."

Shephard grinned. "Now the cowboys are all day traders, one inch away from financial ruin."

"I suppose."

"I find it . . ." He hesitated.

"Hard to see me with someone like that? Cowboys aren't Sally Bowles material? If I remember correctly, she preferred Yale men with failing courage."

"So what was it? Opposites attracting?"

Why *had* she loved Eric? Why did she love him still?

"He made me feel alive," she attempted, as though telling Shephard might explain it for herself. "More alive than I'd ever felt before. Like a pulse was beating right under my fingertips. Eric never thought about his next step—he just took it. There's a huge freedom in that kind of life."

"And terrible consequences."

"Yes—but it's not how I live at all." She glanced at him. "I live in my head. Loving Eric was reckless and intoxicating and *risky*. It had nothing to do with careful consideration. It was complete emotional surrender." *Like a shove off a jump tower from forty feet, fear and exultation rising with the ground.* "I've never felt anything like it before or since."

"And you miss it. Miss *him*. So I guess you were happy."

"Yes and no." She thrust aside the memory of sex like a hand at the throat, sex as ruthless as hunger, sex that cast her up on the sands of morning a bleached and whitened bone. "Eric was difficult. Moody, hard to reach sometimes—he took his work very seriously. But he had a great deal of charm. And a sense of humor. He was intelligent without being well educated; he had a canniness that was pure gut."

Gut. It was carrying her to Budapest.

"A man's man," Shephard mused.

"Entirely. But he was often afraid—*sick* with fear, churning inside. Fighting it gave him a sense of purpose, I think. Aside from a love of good beer and Jack Nicholson, I don't know what else to tell you."

"How long were you married?"

"Just over ten years. How about you? Ever married?"

"Yes." His face tightened.

She thought of the initials engraved on the hip flask and the fact that he carried it everywhere. "Divorce?"

"Breast cancer."

"Ah," she managed.

"You know what it's like to lose someone." His eyes were now fixed on the plane bulkhead. "We went back to the States last posting, thinking she'd get better treatment."

"Strange, isn't it, how you learn that you can't change what's going to happen? That you can only endure it."

"You remind me of Jen," he said simply.

"With blond hair or black?"

It was the wrong thing to have said; she felt it acutely the moment the words were out, but she had done it and now would have to live with the adjustment in his expression, the closing off of feeling. She realized a moment too late that the glib impulse had been self-protective. Tom Shephard was getting under her skin.

He was contentious and irritable and he shot from the hip, but Caroline sensed that what drove him was a fund of caring. He was brutally honest. His gaze was too piercingly intent, his questions too unswerving; he wore his heart on his soiled trench-coat sleeve. Tom was as transparent in his prickly defenses as Eric was opaque. She was afraid she might even be able to trust him.

He reached into his briefcase for a paperback novel and said with deliberate casualness, "Are you going to Marinelli's meeting tomorrow?"

"Yes."

"You think TOXIN will just hand you the Veep?"

"Not without persuasion. Then we follow him into the enemy camp with as much firepower as we can beg, borrow, or steal."

And enough time for Eric to escape. Because if Eric is ever taken by U.S. forces, Dare's precious Agency is screwed.

"I'm beginning to understand your nickname, Mad Dog," Shephard said. And flipped open his paperback.

Caroline sank into her seat and looked firmly out the window. A man as good-hearted as Shephard could not possibly comprehend the violence that had won her the name, or the limits to which she could go. But she was very much afraid that he would discover both before their teamwork was done.

Last night's broken sleep was catching up with her; her eyes burned with exhaustion. She could pick out lights now in the darkness below, and a wide black band that might have been a road or a great wall but which she recognized as the river. The plane window was freezing against her cheek. It would be colder in Buda than in Berlin, and the air would be sulfurous with smoke from the cheap brown coal they still burned all over Central Europe. For an instant she could almost taste it, the damp Hungarian winter of her failed marriage.

TWELVE

The Night Sky, 8:12 P.M.

IT IS NOVEMBER AGAIN, almost four years ago,
November and her feet are scuffling through the dead
leaves in Városliget Park. They are strolling idly along
the winding path around the artificial lake. The fall afternoon slips sadly between boating season, just ended,
and ice-skating, which is yet to come; the lake is forlorn
and deserted under the brooding metal sky, a cup filling
steadily with sodden leaves. Scottie is at Eric's left, and
Caroline is on his right. Scottie sports a jaunty tweed
jacket—green and brown with flecks of plum in it, as
though he has jetted in direct from the Highlands for a
country-house weekend. They have tried to rise to the
occasion his clothes suggest; they have attempted to
make their life in Buda appear an expatriate's dream. For
Scottie, they window-shop for Herend porcelain, they
compare notes on *gulyás,* they sip strong Turkish coffee
amid velvet cushions while a Translyvanian fiddler plays.
Now this walk through the park, a prelude to dinner,
and a foil for Scottie's handling. Because Eric has become his developmental, Eric is his latest hard target.

Scottie has thirty-six hours to give, between a stop in Berlin and a flying visit to Istanbul. He is charming and yet uncomfortable in Caroline's presence; his eyes slide perpetually to Eric's face. She suspects that what Scottie craves is a little private conversation with his main man, the guy he put straight into the hot seat; but Eric's conversation these days is minimal. He has locked some demon so deeply within himself that speech is something to hoard, speech alone might show his hand. He plays the Chief of Station to Scottie's Headquarters Dignitary; he pulls out the stops and hits all the bells and whistles; but he is scrupulous in keeping Caroline by his side. Scottie will not go operational in Caroline's presence. She sees that Eric is using her as a shield, without understanding why. Her position is painful; she has always admired Scottie, after all— he is the father Eric never had, his best friend in the clandestine world. Years later, when Eric is gone and Scottie has abandoned hope, he will turn to Caroline for unconscious comfort; but here in Budapest, on this November afternoon, Scottie eyes her like a delegate from a hostile service. She has turned his Joe.

Scottie is at sea. He hunts perpetually for landmarks, he trolls for intelligence. Beneath the mask of high spirits and bonhomie is a creeping anxiety. He is worried about Eric and all Eric knows; he is afraid that Eric will snap one day like a camel overburdened with straws. A different man might make Caroline his confidante, might break down and ask for explanation—but Scottie knows Caroline for his enemy. She wants to fold up the tent and go home. She wants Eric to quit the Agency.

Eric can no longer say whether home ever existed.

Scottie sees the rifts in marriage before they heave, before the land slides out underfoot; he blames Caroline for Eric's distance.

The folly of Vajdahunyad Castle towers above them like a bit of Disney plunked down on suspect terrain. Caroline fingers a coin in her left pocket. She answers Scottie when he offers a word; she tosses the ball of conversation over Eric's head as though they are conspirators, communicating across a garden wall. Eric, as always, has retreated within. His feet find the path of their own accord. His head is sunk into the collar of his coat. He is searching for threats, mapping out protective cover, his eyes are moving constantly. Caroline is on the verge of screaming, *Talk to me, God damn it, talk or let me go*—but Scottie is admiring the baroque wing of the architectural folly. She outlines the history of Vajdahunyad for his particular edification, she maps whole centuries with one finger in the air.

In Washington the breeze would be sharp with wood smoke, a festive smell that quickens the appetite and sings of winter holidays; but in Budapest the air is yellow and rotten with burning coal. Presently they will put the lake to their backs and turn toward the zoo in the park's northwest corner, not from any desire to see the sad-eyed elephants or the desperate cats pacing in their cages, but because the city's best restaurant, Gundel's, is there in its Art Nouveau palace, and today is cause for celebration.

"How many years has it been?" Scottie asks them now.

"Eight," Caroline says. "Our eighth anniversary."

"You kids." He rests one hand casually on Eric's shoulder, but Eric is staring past him, at a dark patch in the woods. "I don't think even *one* of my marriages has lasted that long. But I hope you've got *years* together. *Really.* I do."

While Caroline was dreaming with her head against the window, Shephard stirred in his seat. He banged his tray table, dropped his book in the narrow space between the rows of seats, and swore under his breath. Caroline never moved. Exhaustion shadowed her eyes; her mouth was parted slightly with deep and even breathing. The plane was starting into its descent. He had to know who Sally Bowles was.

He bent down to retrieve the paperback, and flipped open the leather flap of Caroline's purse. It would be a civilian passport with a blue cover, not her official black diplomatic one.

He riffled delicately through the contents of the purse with his fingertips, tension prickling the back of his neck. There was a zippered compartment. He eased it open with his forefinger, mentally cursing his clumsiness. And felt the folded edge of something.

A matchbook. He thrust it back and felt again—

The two-by-two snapshot was of the woman in the black wig. And the name in the data field was one he had heard only three hours before, on the lips of a wiretapped Palestinian.

Jane Hathaway.

What was the other name Sharif had used? Michael?

Shephard tucked the fake passport back in its compartment and straightened in his seat. His pulse accelerated. *Caroline was working with a Palestinian terrorist.* Sharif had put her in contact with 30 April. And Wally Aronson clearly had no idea.

He drew a sharp breath and ran his fingers through his hair. The plane was steadily losing altitude, and even the flight attendants were strapped in. Was Caroline a terrorist mole in the heart of the investigation? Would she betray them all? Or was she operating under instructions from Washington that no one—not even the Agency's own station chiefs—was privileged to know?

Shephard closed his eyes. He had gone behind her back and been rewarded with dangerous knowledge. He had chosen this sudden mistrust, this creeping sense of treachery. He would have to live with it now.

And watch Jane Hathaway's every move in Budapest.

THIRTEEN
Budapest, 9:30 P.M.

A CRAMPING PAIN CURLED in Sophie Payne's bowels, making her writhe like a creature possessed. For the second time this night, she vomited blood.

From the wall behind her head came pitiful wails, the voices of delirium. She buried her face in the damp pillow.

The sound of a belt slicing down on exposed skin. A squeal of pain, pathetically suppressed. Jozsef was no coward.

"What did you tell her?" Harsh words, in fluent German.

"I never said anything, Papa! I haven't spoken to her in months!"

"You lie!"

The belt. An agonized whimper.

"You lie!"

The blows were raining fiercer now. The boy would be scarred with weals, the blood bright on his translucent skin. "For the love of God, stop it . . ." Sophie whispered.

"You have been talking to your mother," Krucevic muttered viciously into the dark. "Telling her everything. How else could she know? How else could she find Greta and convince her to give up the vaccine? You gave her the information. You betrayed me, Jozsef! Do you know the damage you've done? We must find her! You must tell me before it is too late!"

"I thought you killed her long ago!" A cry of loss and hatred.

"*Killed* her?"

"You *must* have. Why else would she leave me here?"

So it had mattered to Jozsef, this year of abandonment. Sophie thought of his draggled rabbit's foot, the last, pathetic talisman of a normal life. A child's hope against hope that his mother was alive.

"Because she's a coward," Krucevic spat out. "Your mother is too much of a coward to come after you, Jozsef. She would not dare to face *me*."

"Where is she, Papa?"

"You tell me. You're the one who has been talking to her on the sly. Sneaking around, taking my phone in the middle of the night, calling Belgrade. Do you think I don't get the bills? Do you think I don't recognize that number?"

"I did call! I have called her every week since you took me away! But never once have I heard her voice. Never once, the least word. She is not in Belgrade. She is not anywhere. I *do not know where she is!*"

He broke down into a terrible weeping. Sophie's heart burned for the boy, for the lost and fragile child in the room beyond her wall, his thin shoulders spasming with grief. The sound was magnified in her delirium; it swelled, consuming her air, her sight, until the walls vibrated with bitterness and she choked on Jozsef's tears herself. What kind of monster was his father? Didn't he comprehend at all what it was like to be a pawn, a token between two warring parties, one the mother who nursed you and the other the father who demanded your will? Could he see nothing of how the boy was torn? Jozsef was dying for lack of the mother he loved. But he would also die, Sophie felt sure, before he would betray Mlan Krucevic.

The belt sliced down again; the boy cried out.

"That will teach you to take my phone," his father said.

———

From the moment Mlan Krucevic had learned of Mirjana's intrigue—of the brazen theft of his drugs in broad daylight—he had been convinced that Jozsef was the source of 30 April's leak. It was entirely like his bitch of a wife to milk the boy for information. Jozsef was young, he was not yet tough, he could be manipulated by his emotions. That was one reason Krucevic had taken him from his mother. He would not have Jozsef spoiled by a Serbian whore.

But he had beaten the boy almost senseless, and the story had never changed. Jozsef was not the source of Mirjana's information. And what a lot of information she possessed.

Mirjana had known how to find VaccuGen. That could be explained. It was, after all, a private corporation that conducted legitimate business. VaccuGen vaccines ensured that livestock the world over—particularly in developing nations—would not fall prey to a host of diseases. But how had the *žalba* known Greta Oppenheimer's name? How had she known exactly which vaccine to steal?

There was only one answer. Someone within 30 April had betrayed him. And Krucevic had a very good idea who that person was.

He glanced at his watch. Almost dinnertime. Like Christ at the Passover supper, he would break bread with the man who had sold him for thirty pieces of silver. And afterward, he would crucify him.

———

The airport taxi carried Tom Shephard and Caroline Carmichael through boulevards of screaming sirens, around squares of massed police. They passed checkpoints and blockades and forced their way across bridges thronged with people. The false stone facades of the nineteenth-century buildings flickered against a backdrop of flame.

Hungary's Houses of Parliament were burning.

Caroline stood at her hotel room window and watched. The glorious old buildings were ablaze with light, like something from an Impressionist painting, the crimson and gold flames mirrored in the black of the Danube.

"The government fell an hour ago," Shephard said from her doorway.

The flames rippled, reflected, in the black water.

"And the Volksturm land in the morning," she replied.

———

Tonio shivered beside Michael in the passenger seat, the latest of Krucevic's videos resting on the console between them. He had been whistling a tune—something by U2, a B-side recording, he knew them all but not even rock and roll could comfort him tonight.

"Jesus . . . who'd have thought they'd riot over money?"

"Krucevic," Michael answered. "That was the point of the plan, Tonio. Mlan needed an excuse to get the Volksturm into Hungary, and you certainly gave it to him."

"I just do what I'm told." Tonio was defensive. "I just work the keys."

They were close to the city now, and the sky above Budapest glowed like a blast furnace. Tonio shivered. "From the look of that, the place'll be crawling with cops. *Cazzo fottuto.*" He crossed himself, the scars on his wrist livid in the light from the dashboard.

The Italian prison system had not been kind to Tonio.

He jabbed at the car stereo buttons; a czardas filled the car, some guttural words. "They've got shit here for music, you know that? Like their language. And their economy. Pure shit."

Michael reached over and snapped off the radio. "Why don't you sing? A little Paul Simon always works in the darkness."

"I could use a drink," Tonio said.

"It's not much farther."

"There's bound to be roadblocks. Detours. Police barricades. Maybe we should just go back. Tell him we couldn't get close—"

"We'll get close."

Tonio glanced at him. "You know this place, huh? You've been here before?"

Michael looked over his left shoulder, signaled, and moved into the fast lane. Tonio hadn't really expected him to answer. Michael said less than any man he'd ever known—any man without a bullet in his brain.

"Did you know that Mlan is following us?" he asked Tonio conversationally.

"Following us?" Panic, pure and deadly, flooded through his body.

"Or at least Vaclav is. He's driving. I picked him up about fifteen minutes out of the bunker. Otto's in the passenger seat. He looks happy."

Nobody liked it when Otto looked happy.

"Why would they be following us?"

"I don't know. Maybe it's a test."

Tonio swallowed hard on the fear that filled his throat. "What kind of test?"

"For Mlan, there's only one kind."

Michael was right. A year ago, Tonio had watched the boss put a gun to the heads of two men he'd known and liked. "What the fuck have you done, Michael?"

"*Me?* All I did was shoot a little girl when Mlan asked. What have *you* done, Tonio, with your magic fingers? Have you looked somewhere in Mlan's computer that you shouldn't?"

"No! I swear it on the Virgin!"

Michael raised an eyebrow. "Then I guess we've got nothing to worry about. Sing. With any luck, we'll lose them."

He exited the M1 abruptly, well to the west of Buda, snaking the car through the traffic of the side streets and heading downhill toward the bridges over the Danube. They were in the eleventh district now, Gellérthegy, the neighborhood behind the castle's heights, and the broad expanse of Villányi Út was ominously deserted. Then, in the headlights, the plaza that was Móricz Zsigmond Körtér and the police checkpoint.

"Merda," Tonio muttered. He huddled lower in his seat, a furtive rodent beneath a mop of blond curls. "Turn around."

"Absolutely not. We're going ahead."

"Why?"

"Because Mlan never will," Michael answered implacably.

He slowed the Audi to a stop and rolled down the window. An officer approached.

Incomprehensible language, and then Michael nodding.

"Get the registration," he told Tonio.

"What?"

"It's in the glove compartment."

There was a gun in the glove compartment, too—at the bottom, where a casual observer would never suspect, and for an instant, Tonio saw Michael's plan. But the Hungarian cop was staring at him, his cap visor very correct across the brow, and under the weight of those flat dark eyes Tonio could not move, could not seize the gun and shoot the man in the forehead. He had watched while Otto had killed the finance minister, Lajta, he had watched a score of deaths in the past few months, but he could not bring himself to murder now.

Besides, there were other police waiting beyond the headlights, their uniform pants picked out in a halogen glare.

Michael reached across him and took a packet of papers from the glove compartment. Another few words in halting Hungarian.

The cop nodded, flipped through the documents, and then returned them. He barked a word.

Michael produced his passport. "Tonio?"

"What? *Santa Maria—what?*"

"The officer would like your passport."

His brown eyes widened, and he drew a quick breath. Did he have it? Or had he left it in the bunker? Madonna, but Krucevic would *kill* Michael. What if their names were already on a list somewhere—what if these cops followed them, saw the videotape tossed out a window, gave the registration to the Americans—

The cop held out his hand. Tonio reached inside his jacket. His fingers brushed the textured butt of his gun. A few seconds, a flare of light, and Michael could wheel the car up Villányi Út before the others thought to follow. . . .

What then?

He pulled his passport out of his breast pocket.

The cop glanced at it indifferently and then handed them both back.

Michael's window slid closed.

Blindly, Tonio grabbed one of the passports with shaking fingers and stuffed it into his jacket. "What the fuck did you say back there?" he snarled.

"The car's registered to VaccuGen." He turned left into Bartók Béla Út, still heading downhill. "We're traveling salesmen from Berlin. We know nothing about riots."

"Salesmen."

"We know nothing about curfews. We're looking for the Gellért Hotel. It's a few blocks from here."

"*Dio,* I need a drink."

The floodlit facade of the hotel loomed before them, an Art Nouveau confection hard by the Chain Bridge, and suddenly, Michael pulled right and then left, into Budafoki Út. He was still humming "Graceland." Now

Tonio would have the goddamn tune in his head for the next thirty days.

"Here." Michael jerked the Audi into a space at the curb and killed the engine. "You're in no shape for this." He reached into his pocket and handed Tonio some deutsche marks.

"What are you doing?"

"That's Libella." He gestured toward the bar. "Last time I checked, a pretty decent place. You'll like the music. They'll take your deutsche marks gladly and rob you blind in the process, but so what? Money's tight these days in Buda."

"What about the video?"

"I'll deliver it," Michael said curtly. "I should go on foot anyway. It's safer."

"But Mlan—"

"Mlan turned back at the police checkpoint. Mlan will never know. I'll find you in an hour. Two, at the outside. If I'm later than that, take the car and get out."

Tonio swallowed nervously. He could never leave without Michael—not and expect to see morning.

His eyes flicked to the dull gold light pouring from the bar's windows. How long had it been since he'd had a drink? Mlan hated drink like he hated women. He would have to be careful.

Michael was already a block away, heading for the bridge, a shadow under the flame-torn sky.

———

He waited until he stood on the Pest side of the water before pulling out his cell phone. The number he dialed was one Wally Aronson would recognize. For the past four hours, it had been bugged by the Budapest station.

The click of Mirjana's machine. He dialed his access code and waited for the messages. Then Sharif's voice filled his ear.

He listened, the pace of his heart rising slightly as he understood. Then he hung up. His breathing was audible, less perfectly controlled, and he stared intently across the Danube at the distant mass of the Hilton as though he might see her form backlit in a window. The sight of her face on a television screen had been enough to risk a call in the night. Now, knowing that she was here—

A klaxon screamed somewhere behind him.

He turned away from the river and strode swiftly toward the rioters on Szabadsag Ter. They had coalesced, he knew, in front of Magyar Television and the National Bank—one across the square, the other just next door to the embassy. It would be impossible to approach the place without a fight.

U.S. installations throughout Europe should be on alert, their marine guards dying to catch a tourist with the key to Sophie Payne's whereabouts stuffed tight inside his jacket. The embassy was out of the question. Where, then?

For an instant, memories of that other Budapest—of the nighttime surveillance, Caroline beside him, the conversation unwinding as it had always done through the relentless grid of streets—filled his mind. There was the ambassador's residence—he knew it well, a nineteenth-century petit palace in a residential quarter of the city, ringed with a sizeable garden. The marines standing vigil there would concentrate on points of egress, not bushes and flower beds. He could toss the tape over the wrought-iron palings and disappear before he was detected.

But first, another call. He slid into the darkened

doorway of the Hungarian Academy of Sciences and pulled out his cell phone.

"It's me," he said after the beep. "We're in town. Tell Béla to watch his back. And for Christ's sake, be careful."

FOURTEEN

Budapest, 10:53 P.M.

CAROLINE SAT ON THE FLOOR of her hotel room, drapes pulled wide to the glowing sky over Pest. She couldn't sleep. Sleep would be an insult to the ugliness of what was happening in this city, akin to picnicking on the fringe of battle. How had the British slept during that long spring of 1940? Or the Dresdeners gone to bed with carpet bombs? Did exhaustion take over, relentless? Or did you simply grow accustomed to the mutter of unrest, the flare of violence against the night sky?

She swallowed some whiskey from a diminutive bottle, pulled at random from her generous minibar. *Violence.* She had taken it to bed with her amid the Hilton's hushed opulence; it patrolled the corridors and stairwells and banks of elevators. Violence had Eric's alias on a piece of audiotape, it smelled his ruin in the smoke roiling off the Danube. She supposed she had Vic Marinelli to thank for the nondescript man reading newspaper after newspaper in a hard chair in the lobby, or the young woman with owlish glasses who spoke earnestly into the phone. Marinelli was Chief of Station, Budapest. It was his job to send out the best, to place a sympathetic face behind the front desk, a hulking bruiser among the valet parkers. It was a kind of game for Caroline to play, betting the silent odds on exactly who was who. The Agency's net ringed her round with smiling faces, it strangled her with helping hands. If Michael and Jane ever dared to meet, the two of them were as good as bagged.

Yes, she had Marinelli to thank for the last bars of this cage—but only herself to blame. She had not been able to leave Sharif and his friends alone.

She tipped her whiskey bottle up, let the sweet flame flicker along the lining of her throat, and stared at the orange glow across the river until her eyes burned. She could be honest with herself now. She could tell herself the truth. She wanted Sophie Payne alive and bound for Washington on a C-130 transport. But she wanted Eric to walk away clean—free of Krucevic and Agency and Caroline alike.

It was a paradox she could not reconcile. She was Jane Hathaway, bona fide in a box; she was Caroline Carmichael, the baited wife. Her whiskey was gone. She tossed the bottle toward a wastepaper basket under the desk, and at that moment her telephone rang.

She froze. *Eric. Talking in the dark. And Marinelli would have the hotel phone lines bugged.*

She almost didn't answer. Then, as though it moved of itself, her hand grasped the receiver.

"Caroline," he said.

"Scottie . . ." She felt a knife edge of relief—and disappointment.

"Did I wake you?"

"No"—she glanced at the clock—"it's only eleven."

"How's Buda?"

"Pretty hot. People aren't hurling themselves out of windows yet—but then, most of the windows are already smashed. The Volksturm arrive tomorrow."

"Ah," Scottie said with understanding. "Then we can put the Hungarian republic in the chancellor's column."

So Scottie believed it, too. The Third Reich rising like a phoenix from half a century of ashes.

"What's next?"

"If I knew that, you'd be on a plane home. Caroline, you heard about our mess in Bratislava?"

"Yes. I'm sorry." She kept her voice neutral, her words vague, in deference to the open phone line. There was a rustle across two continents as Scottie shuffled paper.

"It's not a complete loss. We traced a phone call to the Big Man himself. And the conversation was extremely interesting. His VaccuGen secretary had to tell him about a delivery that went awry."

Delivery. Caroline pushed herself upright in bed. Had Krucevic planned to dump Sophie Payne?

"Somebody's prescription got into the wrong hands," Scottie continued. "The Big Man was quite upset. We're trying to figure out why."

"Was this medicine intended for our missing friend?" she asked.

"We don't think so. But she may not be doing too well. The specialists on this end are worried about her prognosis."

Caroline's heart sank. Careful as Scottie might be, the message of his last words was unmistakable. Sophie Payne was dying.

"And the secretary? The one who made that call? Could you find her?"

"That's been tried. She's left work under something of a cloud. The Big Man was rather angry, to judge by his tone of voice. Surprised and rattled, even. As though a fly had devoured all the ointment."

"I see. What do you want me to do, Scottie?"

"I may need you to fly to Poland. I'll call you tomorrow if it's necessary."

"Poland?"

"Our friend Cuddy has spotted some activity there. In the accounts he's monitoring."

VaccuGen's corporate accounts. He'd fired up DESIST and found a financial trail. Caroline's heartbeat quickened. "New money?"

"Lots of it. Cash is flooding into a certain German party organization—and from there to friends in Poland. We find that . . ."

"Ironic," Caroline replied. "Given the state of coffers here."

"Well, one market's bear can be another's bull," he retorted lazily, as though he enjoyed this game of charades.

But Caroline was sick of it. "You think our missing friend has gone to Poland, too?"

"Possibly. But she's running out of time." His voice changed. "Have you heard again from the fair-haired boy?"

"No. But I've changed cities. Even he might need some time to adjust."

Which showed how poorly she'd judged Eric.

———

She had closed the drapes against the fading glow of the ruined Houses of Parliament and was almost asleep when the knock came on the door.

Shephard, she thought, and had the impulse to hide under the covers. There was something in the way he looked at her now that made her uneasy. The LegAtt's eyes were too intense, too probing; somewhere in the air between Berlin and Buda, they had lost a professional distance. Perhaps, Caroline thought, it was because she reminded him of his dead wife. She preferred Shephard caustic and uncommunicative; it made him less threatening.

Another knock, louder this time.

She crossed the room and looked for a peephole. There was none. She slid the chain into the bolt and cracked the door four inches, peering out into the hallway.

Whatever she had intended to say died on her lips.

"For the love of God, get me inside before somebody sees me," Eric muttered.

She pulled the chain hurriedly out of the bolt.

He slipped through the door and shut it behind him. He was wearing a white busboy's coat; the dining trolley he'd abandoned in the hall.

Employee entrance, she thought, *and a kitchen computer listing all the guests, for room service.* "You shouldn't have come here. The station's all over the place."

"How did I know you were going to say that?" he asked, and took her in his arms.

The shock of his hands moving over her in the darkness of that room was too much. *Dead hands,* she thought. How many lost nights in the last two and a half years had she cried for Eric's touch, for the solid span of his shoulders beneath her fingertips, the warmth of his face skimming hers? She allowed herself an instant of indulgence and breathed deep of his scent. He smelled of cigarettes and of sulfurous brown coal, of dead leaves and city rain; he smelled of human skin and human hair and the lingering hint of floral-scented soap. He smelled of Budapest and Nicosia and Tidewater, Virginia, of years and heartache and sex and longing. He smelled of life, a life lived without her; a band of pain tightened around her chest. She had mourned the loss of his body as much as his soul—*this* body, strong and controlling, almost feral in the darkness. She shuddered and closed her eyes, feeling his hands on her rib cage, her shoulder, the lobe of her ear. His touch stung her skin with so much rippling life—and for an instant, she wanted to cry aloud with joy, she wanted to forget every unbearable moment of her days without him, she wanted to cradle his head and thank God that he was *alive*. It was what she had prayed for so uselessly during the long nights of grief: a life returned. A second chance. And her prayer had been answered.

But with what vicious reckoning.

This man was no miracle. He was a walking lie.

The rage of the past two years boiled hotly to the surface, so that her own mouth tore back at his, a savage thing that wanted to hurt him. Through the busboy's coat he wore she could feel the thud of his heart, too fast, and the tension in his body, as though he were coiled to spring. But then, Eric was always a predator. She gripped his arms tightly and thrust him away.

"Where is Sophie Payne?"

He was breathless, a diver mad for air. "I can't tell you that. Not yet."

If he refuses to give up the goods, Scottie muttered in her brain, *shut him down, Caroline. Everything else is just crap.*

"Then what are you doing here?"

"*You're* here," he said baldly, and took a step toward her again.

"I'm here to find the Vice President. Your death made me an expert on 30 April, Eric."

"Caroline—"

"Tell me where she is. That's all I want from you."

"I need more time."

"You've had too much time, you son of a bitch!" Tears of rage pricked at her throat—rage at his insouciance, at the way he had walked back into her life as though he expected her to be there, her arms wide open—

She was terrified, suddenly, of breaking down. Rage was her friend. Rage was a tool. Let him believe she was stronger alone than she had ever been in his shadow. Let him fear the High Priestess of Reason.

She moved toward him, her hand punching hard into his chest with each step.

"One call to the lobby, Eric, and I shut you down! *One call.*"

"You won't do that."

"Give me a good reason!" She had one already: Bring Eric in, and he'd damage the Agency irrevocably. She cared little for bureaucracies creaking roughshod over the world, but Dare Atwood, Cuddy, Scottie Sorensen—they were all the people Caroline loved, the only ones left to protect. "Don't you understand? It's *over*. No more vendettas, no more little girls with bullets in their brains. No hijacked VP's. *It ends here.*"

He gave way, a bewildered expression on his face. "Much more is at stake than Sophie Payne. You need Krucevic, Caroline. More than that, you need everything he runs—the bank accounts, the networks, the points of liaison worldwide. You've got to roll him up. That's what I've been working for. Not just Krucevic's life, but everything he's built."

"So work with *me*," she demanded. "Give me the route to his base here in Hungary. Give me the Polish operation. Anything, Eric, that might help."

"You know about Poland?"

Caroline laughed harshly. "What did you think—that only *you* could do this job? We've all been doing it while you were dead and buried. I wish to hell you'd stayed that way."

"No, you don't," he whispered. His face was stark in the orange glow flooding the room from across the river. The light made a death mask of the sharp planes of his face, and she saw how much the past few years had aged him.

But she could not relent. Relent, and she'd lose him. "Where's your base, Eric? Tell me and I'll have a team inside of it before dawn."

He hesitated; he gave it an instant's thought. But the habit of self-reliance ran too deep. "I need a few more hours, Carrie."

"Time's up." Her voice was sharp with contempt. "Now get out of here before I call the cops."

"Caroline—"

"Nothing." It came out with explosive force.

He stopped, frozen.

"Nothing. You. Say. Will. Make. Any. Difference." It seemed important to pronounce each word with equal weight, as though he were deaf, half literate, a confused and pathetic foreigner. The small flower of hope that had bloomed in Berlin turned brown within her and died.

"I know I hurt you," he began. He raised a hand to touch her, and she went rigid.

His eyes—Eric's eyes, bluer than the sea and stark with pain—stared at her wordlessly. Was he begging her? *Her?*

Shut him down, Caroline. Everything else is just crap.

One call. That was all. Let him plead to the station if he was so goddamn desperate.

"Get out," she whispered.

And he did.

FIFTEEN

Budapest, 11:40 P.M.

L ADY. Lady Sophie—are you awake?"
 He was whispering urgently from the hallway.
She pulled herself to the edge of her bed and dangled
one arm toward the floor. If she could roll off the bed,
perhaps she could crawl over and talk to him. . . . She
tested her weight, leaning down on one hand, and felt
her wrist buckle. The effort made her dizzy with exhaustion.

"Lady Sophie!"

"Yes, Jozsef?" she croaked.

"My father is gone. May I come in?"

Despite the pain cramping deep in her bowels,
Sophie smiled. It was like the boy to ask permission.
"By all means. If only I could open the door."

It slid back soundlessly. She saw his small body outlined
against the light of the passage, the remote control in one
hand. In the other, he held a hypodermic.

"I have medicine." He slipped to her bedside still
whispering. He was a boy who would probably whisper
for the rest of his life. "You must take it soon, before it is

too late. There is not much medicine left. And I have had more than my share."

"Your father can make more," Sophie said.

"Not here in Budapest. If he went back to Berlin, maybe, to his lab . . . the Anthrax 3A bacillus is highly secret and very dangerous, lady. Papa does not carry it everywhere."

"Keep your antibiotic, Jozsef."

He frowned. "But you must take it! Do you know what is happening to you? It is very bad, lady. First you vomit blood. Then you vomit your entire stomach. Your heart is eaten away within you. And then at last, in unbearable pain, you die. My father has told me."

"And is your father always right? Was he right about your calls to your mother?"

He looked away.

"Where did he beat you?"

Wordlessly, he lifted the front of his shirt. His abdomen was a mass of red lines.

Asshole, Sophie thought impotently. *He's already bleeding inside.* "No one has the right to keep you from her. She's your mother and she loves you."

"If she's alive," Jozsef retorted, "then why hasn't *she* tried to find *me*?"

"When your father decides to kidnap somebody, he makes sure they're never found. Don't blame your mother. Look what he's done to the marines."

Jozsef giggled—a boyish sound, the first she had ever heard him make—and she was transported for an instant back to her old house in Malvern, before Mitch's death, Peter's grubby hands clutching his father's ankle while Mitch dragged him along, pretending not to notice. Roughhousing. Wrestling. The tumble of boyhood. "Do you want to escape?" she asked Jozsef.

The laughter died. "I could not."

"Do you want to?"

It was easier to be honest in this darkened room, her voice as relentless as the voice of conscience. "How? We can't even get out of this compound. We're locked in. The doors are impossible to force. They're electronic. And you're too ill."

"Then we'll have to make your father give us up."

Jozsef snorted. "My father will never do that. You're too important."

"I don't mean anything to him at all," she said firmly. "I've served my purpose. But you mean the world to him. For you, Jozsef, he would do anything."

"Then why does he beat me? If he loved me, he would not beat me."

"I wish that were true. There'd be far less abuse in the world. But beatings or no, he fears for your life. He fears the illness inside you. That's why he's saving the antibiotic he has for you—and letting me die."

The boy turned and looked at her piercingly.

"Where did you get that hypodermic?" Sophie asked.

"From the supply room, where he keeps the antibiotic."

"Do you have the strength to take me there?"

He did not answer for fully fifteen seconds. Then he said: "Don't do this, lady. It will make him angry. Papa cannot control himself when he is angry."

"I know," she said.

He shook his head. "You know nothing at all. I have seen him kill. I know what he can do."

"Jozsef—do you want to see your mother?"

"More than God Himself," the boy whispered.

"Then take me to the supplies."

———

Anxiously, Béla Horváth scanned the pages of his notebook and then thrust it into the plain black knapsack he carried to the lab every day. It was nearly midnight. The meeting with Vic Marinelli in Városliget Park was only eight hours away, but he was sweating with fear and nausea. The notebook was the embodiment of his betrayal, the embodiment of his faith. It must not come to harm.

He searched his untidy bedroom, eyes straining in the dark. A light at this hour would be a mistake. He had taken a risk even returning to the house. At the thought of Mlan and what he would do if he knew of the notebook—if he knew of the meeting with Marinelli—Horváth's fingers twitched spasmodically. He dropped the knapsack.

He had wanted this meeting, had almost initiated it when the city went up like a torch that afternoon and the laboratory had closed. He had suspected the truth at last tonight, he had tested and retested it out of thoroughness and disbelief, until with a scientist's harsh honesty he understood. Someone had to stop it.

He had bicycled home along the usual streets, crowded with people shouting as they had not done since 1989, since 1956, but those had been questions of politics then—of something worth dying for. This was about money. The ugliness in people's faces depressed him, and he wove in and out among the stalled cars, knapsack tight as a leech against his back, wondering what he hoped to save.

The chalk mark was a red slash trailing haphazardly across a concrete pillar, and for an instant, he was uncertain whether he had actually seen it. He stopped the bike and thrust his glasses higher on his nose, staring at the scrawl on the Vigadó concert hall. The signal was supposed to be done this way—but could it be a mistake? Something to do with the rioting? He was supposed to mark the opposite pillar himself, in blue chalk—he carried it always in a knapsack pocket—but the square, he noticed now, was blocked off by police. They were ranked shoulder to shoulder in front of Gerbeaud's, the coffeehouse. Trapped patrons glared through the broad plate-glass windows; others perused their papers, bored. Horváth felt a bubble of laughter shatter inside him: How like the police to protect their pastry!

He had backed away from the Vigadó, turned out of Vörösmarty Ter, and pedaled home. When he called Mirjana's answering machine, the message from Michael awaited him. He prayed that by now, Mirjana had safely left town.

The sound of breaking glass from the front of the house brought his head up sharply. The back door—

He crept out of the bedroom, turned left in the darkened hall, and saw the gloved hand snake through the shattered living-room window. They would have it open in seconds.

He sidestepped into the kitchen—and there, backlit in the alley streetlight, was the silent shape of a man. He was surrounded.

Horváth looked about wildly. He saw the too-obvious cupboards, the pathetic tray of cold supper his cleaning lady had prepared, the broom closet smelling sharply of vinegar and ammonia. He thrust the black knapsack behind a damp pail at the closet's rear just as Krucevic entered the kitchen.

"Mlan," Horváth said breathlessly, his back to the closet door. "Did you have to break my window?"

Krucevic smiled. "There are broken windows all over Budapest today. Besides, you didn't answer my knock."

"I never heard it," he said. That was certainly true; he

had been lost in a fever of his own making. Horváth gestured toward the tray, the limp slices of meat and the tepid vegetables covered in plastic. "I was just about to eat."

"At midnight?"

"As you see. I—I was working late."

"Poor Béla," Krucevic said slowly. "Always the desperate grind. You should get away for a while. Take a break from all this." He glanced at one of his men—a malevolent-looking bruiser with a shaved head—who stepped forward and took Horváth by the arm. "You haven't said you're glad to see me, Béla."

"I was just surprised, Mlan, that's all. You're well?" The thug's hand was like an iron cuff above his elbow.

"Strange," Krucevic mused. "I'd have said you weren't surprised at all. In fact, you looked like you were expecting me. Perhaps you'll tell me why while we drive."

"Drive?"

"To your lab. I'm afraid, Béla, you took something that does not belong to you. And now I want it back."

ONE

Berlin, 2 A.M.

ANATOLY RUBIKOV CARED NOTHING for the lateness of the hour. Nor for the dull headache that throbbed in his temples, or the sourness in his mouth. He called his wife in Hamburg from the main Berlin train station and felt a shaft of joy at her sleepy hello. Then he told her he loved her and promised he would see her in the morning.

Next he dialed Wally Aronson's cellular phone. Wally answered on the second ring.

"Where are you?" the station chief asked.

"The Hauptbahnhof," Anatoly replied. "I need to talk to you."

"About Lajta?"

Anatoly nodded, as though the man might be able to see his face across the rat's maze of city streets. "I'm scared to death," he told him softly. "I've got to get out. You've got to get me *out*."

"You're still alive. Calm down, Anatoly."

"He threatened my wife. My girls."

"I understand."

"Wally—" The Russian safecracker hesitated, his pride still strong. "I have something for you. In exchange for my safety. I have it here, right now. I will give it to you." His voice rose and broke, which was utterly unlike him. "But you must *help* me—"

"Wait there," the station chief interrupted curtly. "Buy your ticket to Hamburg and wait. I'll find you on the platform."

Anatoly hung up. He glanced around. Two o'clock in the morning in Berlin's busiest terminus, and the place was almost deserted. He saw an old man in a newsboy cap, snoring on a bench. A kid in black leather, the arms cut raggedly away—probably a heroin addict, his eyes had the look of death in them. And a woman. A tired woman with two worn suitcases and a rumpled paperback. She was standing alone on the platform as though she had nowhere to go. And he had thought this morning that she was bound for home.

Their eyes met across the distance. Strange, Anatoly thought, that she had chosen a smoking car from Budapest when she had not lit a cigarette all day.

He picked up his duffel bag and walked casually toward the men's room, praying it would be empty. It was. He walked into the echoing tiled space, registered the window high in the wall. He picked a stall at random and locked it behind him. His fingers, when he unzipped the duffel, were trembling like a drunk's.

Inside was a change of clothing, two packs of Russian clove cigarettes, a magazine. And tucked into the bottom, a sheaf of folded papers. He drew them out.

There were footsteps in the bathroom now, the sound of a urinal flushing. The toilet was old-fashioned, its tank bolted under the ceiling with a chain dangling. Anatoly reached up and pulled the flush. Then he closed his eyes for an instant. Muttered something between a curse and a prayer.

Outside on the platform, Greta Oppenheimer discarded her paperback and walked briskly toward the men's bathroom.

———————

Wally Aronson had spent the past two hours and twenty-nine minutes in a landfill twelve miles outside of Berlin. Old Markus had led the station chief and a team of six FBI evidence technicians into the site, and Old Markus was still there, a rented van at his back and an ancient Mauser rifle in his arms. Old Markus had an acute sense of where the Brandenburg evidence had been dumped; he had taken pictures of the trucks during daylight hours.

Wally clipped the chain-link metal fence and removed a section large enough for the team's infiltration. Spotlights were out of the question. So was extensive examination of the evidence. The Bureau people had decided simply to cart the largest pieces out of the landfill in the hired van for testing at a remote location: an abandoned U.S. Army base in what had once been the Western Sector of Berlin.

The mood among the collection team—four men and two women—was somber. What evidence they might succeed in retrieving would never be admissible in court; it was tainted by removal from the bomb site. But the clandestine trip had helped the frustrated Forensics people put their time to use. And the larger pieces might reveal something of value—stress patterns, fractures, explosive residues—that would shape the FBI's investigation of the bombing. The darkness and disorder of the dump, however, banished all hope of finding anything small. Like the timing device of a bomb.

Wally and the others were tense, waiting for a klaxon alarm, the release of dogs and floodlights, or the disappearance of one of their number into a mountain of stinking refuse. Wally had the most to lose: While the Forensics people would merely be sent home on the next available plane, Wally, as station chief, could be publicly humiliated if he were caught. But the landfill was deserted. Whoever had ordered the evidence removed from the Brandenburg Gate had not troubled with it further.

Wally tucked his cell phone back into the pocket of his black windbreaker. He had never heard Anatoly Rubikov sound so desperate; he would have to drive back to the Hauptbahnhof right now.

"Markus," he told the foreign-service national, "I'm counting on you, buddy. See that these people get back to the ranch, okay?"

———

Sirens were wailing but the police had not yet arrived by the time Wally reached the train station. A kid in black leather was crouched in the doorway of the men's bathroom, groaning as though he was going to vomit. Wally stepped over him and saw the blood just beyond his black-jeaned legs, the corpse in a heap by the open stall door.

"*Scheisse,*" he muttered in German.

Anatoly had been stabbed. The thin-bladed knife was still buried in his chest.

The boy in leather hadn't done it, Wally knew that. The bathroom window was open. Whoever had cut his joe to the heart must have left that way. Wally studied the Russian safecracker, the sprawl of his limbs, the way

he had fallen, and resisted the impulse to close Anatoly's
eyes.

There was not much time.

Wally tugged his winter gloves from his coat pockets
and slipped them on. The boy in leather looked up, eyes
blank with fear. "I'd get out of here," Wally told him in
German. "Unless you want to talk to the police."

The kid stumbled to his feet and ran.

Wally stepped over Anatoly's body and looked into
the stall. There should have been a bag—some sort of
overnight piece—but there was nothing. No luggage to
suggest he had been traveling from Budapest. Wally
studied the stall. The lid of the tank was slightly askew.

He jumped up and lifted the porcelain cover. Groped
inside with his gloved fingers. And then his expression
changed.

The two-note klaxon of an ambulance siren rent the
night air.

Wally pulled the sheaf of papers out of the toilet tank
and slid them inside his coat.

TWO

Budapest, 1:23 A.M.

TONIO WAS SNORING by the time Michael drove up to the underground garage. He punched a key code into a remote-control device mounted on the dashboard and the electronic doors slid open. He pulled inside, and the doors closed automatically behind him. It was then he saw that the space reserved for Mlan's Mercedes was empty.

He killed the Audi's engine, feeling his skin prickle. Krucevic was still mobile. Had he been arrested at the Budapest checkpoint? Or had he abandoned the two of them, Michael and Tonio, now that the Hungarian job was done?

The door to the compound was probably wired to blow.

He glanced over his shoulder at the sealed electronic garage doors, fighting the urge to panic, to gun the Audi in reverse right through them. Think. *Think.*

Krucevic had said nothing about an errand tonight. That was hardly unusual. He never shared his plans until they were ready to activate.

But maybe he had learned at last who Michael really was. Maybe he, Michael, had been betrayed. By an overeager Sophie Payne, or perhaps . . .

He thought suddenly of Béla Horváth, of the unhappy Mirjana. Obvious risks, to themselves and him. His message might have come too late.

You've had too much time, you son of a bitch!

Tonio muttered in an alcoholic dream, his head lolling toward the armrest.

Michael eased open the door. There was a chance he could discover whether the compound was sabotaged before it killed them.

He crept up to the entrance, every nerve in his body screaming. There was no red pinpoint beam of a laser to break, just the camera focused as usual, recording his stealth; he would have to explain that later. He ran his fingers around the doorjamb—no thin copper wire. And no discernible sound from within.

The only way he would know was to attempt it.

He pressed a second code into a keypad by the door, held his finger against a print detector, and waited for the electronic verification.

The door slid open.

Whatever fate awaited him, it was not on this threshold. He went inside.

Jozsef's good-luck charm was resting forgotten on the table in the main room. A curious lapse; he was never without it. Michael pocketed the rabbit's foot and walked down the corridor to his door. It was sealed shut.

"Jozsef? Jozsef?" He raised his hand to knock just as the boy's voice came groggily from beyond.

"Is that you, Michael? What time is it?"

"Nearly two. Go back to sleep. There's nothing to be worried about."

So Krucevic had abandoned them, locked into their windowless cells, the boy and Sophie Payne. Necessity must have driven him. Michael felt a stab of fear for Béla Horváth. If Mlan were to suspect—

He strode back to the main room. Tonio was still snoring in the car. Now for the computer. The payment for Caroline's lost years.

He understood far less about the files than Tonio, of course, but he had been watching, secretly, how the man manipulated his data. He knew how to unlock the keyboard's secrets. Mlan changed the password every day, and only Tonio was privy to it; but Michael had watched his fingers that morning. He thought he could repeat the strokes.

He sat down in front of the laptop. The password was *chaos* today, he was certain—but entry was denied. Had he inverted the *a* and the *o*? Michael swore aloud. Three failed attempts, and the computer would destroy its own hard disk. He willed his fingers to stop shaking and tried again.

This time, like the door to Ali Baba's cave, the way opened. He began to search among the treasures scattered haphazardly on the thieves' floor.

———

"Michael," the voice said behind him.

He jumped involuntarily and snapped the computer lid shut. *Stupid! Stupid not to be more on my guard.* "Mrs. Payne. You should be asleep. How did you get out of your room?"

"Jozsef. He has a remote, did you know?"

She swayed and clutched at the jamb. That quickly he was at her side. She looked ghastly.

"Here. Sit." He helped her to a chair.

"I wish you would tell me why you're pretending to be a terrorist," she said plaintively as she sank into his seat. "I'm almost dead. I deserve to know."

"You're not going to die."

"You don't know what you're talking about. I'm puking pieces of my stomach."

"The medicine," he said. "I'll get you some. He'll never know."

"Don't," she called after him; but he was already in the passage, he had the code punched into the supply-room pad, and it was only when the door had slid open that he understood what she meant. Twelve dozen ampules lay smashed to powder on the floor.

"My God," he groaned, and leaned against the doorjamb. "What have you done, Mrs. Payne?"

Her eyes blazed at him. "I've placed that boy's life in jeopardy, and he helped me do it. I almost lacked the courage. But it had to be done. I had to force Krucevic's hand. Jozsef says there's no more medicine here. If he wants to save his son's life, Krucevic must go back to Berlin. He'll abort this insane campaign."

Michael stared at her in wonder and pity. "He'll slit your throat for this."

"But not the throats of a million Muslims, and that is all that matters. I've been a dead woman since Tuesday." She sank down to the floor, her back against the wall, and took a shuddering breath. "Would you kill me now? Like that little girl in Bratislava? Before he gets back?"

"Mrs. Payne—"

"My name is Sophie. I do not think yours is really Michael, somehow."

"Let me take you back to your room—"

"I'd rather die where I am," she interrupted. "Now get out your gun, God damn it."

"I can't."

"You must. I order you as the second in command of your country!"

He knelt down before her. "I told you once I would not let you die at this man's hands. I'm certainly not going to kill you myself."

"You won't have to. Krucevic will." Her eyes closed tightly; she drew a rattling breath. "Give me your gun, then."

Michael put his hand under Sophie's elbow. "Come on. Let's get Jozsef. We'll leave now."

Her eyes flew open. "Can you get out? Once you're inside?"

"Of course."

"Jozsef couldn't."

"Jozsef's a prisoner," he reminded her brutally. "I'm a jailor." He crossed to the boy's door and pounded on it, hard. "Jozsef. Hurry up and get dressed."

"I can't walk anywhere," Sophie protested faintly. "I'll just hold you back."

"There's a car in the garage. We'll take that to the U.S. embassy. You'll be in a hospital in an hour."

The flash of joy that crossed her face was almost too painful to watch. "Why now?"

He held aloft his computer disk. "Because it's all here—the entire 30 April Organization. In American hands, as of tonight."

"But you won't actually get him, will you?" she challenged. "Krucevic will escape. And he'll wreak havoc for the rest of his days."

"I'll have saved you. That's enough."

Sophie shook her head. "Not for me."

He started to speak—started to tell her that once she was returned safely to the United States, Fritz Voekl and Mlan Krucevic would have the World Court to contend with—but the lies died on his lips.

Tonio was standing in the doorway. How long had he been there? How much had he heard?

"What's going on, Michael?"

"Nothing much. How's your head?" He did not look at Sophie Payne.

Tonio walked toward him, rubbing his eyes groggily. "*Dio,* but it aches. I'm going to bed." His eyes drifted over the room indifferently. They came to rest on the computer. "Who's been messing with that?"

Michael began to move easily behind him, coming around in position behind his head, the butt of his gun in his hand. It was a myth that you could knock a person out with a single blow; the human skull was extremely sturdy. It required a punishing force. Or a knock at the base of the cranium.

"I turned it on," Jozsef said from his door. Little-boy sullenness in his voice. "I wanted to play a computer game, Tonio, but I didn't know the access code."

Sophie Payne had pushed herself, impossibly, to her feet. Her sunken eyes were crazed with fever.

Tonio focused drunkenly on the woman. "What are you doing out of your cell?"

"I wanted to play, too," she said.

Tonio swore viciously under his breath and lifted the

laptop's lid. Before he wheeled to confront them, Michael's gun crashed down on his skull.

And at that moment, they all heard the sound of the garage door opening.

Mlan Krucevic was back.

THREE
Budapest, 2:15 A.M.

M IRJANA TARCIC WAS PARKED in an alley near
Béla Horváth's house, about a hundred feet beyond his small backyard. Vaclav Slivik had never noticed
her, a lapse in his tradecraft and judgment; but Mlan
had given the assassin too little time to reconnoiter.
Mirjana's car was old and indeterminate of color, it was
pulled up in the lee of a battered garage, and a tree trunk
blocked the line of sight from Béla's kitchen door. A
better man than Vaclav would have missed it.

Mirjana had spent most of the day in the emergency
room of a Budapest hospital, waiting to be treated for
bruises and cracked ribs. She had never gone home.
One call to her answering machine had convinced her
that home was a mistake.

Mlan and his men had left Béla's house hours ago.
If she did not move soon, someone would come
back.

She had hoped against hope that it would be Béla
himself who returned—whistling cheerfully as he
walked up the drive, letting himself in through the front

door, putting the teakettle on the stove in the wee hours of morning. That was foolishness, of course.

Her cold hand sought the door handle and eased it open.

The rains had brought down a mass of deadwood from the trees. The crunch of twigs beneath her feet was remorseless as death. She could not allow herself to breathe. She crept up to the back door wondering why his neighbors said nothing, why lights did not go on and alarms sound—and yet, they had suffered the noise of breaking glass without reaction. They were Hungarians. They had grown up under the Party system; black cars in the night had always taken people away. The wisest course was simply to go on sleeping.

Her fingers found the latch. Inside, darkness.

She stepped forward, toward a patch of moonlight bright as halogen on the gray linoleum, and saw a tumbled mass of human hair. The sight stopped her in her tracks.

Not hair. Wet strands of a mop, fallen from the open broom closet. With a ragged breath, she reached for it and propped it inside. What had they wanted with this, in the middle of the night? Or had the broom closet door, poorly latched, fallen open under the mop's weight?

She hesitated, eyes adjusting now to the darkness, and scanned the narrow space. There was the usual broom, a dustpan neatly stacked beside a pail, bottles of cleaning stuff and a carryall filled with clean rags. She knelt and groped along the floor, dreading mice. And touched the square shape of the knapsack.

She had seen him pedaling to work so many times, the knapsack a memory of those university days in Leipzig when they'd all managed to be happy. Béla had hidden it here in his last moments, and Mlan in his viciousness had not understood.

Mirjana clutched the backpack to her chest and ran—heedless of the neighbors, of the branches cracking underfoot—for her life.

FOUR

Budapest, 7:30 A.M.

"I HAVE A THEORY," Tom Shephard said as the taxi pulled away from the entrance to the Hilton, "that a city's soul is something you can feel. It walks the streets, asks you for change on a deserted corner, tells you what song it has to sing. You know what I mean?"

Caroline glanced at him wordlessly. So Tom was a morning person. He had found something to love in this sordid new day, the air rank with burning and the looters asleep in the streets. After Eric had left her, she'd lain awake for hours.

It was impossible not to consider every one of his words, every choice she had made; impossible not to see that she had fucked up abominably. She had drawn Eric straight into her trap, and for emotional reasons, she had let him go. It was unforgivable. *Unprofessional.* It was exactly the kind of example a male case officer would use in an argument against women in Intelligence. Caroline showered blue language on her own head while Tom Shephard chatted genially at her side—Shephard, who had no idea that she had held the Vice President's kidnappers in the palm of her hand and simply waved good-bye. Eric would never contact her again. And Sophie Payne's life was at risk—

"You okay?" Shephard asked.

"I didn't sleep well," Caroline said brusquely. She felt bruised and overly sensitive, as though she suffered from sunburn.

"Take Paris," he went on. "Paris is a wealthy woman with a checkered past. She danced at the Folies Bergères in her youth, then married a besotted *comte*."

"The very opposite of Washington," Caroline managed.

"Washington has the fussy correctness of a bureaucrat's briefcase."

"And a tropical-weight suit," she added, "permanently creased."

"Istanbul—Istanbul is a stalled caravan, hardening in the sun."

"St. Petersburg has diamonds in her hair and a gun at her back."

"So what's Buda's story?" he asked.

She shrugged. "It's part of *your* territory."

"But you've lived here." His look was almost accusing. Intent, invasive, as disturbing as it had been in the plane the previous night. Her pulse quickened. *What is he looking for?*

"I just visit here," he persisted. "I want to hear your version of the truth."

No, you don't, she thought. *My version is a lie.* The taxi had crossed the Chain Bridge and was now in Pest. Here, rioters had spared not a single shop window; shards of glass were flung across the sidewalk like hail. A lavender silk slip trailed across an overturned park bench; more clothes had snagged on trash cans and street signs as the whirlwind of looters had swept through them. Garbage from the dented cans sprawled across the roadbed. A forlorn dog rooted in a sodden cardboard box. Nearby, the sidewalk was stained with what looked like battery acid. Or blood.

The taxi driver grunted and slowed his car to maneuver around an overturned van. Its engine block was still burning. They were the only people moving on the streets—except for a contingent of black-shirted guards. All stared at the taxi suspiciously as it creaked past. Caroline refused to make eye contact. And prayed that she and Shephard would be allowed to proceed.

"Budapest," she told him, "is a middle-aged man in a shabby coat, nursing an espresso at an outdoor café. It is very cold, and the smell of dog urine from the wet pavement mingles with the coffee and the sharp scent of pickled beets from somewhere down the street."

"He's wearing wire-rimmed spectacles," Shephard offered, "and writing in a notebook with a torn cover. His wife left him years ago, but he's haunted by the memory of her laugh."

Caroline turned to look at him. "Is he?" she asked. "Better laughter than tears, Tom."

The hazel eyes did not waver. "What are you haunted by, Caroline?"

It was all there before her suddenly, the concourse in Frankfurt and the man turning away.

"The memory of silence," she replied. And did not speak again until they had reached Szabadsag Ter.

The protesters had abandoned the U.S. embassy. No megaphoned speeches or hurled rocks greeted Shephard and Caroline as they approached. There was a checkpoint, however, backed by the ominous clatter of tanks, so they dismissed the taxi and covered the last thirty yards on foot, their diplomatic passports held high. After a grim few moments of consideration, the guards waved them through.

The stretch of turf that ran between Magyar Television and the National Bank, a modernist cube of glass and steel, was churned to mud and studded with green shards of what had once been soda bottles. The burned trash cans were smoldering now, and stank of seared plastic; a bird, brown as the Danube in winter, pecked disconsolately among the torn seat cushions of a torched car. But the impulse toward civilization had begun to reassert itself; red tape with harsh Hungarian exclamations already cordoned off the worst areas.

Vic Marinelli met them at the embassy door.

"I'm glad you're early," the Budapest station chief said without preamble. "Our meeting's off."

"Because of the riots?" Caroline asked.

He shook his head. "We'll discuss it upstairs. Let's get you through security. Morning, Corporal. I'd like to take these people up."

The marine guard studied their diplomatic passports, then gave them embassy passes they clipped to their clothing. Vic hovered impatiently. He looked, she thought, like a Medici prince—black eyes heavily lidded, full lips set in a permanent curl. She glanced at his hands: the long, tapering fingers of a philosopher-priest.

"Wally Aronson sends his regards," she told him.

"I've already talked to Wally this morning."

"Then he's up early," Shephard said.

"I'm not sure he ever went to bed." Vic looked appraisingly at Caroline. "He thinks a hell of a lot of you."

Tom Shephard was staring through the embassy's front window at the garrisoned square below. "Are those Hungarian tanks?"

"Yes," Marinelli said tersely, "but only a few Hungarians are manning them. Most of those men are Germans. They arrived this morning. The prime minister asked for NATO help two hours before he resigned. He was refused." The station chief's eyes flicked over to Caroline's. "You've heard about the provisional government, of course?"

"Not a word. Tell us."

Marinelli led them down a high-ceilinged corridor, past the state drawing rooms and the ambassador's suite. "Hungarian Pride has formed a cabinet. They seem to have anticipated the treasury heist."

Hungarian Pride was a right-wing faction led by a charismatic and highly articulate history professor named Georg Korda. The group had never boasted significant power, but their nationalist, pro-cleansing rhetoric had steadily gained adherents.

"Korda's hitting the former government over the head for incompetence, and calling for economic austerity. As though belt tightening can protect you from electronic plunder." Marinelli grimaced.

"You believe it, then?" Caroline asked. "That Lajta embezzled the treasury before he killed himself?"

"Somebody did," he said curtly.

The door of the station suggested a closet tucked into the second-floor landing, something to be overlooked. Marinelli waited for her to precede him, arm outstretched in a gesture of courtesy; this was, after all, his domain. But in Caroline's mind it would always be Eric's. She stepped past him.

Every moldy smell, every curling bit of plaster, every length of electrical wire glimpsed under an upturned edge of carpet screamed to her of the days that were gone. Eric had ruled this station for a while—he had breathed, drunk, and ingested it for the length of his tour—and if the soul of that dead time could be said to live anywhere, it was here in the Budapest embassy.

"Okay," Marinelli said, shutting the door behind them, "here's the state of play. DBTOXIN—Béla Horváth—was found shot to death in his laboratory this morning. His house and the lab were thoroughly ransacked."

"Then he's been blown." The sick feeling of disaster tightened Caroline's shoulder blades.

"I'd like to think it was a coincidence, something to do with the riots. But the timing is too perfect. It looks to me as though Horváth was silenced."

"By Krucevic?"

"Or his wife." Marinelli gazed at her levelly. "You know Wally Aronson passed on her number yesterday. A call came through while we were monitoring her line last night. It mentioned TOXIN's first name."

"What exactly did it say?" Shephard was frowning.

" 'It's me. We're in town. Tell Béla to watch his back. And for Christ's sake, be careful,' " Marinelli quoted.

Eric. It could be no one else.

"That sounds like a warning. Not a death threat."

"Perhaps the caller is someone she betrayed," Marinelli suggested. "Just like she betrayed Béla."

"But the *we* makes it sound like one of the terrorists." Shephard's scowl had deepened.

"Or a different group altogether. We can't know for certain." *If Eric could not trust Mirjana Tarcic,* Caroline thought—but no, the very idea was absurd. The woman hated Mlan Krucevic. He had robbed her of her son.

"Is anything missing from Horváth's lab? Or his house?" she asked Marinelli.

"Did they find what they were looking for, you mean? I don't know. I'm trying to get that information from the Budapest police. I have a contact there, but with the riots, the looting—" He shook his head. "I suggested they get one of Horváth's lab partners to go through his things with them. Tell them what might have been taken."

"If Horváth is blown," Tom asked, "do we assume that 30 April has already left Hungary?"

"I sure as hell hope not. Because Wally Aronson just came through with something brilliant." Marinelli reached across his desk for a manila envelope. "Look at this."

A sheaf of blueprints, overwritten with handwriting so fine it was almost impossible to read. Page after page of blueprints—perhaps a dozen in all. Caroline bent over the plans. "What are these?"

"The security details of Mlan Krucevic's Budapest headquarters."

"Jesus," burst out Tom Shephard. "Has anyone called Washington?"

"Of course," Marinelli said patiently.

"I suppose we owe this to old what's-his-acronym," Caroline murmured.

The station chief glanced at her sharply. "Wally got these blueprints from a developmental. A Russian security expert. He's dead."

Tom expelled a gusty breath. "This job just gets less and less healthy. So when do we storm the compound?"

"When we know where it is," Marinelli said crisply.

Caroline and Tom exchanged a look.

"One person might be able to help us," she said. "Mirjana Tarcic."

"We can't trust her." Marinelli dismissed the notion instantly. "It's probable that she betrayed Horváth. If we contact her and she warns Krucevic, he'll be long gone by the time we arrive."

"But Tarcic is all we've got."

Marinelli opened his mouth to argue and then abruptly closed it as the truth of Caroline's words hit home.

Tom looked up from the blueprints. "Are the Buda police searching for this woman?"

Marinelli's eyes shifted away. "I don't know. Maybe they are."

Which meant, Caroline thought, that they certainly were. Marinelli had given his police source Mirjana Tarcic—an even trade for the man's information about Horváth.

"Perhaps we should get to her first," Shephard mused. "Control the situation. The Vice President's fate demands that much."

"I have to agree." And for the first time, Marinelli's medieval face wore a troubled expression. Had he begun to doubt himself?

"Maybe I can help," Tom offered. "I've got contacts here at the Interior Ministry. The Hungarian FBI. Do you have a photograph of Tarcic, by any chance?"

The station chief did.

It was a candid shot, probably taken by a case officer through a car window. She was walking along a city street, muffled in a winter coat; but miraculously the photographer had gotten the angle right, and the woman's face filled the frame. Lank dark hair, deep-set Balkan eyes—it was an arresting face, gaunt with middle age, hollow with anxiety.

Caroline passed the photograph to Tom Shephard. He tapped it lightly with one finger.

"The federal police owe me some favors."

"Let's hope they can keep their mouths shut," Marinelli said.

The Danube Bend, 10:03 A.M.

SZENTENDRE WAS AN ANCIENT TOWN of Byzantine Rite churches, all facing east; of artists and musicians and tourist kitsch. A small jewel of Balkan architecture, it had been founded in 1389, after the Turks won the Battle of Kosovo and the vanquished Serbs fled west and north. Like many places born of exile, it felt more authentic than the original. Most of the Serbs had returned to Belgrade four hundred years later, rather than swear allegiance to the Hapsburg Empire; but a few had remained. Mirjana Tarcic's mother was descended from one of them.

She rented an apartment above an art gallery on Görög Utca, a steep and narrow street running down to the banks of the Danube. Two rooms, with wide-plank pine flooring and red woven rugs, wooden tables painted in the Hungarian folk fashion, and a galley kitchen hung about with antique copper butter molds. Skylights were cut into the sloping roof, and on days of bright sun the rugs fired crimson, the trailing flowers on the painted chair-backs leapt to vivid life. It was a comfortable place for a single woman—or two women, when Mirjana drove out from the city for the weekend.

She had driven out a day early this time, because of the riots. She had driven out of Béla Horváth's alley as though Mlan Krucevic were after her with a chain saw. She arrived at three A.M. and let herself into the apartment with her spare key. Four hours later, her mother found her asleep on the living-room sofa.

Béla Horváth's body had not yet been discovered in the ruins of his lab. She was granted a period of ignorance.

Mirjana slept fitfully, despite the soothing drum of rain on the skylight glass. She awoke with a start to the slam of a door and knew that her mother had left for work. The older woman owned an antiques store on the main street of Szentendre, Fó Ter, a thriving business now that people had cash to spend.

It was already after ten o'clock.

Panic washed over Mirjana. She turned, threw off the wool blanket her mother had tucked around her, and searched frantically for the notebook and ampules. They were there still, on the floor at the sofa's foot, where she had dropped them the night before.

The strong earthen smell of coffee pulled her to the kitchen. Her mind was still dazed with terror. Her ribs, cracked and tightly taped by a Budapest hospital, ached with every breath. Mlan Krucevic lurked in the corners of her brain, in the closets she forced him to occupy; he hammered loudly at her padlocked doors. He knew about her mother. He knew the apartment in Szentendre. What had she been thinking of to draw him this way? *Fool*. She had thrown herself down the Danube Bend in desperation, in the middle of the night, but she could not stay. Her mother—

Where *were* the ampules? The notebook? What time was it, now?

She stared crazily around the room, her throat swelling with fear, then saw them lying where she had left them—on the floor near the sofa. *Thank God*. She wasn't losing her mind. She took a deep swallow of the coffee, choked, and spat it into the sink.

Why was she so afraid of him? He had done almost everything to her body that one man could do. If he killed her at last, it would be nothing more than a single moment of terror in the long line of such moments that had punctuated her life. She was not afraid of pain. She was terrified of *losing*. For once in her life she had the upper hand with Mlan Krucevic—she had the notebook and the ampules, she had knowledge and power over his life. She had a chance to take back Jozsef.

She would find a safe place. She would hide herself and her mother. And then she would contact Mlan— somehow, there was always a way—and tell him what she knew. What she could give to the world, to the United States: the truth about vaccine No. 413.

And at last, after decades of torment and loss and ter-ror, she would grind his balls under her heel, and wear cleats to do it. She would demand the return of her son.

And then? What then, Mirjana? You do not make deals with the devil. Because the devil always wins.

Where is the notebook? The ampules? Da bog sačuva—

There. Near the sofa.

She poured half the cup of coffee down the drain with shaking fingers. And at that moment, there was a knock on the door.

Mirjana went rigid. She could not breathe.

Another knock, louder this time.

And then the sound of a metal pick sliding into the lock.

There was no other way out of the apartment. She was trapped.

Mirjana tore wildly across the small room, whimpering deep in her throat, and snatched up the notebook and ampules. *He will not win.*

She thrust Béla's things under her mother's mattress in a kind of frenzy. She had mounted a chair and unlocked the skylight by the time the front door was kicked open.

Shephard insisted on escorting Caroline past the Volksturm tanks and down Dorottya Utca toward Vörösmarty Ter.

"Are you coming with me?" he asked abruptly.

"To the Interior Ministry?" She was surprised. "I'd just cramp your style. These are *your* contacts, Shephard. You don't need me hovering in the background. I require too much explanation."

"That you do," he muttered under his breath. "So are you off for a quick change in a telephone booth? Caroline Carmichael into Sally Bowles? A meeting with Sharif's Budapest division, say?"

She stopped short. So he had taken Wally Aronson's hints to heart. What else was Tom Shephard beginning to suspect?

"Look," she temporized, "I'm sorry I haven't been completely frank. We work for different agencies. We have different kinds of constraints. I don't expect you to explain your operational code. So don't ask me to explain mine. I promise you that everything I do—with blond hair or black—is dedicated toward finding the Vice President."

His sharp eyes bored into hers, unappeased.

"If you want to nab Mirjana Tarcic, you'd better get going," she said.

"Where will you be?"

"At Gerbeaud's. The café in Vörösmarty Ter. I need some coffee."

"I'll meet you there for lunch." He glanced at his wristwatch. "Let's say one o'clock."

"Done."

She waited on the sidewalk until he was out of sight, despite the raw wind gusting off the Danube. Something in the way he carried himself in his rumpled clothes—graceful as a cricketer in flannels, from an era long dead—lifted her spirits immeasurably. She found that she was actually thankful for him: for Tom Shephard, the millstone around her neck. She had not anticipated how useful he could be. He was, after all, the Central European LegAtt. The security systems of an entire region were theoretically at his fingertips. Mirjana Tarcic was as good as bagged.

She was still gazing after him when Eric's car pulled up to the corner of Dorottya Utca.

He had the passenger door open. She got in.

SIX

Budapest, 10 A.M.

DON'T SPEAK, Eric had written on a scrap of paper. *Car's bugged.*

Caroline held the note tightly in her hand and stared straight ahead through the windshield. It had begun to rain, a fine mist that clouded the glass; the interior of the Audi was musty with wet wool and dead smoke.

He drove fast, toward the Elizabeth Bridge and across the Danube to Gellért Hill, up the winding, parklike roads that switched back and back. In the eleventh century, pagan Huns had rolled St. Gellért down this hill to his death in the Danube. In the nineteenth, the Hapsburg rulers had mounted cannon here and trained them against their own city. More recently, the Soviets had erected statues on the hill, celebrating Communist brotherhood. It was, Caroline thought, a place consecrated in betrayal.

He pulled up at the summit, monuments soaring behind his back. Gellért Hill was deserted at this time of day, in this shower of rain. She got out.

Eric left the keys in the Audi's ignition and joined her. "We don't have much time."

He began to walk, tugging her with him, toward the river roiling gray through the streaming trees.

"What are you doing out here in broad daylight, alone? That's not Krucevic's MO," Caroline said tensely.

"He sent me out." Eric's voice was almost feverish. "He sent me out for a fucking *newspaper,* Caroline. It's a setup."

"Béla Horváth is dead."

He stopped in his tracks, swearing softly, and released her. "Mirjana?"

"Hasn't been found. But Buda station's screening her calls. Don't use her number."

A hundred yards behind them, the Audi they'd left seconds before exploded with the scream of a flying shell. The driver's side door flew off, kited high into the air, and plummeted to the ground ten feet from where they stood.

"Holy shit," Caroline whispered.

———

They stopped running at the entrance to the baths that formed the basement of the Hotel Gellért. Eric paid their admission without waiting for change and they ducked inside, as though intent on some shameful assignation. The air was thick with steam and the pungency of eucalyptus. She looked up, saw the cathedral height of the mosaic tile ceiling, an illusion of sanctuary. And thought, *They are hunting him.*

Eric led her to a table set into an alcove. She sat down, weak-kneed. He remained standing, a man with places to go, always on the verge of leaving her.

"Last night," he said, "after I left your hotel, I drove back to Krucevic's base. He wasn't there. Tonio was dead drunk and the boy and Mrs. Payne were sleeping. I downloaded everything from his computer. Everything that matters. Then I tried to get the Veep and Jozsef out. Krucevic came back before I could."

"And?"

"And he accused me of selling him out to his ex-wife and Horváth."

"Which I presume you've done."

"Systematically," Eric agreed, still in the same intense undertone. "It's the whole point of this operation. I've got a network out there. It's in place. I use it."

"Why didn't he kill you?"

"I told him he was wrong."

She raised an eyebrow. "That alone should have bought you a bullet."

"I pointed out that I had never been given access to his computer. His computer holds everything that Krucevic values. One person alone has access." He leaned closer to her, his blue eyes blazing. "To save myself, I gave him Tonio, who was lying unconscious at his feet, reeking of alcohol. I'd knocked him on the head with the butt of my gun. I told Krucevic that if he was looking for a traitor, he should check first with the man who owned his keyboard. Would you call that cowardice, Caroline?"

"Don't ask me to stand in judgment over anything you do, Eric. I can't grant you absolution."

"The Veep is dying," he said. "She's *dying,* Caroline, and you're right, we're out of time. I can't leave her alone."

"I think you just did," she retorted. "There's no road back from a blown car. Did you push the button, or did they?"

"I didn't wire the car. Let's just call that Krucevic's insurance."

Across the distance of maybe a hundred feet, a wet head was bobbing in the warm spring pool. The echoing vastness of the Gellért baths could play tricks with sound, send deceptive waves curling along the ceiling tiles. But Eric was speaking softly.

"How sick is Payne?" she asked.

"I'd give her twenty-four hours. Less, probably."

"The antibiotic doesn't work?"

"It works for a while. She's had several doses of it, which accounts for the fact that she's still breathing. But Krucevic has cut her off. His antibiotic supplies were limited. He was saving them for his son. And then Payne smashed all that he had."

Caroline stared at him in dismay. "That's . . . that's insane."

"She thought that if Krucevic was out of drugs, he'd trash his campaign. Head back to the labs in Berlin."

"You don't agree."

"Krucevic never retreats, Carrie."

"He'll kill her for this, won't he?"

"I think that's what she wants," Eric mused. "She's got immense courage, Caroline—she's tougher than you'd believe—but she's in enough pain to think death would be a relief. Last night she asked me to shoot her. I probably should have. Now—"

He reached into his jacket and withdrew a small brown envelope. "Get this to Scottie."

"What is it?"

"A computer disk. Everything Scottie needs to know is on it. Mlan's contacts in terrorist organizations worldwide, his complete list of accounts, the way the money flows, the mumps epidemic—"

"*Mumps* epidemic? You mean in Pristina?"

An angel with flushed cheeks sinking on her mother's shoulder. Thousands of sick and dying children, the Muslim horde Krucevic despised. No more sacred to him than firebombed hostels, or dead chancellors, or winsome Dagmar Hammecher, her blond hair shaved and her small hand sawn off. *Of course* the mumps epidemic was no accident. Caroline's anger flared as the random pieces shifted into place.

"And copies of Krucevic's E-mail correspondence with Fritz Voekl," Eric concluded.

"Voekl's sending German medical teams into Pristina with vaccines right now," she said. "Is that the point? Create an epidemic so that Fritz can save a few Muslim lives?"

"You're the analyst."

She stared at him. The disk in her hand held over two years of their lives. Outside the rain beat down on Budapest, dead leaves swirled in the city park. The city park. Where Scottie's ghost still walked in tweeds, an arm around each of their shoulders—

"Scottie knew about you, didn't he?" she said very softly. "All this time. Scottie knew you weren't dead."

Eric went utterly still. His face took on a look of brittle awareness. "He never told you?"

"Told me what?"

Slowly, he reached for the chair opposite and sat down. "Are you saying that Scottie *never told you I was alive*?"

When he could have the most exotic undercover operation ever conceived in his own backyard, subject to no oversight, financed by selective borrowing among the CTC's ample accounts?

With Eric to run and enough room to run him,

Scottie could screw them all—Congress, the guys who'd been promoted past him, Dare Atwood in her cherry-paneled office on the seventh floor. Why tell anyone at all? It was a much better secret savored in silence. And with a little luck and expert timing, Scottie might even catch Mlan Krucevic, certified sicko, with all the adulation that could bring.

Deception was second nature to Scottie; he had compartments to spare in his sinuous brain. Eric fit so conveniently into one of them. Caroline felt suddenly giddy with hilarity. *Of course Scottie told nobody.* This thing was as sexy as a stripper in the living room, it was the wet dream of a case officer's long, dry career.

"What do you think Scottie is," she replied with a shaky laugh. "Unprofessional?"

Eric stood up suddenly and tossed the small table aside like so many milk cartons, tossed it at the tiled wall of the baths with a violence that echoed and reechoed under the streaming ceiling. Her second explosion that hour. And seized her by the shoulders, oblivious of the bathers watching them now.

"You honestly thought that I would leave you—spend all this time under cover—without a word? You think I would do that? You think any kind of operation would be worth that kind of pain?"

"I had nothing else to believe."

"Thirty months." He paced viciously away from her. "Thirty months of hell, of being not what I am, of plotting and calculating and hoping there's some kind of God between me and death, of thinking, *Caroline is there. She is there. I will get back to her—*"

He stopped.

"Only that was never part of the plan, was it? That's

why he didn't tell you. Scottie never thought I was coming back."

"Eric," she said brusquely, "you're dead and buried. And believe me, right now, everybody at the Agency would prefer you stayed that way. No one's prepared to offer an explanation for your survival. The truth has never had much to do with Operations, has it?"

"But this is *Scottie* we're talking about." He stared, unseeing, at the steam rising like cumulus from the surface of the pool.

"There's no way he could have told me. I'd have rejected the entire idea. Or I'd have shared the secret—with Cuddy, maybe. You know I would."

"Cuddy doesn't know?" Eric stared at her blankly. "What about Dare Atwood?"

"She sure as hell knows *now.*"

"You all wish I were dead." Accusing now, with herself as proxy for the man he couldn't strike. "That's what you want."

"Well . . ." She rose and went to him, afraid of the high-vaulted chamber's effect on sound. "Nobody was thrilled to see you alive and well and kidnapping the Vice President, understand?"

Eric wheeled away from her. "He *used* me. Completely and utterly. And I volunteered for the privilege. I was so proud that he *trusted* me. . . ."

"Are you saying that Scottie engineered the hit against Payne?"

"That would be Oliver Stone's version, Caroline. Don't be paranoid. Scottie put me under deep cover, working for Krucevic. And told me that when I had what I needed to nail the asshole, he'd get me out."

What had Scottie said only Tuesday morning? *He's a*

killer, Caroline, and he's out in the cold. It wouldn't be Scottie who brought Eric home. Scottie had run a rogue operation. As a result, Vice President Sophie Payne was dying.

But Scottie had complete deniability—as long as Eric was silenced forever.

———

They crept through the Var, the Castle District, scorning the open expanse of the Danube ramparts, the funicular railroad, the places where tourists thronged. They took the side streets and alleyways beyond Gellérthegy until at last they emerged at the north end of the Var. This part of Buda had been destroyed and rebuilt so many times—by Mongols and Turks and Austrians and Nazis—it seemed a fitting place to turn over the rubble of their lives. A place where the appearance of order was all that remained.

"There was a girl," Eric said as they walked, "at the university. A graduate student in molecular biology. Her name was Erzsébet Király."

"What about her?"

"She worked part time in Mlan's lab. I recruited her there, before the end—before MedAir 901. She was sharp and funny and you would have liked her, Caroline, with her peasant skirts and her long red braids hanging down her back. She knew something was wrong with Mlan's vaccines."

"You mean the mumps?"

"His small contribution to the Muslim problem." Eric looked at her searchingly. "It's all on the disk. Make sure you get it to Dare. *Not to Scottie.* Is that understood?"

She nodded. He walked on, head down, hands thrust

in his pockets. She tried not to look over her shoulder for a man with a gun.

"Three years ago, I started paying Erzsébet to smuggle information out of the lab," Eric said. "She did a good job. So good, Mlan chose her to carry his germs to Turkey."

"On MedAir 901?"

"It made excellent sense." Eric kicked at a paving stone and watched it skitter into the street. "Airlines don't x-ray boxes of certified medical supplies. Not vaccines. Not when the boxes come with the right government seals and stamps. They're too afraid that radiation will destroy the drugs. Do you see?"

"There was a bomb in the VaccuGen cargo and Erzsébet put it on the plane," Caroline said flatly. "Why weren't you on that flight, too?"

"I was. I gave up my seat." His voice was still flush with amazement at it, the narrowness of chance. "I gave up my seat to a woman with a sick child, a woman who needed to get back to Istanbul. The baby was wailing. A flight attendant stood at the front of the plane and asked for volunteers. I went."

"They didn't bother to pull your boarding pass?"

"This was not an American airline, Carrie. It was a third-world plane with about forty seconds to hit its takeoff slot at one of the busiest airports in the world. They sent me to the counter to rebook and plunked the woman and baby down in my seat. Never took my name off the 901 manifest."

"But you didn't rebook."

"I went first to your gate. Your plane had already pulled back. So I got lunch instead."

"And thirty-three minutes after takeoff, MedAir 901 exploded," Caroline finished. *Life as I knew it, shot down in flames. The jetway at Dulles seven hours later, Scottie and*

Dare waiting with the news. I didn't believe it. I didn't believe it. And then Scottie's face—grief on that perfect forehead. Mourning the only thing that mattered. His Eric. Then I knew it was true.

"The plane blew up with Erzsébet and the woman and her baby on board," Eric said. "I called Scottie as soon as the news came through."

"Why didn't you call *me*?"

"You were somewhere over the Atlantic. And Scottie promised he'd explain."

Explain. As though I were a lunch date skipped for a perfectly good reason. She raised her fists and beat them against his chest in fury. "You did this for Erzsébet Király? You traded *me* for *her*?"

He circled her wrists and held them tightly. "I paid her to betray Mlan. I caused her death. A twenty-one-year-old girl. I owed her something, I think."

"Your life for hers. Our marriage." Caroline's voice was lacerating. "So was it worth it, Eric? Your payment in blood? Are you happy with the bargain?"

His eyes were shuttered. "Happiness was never the point, Mad Dog."

"No. I see that now."

———

Three blocks from the Hilton he stepped into the doorway of a vacant storefront and pulled her roughly against him. The embrace was cover, she thought; there was no emotion behind it. Just a piece of business in case anyone was watching. The cold hollow in the center of her chest widened and spread, dulling her senses.

"I've got to leave you here," he said, "and get back to Sophie."

"Back? That's insane! Krucevic will kill you."

Caroline gazed at Eric's face and saw the wind howling in his bones. He was only forty. He looked far older. He had no way in from the cold, and he knew it. He would live for a while, a hunted man. And then he would die in the dark, far from home. This time, no one would break the news.

He reached into his pocket, his eyes scanning the street beyond her head. "Take this. It's a map to Krucevic's Budapest base. Take it to your COS"—he was dissociating himself now, he wanted nothing to do with the Agency apparatus—"and get a raid going. But do it fast. You haven't much time."

Caroline glanced at her watch. It was 12:32 P.M.

"The place is an arsenal—"

"I know. We have the blueprints." She clutched the paper between chilled fingers. "Eric, Krucevic blew your car. He wants you *dead*. Béla Horváth may have told Krucevic everything before he died. You can't walk back into that sort of situation. Unless you have a death wish."

"Sophie Payne is alone, Caroline."

"We'll get to her. In a matter of hours. But it's time you walked away. Anything else is just ego. The Eric Carmichael I knew would never throw himself away on pride."

"We both know there's no going back, Mad Dog." And at last, she heard bitterness in his voice. "To survive evil, you have to become its friend. You have to take its hand and walk with it a ways. And then the path behind is barred to you. You're no longer the person you were, the person who would never think of putting a silencer to a little girl's head. You can't wake up on a Saturday morning in the suburbs of Washington and take a run along the canal or chat over coffee about the Super Bowl—not if you have the remnants of a soul. You're too guilty for peace."

"It's as though you really did die," she said.

"I've done some terrible things, Caroline. I don't live with them easily. I can't wipe them off my soul."

It was true, she thought, with infinite sadness; and there was no going back to her marriage, either. The man she had loved—yearned for in death, and desired in life—was gone.

"Take this." He was holding out a beeper. "It's a homing device for a transmitter I planted. Highly sophisticated—German technology. If you're within two miles, it should lead you to the Veep."

Her fingers closed around it. "Promise me you won't return to that bunker."

"What promise could I possibly make that you would ever believe?" He studied her narrowly. "Krucevic suspects he's been betrayed. He may already have left Budapest. If the map's no good—"

"Then what? Berlin? For more antibiotic?"

He shook his head. "Like I said, Mlan doesn't retreat. He'll go onward, not back. There's only one place left."

Caroline's brain raced furiously. To Poland, where Cuddy had traced the Hungarian treasury funds? But Krucevic had no lab in Poland—or none that she had ever identified. If Krucevic cared at all about Jozsef—

"He'll go to ground," she murmured. "Like a wounded animal. He'll go *home*, won't he?"

Eric nodded. "To Bosnia. Živ Zakopan. The old death camp south of Sarajevo. He's got a lab there, set high in the hills."

She took a step backward, her breath catching in her throat. *Živ Zakopan. A place so terrible, even rumor spoke in whispers. A place no prisoner had ever left alive.* "It really exists?"

"It must," Eric said bleakly. "I've been there. Now listen carefully, Mad Dog. I'm going to tell you where it is."

SEVEN

Budapest, 1:03 P.M.

IN THAT LAST MOMENT, when Eric turned to walk away, Caroline reached for him and held him close. She was done with bitterness and rage. Done with weighing her options, cataloging pain, attempting to control the future—it was enough, in that moment, to feel the heart of the man she loved beating close to her own.

"God, don't leave me," she whispered. "I can't stand it, Eric."

"Neither can I," he muttered into her hair. "You tear the soul from my body, Carrie."

"Then take me with you. We can run together."

She felt no loyalty now to the Agency that had betrayed him.

He loosened the hands she had locked around his waist and held her at arm's length. For perhaps three seconds, she watched him consider her offer. Then he shook his head.

"It's not finished. This business. Running won't end it."

"You've done enough!"

"Remember Sophie, Caroline. *Sophie.* I owe her a chance. And I need you to help me."

Caroline's protests died on her lips. She dropped her head to his chest, as futile as pounding a brick wall. Sophie Payne was more innocent than Eric. Sophie Payne demanded retribution.

"Let it go, Mad Dog," he said quietly. "We live the lives we're left with."

"We will not let him win, do you hear?"

"Mlan?"

"Scottie," she said fiercely. "*Scottie.* We will not let him ruin us and walk away clean."

He smiled at her, but there was no belief in his eyes. She felt like a child he was humoring. She snatched at his wrist. "Damn it, Eric. I won't let you just lie down and *die.*"

"No. You never would. My mad dog—"

He leaned forward and kissed her full on the mouth. The savagery behind it was like an electric shock.

"Do you still have your grenade pin?" he asked her.

She nodded, too breathless to speak. *The cunning and unlikely grenade pin.*

"Here's mine."

It dangled before her nose, an olive drab metallic ring broad enough to circle a man's finger. She reached a trembling hand to his, and their fingers locked.

"I've kept it all these years," Eric said. "My link to the past. To *you.*" His grip tightened. "If we both survive this, Mad Dog, I will find you. *Believe that.*"

And then her hand was hers again. The grenade pin slipped back into his pocket. She watched him walk away, hoping he would look back—but what would she do if he did? To stand stock-still on the paving stones of

Budapest while Eric left her once again was much more difficult than running. *Caroline is no trouble,* whispered Uncle Hank in her ear. *Caroline does the hardest thing, always.*

Eric did not look back.

When he had turned into a side street and vanished from view, she took a shuddering breath and thrust her hands into her pockets. The sharp, clean edge of his computer disk. The homing device. And the folded piece of paper that was the key to Sophie Payne's prison.

Time was short. She would need an explanation for the map's existence—Vic Marinelli would demand it. Heading for her hotel, Caroline crossed the street at a run.

————

Tom Shephard was sitting inside Gerbeaud's with a copy of the *Herald Tribune* spread open before him. He had consumed almost all of a chocolate torte and, to Caroline's surprise, had taken it with tea. A pot of Earl Grey still perfumed the air gently with bergamot.

"You're late." He tossed his napkin aside. "I haven't got much to tell you, I'm afraid. Mirjana Tarcic was treated in a hospital the day of the riots, then disappeared. The federal police think they might have a lead—"

"Have you paid, Tom? I've got a taxi waiting."

The impatience in her face stopped his objection. "What is it?"

"Krucevic." She held aloft a slip of paper. "His Budapest base. The one that matches Wally's blueprints."

"Jesus." Shephard emptied his pockets of loose change. "How the hell did you find that?"

"Call it a gift from Mahmoud Sharif's Budapest division," she said.

Vic Marinelli came to attention in his chair. "A map?" he said into the receiver. "Right—it's coming through the secure fax right now. Jesus! What do we do with it?"

"You wait for Atwood and Bigelow to come on-line in the VTC room," Cuddy Wilmot told him, "and then you conference."

Marinelli was already staring at the rough line drawing of the northwest sector of Budapest, a neighborhood of warehouses and commercial trucking. The map was furred and ratcheted with electronic interference, but he could piece his way, bit by bit, to the center of Krucevic's heart. His own began to thud with excitement. Headquarters had finally done its job. "What time's the teleconference?"

"One-thirty. Have Caroline and your LegAtt in the vault three minutes before."

"Caroline? You mean your analyst?"

"Of course."

"Do you think that's wise?" Marinelli's tone made it clear that he did not. "This is *operational*, Wilmot. She shouldn't have access."

"Caroline is an expert on Mlan Krucevic," Cuddy replied patiently, "and she's already seen the map, Vic. I sent a copy to her hotel."

"You *what*?"

"I thought she'd be able to tell me whether the details made sense. She thinks that they do."

"But she's an *analyst*," Vic repeated in disbelief. "Not a case officer. What were you thinking?"

"We don't draw those lines so strictly here at the CTC." Cuddy sounded almost amused. "We use an interdisciplinary approach to cases. And you owe the map to Caroline in the first place. It was at her suggestion that we queried this source."

The source, Cuddy had already explained, was an American citizen they would call the Volunteer. He was in the habit of dealing gray arms to dubious clients, but from time to time, he offered information to the CIA in recompense for his sins.

"This is un-fucking-believable," Marinelli muttered.

"Caroline thought of the Volunteer immediately when she saw Wally Aronson's blueprints. But she was worried about turf—who handled the guy, what she was allowed to tell you. So she called me."

Marinelli's eyebrows lifted satanically at a target six thousand miles away. He'd spent enough time in the game to know when Headquarters was trying to upstage him.

"Luckily, the asset was available for questioning— he's being held in a medium-security facility in West Virginia."

"And he just . . . *volunteered* . . . the route to 30 April's bunker," Marinelli mused. "*Lucky* doesn't even begin to describe it, Wilmot."

"Strap one on, Vic." Now the amusement was obvious. "We'll be pulling for you back home."

In Washington, D.C., it was only seven-thirty in the morning. Caroline studied Dare Atwood's face on the secure video monitor and found new lines of weariness and strain. The Vice President of the United States had been kidnapped seventy-two hours ago. Since then, Dare had probably briefed Congress once or twice, met or avoided a legion of reporters, held endless meetings with her Intelligence chiefs, and taped a political talk show appearance for airing on Sunday morning. In between, she would have eaten badly, dispatched aides to her Georgetown home in search of a fresh silk blouse and pink lipstick, and taken the long walk from the East Gate to the White House six or seven times, briefcase in hand. The possibility that Eric might go public about his Agency affiliation would have destroyed what little sleep Dare had. The appearance of this map to 30 April's bunker should have come as an enormous relief. But gazing at the monitor, Caroline couldn't find relief in Dare's face.

Jack Bigelow, on the other hand, looked as though he were wired for sound. His image nearly catapulted through the television screen. He'd slept well, had a big breakfast, and was goin' out huntin', loaded for bear.

"Hey there, folks," he drawled genially when Embassy Budapest came on-line. "Hear y'all been doin' yer jobs real well fer a change. Soph's gonna be pleased as punch when y'all come knockin' at the asshole's door."

"Good afternoon, Mr. President, Director Atwood," said Ambassador Stetson Waterhouse. He was a recent political appointee to the Buda post—a lifelong fly-fishing buddy of Jack Bigelow's—and a man crucified by concern for protocol. "I have with me COS Vic Marinelli; the Legal Attaché for Central Europe, Mr. Tom Shephard; and Ms. Caroline Carmichael, of the CIA's Counterterrorism Center. Are we coming through clearly on your end?"

"Clear as mud, Stetz," said Bigelow. "DCI's gonna give us a little summary."

"Mr. President," Dare began, "it is our view that Vice President Sophie Payne may presently be held at 30 April's Budapest headquarters, a warehouse with underground facilities located in an industrial sector of the city. You have a copy of the map to that warehouse in front of you. Our sources suggest that Payne was present at that site as recently as three hours ago. We have a fix on the facility's location, and blueprints of its security systems. We do not yet know, however, whether the terrorists and Mrs. Payne are still there."

The DCI had barely finished before Bigelow's voice cut over hers. "You guys on the ground got any ideas?"

Ambassador Waterhouse looked around at the three of them, flummoxed.

"Mr. President," said Marinelli, "we received the map only fifteen minutes ago. I—"

"Get some surveillance on the place."

"Yes, sir." Marinelli reached for a phone on the desk before him; he dialed an internal embassy number.

"And make sure yer watchers are armed, son. We don't want another Bratislava."

Bratislava. The memory of two case officers shot to death in a plumber's van loomed large in all their minds.

Caroline kept her eyes on the screen. Since her return to the station, the COS had been treating her as though she carried the plague.

A gray-haired man in uniform who sat at Bigelow's left stabbed his microphone button abruptly. She recognized the chairman of the Joint Chiefs.

"We can send up some AWAC planes," Clayton Phillips barked. "Intercept all electronic emissions coming out of Budapest. There are NATO crews on the ground already in Hungary."

"But you'll have to get NATO consent," objected Matthew Finch, the National Security Advisor. "That means giving NATO a reason for the intercepts. Sharing the truth. And losing control. Could be a big mistake."

"What about Delta Force?" Bigelow asked.

"If we had more time—" Phillips began.

"Then what about Germany?" Bigelow was getting impatient. "Ramstein Air Base. Scramble a bunch a guys outta there."

"Again—to assemble the team, get them in a plane, send them to Budapest, and deploy them at the site," General Phillips said, "you're talking three hours."

"Three hours." Bigelow glanced at his watch, then squinted at the video monitor. "What time's it over there?"

"In three hours, Mr. President, it will be almost five P.M.," Stetz Waterhouse told him.

"Gettin' dark. That'll have to do. Unless—"

The President released his mike button and leaned to whisper in his security advisor's ear.

"Ms. Carmichael," said Matthew Finch, "in your bio of Mlan Krucevic you state that he never negotiates. Could you amplify on that point?"

"Certainly." She threw a glance at Marinelli; his expression remained wooden. "Negotiation is a nonstarter for several reasons. First, Mlan Krucevic would have to come out in the open—speak under the eyes of the world press—as Mrs. Payne's kidnapper, and he shuns that kind of publicity. He'll avoid it at all cost. Second, negotiation means Krucevic gives up Mrs. Payne in order to get something else. We have nothing to offer Krucevic that he wants. And it's a point of honor to the man that he does not concede."

Marinelli snorted beside her. "Put a gun to his head. He'll concede in a heartbeat."

"Third," Caroline continued, "in order to negotiate at all, Krucevic would have to recognize his counterpart as an equal. He'll never do that."

"Even if he's negotiating with the President of the United States?" Jack Bigelow's voice was still genial.

"Seems to me he's been negotiatin' with every one of those videotapes."

"I would consider those more in the form of direct insults, Mr. President," Caroline said. "He intends to taunt and humiliate you by displaying Mrs. Payne's subjugation. He believes this could make you feel frustrated and powerless. The videos are one of Krucevic's instruments of terror, not a method of brokering a deal."

All three men in the White House Situation Room were listening to her now. Dare Atwood, on the Agency screen, had a faint smile playing about her lips.

"But let's just say," Matthew Finch argued, "that we pretend to negotiate in order to buy some time. Keep Krucevic focused on the dialogue while Delta Force gets their act together. Then we'll have tried the diplomatic option—and the world will know it—and we can go in shooting."

Caroline shook her head. "Go in shooting and all you'll find is bodies."

Finch threw up his hands and stared at Jack Bigelow.

The President smiled at Caroline through the secure video feed. "You're pretty damn sure of yourself, young lady."

"Mr. President—" She sighed and searched for a succinct way to explain. "For the past five years, I've followed Mlan Krucevic and 30 April. He's a tough man to pick out of the crowd. But I've done it. It's my job. I've read every scrap of classified and open-source material on the man, I've researched his childhood, I've placed him on a couch and trotted out the psychiatrists. I know more about Krucevic than anyone, with the possible exceptions of his mother and his wife. His mother's dead. His wife is missing. I'm all you've got."

"How can you say he'll never negotiate?" Matthew

Finch was still resistant. "This could mean life and death to the man."

"The value of a life is relative, Mr. Finch," Caroline said patiently. "Mlan Krucevic has known that from birth. His father was a member of the Croatian Ustashe—the fascist allies of Nazi Germany. Anton Krucevic is believed to have been in charge of a concentration camp somewhere near Sarajevo that was built entirely underground. Everyone connected with the camp's organizational hierarchy was ordered to commit suicide at the German surrender, and the location of the camp itself has never been positively identified—but estimates of the number of Serb partisans executed there range from several thousand to nearly one hundred thousand."

"In Krucevic's biography," Finch noted, "you say he's fifty-eight. That means he was born during the war."

"Krucevic reportedly lived out his babyhood on the camp grounds," Caroline affirmed. "He grew up watching people die rather horrible deaths. Mlan's father, in his eyes, must have seemed like God himself. He held people's very lives in his hands. *No one survived Živ Zakopan.* Rumors of the place circulated during the war, and that's what historians are left with. No witnesses surfaced to tell the tale of the camp's horrors—unless you include Krucevic himself."

"What happened to his father?" Jack Bigelow asked.

"He shot himself—and his wife—when the Russian liberators came for them."

"But not the boy."

"Krucevic was found bleeding in his dead mother's arms. He has a bullet scar to this day on his temple. He's on record, Mr. President, as saying that death is always preferable to failure."

Jack Bigelow scowled. "Too bad the bastard's had such a string o' good luck."

Matthew Finch looked down at his notepad.

"So what do you think will work, Caroline?" Dare Atwood asked. As though the Director of Central Intelligence routinely deferred to her junior analysts.

Caroline hesitated an instant before replying. She would not allow herself to consider Eric. If he had returned to 30 April's bunker, he had placed himself beyond all protection. The High Priestess of Reason was back in the briefing room; what the Policy-makers did with her information was their affair.

"If we announce our presence—try to negotiate—he'll divert us long enough to launch a counterattack. If we land a helicopter on his roof, he'll kill Mrs. Payne before we've killed the rotors. Our only hope lies in stealth."

Matthew Finch looked straight into the camera. "Thank God. I thought there *was* no hope."

"We need to use the blueprints Wally Aronson gave us. We need a squad of professionals trained to infiltrate electronic barriers," Caroline persisted. "Pros who can creep up to the bunker, find the air vents we know are there, and drop canisters of chloroform right into Krucevic's living room. We need to take out 30 April before they even know they're blown—and free the Vice President without a shot being fired. But we need to do it *now*."

Jack Bigelow rocked back in his conference chair. "Get the AWACs in the air, Clayt. Tell NATO whatever ya like. Scramble a Delta Force team from Ramstein or wherever else you got 'em hidden. And make sure they bring their chloroform, hear? 'Cause they ain't getting off the plane without it."

When the screens had gone blank and the ambassador had scurried away to his round of appointments with the new Hungarian government, Tom Shephard stood up and held out his hand. Caroline took it in surprise.

"What's that for?" she asked him.

"Work well done."

"You coming?" Marinelli barked from the doorway of the vault.

Shephard turned. "Where to?"

"Surveillance. I'm going to watch the bunker until those flyboys arrive. Just in case Krucevic tries to split before it's convenient."

Tom vaulted a stray chair and was at the station chief's side. "You think I'd miss that?"

Marinelli clapped the LegAtt on the shoulder. Then his gaze drifted over to Caroline. "I'd appreciate it if you'd stay behind. This is entirely operational, you understand. And while you convinced the President you know your tradecraft, I'm not entirely sure. I like my visiting analysts safely behind their desks. It saves a lot of explanation back at Headquarters when things go wrong."

The hostility was unmistakable. Tom Shephard's eyes widened in surprise. But this was neither the time nor the place, Caroline knew, for a bureaucratic squabble, for a drawing of the line between Analysis and Ops. Too much was at stake.

"Right," she told Marinelli through bitten lips. "You're the station chief. I take my orders from *you*."

"'Bout time," he retorted, and swung into the hallway.

The screaming had been going on for what seemed like hours now, beyond the sealed door, and even Jozsef was done crying.

Krucevic had thrust the boy into Sophie's room without a word of explanation earlier that day—she did not know what time, she had no clock and no window, nothing but a sense of having slept badly and in increasing pain. She had held Jozsef close to her fevered body, held her hands over his ears to stop the noise, cursing vividly and relentlessly under her breath to drown out the screams. She poured forth a torrent of vituperation into the dead air while Jozsef shuddered with sobs and the screams went on—varying sometimes in pitch, sometimes in duration, but inevitable, as though the tortures they subjected him to had a preordained rhythm.

He was singing now—a broken, dying tune. Paul Simon's "Graceland."

"What did he do?" she asked Jozsef at one point. "What could he possibly have done to deserve this?"

The boy had shuddered. "He betrayed Papa."

Even the singing, now, had stopped.

EIGHT

Budapest, 3:13 P.M.

DUSK FELL SWIFTLY on a November afternoon in Central Europe, and dusk was their ally.

Tom Shephard studied the pale profile of the man crouched next to him in the back of the armored van. Vic Marinelli was roughly the same age as Tom, but he was in better shape and he had once been a SEAL. That fact alone gave Tom some comfort. The Agency, as a rule, didn't deal in guns. The FBI did. But a SEAL— even one who'd been out of the navy for the past ten years—knew what the hell he was doing. And Tom, at this moment, felt as though he was flying by the seat of his pants.

Krucevic's stronghold was innocuous in appearance—a loading dock in a neighborhood of warehouses, accessed by an alley. One of Marinelli's case officers had parked the station's van in front of an animal-feed-supply warehouse perpendicular to the bunker. The CO jumped out of the cab and made a great fuss over his cousin, another young Hungarian laborer who had just driven up in a shining red Volkswagen Passat. The CO pulled off his work overalls, secure in the knowledge that no one could be watching; threw on a clean shirt; dragged a comb through his hair; clapped his putative cousin on the back; and slid into the Passat's passenger seat. The two men drove off into the darkness, intent on beer, lap dancers, and oblivion.

The van was left locked and apparently empty in front of the warehouse. Except that Marinelli and Tom were crouching inside. Their position in the back of the armored van was an uncomfortable one: The last team dispatched to monitor the Veep's kidnappers in Bratislava had been murdered as handily as wild geese under a low cloud ceiling. Neither Tom nor Marinelli troubled to make much small talk. Each had brought a personal weapon. They kept their eyes trained on the surveillance equipment that was the key to Krucevic's kingdom, while silence gathered between them like dead leaves.

Marinelli was the master of a formidable array of electronics. He had eyes that could see and ears that could hear through layers of protective steel. He had hidden antennae and radar and television monitors. Tom heard a warehouse's metal door slide down with a crash; a truck creaked past, looming like a leviathan on the van's black-and-white screen. Snatches of Hungarian sputtered in their earphones. If a dust mote were to settle on the van's roof, Tom thought, they would know about it.

But precious little emanated from the bunker. When Marinelli's beams intersected Krucevic, they fell dead.

"This guy's already walked," Marinelli muttered as he turned a dial. "All that bowing and scraping before the Joint Chiefs, and we're gonna look like idiots. It won't be your friend Little Miss Muffet who takes the fall, either. It'll be *me*. Because *I* didn't get surveillance out here before the ink was dry on that map. Sometimes I hate this fucking job."

"The entire U.S. Army couldn't find Saddam Hussein, Marinelli, when it was parked in his front yard. Sometimes people defy technology. You know that."

The station chief slammed the palm of his hand against the recalcitrant dial he was tuning. "Hell, yes. And sometimes technology isn't worth shit. I'm just pissed off about that chick in jackboots, Tom. She had Bigelow eating out of her hand. Why do they let women anywhere near Intelligence? They don't know dick about operations."

Shephard smiled faintly, remembering the steel gray Mercedes and the little black wig. "Caroline doesn't roll over. She looks at you with those cold blue eyes—she lets you dig yourself in deeper as you try to justify your existence—and then she walks right around you."

"You just want to get into her pants."

He frowned. But it wasn't Shephard's job to explain Caroline Carmichael to the station chief. He had harbored enough doubts about the woman himself. Her conjuring of the map, however, had buoyed his confidence. Whatever her deceptions, her closet loyalties—the things she would not explain—Caroline had gotten the job done.

Marinelli flipped a switch on a scanner; static crackled. "He's blocking us. Son of a bitch is blocking us."

"That's the least of what he's doing."

They had both studied the blueprints of Anatoly Rubikov's security system, the blueprints Wally Aronson had fished out of a train station bathroom at two A.M. A U.S. government–issue scanner was about as effective against Krucevic as a slingshot and dried peas.

"He's not *in* there," Marinelli repeated tensely. "He's blown this hole while we watched Mary Sunshine cream the Prez."

"You don't know that."

The afternoon's misting rain had changed to a downpour. Outside the van, darkness was almost absolute. A few spotlights lit isolated corners of the warehouse district—Tom could see them when he panned the surveillance cameras wide—but none had survived Krucevic's installation. The loading dock was blanketed in shadows.

Marinelli bent over a small square item that looked like a viewfinder.

"What is that?"

He glanced up. "Infrared detection device."

"You're looking for heat?"

"It's November in Budapest. Coming on for dark. Temperature is dropping to thirty-nine, thirty-seven degrees. The heat should be on in that bunker."

It should be flying through the seams of the loading-dock door like a sonic wind, Tom thought. Marinelli stood aside; Tom peered through the infrared viewfinder. The outline of the garage door glimmered coldly.

"It's dead," Marinelli told him. "Shut down. I'd bet my life on it." The station chief pulled gently on the van's rear-door handle, eased it open.

"Are you nuts?" Tom hissed.

"We've got Delta Force on the wing, Shephard, and the Veep's not here. That map was a fucking diversion. It got us looking at where 30 April *was,* not where they are. If I'm not back in fifteen, call the station." He slipped through the door as softly as a whisper.

Marinelli, Tom fumed, was like all of these goddamn Agency people. He was not what he seemed. He'd perfected the art of appearing to be other than what he was—perfected it so well that he made you believe he was a Medici prince when in fact he was nothing but a goddamn cowboy. An adrenaline junkie. Like Caroline

Carmichael in her red beret, stepping out of a terrorist's car—

Tom bent over the infrared oculars. He tracked Vic Marinelli through the darkness and rain, the heat of the man's body flaring against the green crystal screen. The station chief eased his way from warehouse doorway to trash bin to utility pole, all of them cold under the lens. Tom scanned the roofline, the corners of the building where the blueprints showed fiber-optic cameras to be. And then he saw it, like a wink in the night. A red laser eye that opened once, then closed. Marinelli had missed it.

The heat might be off—the bunker empty—but something was wired to blow.

––––––––––

The federal police caught up with Mirjana Tarcic twenty-three minutes before her aged mother mounted the steps to her quiet two-room apartment and found the door standing wide open.

There were three of them: Ferenc Esterházy, who was in charge, and two deputies named Lindros and Berg. They wore charcoal-colored wool suits redolent of nicotine and sausage, petrol fumes, and rain. Esterházy's features were heavy and his pallor unhealthy; he smoked unfiltered cigarettes and had spent fifty-three years in a country where life expectancy for men was fifty-eight. His tie was bright green; his wife had bought it in Prague last Easter. Lindros and Berg were less obviously natty.

The three of them moved, through long habit, in an arrowhead that pierced the foot traffic on Szentendre's streets: Esterházy to the fore, his deputies flanking each side, none of them requiring direction or even much speech. They had parked the dark blue sedan two blocks above the art gallery on Görög Utca and crossed to the far sidewalk. None of them carried an umbrella.

Esterházy mounted the narrow staircase first. Lindros drew his gun and came behind. Berg looked for a second exit to the street, found none, then posted himself at the foot of the stairs. It was quiet enough in the apartment above that when Esterházy kicked open the door, the sound exploded in the passage and brought Berg around with his gun raised.

The door was unlocked.

It bounced hard against the interior wall and slammed shut in Esterházy's face before he had a chance to slide through the opening. But not before he glimpsed what lay within.

The body of a woman, sprawled on the floor. Her face was a mask of blood.

Lindros was already beside him, pallid-faced but silent. Esterházy clutched the doorknob, raised his gun in his other hand, and slid quietly into the room. Lindros followed.

The apartment was cold and raw, a gusting draft pouring in through the ceiling. He looked up and saw the skylight open. There was a chair overturned like a second body near the woman's corpse. She had been trying to escape through the roof when her killer caught up with her. Esterházy's gaze slid away from the ruin of her face.

He made his way along the living-room wall to the bedroom doorway, then swung inside with gun raised.

No one was waiting for him.

His heartbeat thudded in his ears. He searched

quickly under the bed. Behind the closet door. Through the bathroom.

No one.

Lindros was crouched at the woman's side, checking for a pulse. Esterházy could have told him not to bother. He pulled a photograph from his breast pocket—the candid shot of Mirjana Tarcic that Tom Shephard had given him four hours earlier.

"Mirjana Tarcic?"

Lindros shrugged. "Who knows?"

Her face had been crushed to a pulp with something heavy—a crowbar, a vicious boot. Fragments of the woman's skull and teeth were scattered about the wide-plank floors. The bright red rugs were clotted with blood. And the rain had dripped steadily through the open skylight, washing the gore across the room toward the galley kitchen—she must have been killed hours before. In the morning, when they still hadn't known enough to look for her.

Lindros pointed to the corpse's neck. "Look at that, boss."

A silk scarf was tightened like a tourniquet around her windpipe, crimson with blood. Esterházy looked at Shephard's photograph once more. Mirjana Tarcic wore a white silk scarf.

"Boss!" yelled Berg from the foot of the steps. "There's an old lady down here, says she lives up above! You want to see her?"

The mother. Bassza meg.

Esterházy's stomach heaved. He ducked back into the bathroom without a word.

———

Tom Shephard could not have reached Marinelli before the red eye blinked, before the laser beam he could not see was intersected and the explosive circuit completed. But he ran anyway, his mouth open in a yell against the stupidity of all cowboys, the bravado of SEALs, toward the Medici prince outlined for an instant against the mouth of hell.

NINE

Budapest, 6 P.M.

EMBASSY BUDAPEST OFFICIALLY CLOSED for business at five P.M., but no U.S. installation in a rioting city, with a hostage Vice President and a rescue mission in progress, simply shuts its doors and sends its people home. Caroline had company in the station vault: Vic Marinelli's secretary, an efficient woman in her forties named Teddy, who scrupulously organized files while waiting for news. Teddy was slim and stylish in her long, narrow skirt; she shifted paper with quick hands that never mistook their purpose. Caroline would have been grateful for a distraction—she was tense and apprehensive—but Teddy seemed disinclined to talk.

In her mind, Eric walked slowly away down a rain-washed street.

Christ, Eric, I won't let you just lie down and die.

No. You never would.

She pushed him aside with difficulty, pulled up a chair to a computer terminal, and began composing a cable for Dare Atwood.

Classification: Top Secret. Routing: the DCI's personal channel. Caroline added her Cutout slug, which would limit access to Dare Atwood alone. Then, confronted with the body of the cable, she typed:

The following is information received from Michael O'Shaughnessy, an operative working under nonofficial cover who penetrated the 30 April Organization. During the past thirty months, C/CTC handled O'Shaughnessy in place. This intelligence was secured at C/CTC's direction from 30 April's main computer database.

C/CTC meant "Chief, Counterterrorism Center." Dare would know immediately what Scottie Sorensen had done, from the moment of MedAir 901's explosion; Dare was a High Priestess of Reason, too. She would unravel the knots faster than Scottie could tie them.

Caroline retrieved Eric's disk from her coat pocket. Downloading foreign data onto a secure Agency computer was technically forbidden; the fear of electronic virus transmission was too great. Caroline suppressed a qualm and pulled up the disk's file list. She began systematically copying it into the DCI's cable.

A phone pierced the station's stillness. Teddy cut it off on the first ring.

"Caroline? Could you go down to Reception and talk to a guy from the federal police? He asked for Shephard or Marinelli, but I said they were unavailable."

Mirjana. She stood up, her pulse accelerating, and hit the computer's screen saver. "Please don't secure the vault, Teddy. I'm still cabling Headquarters."

———

The visitor, a broad-shouldered, stocky man in a rumpled wool suit, was pacing by the time she got to the marine guard.

"Caroline Carmichael," she said. "How may I help you?"

He shook her hand mechanically, but his face remained guarded. "Where is Shephard?" he asked in halting English.

"We expect him momentarily. I work with Mr. Shephard. I'm happy to relay any message—"

"You are FBI?"

"Department of State," Caroline said smoothly. "Temporary duty from Washington. And you are—?"

"Esterházy."

He flipped open a badge; she studied it briefly. "Shephard brought you a photograph this morning."

His eyes widened slightly. He nodded.

A few chairs were ranged against one wall of the reception area; Caroline turned, and Esterházy followed her. They sat down fifteen feet from the impassive marine guard.

"Tell Shephard the woman is dead," Esterházy said softly.

"Mirjana Tarcic? *Murdered?*"

"But yes."

"Was she shot? Like Horváth?"

"She was beaten. A scarf around her neck, tight. You do not want to know. . . ."

"You found her in Budapest?"

The man had no reason to tell her anything. His gaze slid uneasily around the foyer; then he seemed to concede. "In Szentendre. A small town on the Danube Bend."

"I know it." Two Sunday-afternoon trips in search of antiques, spring wind in her hair and red wine in her veins. Back when she and Eric had a home to fill.

"Her mother has a flat there," Esterházy said. "We learned of it this afternoon. Someone else got there first."

Krucevic. Or one of his men—Otto, perhaps. He'd have en-
joyed choking the woman to death.

Caroline swore under her breath. Eric's network had
been rolled up inside of a day. And Eric—

"We found some things stuffed under a mattress. One
was a book. . . ." Esterházy gestured, groping for
words. "In Horváth's writing. From his lab—"

"Notes?"

He nodded. "I want Shephard to see. Is evidence,
you understand, he cannot have this book—but I wish
his opinion—"

"Of course. Did you find anything else?"

The man scrutinized her nervously. "Glass . . ." The
word escaped him. He held up his fingers four inches
apart. "So big. Filled with . . . we do not know what.
Six of them. These we send to our police lab for study."

Somebody's prescription got into the wrong hands, Scottie's
voice whispered in her mind. *The Big Man was quite up-*
set. Drugs from VaccuGen's Berlin headquarters had
been stolen two days before. Not the anthrax vaccine,
Scottie had said. So what else would be worth the murder of two people?

Erzsébet knew something was wrong with Mlan's vaccines.
What would Krucevic kill to conceal?

Mumps. His small contribution to the Muslim problem.

"I'll tell Shephard." Caroline stood up, intent upon
the answers she knew she'd find on Eric's disk. "He'll
contact you as soon as he can. And Mr. Esterházy—"

"Yes?"

"Tell your lab to be careful with that glass."

———

She knew disaster well—its look, its smell, the way the static
charge of air itself changed in disaster's presence—and the

station was filled with it when she returned three minutes later. Teddy was standing behind her desk, the phone pressed against her shoulder. She stared unseeing at Caroline's face, then dropped the receiver with a clatter and sank into her chair.

Caroline snatched up the phone. "Carmichael."

"It's me," Shephard said.

"Where are you?"

"Marinelli's dead. Bunker was wired. Blew sky-high."

"You should have *known* it would be wired! You had the goddamn blueprints—"

"Don't yell at me." Shephard cut across her viciously. "I nearly died tonight, okay? Because of a guy who should've known better. Hell, we *all* should've known better. That map was a dangle. Krucevic was long gone."

Dangle. A deliberate plant. Had Krucevic suspected, then, what Eric was doing? Had he known *everything*?

"You searched the bunker?" she asked Shephard.

"Once the flames were out. Flames have a way of drawing police, even in Budapest, even in the midst of riots. Try explaining that one, Sally. Just try explaining what the hell the U.S. Legal Attaché for Central Europe is doing with explosives in Buda. Christ."

"Tom—"

"So I told the fucking police the truth. That we thought the warehouse held the Vice President. They were not impressed. It took every string I could pull to get me off the hook, every apology I could think of in three different languages, before they'd let me go into the place with the firemen."

"You went in."

"I stepped over what was left of Vic Marinelli, Caroline, and I crawled through a shitload of wreckage." The savagery in his voice scalded her. "You never told me Krucevic had an American in his entourage. But then there's lots of crap you've never told me, right? Like your alias. Jane Hathaway. The name Mahmoud Sharif used in Berlin to set up contact with 30 April. What the hell are you playing at, Caroline? And when are you going to come clean?"

"What American?"

"One Michael O'Shaughnessy, from the passport in his breast pocket. A blond guy in his mid-thirties. But you know that, don't you? Michael was Sharif's other bona fide."

Her legs nearly folded under her. "You saw him?" she whispered.

"What was left of him, yeah. Krucevic tortured him, then strapped him to the door and set it to blow. There was a grenade pin still dangling from his finger."

Caroline cradled the receiver and walked unsteadily away from Teddy's desk. She groped her way to the computer. Her face was a mask, her mind screaming his name.

She had already mourned Eric once. She knew how it was done. But this second time felt like a thin steel blade twisting between her ribs, a torment she could not grip strongly enough to tear out.

Remember Sophie, Caroline. Sophie. I owe her a chance.

He had gone back, despite her best arguments. While she waited for Shephard to pay his bill at Gerbeaud's, they had nailed him to the cross.

Good-bye, dear love. Good-bye.

And then the word *torture*—that idle little word on Shephard's tongue—flooded her senses. She gasped, leaned hard against the desk, gripped it until the pain knifed upward through her shoulders and she knew that she could feel.

For the past four days Eric had dominated her thoughts, her work, her sleep, her heart. She had flown out of Washington in a fog of bitterness, suppressing emotion like a terminal illness. The High Priestess of Reason had no time to *feel*. Love could never be as strong as rage. Caroline had had no room for empathy, no thought for Eric's torment during the past thirty months. Retribution was what she wanted, payment in blood for the agony he'd caused.

She had seen him clearly for the first time in years. Calculating. Morally equivocal. Ruthless. A man for whom, nonetheless, justice had still meant something. He had thrown them both into this final battle because he thought it was more important than love or happiness. He had never asked permission. He had assumed that she would understand.

The one woman I could trust in the depths of hell, the woman who would believe, regardless of everything.

She had never justified that trust. She'd punished him like a spiteful child.

And Krucevic had tortured him. The grenade pin—

She drew a shuddering breath, her throat so choked with unspent tears she could not breathe. It was too late for regret. Too late for love. What remained must be a settling of accounts, for Eric's sake.

It was the consummate Agency word, *account*. She and Eric had shared one for years: 30 April. It was time to make Krucevic pay.

Teddy was weeping harshly for Marinelli in the outer room. Caroline pressed her fingers against her burning eyes and steadied herself. Then she stared once more at the computer screen. Clicked back into her cable. And began to learn what Eric had died for.

TEN

Živ Zakopan, 9:30 P.M.

SOPHIE PAYNE REGAINED CONSCIOUSNESS as the helicopter landed in the clearing beyond the trees. Pain tore at the lining of her stomach like talons; pain rattled in her lungs with every breath. For hours now she had drifted in a delirium where the voices of her son Peter and the terrorist named Michael blended with the face of her dead husband. *I'm coming, Curtis,* she told him, and was vaguely irritated by his impatience, by the way his looming form twisted and vanished before her eyes. It seemed desperately important that she reach for Peter; she clung to him, and held him tight, and felt his thin, little-boy bones tremble in her arms. And then, when the darkness cleared and Curt's face receded, she knew that it was young Jozsef she clasped, not her son, and that her filthy sweatshirt was damp with his sweat and spatters of blood. The boy was burning with fever.

When Vaclav killed the rotors, Otto and Krucevic carried her from the chopper. Jozsef whimpered as she was taken from him—he clung to her like a small bird, as though he knew that he would never see her again—

but in her illness she was no proof against the men's strength. She squeezed his hands tightly once in parting and felt him press something small and hard into her palm. The rabbit's foot. He had given her his most precious possession. She clenched her fingers around it and did not look back.

They dumped her unceremoniously on the ground. She lay there, curled in the fetal position, thinking of water. Cool water that trickled down the throat, still tasting of the ice it had once been. Water that gurgled over stones in the paddock at Malvern. It had its own language, that stream, an inconsequential chatter of horses' mouths dipped and lapping, the scarlet flit of a cardinal's wing, the slow, sinuous glide of a trout. Leaves spiraling in an eddy and the puncture point of a raindrop, Peter's boats made of empty egg cartons, a toothpick for a mast. Sophie's parched throat ached with the taste of blood.

The thin beam of a pocket torch picked out a tumbled stile, a heap of scattered stones. Otto heaved the latter aside with a grunt. Beneath them was a manhole cover fashioned of solid iron. It took Otto and Krucevic pulling together to haul the thing out. Rust stained their hands corrosive orange. Then Otto turned and looked at her. He smiled.

Oh, Michael, Sophie thought uselessly, *you were wrong. I am going to die at this man's hands.*

Slung over Otto's shoulder in a fireman's carry, she flailed out with her fists against his back . . . but she might as well have been the summer rain in the paddock stream, for all that she diverted him from his course. He dropped feetfirst into the manhole, his face against a ladder, so that her dangling head and back filled the passage's remaining space. Her legs were pinned between the tunnel wall and Otto's chest. There was barely room for one large man, much less the burden he carried; Sophie's hair snagged on old concrete, she smelled dirt and mold and felt the small creatures that live in mold scatter at their passage. Where his shoulder jutted into her abdomen, pain shot upward and radiated, as severe as the contractions of labor. A trickle of blood oozed from the corner of her mouth. She could not wipe it away.

They went down and down, Krucevic following, maybe thirty feet into the earth—until the dying darkness at the tunnel's mouth became impenetrable and the air was stale and decades cold.

Otto dumped her on the tunnel floor. She retched, whimpered, and vomited blood.

Somewhere above, Jozsef lay dreaming in the field. She had done this to him with her violent fingers, she had dashed to the ground the drugs that could have saved him, and he had watched her, silent, with the mute submission of a child whose life has always been determined by other people. Would she have risked so much if the boy were her son?

The passage before them had once been concrete, or something more akin to the earth, like stone. She could see nothing until Krucevic's flashlight played over the wall in front of her. An archway, perhaps five feet high, yawned like the mouth of a whale. Beyond it, only darkness and the fear that thrives in darkness. It reeked as a catacomb reeks, as all the dead spaces where civilization ends. Uncontrollably, Sophie began to shudder.

She had thought that the vials of crushed antibiotic would force Krucevic's hand, that to save his son he would abandon his mad quest to purify Europe. She had not reckoned with obsession. And now Jozsef was dying. His blood on her soul.

Otto dragged Sophie forward, past openings narrow

as cannon ports in the cold stone walls. Krucevic stopped suddenly and shone his beam into one of them.

"Welcome to Živ Zakopan, Mrs. Payne."

Sophie squinted against the light, pain shooting through her eyeballs. The beam picked out a heap of skeletons, innumerable, splayed across the dirt floor of the low-ceilinged space. They had probably been shot, and died where they lay: Half a century later she had a snapshot of how it had been—the moment of their murder.

"What is this place?" she croaked.

"It is the most hallowed ground of sacrifice in Bosnia," Krucevic replied, "which is saying a good deal. Do you know what happened here fifty-eight years ago?"

"The war."

"The war." Krucevic's laughter was brittle with contempt. "Mrs. Payne, there has been war in these hills for centuries. But in 1942, Živ Zakopan was a Croat place. It was part of the Independent State of Croatia, which for three glorious years ruled this country."

"Ustashe," Sophie muttered.

"Ustashe, which in the Croatian language is another word for fascist. Yes, Mrs. Payne. Živ Zakopan was established with the help of Nazi commanders and with the leadership of our great Ante Pavelic, the father of independent Croatia. We swept the Serb hordes out of Bosnia, we threw their women and children off our cliffs, we converted the Orthodox to the one true Catholic faith, and then we sent them to meet their God. There are the camps that everyone knows about— Jasenovac, near Zagreb, and Stara Gradiska—but at Živ Zakopan, we destroyed our worst enemies, the partisans ruled by Tito, the faithless ones. We left them here to rot in the bowels of the earth, already less than human. And the world did not care."

"No," Sophie protested. The pain was growing inside her like a swarm of bees, angry and intense, on the verge of bursting. "We would have known. This place—"

"This place has been buried for half a century, and it will be buried long after your name is forgotten," he said implacably. "Do you think they remember history in your country, Mrs. Payne? Everyone who knew about Živ Zakopan is dead. Except for me."

Half a century. Of being classified as *Missing, Presumed Dead*. Of no one knowing. Her gaze met the hollow eye sockets of a skull, inches from her face, flooded with Krucevic's beam. A thousand jaws, gaping wide in terror. No one walking in the fields above had even heard these people scream.

"Do you know what it means in English—Živ Zakopan?" Krucevic stared into her fevered eyes. "Literally it means 'buried alive.' But a more elegant translation might be 'Living Grave,' Mrs. Payne."

Sophie knew, now, why she was here.

Otto dragged her away from the charnel pit.

They reached what must have been the central room, the command center, twelve feet by twenty, with two wooden tables and a scattering of chairs, some broken and canted on their sides. Krucevic stopped short in the entryway, sliding the beam around the walls, his breath rapid now and shallow with excitement. "The Kommandant lived in Sarajevo, but his days were spent here—his days and many of his nights. Underground, all hours are the same."

"You can't know that. You're older than I am, but you probably weren't even born in World War Two."

"I was three when the Kommandant was taken. Old enough to remember the door to the tunnel, to remember these fields."

"Your father?" Sophie gasped.

"He denied them the final victory, Mrs. Payne. He died in captivity, by his own hand." Impossible now to read the crazed eyes under the clipped black hair. But she could feel the singing tension in the dank air of the chamber, the crackling of obsession barely suppressed. Krucevic was at his most dangerous.

"A son should know his father's greatness. A son should live to see his father avenged."

"You will never live to see your kind of vengeance, Krucevic, unless the world runs mad and everything good and true is utterly destroyed."

He turned the torch full on her face, blinding her. "You are dying, Mrs. Payne." His voice was utterly indifferent. "I want you to die knowing just how wrong you are. You destroyed those vials of antibiotic— yes, Tonio told me how it was done—in the hope that Jozsef's illness would stop me. You thought you could crush my vision of a new Europe with the ampules under your heel. *You tried to kill my boy.* For that, you forfeit any right you might have had to consideration. You deserve to be tortured, Mrs. Payne."

"I have been," Sophie muttered. By the thought of what she had done to Jozsef.

"You deserve a public execution." His face was close to her own now, his eyes shining in the torchlight. "But execution is too painless. I want you to die slowly here, I want you buried alive. And while you struggle for breath—while you crawl through the dirt—I will go on. I will save Europe. And my son.

"Otto—let us see whether Mrs. Payne is able to stand."

Otto heaved her to her feet, then backed away. Sophie swayed and clutched at a chair; it toppled over as she fell.

"I should judge her in no danger of escape," Krucevic said.

ELEVEN

Langley, 2:46 P.M.

"THE CALL JUST CAME THROUGH FROM STATE,"
Scottie Sorensen told the DCI. "Marinelli's body
will be on a plane home tomorrow night."

"And Michael O'Shaughnessy?" Dare didn't turn
away from her view of the pin oaks bordering the
chasm of the Potomac River. "Does his body come
home, too?"

The news of Eric's death had filtered through to
only a few of the Agency faithful. It had come in a
roundabout fashion, as such news must, because the
passport he held as Michael O'Shaughnessy bore a
next-of-kin notification number that ended eventually
at the CIA. The person designated to take such calls—
from the State Department's consular section—also had
access to the bank of real names associated with false
passports. Haley Taggert could now be included
among the number of those who knew that Eric
Carmichael hadn't exactly died two and a half years
before.

In a private session in the DCI's office, Dare had tried

to impress upon the administrative assistant that the matter was compartmentalized beyond her level of security clearance. Haley didn't know where Eric's body had been found or under what circumstances. With any luck, Dare could keep that information a close hold. But luck depended in part upon the Central European LegAtt's control of the Hungarian police and the press corps milling through Budapest. Dare figured her luck had run out.

"O'Shaughnessy's body will be on the same plane," Scottie told her.

"Good. You'll meet both caskets."

"Marinelli's brother will be there."

"Then meet Eric's. You owe him that much."

"I'm sorry, Director, I—"

Dare wheeled around. "Don't want anything to do with him? It's a little late for that, Scottie."

He rocked a little in his Cole-Haan loafers, as he might have done in a White House receiving line, then bent his head attentively toward the DCI. She was suddenly sick with fury at the man—the man who thought he had her snowed, had her right where he wanted her, the man who probably laughed each night in the privacy of his own bedsheets about just how thoroughly she was screwed.

"Sit down," she said wearily, "you goddamn son of a bitch."

Scottie sat.

Dare moved purposefully behind her desk. She found the hard copy of Caroline's Cutout-channel cable, the cable filled with the past thirty months of Eric Carmichael's life and enough intelligence to roll up Mlan Krucevic's networks worldwide. Before she handed it to Scottie, she said, "Caroline is missing."

Concern furrowed the CTC chief's brow.

"I called Embassy Budapest when I got the news

about Eric. Caroline is gone. She's checked out of her hotel."

"I'll alert our friends at every border crossing," he said immediately. "Notify the airlines, the trains—"

" 'Mad dogs and Englishmen come out in the noon-day sun,' " Dare quoted softly. "I've already talked to Hungarian border control. I don't want Caroline stopped. I want to know where she's headed."

He stared at her, perplexed.

"Tell me something, Scottie. That nickname of hers. Do you know how she got it?"

"Eric gave it to her."

"But *why*, Scottie? *Why?* You don't know?"

Dare waited implacably. She had a forbidding face in the best of circumstances, a voice like rain-drenched gravel. Scottie lost some of his self-possession. It dissipated, like bubbles in warm champagne.

"Let me tell you a story," she suggested. "About a woman run mad. You've got all the time in the world, Scottie. Eric's dead and now it's Caroline's word against yours about all the dirty tricks you've pulled. We don't place people on trial here; we simply send them to Tbilisi and Uzbekistan and all the other shitholes in the world until their time runs out. It's a long list, the list of shitholes, Scottie; and you have all the time in the world to consider it. So listen.

"Caroline Carmichael lives by her wits. She prides herself on being logical. On remaining calm in any crisis. On finding objective truth through her subjective lens. She's so good at projecting complete control that you have to know her well to see the fault lines inside, the places where surfaces shift and crack. There are forces in the earth, Scottie, that even Caroline can't suppress, and sometimes she remembers it."

Dare stopped, expecting him to object—to squirm in his chair or express annoyance—but he was paralyzed for once. Tbilisi had taken the wind from his sails.

"You know the training she's had. Denied Area Penetration, Terrorist Tactics and Countermeasures, Isolation and Interrogation—every course Eric scheduled before he went out to Nicosia, Caroline had, too. They trained *together*. Eric the teacher, Eric the Green Beret, just another student like his logical wife.

"Tell me, Scottie—how does the training go in Isolation and Interrogation?"

He crossed his right leg over his left. Unconsciously protecting his crotch from a ball-breaker, Dare decided. "The trainers try to find a person's vulnerability. Show him just where he's weak. So that the weakness can be corrected . . . or avoided."

"They put Caroline in isolation for three days. She was told, going into the cell, that there was a way out if only she could find it. She analyzed every square inch of the place, looking for a method of escape. She had no furniture, no bedcoverings, only a pot in the corner and one window. A window that showed her *Eric,* lashed upright to a pole and periodically subject to abuse from a gang of soldiers.

"After the first day, a trainer visited Caroline. He told her she could leave as soon as she confessed to her crimes—espionage, conspiracy, the usual gamut of trumped-up charges. He drew her over to the window and showed her Eric, who by this time was semiconscious, his head hanging, dried blood smeared above one ear. Eric would go free, the trainer explained, once Caroline confessed. She refused. She knew that they expected her, as a woman—a supposedly emotional creature—to find the sight of Eric's suffering unbearable.

"The process was repeated over two more days. By

that time Eric's moaning could not be shut out; it filled her head. She recited poetry aloud. She screamed. She ripped her clothes and stuffed scraps into her ears. When the trainer walked in on the third day, Caroline was already waiting at the window. He approached her carefully. She allowed him to come close; she seemed oblivious to everything around her. When he was within two feet of her right hand, she reached out and snatched a live grenade off his uniform belt.

" 'Cut Eric down or you die,' she said. Completely calm. Utterly logical. And twenty seconds from annihilation."

"Mad dogs and Englishmen," Scottie muttered. "So? What happened?"

"Her trainer screamed an order through the window. Eric was released. Caroline tossed the grenade through the bars of her cell and it detonated in the air. The prison shack collapsed. Caroline was pulled from the rubble along with her trainer, both of them concussed."

"I'm surprised she wasn't fired," Scottie said.

"She nearly was. I intervened. I had the power to do that, even then. She was my analyst. My office owned her. I forced her to submit to a complete psychiatric evaluation, and the docs vetted her clean. She had just been pushed, they said, a little too far. And Eric went to Nicosia alone. She was allowed to visit him, of course. They gave her Budapest's analyst-in-station post two years later, for good behavior."

Dare came around the end of her desk. "So what's the moral of the story, Scottie? Now that Eric's coming home in a body bag and Caroline is AWOL in Central Europe?"

"Beware men bearing live grenades," he suggested roguishly.

The DCI raised her right hand in an arc as though she might actually strike her counterterrorism chief—and then she stopped short. Dare, too, could be pushed too far.

"The moral, you stupid ass, is that Caroline fights for what she loves, sometimes beyond the point of reason. She's done trusting the Agency—the Agency, in the form of Scottie Sorensen, sold her husband out. She's on her own now. And she'll bring the prison house down around her if she has to, to save Sophie Payne. It's the only thing she can do to restore Eric's honor."

"She should be fired," Scottie said, tight-lipped.

"And it would suit your purposes nicely if Mlan Krucevic killed her," Dare retorted. "But if anything happens to Caroline—if she's hurt in the slightest way—I will hold *you* personally responsible."

"May I remind you, Director, that it was your decision to send her to Berlin?"

"You decided for all of us, when you made Eric a rogue operator thirty months ago. In a different country, another century, you'd have been executed by firing squad at dawn, Sorensen."

Scottie's mouth opened, then shut without a sound. He looked as though she had sucker-punched him. He understood, finally, all that Dare Atwood knew.

But he had been too long a professional dissembler to consider honesty now. He rose and stood before her, the last true scion of the old-boy net. "If you're unhappy with my performance, Director—"

"Then I can take your SIS slot and hand it to the next available warm body," she agreed. "That's always been the case. You just never thought I'd do it."

Dare reached for the Cutout cable and tossed it in

Scottie's lap. "Read this. And if you decide to shoot yourself in a stairwell, call me first, okay? I'd like a front-row seat."

When the CTC chief had scuttled out of her office like a whipped dog, Dare picked up her phone and called Cuddy Wilmot. She had sent him a copy of the Cutout cable as soon as she saw its importance.

"Well? Have you read it?"

"Five times," he muttered. "There's so much here, we can't digest it fast enough. Networks, operations, fund transfers—"

"Where will Caroline go, Cuddy?"

"Wherever Krucevic leads. She's on a vendetta now—you realize that, Director?"

"And where will it take her?"

Cuddy hesitated. "To a place we've never located on any map; Mlan Krucevic's boyhood home. Živ Zakopan."

"Caroline knows where it is?"

"Eric certainly did." Cuddy's voice was like flint. "It's clear from the Intel contained in this cable that he saw the place."

"You thought Krucevic had plans for Poland. You watched money flood into coffers there."

"I did," Cuddy admitted. "But the funds have stopped moving and everything's quiet, from Danzig to Krakow. Poland's as dead as that Budapest bunker."

Dare debated the point. It was a risk, throwing time and resources at a guess; but Sophie Payne's kidnapping was eighty hours old and the President was losing patience. "You're sure in your mind?" she asked Cuddy. "You stand by this judgment?"

"I do," he replied. "God help me."

"Any idea at all where this camp might be?"

Cuddy hesitated. "During World War Two, it was thought to be somewhere on the outskirts of Sarajevo. But we only have whispers and rumors, Director. And what happened there occurred over fifty years ago. So much of Yugoslav history was distorted after 1945—made the tool of Communist ideology—that for a long time, the whole idea of Živ Zakopan was discredited. Western historians called the story antifascist propaganda. But since the fall of Communism and the Bosnian war, the rumors have resurfaced. And Krucevic is always at the center of them."

"Sarajevo," Dare repeated, clutching at the one element she needed to understand. "We still have NATO peacekeeping planes on the ground there; I'll request AWAC coverage in a hundred-mile radius around the city. Retargeting overhead recon will take too much time."

"Caroline may call in," Cuddy said, "and give us a fix on her location."

Or the border patrol may find her. Two passports I know of, two possible names. But what if there's a third identity she hid from all of us?

"We don't have time to wait." Dare's tone was brisk. "Dig your tie out of a drawer, Wilmot, and put it on. We're going to brief the President."

TWELVE
Sarajevo, 11:43 P.M.

For a moment, holding the opposing currents between her fingers as she hot-wired the Skoda, Caroline was thrust back into a Tidewater May. The streaming curb of an ill-lit Sarajevo alley was transformed without warning into morning sunlight, kudzu and midges, the sharp green smell of bruised skunk cabbage underfoot. Forty people were somewhere in the woods around her, forty people attempting to cross the Farm's ten thousand acres to a pinpoint on the map where a chopper would be hovering—and Eric was hunting them from the air.

He had a machine gun mounted in the belly of the Chinook, he had forward-looking infrared, he had aggressors on the ground in jeeps and crawling on their bellies through the underbrush. He had radios and flare guns and diversionary tactics. His squad had nothing but the camouflage on their backs.

They crouched in a gully, Caroline and three friends, their eyes barely visible above the tips of the wild grasses, watching a dirt road they could not avoid crossing.

Suddenly, a green army jeep roared out of nowhere and skidded to a stop. The driver jumped out, his M-16 pointed to the sky. Caroline noted his cap, soiled with sweat above the brim; she saw the toothpick in the corner of his mouth. His name was Carl. He had a baby about twenty months old. And, fake bullets or no, he was going to shoot them down.

Two men burst from the trees behind Carl and flung themselves across the road. The driver turned and gave chase.

The keys to the jeep were still in Carl's pocket, but Eric had taught her which wires to choose, which ends to touch. Holding her breath, she fired the ignition, a prickling of fear striding up her back, and even when the engine turned over and she whipped the jeep around in the dust, she waited for the sputter of Carl's M-16 and a radio call that would end the exercise for all of them.

Nothing but midges and a cooling breeze across the windscreen, high cirrus curling above.

She drove to the pickup point eating the lunch Carl's wife had probably packed that morning, sharing it with her friends—potato chips, a fat ham sandwich, and three chocolate cookies scrupulously divided. They had not eaten in two days.

The jeep they abandoned in the middle of the base's main road, where someone was sure to find it. They slept away the afternoon among the dandelions and headstones of an abandoned graveyard. Caroline awoke at three P.M. to the sound of rotors churning the humid air.

Carl demanded a confession. He demanded an apology. He declared the theft of the vehicle to be against the exercise rules. The rules dictated that one should suffer in order to survive. Caroline admitted nothing.

In the field, Eric told her, *you do whatever it takes. If the car means you live and somebody else doesn't, you take the car. You don't stop to think about whether the guy will miss his next meal.*

The Skoda's engine turned over. She raised her head above the dashboard and stared out at Sarajevo.

———

Caroline had been on the road now for nearly four hours. She had formed the vaguest of plans—a hash of hope and guts—thrown together as she scrolled purposefully through Eric's files on an embassy computer. As she read, her mind dazed and jumping with violent death, the superstructure of Krucevic's plan appeared beneath her fingers, like a stockade of privets shaken free of snow. She saw the brilliance in his simplicity, the tragedy he had engineered. And saw how his dead wife could be used against him.

She left Embassy Budapest and hailed a taxi. She had the presence of mind to go back to the Hilton before heading for the airport—she needed a change of clothes and her Walther, comfortable shoes, some extra cash. She checked out of the hotel and left her luggage with the bellman. To be called for later, if she survived.

Caroline had absolutely no right to decide the Vice President's fate in the backseat of a Hungarian taxi. She had no business keeping vital information, such as the location of Krucevic's lab at Živ Zakopan, entirely to herself. The High Priestess of Reason stood back in judgment, showing Caroline the flaw in all she did; she scolded her and pleaded with her to call in reinforcements—Caroline almost tapped the taxi's glass partition and sent the driver back to the Hilton. She should be awash in self-doubt. She was an analyst, after all—one who demanded time, one who required more pieces of the puzzle.

But recklessness sang in her veins. Mlan Krucevic and Scottie between them had pushed her past her breaking point, and she would have juggled grenades if a few had been handy.

If she failed in this last great act of hubris—if she swung out from her trapeze and found no hands dangling—she would be destroyed. Failure, thought Caroline, was the headiest prospect she'd been offered in years.

She wanted to go home. She had no home any longer.

Hank, she prayed as her driver leaned on the horn, *I promise I will call you if I manage to survive.*

When she closed her eyes, she saw a man in black leather walking slowly away. Did he wave once, in farewell? Or was he motioning her onward?

The one woman I could trust in the depths of hell, the woman who would believe regardless of everything.

What, Caroline thought, would Eric do if he were alive tonight and sitting beside her? He would trust her to follow her particular instincts, the ones she never believed she had.

Remember Sophie, Caroline. Sophie. I owe her a chance.

She should contact the Agency. Tell them how and where to throw raiders into the breach. She should give them the location of Živ Zakopan. But Caroline was uncertain whom to trust at the CIA. Twice in the past four days, rescue operations had failed horribly. Eric was dead and Sophie Payne close to it. The military option was dicey at best; even the reluctant High Priestess in her head agreed.

Not Tom Shephard, she thought as the taxi careened

over the northwest highway. *I cannot trust Tom with his questioning eyes and his way-too-obvious suspicion. Not Cuddy—not poor loyal Cuddy, with one thumb on his glasses and his pulse on the polygraph. Not Dare, who has her position to think of. An entire bureaucracy to protect. And never Scottie.*

Scottie of the debonair suits and the poker face, Scottie who ran agents the way a child threw toys into battle—Scottie danced among shadows of his own, a parallel kingdom within the Agency itself. In a world where who you are depends upon what you know, Scottie had always known the most.

Now, for the first time, Caroline knew more.

She had a fix on 30 April's location. She had a homing device for tracking the Vice President. And she knew what Mlan Krucevic did not: that Béla Horváth's lab notebook and vials of stolen vaccine—mumps vaccine No. 413, according to Eric's disk—were in the possession of the Hungarian federal police.

Krucevic feared that notebook and those vials more than Chinooks on the roof or Delta Force troops in the heating ducts. He feared them more than losing Sophie Payne. He had killed his wife and his oldest friend to suppress the truth. And now Caroline was going to inform him that he had failed.

She made the last plane out of Budapest that night— the last plane that week—bound for Bosnia. She bought a ticket in her true name because she had no intention of leaving the Walther in Hungary, and her paperwork for the weapon read Caroline Carmichael. The Agency was already tracking her—the look on the face of the Hungarian border control guard told her that. Her alias was probably compromised as well. He did not have a poker face, that passport official; it was rumpled like a used paper bag, his eyes two small prunes. He studied her

malevolently, glancing from passport to woman and back
again. The question in the back of Caroline's mind was
why he didn't simply bar her from the plane. Nothing
was easier. A polite word—a hand on the arm—a tedious wait in a featureless office—and her documents returned when the flight took off.

The answer, she knew, was because he didn't care
where she came from. He wanted to know only where
she was going. And so an hour later she bundled Jane
Hathaway into a garbage can at Sarajevo Airport and
became someone she had almost forgotten: Caroline
Bisby, High Analytic, with her finger on the afterburner
and contrail streaming. The stuff of which mad dogs are
made.

She pulled the hot-wired Skoda away from the curb
and drove deeper into the city, feeling her way. She knew
Sarajevo only as a series of images on a television screen, a
garble of names too difficult to pronounce. It was a
European city, beautiful in the Baroque manner of Vienna
and Prague and old-town Bratislava, a small city cupped in
a valley ringed by mountains. On the hills above the red
tile roofs, the army of neighboring Serbia had erected
siege guns and positioned tanks. Each day between 1992
and 1996, the Serbs had bombarded Sarajevo with four
thousand shells. It was the longest siege in modern memory, longer even than the vicious Nazi siege of Leningrad;
but in the end, NATO marched in and the Serbs
marched out.

The Stabilisation Force peacekeepers were still there,
afraid of what might happen if they left.

The Skoda bobbled and dipped as she drove across a
shell hole. Someone had filled it with bright red epoxy,
a cartoon attempt at public works. As far as the eye
could see, brilliant gouts of blood dotted the street.

She was looking for the university on a map spread across her knees—which was in Croatian with Hungarian translation, neither helpful—while driving through the darkness of a city that seemed to have had most of its street signs blown away. But the university must surely possess a student center that never closed down, a place where coffee could be bought and politics debated and a laptop connected to the World Wide Web. Caroline had memorized Mlan Krucevic's E-mail address. It was there like a lost pearl among the terrorist's messages to Fritz Voekl, part of the archives Eric had managed to steal.

"Papa," Jozsef croaked through his swollen lips, "what have you done to the lady? Where is she?"

Mlan Krucevic laid his cool hand on his son's forehead and brushed back his sweat-soaked hair. The antibiotic for which he had retreated to Živ Zakopan was already streaming through an IV into his son's veins, but it would be hours before he glimpsed signs of improvement in Jozsef. He refused to consider that improvement was beyond him, that Jozsef might have slipped too far into the maw of the disease. Mlan Krucevic had not played God for so many decades to succumb to failure now. He had not built this new Živ Zakopan high above the old killing ground and labored patiently for years in its laboratory to be defeated by a germ of his own making. He would not pay for immortality with the blood of his son.

"Shh," he said. "You must rest. You are safe now. I have *saved* you."

The boy squirmed fretfully under the sheet, tugging at the tape that secured his arm to the bed, the precious IV feeding into his wrist. "Sophie," he murmured, and then the sheet above his abdomen blossomed like a flower, a spreading stain that darkened as it grew, first peach and then salmon and then a rusty orange. Jozsef was pissing blood.

Krucevic shuddered. He sank to his knees on the cold cement floor. He gripped the metal rail of the boy's bed until his hands lost their feeling, and this alone must be his prayer, the prayer of a man who acknowledges no god. He was crouched thus, doubled over with grief and rage, when Vaclav appeared in the doorway.

"Don't bother me," Mlan spat out.

"There's something you should see."

"Go away."

"But Mlan—"

He came to his feet with a howl, whipping his gun from its shoulder holster. Vaclav was twenty-two inches removed from a bullet in the brain. The cherub-faced Czech stared the gun barrel down.

"You should, Mlan. See this."

Krucevic drew a shuddering breath, holstered the gun, and followed Vaclav down the hall.

Otto was seated in front of Tonio's laptop, his forehead almost touching the screen. "It's from the university. How the fuck did some college kid find Mlan?"

Krucevic stood behind him and read the E-mail.

Béla's blood is on your hands, Mlan. Mirjana's dead. But I have Béla's notes and vaccine No. 413. Come and get them, if you can find me.

"The *žalba* told someone," he whispered.

———

Caroline left the university student center immediately after sending the first message. Time was of the essence: If her ruse was to help the dying Vice President, it must be effected quickly. She drove to the Sarajevo Holiday Inn, temporary home of war correspondents and relief

workers, where a third of the three hundred and fifty
rooms still showed damage. Patches in the curtains covered machine-gun holes, concrete crumbled under the
hallway carpets, and a bored cocktail waitress chain-
smoked through the lobby at 12:03 A.M. Caroline ordered a large cup of coffee and found an Internet port.

---

*The worst of it isn't the epidemic itself—those thousands of chil-
dren dead in Pristina, the disease spreading like a red stain on
the snow. The real horror, Mlan, is the salvation you offered. Vaccines. Your special vaccines. Flown into Pristina on German
planes, administered by the most selfless doctors the world
has known—Nobel laureates, above reproach, Doctors Without
Borders.*

What happens to some boys who contract mumps in
childhood? *What happens to every boy inoculated with vaccine No. 413?*

*Sterility, Mlan. Your small contribution to the Muslim problem,
as the man called Michael once said. A generation of Albanians incapable of reproducing itself. Genocide without camps, a bloodless
wave of cleansing. No one will even suspect the damage for another
fifteen years at least. And by then it will be merely a flaw in the science. Regrettable. But hardly a crime.*

*And all those toddlers rotting in mass graves, all the parents
destroyed with grief—just so much wreckage along the way.*

You sicken me, Krucevic.

*I'm going to the press. To the Americans. I have proof, and I
want to see you burn.*

"Michael," Otto murmured. "Of course it'd be Michael
who sold us out. He must've talked to a friend. *An asso-
ciate.* His little form of insurance, in the event of death.
And now that prick's got your E-mail address."

" 'I'm going to the Americans,' " Vaclav repeated. "So he's not American himself. A free agent? One of Michael's Arabs?"

"He's a prick, whoever he is," Otto insisted.

"A clever one. He sent the first message from the university. This one's from the Holiday Inn."

"All he wants is money." Krucevic stared at the text on the screen, weighing his options, then turned his back and headed for Jozsef's room. "Ask his terms, Vaclav."

"What makes you think Mr. Prick wants to deal?"

Krucevic smashed his hand once against the door frame, and the supporting wall shuddered. "Nobody telegraphs a punch, idiot, unless they expect it to be dodged. He could have gone to the press and the Americans hours ago. So find out what he *wants*.

"Then we'll give him what he deserves."

Part V
SATURDAY, NOVEMBER 13

ONE

Sarajevo, 12:33 A.M.

CAROLINE TYPED OUT HER LAST MESSAGE at the Sarajevo airport.

My terms? she wrote after an instant's thought. *I want Mlan Krucevic's head on a platter. I want the pleasure of watching him beg for mercy, the pleasure of refusing his dying wish. I want justice for MedAir 901 and for the Brandenburg Gate and for all the children who will never have children.*

But I'll settle for the release of Sophie Payne.

Bring her to the Tunnel by 2 A.M. I will be waiting alone with the vaccine. If you are not there by 2:30, I will take what I know to the people who will destroy you.

"The Tunnel" required no explanation. Everyone in Sarajevo knew about the Dobrinja-Butmir Tunnel. Four feet wide and a quarter of a mile long, it was little more than a culvert that had been clawed under an airport runway during the height of the siege, a culvert that had been shelled by the Serbs for months and that served as the beleaguered city's chief link to the outside world. The Tunnel was a black-market conduit, a ribbon of commerce in a state of war; it was a thoroughfare, too, a communications link, a rite of passage. When bureaucrats from elsewhere in Bosnia needed to reach the capital, they used the Tunnel; even the American ambassador had pushed his way through whenever he was forced to leave the city. No one's dignity was beneath Dobrinja–Butmir.

Caroline hesitated. Could Krucevic possibly believe she was so stupid? The taunts in her message were in-cautious to the extent that they ought to amuse him. The author of such a message was intoxicated with her own power; in possessing the vaccine, she believed her-self invincible. Such a person never considered that Krucevic made no deals.

Caroline, however, was not intoxicated. She was the very opposite of stupid. She was shrewdly calculating a risk. She had spent years studying Mlan Krucevic's personality—reconstructing his behavior, assessing his deeds—in an effort to predict how he would act when it really mattered. She was about to find out just how good an analyst she was.

Krucevic, Caroline believed, would never bring Sophie Payne to the Tunnel on so slight a lure as her of-fer. He would keep his hostage safe at Živ Zakopan; he would send his men to hunt down the vaccine. If the E-mail bargain was in fact a setup, he might lose a few men, but nothing more. If Caroline were alone, as she had promised, he'd order her brought back to his base for questioning. And after the questions, he'd kill her.

Only Caroline would not be crouched in the mouth of the Dobrinja–Butmir Tunnel. When Krucevic's men appeared for the rendezvous, she would be on her way to Živ Zakopan, where only Krucevic himself might guard the Vice President. It was dangerous, of course; she could not know how many men Krucevic would send for her and how many would remain behind. She was feeling her way toward Krucevic's camp. She did not have the luxury of playing 30 April like a fish. She no longer had the indulgence of time.

Caroline glanced at her watch. 12:40 A.M. Roughly twelve hours earlier, she had said good-bye to Eric. He had told her then that the Vice President could not live long.

Sophie had managed to crawl through the darkness of her prison, pulling herself forward with excruciating effort, her belly on the ground. She had crawled past the opening of the martyrs' charnel house, her skin prickling with horror at the bones beyond the wall, everything in her mind and body screaming. It was important, she told herself silently, not to consider what might lie on the floor around her. It was important to think of other things, to keep from going mad.

She had never been a person who minded the dark. At the house in Malvern she would lie restless in bed, long after Curtis had fallen asleep, his face turned into his pillow. She would listen for Peter's dreaming sigh from across the hall, then get up and walk noiselessly through the house. The things she had chosen and placed in these rooms were like strangers in the moonlight. She would caress the burnished arm of an antique chair, pick a feather from a cushion. And then, like a shadow, she would catch her reflection, a muted form shimmering in the mirror, only her eyes still luminous. She had liked to think that a century hence, on moonlit nights, her image would gaze out from the gilt frame.

Her eyes were tightly closed now. The difference between the darkness of Malvern and the night of Živ Zakopan, she knew, was the silence. Here she was an amoeba suspended in water, a yolk inside an egg. There was no ancient house settling on its stone foundations, no wind sighing through the elms. No Peter dreaming across the hall—

The anguish at her core when she thought of her son was unendurable; it sharpened the pain of her sickness, the slow agony of dying. Peter, with his eyes the color of moss, his quick speech and laugh of deprecation. Peter, whose square chin was Curt's chin whenever he was angry. Peter, who needed Sophie more than he could admit now, at the age of twenty—Sophie, who was his only family. She clenched her teeth on the thought of Peter, burrowed deep into the pain, and used her son's face to keep the ghouls of Živ Zakopan at bay.

She was very weak, and her throat was so parched that she could no longer swallow. At intervals she slept, then awoke with a start, cheek pressed against the filth of the stone passage, and sensed that she had been unconscious. It was probable, she thought, that sometime soon she would never wake again. But still she dragged herself forward, toward the manhole cover and the air above.

Her journey covered perhaps ninety feet. It took over three hours. She collapsed for the last time at the foot of Otto's ladder. But the rabbit's foot she still clutched in her hand pulsed steadily through the night, transmitting its signal like an unquiet heart in the grave.

———

Živ Zakopan is twenty-three miles south, Eric said in Caroline's mind, *along the road to Foča. You climb out of the city and then descend through the pass. After maybe ten miles you'll see a power plant and an explosives factory. The road's shit to begin with, but by the time you're thirteen miles out of Sarajevo, it's pretty smooth.*

You're in a valley, it runs down to the Drina River. About mile nineteen you'll start to pass collective farms, or what's left of them. The buildings are burned-out shells. Four miles beyond, on the left, is a rutted dirt road. Don't miss it in the dark. That's the turning for Živ Zakopan.

She drove south through the night, along a road littered with derelict tanks and abandoned gun positions and the refuse of war that time had not yet buried. NATO had condemned the Serbs for what they did in Bosnia, and later for the atrocities of Kosovo, but the world did not remember the Ustashe terror of World War II; it knew absolutely nothing about the horrors committed by Croats at Živ Zakopan. The world had the luxury of simple solutions.

Caroline allowed her gaze to veer for an instant from the empty ribbon of shell-pocked road, to take in the midnight landscape. She thought of postwar movies, still ardent with propaganda. Of desperate partisans allied to the British, of Chetniks who died on behalf of King Peter while he slurped oysters in London and danced at the Ritz. There were no angels in the Balkans, no heroes one could name. This was not a place for choosing sides. It was a place to abandon hope.

"Tell me about Živ Zakopan," she commanded Eric's ghost.

It was a Ustashe killing field. The earth there is riddled with tunnels—ancient holes gouged into the hills. The Romans built them. The Hapsburgs hid an army there. And the Ustashe tortured partisans far below the ground. Mlan's laboratory is hidden among the cliffs that soar above.

"A bunker, like in Budapest?"

He shook his head in the shadows. *A concentration camp. Barbed wire, electrified fences, searchlights, armed guards. One woman equipped with a double-action Walther TPH, accurate range maybe twelve feet, will never storm the fastness alone. Even if she's as steady with a handgun as you are, Mad Dog.*

"What's he use the place for?"

Experimentation. He tests his vaccines, his drugs, his chemical weapons, on Serb and Muslim prisoners.

"And nobody comes looking for these people?"

They're the Disappeared, Carrie. Taken away at gunpoint in the middle of the night. And who knows where they end up? Nobody ever leaves Živ Zakopan. There's a reason the place is called "Living Grave."

They came up suddenly—the abandoned collectives, the burned outbuildings. A tractor's skeleton loomed like an iron gibbet near the verge of the road, whispering of ancient crimes. Caroline glanced at her odometer to calculate the distance; when three and a half miles had worn away, she pulled the car to the shoulder and slowed to a stop. From here she would go forward on foot.

She was wearing black microfleece leggings and a pair of running shoes—workout clothing that would have to double as combat wear. The Walther she pulled out of a black nylon shoulder bag—the only luggage she'd brought with her from Budapest—and strapped it to her thigh. She practiced drawing the weapon from its holster a couple of times, the mechanics a cover for her increasing nervousness, the acceleration of her pulse. She was alone in the middle of dumb-fuck nowhere, with a ghost and a .22-caliber gun for company; she had, at last count, six rounds in the chamber and thirteen extra bullets. Above her head the stars shone with a brilliance that was excruciating; they reminded Caroline of nights in Southampton, the sky deepening after sunset to ink blue rather than black, the constellations whirling to the sound of her great-uncle's voice. The chink of ice cubes. Cicadas. A splash of Bombay Sapphire. *Hank,* she assured him, *I'm thinking seriously of law school. I just might take you up on it.*

A pinprick of light scintillated in her palm. Eric's homing device, registering a signal. Sophie Payne was within range.

"After you," she told him.

And followed where he led.

TWO

Živ Zakopan, 1:23 A.M.

JOZSEF'S EYELIDS FLUTTERED OPEN, and he stared up at the ceiling. The room had no windows. Light, such as it was, came from a pair of gas lanterns propped on a crude table made of packing crates. Shadows, primitive and strangely comforting, flickered on the wall like the Indonesian puppet dance he'd once seen; for a moment he could not imagine where he was. The haze of delirium receded slowly, the way water drains from a basin—imperceptibly at first, then in a final rush that sweeps everything with it. And when that rush to consciousness came, Jozsef sat up abruptly. There was the helicopter, the lady torn from his arms, the rabbit's foot pressed into her hand. And then the dash from the landing pad to this room, the lines of barracks whirling about him, the faces thrust against the chain-link fence. He was alone in a room on top of a cliff. He was at Živ Zakopan.

"Papa!" he cried out.

Krucevic appeared in the doorway.

Jozsef kicked away the soiled sheet and wrestled his

wrists free of the tape that restrained them. "Where is the lady? What have you done with her?"

"She is dead and buried," Krucevic replied.

"That is a lie. I know you lie!" Never had he spoken with such venom to his father, and for an instant, the boy felt sharply afraid. He cowered backward, white-faced and trembling, waiting for the punishment that would surely come.

"If she was not dead when I left her, she is certainly dead now," his father told him calmly. "You should rest. You're still quite weak. Get back in bed before you disturb your intravenous feed."

Jozsef set his foot on the floor. His muscles screamed as though they had been crushed under the wheels of a truck. He tasted blood, felt himself sway, and clutched at the mattress.

"Get back in bed." His father came nearer, looming over him. "You were close to death yourself."

The boy stared at his own hands, clenched around the sheet to keep from trembling. "You cannot leave her in the ground, Papa. It is not right."

"But it is done," Krucevic said, "and nothing will change it now." He closed his fingers over Jozsef's wrist, pried his weak hand from the sheet. Then he gathered up the boy and laid him carefully back in the bed, drew the sheet over his body. Jozsef closed his eyes on a surge of rage and anguish; he could not look at his father's face, could not trust himself to speak without sobbing. A tear slid from under his lashes and lay wetly on his cheek. He turned his face into the pillow.

"I am sorry for your pain, my son," Krucevic said.

It was the first and last time Jozsef would ever hear an apology on his father's lips. He did not answer him.

Krucevic turned away.

And at that moment, a shout went up from Vaclav at his security station down the hall.

———

She found the entrance to the ancient tunnels where Eric had told her it would be.

It's Milan's escape route from Živ Zakopan. He'll be certain to keep it in good repair.

"He only has one?"

By land. But there's always the air.

Caroline glanced swiftly toward the dark hulk of hillside rising above the ruined barn. No lights, no sound from the heights, to suggest an armed encampment. Just the transmitter signal pulsing strongly in her pocket now, reason enough to keep going.

She crept forward through the withered November grass, the dead stalks rigid with hoarfrost. The smell of damp earth mingled with the sharp scent of distant snow—a fresh, nostril-flaring whiff that, absurdly, charged Caroline's blood with hope. The barn door's frame was blackened, the space beyond impenetrably dark. If Krucevic was waiting for her, this would be the moment for ambush—for some explosion of light and sound as death came shooting through the shattered door.

The floor of the barn disintegrated in the blaze, Eric reminded her. *It fell into the sheepfold below. The drop's maybe eight feet. You can manage it. Drop close to the wall and walk around the foundation to the right. He's mined the center, where the going looks easiest. Remember, Mad Dog, never take the path somebody carves for you. It's there for a reason.*

She balanced on the ruined threshold carefully, her gun in her hand.

The floor of the barn was a mass of rubble—tumbled

bits of wood and stone, the shafts of a plow, glimpsed fitfully in the starlight streaming through the gutted roof.
An iron bar, set into the dirt in the far corner—

"I know," she told him irritably. "I see it, okay?"

"Mlan," Vaclav said, his eyes on the screen, "there's an
infiltration. At the tunnel entrance in the barn."

Krucevic was at his side instantly.

"It looks like a woman."

"A *woman*?" He peered at the monitor with narrowed eyes, disbelieving. "Probably some dick with
long hair."

"Do you want me to go down?"

They were short of men. Otto and two others—Živ
Zakopan guards—had driven north to Sarajevo Airport
to meet the author of the E-mail messages. They had
not yet returned. Six men patrolled the barracks area
where the prisoners slept fitfully; another guard was on
duty in the hospital ward. He could not spare Vaclav,
who alone was monitoring the new security system. If
the woman had penetrated the barn, others would be
climbing the cliffs.

Krucevic glanced swiftly at each of the video display
screens—there were four in all, facing every possible
means of ascent to the fortified aerie. Blank. No triggered alarms, no red lights blazing. He slapped the panel
in frustration. Where the hell were they? Nobody attempted an assault alone.

The helipad. Da bog saçuva! If they had already landed—

But the security monitor showed him a quiet compound, two guards patrolling with machine guns at the
ready. No rotors *thunk-a-thunk*ed through the clear
night air.

"Stay on the screens," he told Vaclav. "I need you to follow the assault."

———

From his bedroom doorway, Jozsef watched his father wheel around, gun in hand, and race down the hall to the supply closet. He knew the tunnel ended there; he had often been locked in the dark and crawling passage as punishment when he was just a small boy. A woman was climbing steadily through the earth.

Mama, Jozsef thought, *you came for me at last. You came for me.* And his father meant to kill her.

Eyes huge and dark in his ravaged face, Jozsef lifted his hand from the support of the door frame. He swayed an instant, dangerously. Then he tore the adhesive tape from his wrist and threw the IV feed to the floor.

———

The dirt walls of the tunnel were crudely carved and narrow. She crawled on her knees toward an uncertain end, a passage that could be blocked, a possible cave-in. She had no flashlight; the first law of infiltration is never tell them you're coming. The dark was so profound that Caroline was disoriented; for a time she had no idea whether the passage was in fact rising or whether she was falling with infinite slowness toward the center of the earth. She closed her eyes and crawled on.

The tunnel widens at the end so that you can comfortably stand, Eric whispered. *But for God's sake, be careful.*

Caroline stopped a moment to catch her breath. The darkness was smothering. Blood pounded in her ears, a throbbing cadence, adrenaline-fueled, and so loud it must tell the entire terrorist world, *Here I am, why not kill me?* She drew the homing device from her pocket. Soundless, vibrating, a needle point of red light—but the signal was fainter now. As though the transmitter was farther away. Apprehension knifed through her. *What if I'm headed in the wrong direction? Shit.*

Then her head came up. She sniffed the air. It was less heavy, less weighted with earth and disuse. She was only feet from the tunnel mouth.

She tucked the homing device away. She willed her heart to stop pounding. It ignored her. So she crawled on anyway.

Jozsef moved like a sleepwalker, like a child learning to toddle, his legs barely obeying his will. He moved out of his room toward the hospital ward three doors down the hallway. Vaclav was staring at his surveillance monitors; the corridor was deserted.

At the entrance to the ward Jozsef stopped and clutched at the door frame. There was screaming behind him, his father's rage, a sharp cry of terror.

Mama—

He fought the mad desire to run to her, to hurl himself at his father and save them all—because failure lay that way. Jozsef did not have time for failure. He drew a shuddering breath and stepped across the threshold.

There were sixteen of them strapped into beds, arms handcuffed to the iron railings. The livid glow of a fluorescent light spotlit their faces. A guard Jozsef did not know sat in a chair with a tattered copy of a Sarajevo newspaper spread open on his knees. He was in the act of rising, alerted by the screams, when Jozsef appeared.

"Go!" the boy commanded. "My father needs you. We are betrayed!"

The guard tossed aside the newspaper and reached for his gun.

"Give me the keys." Jozsef thrust out his hand. "My father's orders."

The man looked doubtful. "Are you well enough?"

"The keys!" Jozsef snarled.

The man hesitated, then slapped a metal ring into his palm and dashed through the doorway. Jozsef shut the door behind him and locked it. Then he turned to face the damaged things lying in the beds.

Two old men he discounted at sight; both were obviously adrift in coma. A girl of perhaps five stared sightlessly upward while her fingers plucked at the thin sheet. A woman was moaning, the sound repetitive, maddening—she had already lost her mind. But the rest, three women, two boys his own age, and seven men—were staring at him with expressions ranging from curiosity to open hatred.

He moved toward the first as quickly as his own illness would allow, fingering the keys. *No time.* No time to test them all, with these people helpless and his mother's screams silenced.

"That one," the man before him muttered in Serbian. He had bright blue eyes, impossibly blue eyes, under a mat of filthy black hair. His face was scabbed and bruised. "The one between your fingers. No—the one you just let go. It is the skeleton key."

Jozsef's hands were shaking uncontrollably. He thrust the key into the lock, turned it to the right, and heard the click. The cuffs fell away. "You must fight," he said haltingly in his mother's tongue. "Fight for your life. Can you do it?"

The man sat up and rubbed his aching arms. Then he stared at the door at the end of the hall, the one Jozsef had not yet locked. "There are guns in that storeroom. But it will be guarded."

"Then we must draw the guard to us," Jozsef told him. He had unlocked four more sets of cuffs; all the prisoners capable of listening were listening now.

He nodded at one of the women—dirty-blond hair chopped any which way, bright spots of color burning in her cheeks. She looked more alert than the rest. "Scream as though someone wanted to slit your throat. Break some glass. When the guard comes through that door, we will be waiting."

The blue-eyed man found a scalpel on a shelf. And when the woman screamed and the gun-room guard raced in with his automatic leveled, the man stood ready behind the door.

The guard fell with the scalpel through his neck.

Jozsef steadied himself against a bed. Stars were exploding behind his eyes. *I must not faint.*

The blond woman's hand gripped his shoulder. He saw, as from a great distance, that three of her fingers were missing. In her other hand she held a knife.

"What now?" she asked. As though he were a grown-up. Someone who knew what should be done.

"To the barracks," he cried. And heard his father in his voice.

———

Caroline crouched with her ear against the tunnel door, listening intently. Her gun was raised. Beyond the flat panel of wood must be the supply closet; beyond that, a silence that made her flesh crawl. Too tight. Too heavy. A silence screaming for air.

Someone was waiting beyond the closet door.

Of course he's waiting. You didn't really think this would work, did you?

Shut up. I don't have time for this now.

Caroline clutched her Walther more firmly and thrust aside her fear. She was within an inch of death and singing about it, she was intoxicated with derring-do. For an instant she stood alone on a forty-foot jump tower in deepest Tidewater—only this time there was no Eric to shove his hand into the small of her back. She took a deep breath. Felt for the latch of the tunnel door. And hurled herself off the platform—

He must have expected her to ease the door open gently, to peer around the edge, a deer in his headlights, while he pumped a round of bullets straight into her face. Instead the tunnel door slammed open and Caroline propelled herself, still crouching, straight at the man's knees. He lost his balance and swayed heavily against a shelf, raining boxes and vials to the floor. The crash of glass. Caroline screaming, a guttural, wordless battle yell.

It won her a few seconds longer.

She saw the man's dark eyes, the close-cropped hair, the healed white sickle at his temple where a bullet had traveled long ago. Mlan Krucevic. The man she had hunted obsessively for years, the man whose face she had never seen. The man who had strapped Eric to a door and waited for it to explode.

His foot swung in an arc toward her head. She had no place to roll in the closet's narrow space, no place to dodge. A piece of glass knifed into her bicep—

She thrust herself upward and fired.

If you're going to use a Walther, Eric murmured to her, *a closet's the only place to do it.*

Krucevic grunted with pain. Then the boot completed its arc and smashed into her cheekbone. Pain exploded behind her eyes, her hands came up to her face, she was curled in a fetal ball on the floor. He kicked her again in the kidneys. Then his hand was on her wrist, twisting. The delicate bones snapped under his strength—and she let go of the Walther's grip. Two iron talons grasped her shoulders and hauled her to her feet.

In an instant he would put his gun to her skull and pull the trigger. The pain was a dull roar in the back of her ears, like the sound of the sea captured in a shell.

"Where are they?" he screamed in German. "Your team. *Where are they?*"

Her bullet had struck him in the abdomen. Blood spread like a map across his stomach, it stained the dark gray sweater he wore to black. Why was he still standing?

"Where are they?"

The sound of a gunshot, and a man's brutal scream, from the hallway beyond.

His gun smashed again into her battered cheekbone. Agony cut like a jagged knife through her brain. She summoned her last shred of strength—and shoved her knee straight into the dark stain at his abdomen.

He howled and doubled over, still clutching his gun. She kicked backward and scrabbled for the missing Walther.

Footsteps pounded toward them.

"Papa!"

Her skull still ringing, Caroline glanced over her shoulder and saw a thin kid in underwear, his eyes two charcoal holes in a bone white face. *Jozsef.* He had called Krucevic *Papa.* Behind him were other faces—haggard, deranged, a crowd of eyes burning. He had brought the whole camp with him.

"Vaclav!" Krucevic yelled hoarsely. One hand clutched his stomach, his gun was still potent in the other. *"Vaclav!"*

Caroline rose slowly to her feet, her eyes fixed on

Krucevic. He had sunk to the floor, and the Walther was pinned beneath him. There was no salvation that way.

Blood spilled between the fingers he pressed against his shirt. His teeth were clenched in a snarl. But still he raised his gun—

"Papa!"

The boy slid across the floor to huddle at Krucevic's side, his face a mask of fear. "You're bleeding!"

Krucevic clapped a crimson hand on his son's shoulder. He turned Jozsef around to face Caroline and the throng of silent inmates standing twelve feet away. She saw now that they were armed. There would be no reply from Vaclav.

Krucevic raised his gun to Jozsef's temple. He gasped out something in Serbian. Caroline could not understand the words, but she caught the meaning. He would shoot the boy in the head if they came any closer.

The value of a life is relative. Krucevic has known that since birth. He's on record as saying that death is always preferable to failure.

Jozsef's lips parted, but no sound came. And then his eyes slid closed with a terrible weariness. He leaned his head into the barrel of his father's gun and sighed, a child up too long past his bedtime. And Caroline at last understood. He was Krucevic's son, as Mlan was the child of *his* father. Jozsef was waiting for the death he had always known would come.

Fury swept over her like a wave of heat: fury for this boy who had always been trapped, exchanged like a prisoner of war between parents who never loved him enough. Fury for Eric, who was Jozsef grown up. Fury for herself, and what she had become.

Krucevic muttered something more. But his hand was shaking and his voice was faint. He had lost too much blood.

Caroline felt a spark of satisfaction—her one bullet had evened the odds—and then she threw herself at the pair of them without pausing to think, as though Krucevic were just a trainer in a prison shack, the grenade dangling temptingly from his munitions belt. She fell on top of the boy, her hands clawing at Krucevic's face.

His gun went off.

The bullet winged her, then plunged over her shoulder to bury itself in the closet wall. She tore the boy from Krucevic's arms and rolled backward, fighting her own pain. The gun fired again—

A woman with ragged blond hair and intense green eyes leapt over Caroline and fell upon Krucevic. Caroline saw the knife in her hand rise—then rolled again to shield Jozsef from his father. She had managed to thrust them through the closet door. She dragged herself to her knees, her arms still around the boy's frail body, as the horde of crippled things Mlan Krucevic had made surged past them.

Caroline pressed herself flat against the wall, pain stabbing through her shoulder, and took a dizzying blow on the side of the head. They were like animals, like brutes, their hatred and blood lust destroying reason; she would be overwhelmed and then she would die.

"Papa!" Jozsef's voice, pinched and shrill with terror.

A hand scrabbled at her neck, gripped hard on her collar. She screamed into a pair of shocking blue eyes, a mouth open in a snarl; then the man yanked her ruthlessly toward the hall. One of the camp's inmates.

Krucevic was being bludgeoned with pieces of chairs, with laboratory tools, with shattered frames torn from the windows. The inmate dragged Caroline forward, stumbling, through the insane tangle of bodies. She could not fight him. She could not feel the fingers of her right hand. Blackness clouded her vision. She tripped over a leg. A child's leg, bare to the edge of his filthy shorts.

The dark-haired man lifted Jozsef in his arms and shouted at Caroline, an incomprehensible word. He was gesturing for her to follow.

A terrible, high-pitched cry rose from the knot of bodies behind. *He's dead,* Caroline told the leather jacket receding in her mind. *Mlan Krucevic is dead.* But Eric did not turn to look—he had better things waiting down the road ahead—and in the end, neither did she.

THREE

Živ Zakopan, 2:52 A.M.

AN ARMY OF THE DISAPPEARED had seized the hallway ahead. Caroline caught sight of the man who had saved her, his black head and wiry body pushing a tortured path through the shrieking faces. Fear and pain overwhelmed the adrenaline surge that had propelled her out of the tunnel mouth; a few more minutes, and she might crumple to the floor. She tried to keep the black hair in her sights, wavered, and then toppled against the wall, waiting for the dizziness to pass. A screaming woman clutched at Caroline's wounded right arm. She cried out in pain, and felt the blackness roll up to claim her.

Blue eyes, fierce and relentless. He had come back. The man threw his arm around her waist and pulled her forward through the chaos. The wall beside her disappeared and abruptly, Caroline was falling sideways. The doorway to a room. She landed hard on the floor and rolled over. The door behind her slammed.

Darkness. Not the heavy weight of unconsciousness, but the absence of all light. The man flipped a switch on the wall; nothing. Someone had gotten to the camp's generator.

Caroline glanced swiftly around, her eyes adjusting to the gloom, and staggered to her knees. She was in a cubicle, a room with one unshaded window, a metal cot, an IV stand, some crates for a table. The blue-eyed man threw a torrent of Serbian at her. Useless.

A boy's voice answered, broken with exhaustion and grief. *Jozsef.* He lay in a heap at the foot of the cot. Caroline pushed herself toward him, but he flung out a hand in mute warning. He did not need this stranger. What she could see of his face was blank with shock.

There was a clatter behind them, a spattering of words. The blue-eyed Serb had turned the crates on their sides and jammed them against the closed door. Then he pulled the sheet from the cot and tore at it with his teeth. A roll of cotton from the room's supplies was already in his hand.

He was making her a bandage.

The Serb pressed the folded linen against the shredded fabric near her collarbone. Caroline's breath hissed raggedly through her clenched teeth. It was an awkward area to dress—but the man wrapped cotton gauze several times around her armpit, then tied it off with ruthless force. Caroline bit down so hard on her lip that blood oozed under her teeth. Unhygienic, inexpert— but it would do. She grabbed his hand as he stepped away, looked up into his eyes. She knew not one word of Serbian. "Thank you."

He nodded, then crossed the room and thrust up the window. He held out his hand to Jozsef.

Unable to stand, the boy crawled.

"Halt," Caroline said hoarsely. *"Sophie Payne. Wo ist Sophie Payne?"*

The boy's head came around; his eyes widened. *"Sie konnen die Dame?"*

"Yes," she answered. "I know the lady. Jozsef, I'm Michael's wife. I came to help you."

The Serb prisoner stared at Caroline, uncomprehending, then spat something harsh and desperate in his own tongue. Fists pounded against the locked door. The wave of violence sweeping the camp was indiscriminate, now; the only sane thing to do was flee.

"You killed my father," Jozsef whispered in lacerated English. "You are the one who shot him like a dog."

"The camp killed him. I came for Mrs. Payne." With her left hand—Krucevic had broken the other wrist—Caroline pulled Eric's homing device from her pocket. The signal was fainter than in the fields below the compound.

"Jozsef, where is she?"

"Ich weiss nicht!" The twelve-year-old was sobbing, his hands beating the cement floor, on the edge of hysteria. And why not? A few minutes ago, his father had held a gun to his head. And now his father lay in pieces somewhere down the corridor.

"She's not with you?"

Jozsef shook his head.

Caroline crouched close to the boy and held out the homing device. "See this red light? It's a signal. Michael buried a transmitter somewhere in her things."

"The lady has nothing," he said dully.

The Serb prisoner tossed two words at them and then thrust himself through the open window. At that moment, the door frame shattered and the wooden crates were pushed backward into the room. Caroline seized Jozsef's waist—he was as light as a cat from illness, a bundle of sticks to be tossed on the fire—and hurled him at the sill.

"He left her down below," the boy said against her cheek. "He told me she was dead and buried."

Dead and buried. The tunnels of old Živ Zakopan.

There was a six-foot drop from the windowsill. He sat for an instant, weak legs dangling, then crumpled to the ground. Wishing uselessly for her Walther, Caroline thrust herself face first through the window, kicking at the frame. She dropped with a sharp jolt onto her left side, and her collarbone creaked and shifted under her skin; she cried out, then clamped down on the pain searing through her chest.

She felt for Jozsef.

"Here," he breathed, and she saw his eyes peering through the slit of a doorway opposite. She crawled over and ducked inside the small shed.

The stench was overwhelming. He had hidden in a latrine.

Caroline held her breath against the sour odor. Feet thudded past them. Something crashed into the door of the latrine with a piercing shriek, bounced away, fell silent. Jozsef shuddered and pressed against her. Caroline put her good arm around him.

They waited for what seemed hours, probably no more than eight minutes. The smell of excrement and lime would cling to her clothes and hair, Caroline thought, a stink so solid she would taste it for days to come. If she survived. Her collarbone was numb, and the bandage had stanched the flow of blood. But she was weakening. Her eyelids drooped. Maybe she could sleep for a while and look for Sophie Payne in the morning.

"I gave her my rabbit's foot," Jozsef muttered. He seemed to have slipped sideways, down the current of a dark river. She groped her way back to him.

"What?"

"My good-luck charm. The lady needed it more than me. But what if the luck fails?"

Dead and buried. The tunnels . . . Caroline roused herself with effort. The screams from the compound were fainter now, the pounding feet gone elsewhere.

"Jozsef—can you show me the gate?"

He reached for her hand. "I do not think it will be guarded any longer."

It took them thirty-three minutes to descend the narrow path through the rocks. Caroline's vertigo returned, and Jozsef fainted halfway down, a dead weight dragging on her left arm. She stopped to revive him, chafing his wrists and slapping him methodically; and remembered, as he lay senseless, the antibiotics in Živ Zakopan's labs. Antidotes to anthrax that might have saved two lives. They were probably smashed to pieces by this time.

Caroline cursed viciously. It was too late to go back.

Jozsef's eyes flickered open. She crouched beside him.

"I can't carry you." Blood had soaked through her makeshift bandage. "You can stay right here. Close to the cliff face. I'll come back soon with help."

She had no idea whether she would find Sophie Payne or how to summon help, if any was at hand; but there was nothing else to tell the boy.

Jozsef struggled to his knees. And began to crawl.

The Skoda still sat where she had left it, wide open to the world. No one had seen fit to use it for a getaway. Despite the slow torture of the hillside path, they were the first to descend from Živ Zakopan. The rest were too intent on blood and vengeance.

Jozsef heaved himself weakly into the back of the car and lay motionless. Caroline fumbled in her pocket for the homing device and held it to her ear.

The signal was stronger than it had been in Krucevic's camp.

"Don't leave me," Jozsef said weakly. She looked down and found his eyes upon her. They were bright with fever and anguish and death.

They struggled across the field together, in search of the signal's source. It was 3:07 A.M. In a little while the birds would sing.

———

"Mrs. Payne."

Nell Forsyte, the same Nell Forsyte she had seen murdered in Pariser Platz; Sophie heard her voice with a flush of joy. She loved Nell. Nell had died for her, a senseless sacrifice. But they would be together always. She reached out her arms to hold Nell close. It was so dark in here. She had thought she was buried alive once, in the trunk of a car.

"Mrs. Payne. Can you hear me?"

She tried to open her lips. She may have moved her head. A faint sound, like the mewling of a cat. Then a steel rod was thrust under her back, agony exploded in her skull. Blood surged from her abdomen to her mouth, flooding between her lips. She choked on the words she needed to say.

Someone was crying. Small, little-boy fingers fluttering on her cheek. She would kiss Peter's knee and make it better again.

Mrs. Payne, Nell called again, with that gentle insistence of the professional bodyguard, the untitled nanny.

I'm coming, Sophie answered gaily, and took one last

look at her reflection in the golden mirror. It was hard to see anything at Malvern tonight. Especially from such a distance.

———

Panicked, Caroline searched for a pulse in the wrist and neck. She laid her head on the woman's blood-soaked sweatshirt and listened. She felt with her fingertips for a wisp of breath, frantic to snatch this life back—for she had found Sophie Payne *alive,* and the woman had slipped through her fingers. Water in a bowl of sand.

She stared down at the Vice President and thought of Eric, whom she had failed. Not Jack Bigelow or Dare Atwood or even, really, Sophie herself—but Eric, who had placed the map and the transmitter and the woman's life in her hands. Caroline wasted no time debating whether such a burden was fair. She did not hate him for it. It was the burden she had chosen.

She closed Sophie's eyes and left her alone at the base of the ladder. Without help from Sarajevo, there was nothing else she could do. Then she climbed slowly toward the surface, her left hand cramping on the ladder's iron rungs. Tears seethed at the back of her throat.

"You found her?" Jozsef asked. He was huddled against the stile near the iron manhole cover, filthy and stuttering with cold.

"We should hurry and get help," Caroline told him.

He sat up, eyes vivid with hope. "She's alive?"

Caroline opened her mouth, then shut it again. Not for this boy the kind prevarication, the words better left unsaid. She shook her head.

He went very still. Everything in his face died. Caroline crouched down and drew him close.

Terrible, these tears so long unshed, falling now on a

stranger's neck. The fierce, inhuman sobbing of grief. Jozsef wrapped his arms around her and said nothing while she cried.

At 3:32 A.M., the first wave of NATO helicopters thundered overhead.

FOUR

The White House, 12:34 A.M.

JACK BIGELOW GOT THE NEWS from the White
House Situation Room two minutes after midnight.
He had attended a reception for the president of
Somalia; he had listened to a large young soprano sing
arias in Italian; he had stood near his wife and smiled
tirelessly into the eyes of people whose names he occa-
sionally remembered. Now he sat alone with his bow tie
undone and his dress shirt half open, a glass of ice water
in his hand. He was reading three paragraphs of an arti-
cle on the backswing in *Golf* magazine.

The news came with a ring of his internal phone
and the hesitant voice of a detailee from the State
Department. Dare Atwood, she said, was on her way
over.

Bigelow closed the magazine, his forefinger resting
for an instant on its glossy cover; then he whipped off
his tie and dress clothes and threw on a polo shirt and
khakis. He would have to call her son. Peter had arrived
at his mother's residence—the Naval Observatory—that
afternoon. Should he do it now? Or let the boy sleep?

Terrible, if Peter heard it first from a television screen. Like the outcome of a close election.

He fumbled with his belt buckle, and then his fingers stilled. Sophie was dead. Throughout each hour of the past five days, he had known it was a possibility. But the fact of her death threw his crisis management in a harsher light. Death demanded reevaluation. Where had they gone wrong? The pundits would certainly ask. And the next question was inevitable: Who would pay?

"So Krucevic is dead?"

"We have confirmation of that, yes. From Caroline Carmichael."

"The woman who found Sophie."

"My analyst," Dare Atwood amended. "And our Budapest station managed to collect a remarkable amount of intelligence from . . . the 30 April bunker in Hungary." This was technically true; she saw no reason to explain exactly how Eric's disk had survived the explosion. "We're rolling up Krucevic's networks all over the world. Thirty-five arrests have already been made, in fourteen raids."

"Do we have enough to screw Fritz Voekl?" Bigelow asked pensively.

"I believe we do. He's clearly implicated in the VaccuGen mumps scandal—the records of E-mail correspondence between the chancellor and Mlan Krucevic confirm his full knowledge and support of the vaccination campaign. And then there's the Brandenburg dump."

"What dump?"

"Voekl ordered all evidence from the 30 April bombing destroyed. Our station chief in Berlin, Wally Aronson, has found out why."

"Go on," Bigelow ordered.

"You may remember that Fritz Voekl got his political start running a munitions plant in Thuringia."

"Best little gun shop in the GDR."

"The FBI's forensic technicians have traced chemical residues from the explosive responsible for the Brandenburg Gate's destruction directly to plastic explosive produced in that plant."

Bigelow whistled softly. "It ain't exactly proof the man planned a hit on his own capital. . . ."

"And it won't be admissible in court. But it's as close as we'll ever get to a smoking gun."

The President swiveled in his desk chair thoughtfully. "We're not goin' to court, Dare. What we want is Fritz Voekl outta office."

"For that," Dare replied, "you need only public outcry. Give the mumps epidemic to the press, Mr. President, and you'll have it."

Bigelow glanced over at his DCI. "We owe that much to Sophie. Having failed her in every other respect."

Dare Atwood bowed her head. "May I say, Mr. President, how deeply I regret the Vice President's death?"

The President stared out the Rose Garden window. At this hour of night, a spotlight lit the bare canes; they threw a shadow like barbed wire across the withered lawn. "I know you did everything possible," he said. "Don't know what else we coulda done. But I'm sure I'll be reading about this fiasco in the *Washington Post* for the next six months."

So much, Dare thought, *for mourning Sophie Payne.*

"How much access should the Agency afford the press, Mr. President?"

He studied her. "The Agency? Or your analyst—the Carmichael woman?"

"She *is* something of a heroine," Dare observed delicately. "The fact of the Vice President's death takes nothing from the extraordinary courage and brilliance Ms. Carmichael displayed. That should not go unrecognized."

Jack Bigelow considered the point. A heroine might be useful at dispelling the funk of failure. But they would have to be careful how they handled Carmichael.

"There's just one question I gotta ask, Dare."

"Yes, sir?"

"The Sarajevo cable says she used a homing device to find Sophie in that tunnel. But who planted the transmitter—and where, exactly, did your gal get the device?"

Dare felt a tremor between her shoulder blades and stood a little straighter. "From someone within the 30 April Organization, sir. That much is obvious. If difficult questions are asked, I suggest we refer to our constant need to protect our Intelligence sources and methods. That tends to put an end to certain conversations."

Bigelow tossed a copy of the *Financial Times* across his desk. Even upside down, Dare knew what the headline said: AMERICAN'S BODY DISCOVERED IN TERRORISTS' LAIR.

"You realize the kind of stink this could cause?"

Dare returned his gaze steadily. "I haven't read that piece yet, sir."

"You in the habit of runnin' rogue operations, Dare?"

"Absolutely not, Mr. President." She hesitated. "The groundwork for that . . . *operation* . . . was laid during my predecessor's tenure."

Bigelow scowled. "And no one saw fit to inform you of it?"

"No, sir."

"Wonder how many other DCI's that bastard Sorensen has end-run."

Dare had asked herself the same question. Had Scottie made a practice of deceiving his superiors? Or was her case special—a higher threshold of mistrust—because she was a *woman* with no operational experience?

"Mr. Sorensen has already proffered his resignation," she told the President.

He shook his head. "We can't accept it in the present climate. Too many questions would be asked. And Sorensen might feel obligated to answer them."

"I agree."

The President crumpled the *Financial Times* and tossed it in his wastebasket. "Watch your back, Dare," he advised her. "You're not careful, son of a bitch'll have *your* job next."

"Yes, sir," she replied.

————

Tom Shephard caught up with Caroline thirteen hours after Delta Force did.

He stood in the doorway of her room—the embassy had pulled rank with the Sarajevo hospital and insisted it be private—and studied her. She was sound asleep. Her head lay slantwise across the pillow, her blond hair lank from several days' neglect. The bandaged collarbone was just visible through a gap in her gown. The room was filled with dusk and the green glow of a fitful fluorescent tube, so that the quality of her skin was cadaverous; nothing of Caroline's force or spark remained.

He had not entered a hospital since the day five years before when his Jennifer had died. He found he was still not ready. With a flutter of panic, he turned to go.

"Hey, Shephard."

Perhaps it was her wound that had stripped her of all defenses, or the fact that the long, hard quest was done. Whatever the reason, she looked at him baldly and stretched out her hand. He understood then just how lonely she was—how much in need of human contact.

He took her fingers between his own and squeezed them gently.

"Couple of inches to the right, Mad Dog, and you wouldn't be here," he said with a nod toward her bandage.

"Couple of inches to the left, and I'd be home by now," she retorted.

He grinned at her, his spirits rising suddenly, the ghost of that lost other love lifting as quietly as a bird from his shoulders. He pulled a chair close to her bedside.

She studied his face as though nothing but the truth could possibly be read there. He wondered if she understood how much he had mistrusted her—and how much he had wanted to believe. He decided that neither was worth saying right now.

"How's the boy?" she asked. "How's Jozsef?"

"Not good. They've got him pumped full of drugs from the embassy stores—but he hasn't turned the corner yet." The corner being an S-bend between death and life, sharp enough to derail a train. "We're thinking about airlifting him to Germany."

"No."

"Caroline—he needs an ICU worthy of the name."

"He'd get far better care in the U.S."

"But it's farther away. He could die in transit."

"We are *not* sending him back to Germany. Not even to a NATO base. He has no one left, Tom—*no one*. You heard about Mirjana?"

"There may be supplies of the Anthrax 3A–specific antibiotic in Berlin," Shephard attempted. "At Vac-cuGen."

"So get your buddies in the BKA to break into the warehouse! Send some drugs home! The CDC would *kill* for a sample."

Dare Atwood, Shephard reflected, had already suggested something similar in a teleconference with Embassy Sarajevo.

"But don't drop that kid smack in the middle of Fritz Voekl's camp," Caroline insisted. "He deserves a break. Sophie Payne would have wanted that much—" She broke off and bit hard at her lip.

"Fritz Voekl shot himself two hours ago."

Caroline's eyes widened fractionally. Then surprise gave way swiftly to calculation, so that Shephard might almost have believed they were back in Berlin, briefing Ambrose Dalton. "Who took over? His deputy party chief, or—"

The corners of Shephard's mouth twitched. Her case could not be that desperate if she was already analyzing.

"Get some sleep, Carrie," he ordered. "I'll talk to the ambassador about Jozsef Krucevic."

"Talk to the BKA," Caroline ordered, "then come back and tell me who's running Germany. I want to know!"

"But you don't *need* to know, Mad Dog," he said. "Not yet."

———

The body of the Vice President of the United States was returned to Washington two days later. Jozsef Krucevic accompanied his lady on the plane, a dirty white rabbit's foot clutched tightly in his hand.

Jack Bigelow and an honor guard were waiting on the tarmac. So were the press crews of thirty-four nations and a crowd of nearly a thousand people, held back by a phalanx of helmeted police. The coffin was draped in the American flag; the mood was solemn. Peter Payne laid his cheek on Sophie's casket before fifty million television viewers, then paced slowly behind the honor guard to the waiting hearse.

Jack Bigelow put his arm around the young man's shoulders and said a few words the microphones could not catch. Something, probably, about sacrifice and sorrow. Peter Payne nodded and extended his hand.

Later, the pundits would say a torch of some kind had been passed.

But before all this occurred—before the motorcade to Arlington and the *Newsweek* cover of Caroline Carmichael, before the presidential letter of appreciation and the Bronze Intelligence Star—there was a different sort of homecoming, in a freight hangar at Washington Dulles, and Scottie Sorensen was the only person there.

———

He stood with his hands in his pockets while they wheeled the coffin forward on a gurney, a medical examiner at his side.

"Are you ready, sir?" the attendant asked him. Sorensen nodded, his expression debonair as always. He was not required to make a formal identification of the body. It would probably be unpleasant. There had, after all, been an explosion. But Scottie thought he might sleep better, nights, if he knew for certain that Eric Carmichael was dead. Eric had possessed too many secrets.

They lifted open the casket's cover. Scottie stared down at the blond hair, the corpse riddled with shrapnel. Most of the facial features were missing. He studied one hand and an arm. Ugly red weals crisscrossed the wrist. Eric had, after all, been tortured; but these scars were old. These scars had healed years before. They were the marks of a razor blade inexpertly applied by a man who hadn't really wanted to die.

He took a step backward. He motioned that the casket should be closed. He drew a clean white handkerchief from his pocket and pressed it delicately against his nose.

"Can you identify this man as Michael O'Shaughnessy?" the medical examiner asked.

Scottie hesitated. There were so many possible answers.

"His name is Antonio Fioretto," he said at last. "An Italian national, and a terrorist."

And for a wild instant, he almost laughed.

ABOUT THE AUTHOR

FRANCINE MATHEWS spent four years as an intelligence analyst for the CIA, where she was trained in Operations and served a brief stint in the Counterterrorism Center assisting the investigation into the 1988 bombing of Pan Am Flight 103. The author of ten previous novels, she lives and writes in Colorado, where she is at work on her next thriller, *The Secret Agent*.

Visit Francine Mathews's website at
www.francinemathews.com.

If you enjoyed Francine Mathews's
THE CUTOUT,
you won't want to miss her next tantalizing novel
of international intrigue and suspense,
THE SECRET AGENT.

Look for THE SECRET AGENT in hardcover at
your favorite bookseller's in Summer 2002.

And turn the page for an exciting preview of

THE
SECRET AGENT

by

Francine Mathews

Coming soon in hardcover!

ROSE COTTAGE, MARCH 26, 1967

HE HAD NEVER BEEN A MAN who minded the heat. In Bangkok he disdained air conditioners and forced his houseboy to cook nightly over a charcoal brazier, the flames flickering like knives on the man's burnished skin. By day he slipped through the humid, sweltering streets when the sun was strongest, silk suit tailored close to his lean frame. His face was deeply tanned from sitting by the pool at the Royal Sports Club, his brow furrowed from staring into the light.

They called him many things in Bangkok: the Silk King, the Boss, the Quiet American. The braver ones called him Spy and Devil, and he admired their courage and honored their names in turn. He fashioned a life from myths and lies over the course of twenty years; he bought and sold entire villages, entertained everyone who stumbled into Southeast Asia, advised ambassadors and court potentates, dried the tears of women desperate for love. They had always whispered behind his back in Bangkok and the names they called him were proxies for one word: *Power*. He relished this about Siam the way he loved the stench of the klongs and the liquid snatch of raw silk through his fingers: Siam was ruthless, Siam cared for no man not born of the River of Kings, Siam bowed only to secrets and the power secrets held.

He was a man who could buy anything with money; but secrets were traded in blood and that was why he cherished them.

This afternoon, alone in the blessed quiet that is granted to those who remain alert while the rest of the household is napping, he sat on the terrace and turned a cigarette in his restless fingers. His doctor insisted that he quit smoking—but he was past sixty now and far beyond a human caution. He had lost too much in recent days to give up anything by choice.

The sun was fitful and the air was chill, six thousand feet above the Malaysian coast. He shivered slightly, closed his eyes, and thought of monsoons—of moist warmth, of stones streaming with fragrance. Of skin wet and shining in the garden torchlight, her head rising like a serpent's from the filthy water of the klong—

He discarded the cigarette in a burning arc.

He was alone at last after the fuss and clatter of Easter morning, the service at the Anglican church in Tanah Rata, the picnic later on a distant hillside. He knew that his urgency had disconcerted them—the way he hustled them through the meal, packing up the plates and glasses as soon as the last morsel was consumed, shooing them back to the car without explanation. It was a sign of advancing age, this lack of courtesy; a slip in tradecraft. He was stripped raw with tension, his ears preternaturally alert, a fine beading of sweat at the hairline—he, who had never minded the heat.

Tradecraft had got him this far. It would take him no farther.

He glanced at his watch. Time to rise and push back

the chair, time to set off purposefully down the gravel drive toward a man he had not seen in years and might be forgiven for failing to recognize. It was his last possible chance at a meeting. He had cased the route earlier in the day, refusing the car that would have conveyed him to church, joining the others at the foot of the road that wound past the golf course. He would take nothing with him now but the briefcase brought from Bangkok—the briefcase, and every mortal lust or fear that had propelled him through two decades of life in Asia.

His eyes narrowed in the failing light. The road was deserted, the whole world asleep. He set off.

———

Later, they would admit that they heard him go. His footsteps, even in their dreaming ears, could be those of only one man. The girl he had brought with him from Bangkok turned restlessly in her sleep, arm lifted in a gesture akin to dancing. Her lips might have formed his name.

She slept on.

Part I

MAX

CHAPTER ONE

THE ORIENTAL HOTEL in the heart of Bangkok is a name to conjure history. It recalls a time when tourists were travelers, when steamer trunks came by long-tail boat up the Chao Phraya, the River of Kings; when stoic male writers and legends of the Asian bush crawled out of the jungle to swap stories in the Bamboo Bar. Somerset Maugham almost died of fever there, in the nineteen-twenties, and Joseph Conrad tossed sleepless on a sweat-soaked cot; Hemingway ought to have seduced a legion of hard-drinking women behind the swinging shuttered doors, but apparently never did. During the Second World War the natives of Bangkok edged warily around the place, which had become an object of fear under the Japanese; and when Thailand capitulated to the Allies, the Oriental turned hostel for U.S. and British officers.

They must have felt right at home, those Allied soldiers, between the French doors and the lawns running down to the swollen brown river. Orchids bloomed as profusely as English violets at the foot of the towering palms, and the whistles of the boatmen flew over the water like lark song. Under the drift of electric fans they drank deep of gin and Pimm's, and composed letters to women they hadn't seen in years. They imagined themselves conquerors, without having fired a shot.

This is the trick of Thailand, and of the Oriental Hotel: to make a guest feel at home without ever implying he is anything but a guest. But like all great hotels, the Oriental is a stage for public drama: it demands a decent performance from the people who walk through its doors. The right to enter history comes at considerable cost, and style is the preferred form of currency. Shorts and backpacks—those hallmarks of the indigent tourist desperate for an hour of quiet and air conditioning—are strictly forbidden in the main lobby of the Oriental.

Stefani Fogg had stayed at the hotel before. She had read the dress-code notice etched politely near the revolving main door. But she was the sort of woman who rarely apologized, particularly to the hired help. And so this morning she hitched her backpack higher on her shoulder and swung her long, bare legs out of the taxi.

"Welcome back to the Oriental, Ms. Fogg," the doorman said, and bowed low over his steepled hands.

She took the spray of jasmine he offered her and raised it to her face. The scent was elusive—the essence of untimely death. She nodded to the doorman, paid off the taxi, and stalked inside.

She may have been conscious of the eyes that followed her as she crossed the spotless carpet. If so, she ignored them. She ignored the soaring windows, the comfortable chairs swathed in silk, the towering arrangements of lilies, the four different employees who bowed in succession as she passed. She ignored the powerfully built man with the gleaming black hair, who sedulously scanned his newspaper at a desk opposite the magazine kiosk, although he was the only person in the room pretending disinterest and thus ought to have been alarming. Stefani was too tired to care. The rigid set of her shoulders and the thin line of her mouth screamed exhaustion. During the past week she had slept badly and in the previous twenty-seven hours, not at all.

"Mr. Rewadee," she said by way of greeting to the Manager of Customer Relations. The backpack slid from her shoulder to her feet.

"Ms. Fogg! Welcome back to the Oriental!"

This phrase—or variations on the theme—was a gamut she was forced to run every time she reappeared on the banks of the Chao Phraya. But she liked Rewadee, with his correct navy suit and his beautiful silk tie, his smooth, tapering fingers; so she stifled her annoyance and forced a smile, as though her clothes did not stink of mildew or her feet require washing.

The manager's plum-brown eyes crinkled at the corners. He waggled a finger at her. "You're three days past the date of your reservation. We'd almost despaired of you. We even went so far as to *talk* of calling New York."

"I'm sorry. I was trapped in Vietnam. A flood."

"I had no idea there was a problem. Typhoon?"

"Yes," she said abruptly. "You still have my room?"

"Of course. For *you*—"

He waved vaguely in the air as though to dispel doubt, or perhaps the persistent odor of damp and decay that clung to her clothing. "I shall escort you to the Garden Wing myself."

He came from behind the counter, reached delicately for her backpack, and hoisted it waist-high like a fish unaccountably snagged on his line. Stefani did not protest. The strict tension holding her upright had begun to dissolve in the jasmine-scented air, the hushed quiet of deep carpets. She followed Rewadee without a backward glance.

The powerfully built man at the writing desk folded his newspaper carefully as he watched them go.

————

The rain had started during her eighth day in Vietnam, after she left the Mekong Delta behind and headed north along the coast. Before Saigon there had been Vientiane, the backcountry of Laos, and the old trade routes that once ran between Burma and Angkor Wat and were slowly being reclaimed for capitalism from the guerillas and the drug lords. It had been seven weeks exactly since her last stop in Bangkok, seven weeks of monsoon, not the best time of year to travel. Vietnam and Laos have no national weather services. Predictions are made on the basis of hope, not science. Stefani traveled in ignorance, as people have traveled for millennia; and she learned to judge the feel of the air against her cheek, the color of clouds in the banded sky, and to guess the degree of wetness coming. The rainy season varied from place to place and she was alternately sweating under a humid sun or pounded by cloudburst.

She was too travel-worn to worry when the rain fell in torrents just south of Hoi An. She stared out the car window at the endless fields of rice, rainwater lapping the dikes where the local peasants buried their dead, the stone monuments too solid and square among the feathery tips of green. Only one highway ran along the coast of Vietnam, a winding strip of macadam that uncoiled as innocently as a snare through the sudden peaks and dipping plains of the Truong Son Range. The South China Sea was creeping over the white strip of beach and encroaching upon the road; seawater licked at the hubcaps of her hired Mercedes. The car hood thrust through the small fry of pedal bikes and motor scooters like a blunt-nosed shark; enraged cyclists slammed their fists against the windows as she passed.

They pushed on from Da Nang, Stefani and her Vietnamese driver, through the water that flooded the coast road until it fanned from their fenders like a ceremonial fountain and the green tips of the rice paddies were entirely submerged. By the time they struggled over the Hai Van pass and descended into Hue, the ancient Vietnamese capital, it was pitch dark and the driver was swearing.

The Morin Hotel had a sluggish current streaming

before the reception desk, the Century's entire ground floor was under water; and while they stood on the soggy carpet, watching the rain drip from the ceiling tiles and gush down the banisters of the grand staircase, the first refugees arrived by boat.

After that, Stefani abandoned the banks of the Perfume River and sought out the private home of a man she knew, a surgeon in the hospital in Hue, who lived on higher ground. Though it was nearly midnight, Pho was standing outside his house as they approached, his wife and four children busy on the flat roof of the single-story dwelling. They had managed to rig a tarpaulin (old U.S. Army combat green), and most of their belongings were already piled under it. Stefani got out of the car and helped haul a basket of trussed chickens up to the roof.

Her driver dropped her pack on a plastic deck chair and wallowed down the hill in his flooded Mercedes, never to be heard from again.

"You will eat rice with us?" Pho asked. His English was halting but thorough; at thirteen, he'd carried a gun for the South Vietnamese Army.

"I would be honored," Stefani replied.

Pho's wife boiled rainwater over a kerosene burner, and rice is what they ate for the next five days—rice and a few eggs produced by the querulous chickens, while the Perfume River engulfed the Imperial City. They were cut off on a shallow island without a boat, and the river rising.

That first night no one slept out of fear that even the roof would not be high enough. Pho's wife kept her youngest child strapped tightly against the wet skin of her breast and rocked without ceasing as she hunkered under the tarp. Stefani paced off the roofline and found that the world had dwindled to eighty square feet. By day, they saw the houses of less fortunate lowlanders sweep by on the current. Boxes, rubbish, a flotilla of dead cats. Pho's neighbors called shrilly from other rooftops, traded rumors and news and what food they had. The children squabbled and fished ineffectually for the cats. Stefani tried to make a cellular phone call and found her battery was dead. By late afternoon, boats crowded with the homeless were poling through the flooded trees.

She scanned the skies for helicopters and saw nothing but layers of cloud. The sound of rain pattering on the tin roof under her was slowly driving her mad. She wanted to stuff rags in her ears, to scream words above the din; she fought the impulse to dive like a rat over the side of the sinking house. No helicopters appeared. The surging current was only eighteen inches below the roofline. The rain went on.

A palm tree in Pho's front yard served as her high-water marker. When the flood began, two feet of trunk were submerged. At 2:53 A.M. on the third day, at the height of the typhoon, she shone a fitful flashlight on the swaying palm and guessed that eight more feet had vanished. Thirty-one hours later, when the river was within five inches of Pho's roof, the rain turned to drizzle and the water began to recede from the hilltop. Stefani thought of arks and of doves and of eating something other than rice boiled in rainwater. When the house's ground floor appeared thirteen hours later, she helped Pho sweep the stinking mud and a few drowned chickens from his house while his wife burned incense to the river god.

That afternoon, Pho waded down to the open-air market and bought vegetables and more kerosene. Stefani went with him, sloshing through water that surged to her thighs and trying not to think of snakes. She watched shoe salesmen hose the mud out of ladies' pumps and men's sneakers, she watched hawkers sell plastic ponchos and tourists film the wreckage with Baggies strapped over their video lenses. The bodies of the drowned were beginning to surface. Children sold chewing gum and the more enterprising cycle drivers charged journalists ten bucks apiece to view the corpses.

Later, she pressed two hundred and six dollars—all the hard currency she had—into Pho's palm and pulled her backpack onto her shoulders.

She fought her way onto a public bus and traveled south at a snail's pace, back to Da Nang, the only airport within reach that possessed a jet-length runway and a connecting flight to Bangkok. The trip usually took three hours; she stifled in the bus for ten. The narrow highway was still drowned under a yard of water. To the right she spied the railway line, impassable now, whole sections of track torn off and dangling. There were rumors of passengers stranded for days in the packed train cars.

"Not your usual room," Mr. Rewadee said now as he thrust a key into the Oriental's bedroom door, "but exactly like it in every particular. I've placed a bottle of Bombay Sapphire and several of tonic at the bar, along with some limes."

The suite was four rooms on two levels: a breakfast area near the pale green sofa, the bedroom and teak-lined bath up a short flight of stairs. Kumquats flushed orange in a porcelain bowl. She knew, now, that seven people could survive for days in a space of eighty feet square. Maybe she should invite all of Bangkok in for a party.

"Mr. Krane has called several times," Rewadee observed delicately. "I would be happy to inform New York that you have arrived—"

"I left two suitcases with the bellman a month ago."

Mr. Rewadee bowed.

"I'd like them brought up right away. Also a cheeseburger and a beer. And could you book me a massage for this afternoon?"

One entire wall of the room was glass. Stefani pulled wide the raw silk curtains, saw the long-tailed boats churning across the River of Kings—and leaned her forehead against the window. Just what she needed. A view of the water.

"Welcome back to the Oriental, Ms. Fogg." Her personal butler held out a silver tray with a glass of orange juice and a copy of the *New York Times*.

Stefani Fogg was thirty-nine years old. She had a slight frame that encouraged most people to think she was frail. She was a pretty woman with the face of a pixie: heart-shaped, smiling, a hint of hilarity and high living in the sharp cheekbones. Like her body, it was a face calculated to deceive. Under the fringe of jet-black curls her brown eyes were assessing and shrewd.

"Wharton School," Charlie Krane had murmured over lunch in his corporate headquarters seven months before; "and prior to that, Stanford. I can see you in California, Stef—but *Philadelphia*? Come on." He consulted no résumé; it was his habit to remember everything. The most secure intelligence network in the world, Charlie Krane liked to say, was the human brain—provided it was properly handled. "Iconoclast. You did the Lauder Program instead of a Harvard M.B.A. I like that about you; you never quite run to form. You speak German, I understand? Though you're said to prefer Italian."

She shrugged. "Better wine."

"Pity you didn't work up some Russian. Or Chinese."

"But then I wouldn't be just another pretty face, Charlie."

"Balls," he'd retorted sharply. "You don't run a fund for a major investment house—and get a seventy-eight percent return over five years—with just another pretty face."

He peered at her forbiddingly through his tortoise-shell glasses.

"I want you for Krane's, Stefani, and I'm willing to bet I've an offer you won't refuse."

"That's your job, isn't it?—Predicting the level of risk?"

She had tilted her pixie face and thrown him that disarming smile; he'd stared her down. Charlie had done his homework, of course; he knew the exact extent of Stefani's personal holdings. Something under eleven million dollars in various funds; an eight-room co-op on Central Park; a summer place in Edgartown; a ski condo in Deer Valley. He would know that mere money wasn't enough to scuttle her present job. She'd had money for years and was bored with it.

The walls of the small dining room were lined with cobalt blue velvet. Only one table—theirs—was placed in the center of the maple floor. The view from the fifty-fourth story was blocked by sheer silk curtains in a color that shifted under the eye like seawater; a screen, no doubt, for Charlie's varied electronics.

He had given her sushi, tempura prepared at the table, a fan of fresh vegetables, and a glass of Screaming Eagle. When she had refused a passion-fruit flan, the head of the firm leaned across the table and ticked off his points in a voice that sounded pure BBC, though it was probably born in Brixton.

"Point the First: Stefani Fogg when she's at home. Likes to describe herself as bright but shallow. Raised comfortably in Larchmont, Princeton, Menlo Park. Father a chemical researcher and large-animal veterinarian. Mother rather determinedly hip. She's a clever girl, our Stef, but gun-shy where commitment is concerned. No lover, no child, not so much as a small white dog for messing the carpet with. Appears to choose men by their shirt size rather than their IQs—the odd fitness instructor or bartender, a hapless musician. In the past seven years, no relationship longer than four months.

"Frequently described by the admiring epithet of *bitch*. Roughly translated: she has committed all the sins available to a woman in a man's world. Restless, impatient, ruthless, and ambitious. Sole weakness a reckless streak you could drive a semi through. Two hundred years ago, she'd have been burned at the stake as a heretic and a witch. The girl has intelligence, of course, and courage; but if she has a soul, nobody's saying. I do *not*," he added sternly, "consider charm to be evidence of a soul."

"Thank you," she murmured.

"Point the Second: Stefani Fogg rumored to have turned down the chairmanship of FundMarket International last year, when it was offered her on a plate. Pundits confused.

"Point the Third: Stefani Fogg supposedly in play for CFO of at least three major multinationals, none of which succeeded in bagging her. Pundits agog.

"Point the Fourth: *Galileo Emerging Tech*—the fund Stefani Fogg manages at FundMarket—has lost nearly sixty-seven percent of its high-market value over the past three weeks. Rumors flying within FundMarket and without: Fogg is slipping, Fogg is asleep at the wheel, Fogg may be out on her arse next Tuesday. Pundits immensely gratified."

He sat back in his seat and stared at her with satisfaction. "Missed anything?"

"Just my soul. I keep it beneath the floor of a warehouse off Canal Street." She toyed with the Screaming Eagle. "About *Galileo*—The tech market's volatile, Charlie. You want big returns, you run major risk. Sometimes that means short-term loss."

"And you've generally defied the odds, haven't you? So what's gone wrong this month?"

She didn't answer.

"I have a theory, old thing. I won't bother to ask whether you'd like to hear it."

"Well, you *did* give me lunch. I can spare you a few more minutes."

"Stefani Fogg is bored off her nut and desperate for fun," he suggested. "*Galileo* is sinking because she no longer gives a diddly. I could offer the girl a spot of larceny or a fast plane *to a desert island, and she'd snatch them both out of my moist little palm. Any sort of diversion would do, provided* it were dangerous enough. She's toyed with electronic fraud, with faking her own death, with ripping off Tiffany's in a cat suit at midnight—but the payoff is never quite worth the risk. Our Stef has her reservations. She knows that crime, however enchanting, however *séduisante*, can rather get one's hair mussed. Crime carries with it a measure of annoyance. There's the enforcement chappies, of course; there are turf battles between kingpins she doesn't even know, potentates she could easily offend. There's the possibility of maiming or a sordid public death. Our Stef re fuses to pay the earth for a casual fling. She's looking for bigger game. Something with staying power. A challenge to match her peculiar wits. Am I right, dear heart? Have I hit the target bang-on?"

She went very still, watching him. He was a mild-looking man in his late forties: slim, loosely tailored in medium gray wool, his fair hair clipped short over the temples and rakishly long at the brow. The tortoise-shell glasses partially concealed intense, caramel-colored eyes. Altogether a sleek kind of cat, his tail practically twitching as he surveyed her. He *had* done his homework.

"So you have the antidote to boredom, Charlie. What could you possibly offer that I need or want?"

"Fun, intrigue, and high jinks on six continents," he replied promptly. "A floating bank account accessible at all times for expenses that would never be questioned. Counsel from the main office whenever you want it, but no handcuffs or second-guesses or attempts to drive your car from the rear. An unwritten brief. A handful of clients. Stimulation. A direct line to my desk, night or day. Gut decisions. Unlimited spa time in exotic places. *Power.*"

"To do what, exactly?"

"Beat crooks at their own game. Much more exciting than joining them, I always think. You could spy and seduce and manipulate empires—all in the name of defending commerce. With your talent and brains, Stef, you could write your dossier."

"But why *me*, Charlie? Why the bitch with the lousy returns?"

"Because they'll never see you coming, darling," he answered softly. "You're a bloody great gold mine. Smart and chic and too damn bored with your own wealth to be corruptible. You'll have your teeth sunk into their necks before they even catch your scent." Charlie's tawny eyes flicked across her face with brutal candor. "And there's the added advantage that I love you, ducks. As far as the world of High Finance is concerned, we've never even traded so much as an air kiss. I'm not offering you a title and a desk with a plastic nameplate. I don't want you in New York. I want you bumming around the world on extended holiday."

"Anonymity and carte blanche," she mused. "A high-wire act without a safety net. If I fail, I fail alone."

"Of course. Where would the challenge be, otherwise?"

A silence fell between them.

"Don't refuse me before you've had ages to think," Charlie suggested soothingly. "It wouldn't be the first time a woman's done that, I grant you—but for Stefani Fogg, I'm willing to wait."

"Until *Galileo* craters?"

What had he said? Charm was no evidence of a soul?

He smiled, and pressed a small button under the table. A waiter appeared within seconds, on soundless feet.

"You've had the glamorous turn, old thing." Charlie's voice was like a croon. "You've had the usual stiffs in the Wall Street clubs with their fast cars and limp members. Now you want to run with the wolves. Don't you? *Confess* it."